CHRONICLES of GALAXY OSMARON

The Solarian Empire

They were receding ever further from the ledge. The rough shoulder of rock continued to widen, as if guiding them on purpose from the rocky ledge towards the centre of the darker sands. Bravely they continued onwards, still hugging the rough shoulder of seemingly solid and slippery rock material.

When it happened it was sudden. They froze in their tracks. The ground ahead opened up, as a deep chasm irreversibly began to move towards them. They were stunned in their tracks and too tired to take any abrupt action, even to turn around and flee. They found themselves falling from a great height into a large elastic net or web of some kind.

The Chronicles of Galaxy Osmaron Series

First Edition

CHRONICLES OF GALAXY OSMARON

The Solarian Empire

Earth is regenerated - A new Empire is born

by

Adrian Graye

Nutralian Publishing
http://nutralianpublishing.com

nutralian
An imprint of Nutralian Publishing
5 Bradford Square, London E1 0SG
http://nutralianpublishing.com

This paperback edition 2008
B00005555

First published in Great Britain by
Amazon KDP 2024

ISBN 978-1-0687902-3-2

Printed and bound in Great Britain by Amazon KDP Publishing.

A CIP catalogue record for this title
is available from the British Library.

This book is dedicated to my friends

&

To all those who believe in universal existence
and appreciate the lowliest of life, for like babes,
they are the beginning

TABLE OF CONTENTS

BOOK 1
A new beginning

The painful race of life

On every living thing a little rain must fall,
And every drop will help, even the smallest tree grow tall.
For even in the darkest night,
The stars above will still shine bright,
And if we wait until the morn,
A glowing sunrise may adorn.

So trust in God, but do your best,
And with strong endeavour you'll win the test.
For life's a race only few attain,
So even if you fail, try and try again.
Because the entire point of life,
Is within the Eternal Race we strive

Victor E. Roche

Prologue

Under quite strange circumstances, Plato, one of the Andromedan visitors meets the President of the USA and arrange to have dinner at his country residence.

During dinner he is shown a replay of the destruction of Plato's people on a planet call Caefon within the galaxy of Andromeda. This event took place about three thousand years ago. The alien nano-bot monsters were called Javols and constructed from metallic microid robots, each smaller than the size of a single human cell. They were difficult to kill and preyed on all biological life for food. The Javols are presently on their way to our galaxy, known to the Andromedans as Osmaron, and will destroy all life in their wake.

During the intervening period we are to find ways to fight and resist them, if we are not to go the same way as the Andromedans and their galaxy. Gerald Fraser, the President of the USA, known to his friends as Jerry, acknowledges the grave problems ahead, but realizes he cannot tell his public. He decides to go on a special inter-stellar journey in order to observe other life within his home galaxy and hopefully gain some insight in cosmic matters before serious decisions are taken with regards to Earth.

Having made arrangement for a duplicate actor to take his place while on sick leave, Jerry and his wife, Sharon, have departed on their first inter-stellar journey for a space-picnic with some surviving Andromedans. Hopefully this trip will last for one week, during which time they will visit many stellar systems. However several challenges occur on route and decisions are made that will transform the role of mankind within Osmaron (our Milky Way galaxy).

Introduction

Lord Vektron meets the president

It was time to begin the next phase of the master survival plan, whatever it was. Plato asked Lumak whether he should call the group together and Lumak advised him to do whatever he thought necessary, so he had a silent word with Jerry, who clapped several times to silence his guests.

'Everyone, please! Plato would like to say a few important words!' They decided to listen to what Plato had to say.

'Mister President, associates, colleagues and friends. On behalf of my people and others here, I sincerely thank you for your kind invitation, your generous hospitality, this most splendid meal and the great honour you have bestowed upon us, in every respect. However, before we part company this day you also have a right to know of your purpose within the greater survival plan.'

Plato pressed the large winged buckle on his previously hidden belt and suddenly a greenish glow appeared ahead of them, about two metres above the floor. The group suddenly moved backwards, fearing whatever was happening within that area. As the glow decreased, a black sphere took its place, revealing a winged insignia at its very front.

The sphere spoke English in a strange way, as if eating its words.

'Ah, Plato. I see almost everyone in the master plan are all together and in one place, even Siend Lumak, our most important Shadite. You obviously need my contribution at this juncture of the master plan.'

He bopped up and down as if observing the whole group, but also in an excited state. He floated closer to them in frivolous manner. Then Lord Vektron the Ploran began to speak again:

'*Mr President, I trust you and your colleagues are not too alarmed by my presence.*

'*You know, appearances are related only to form and we are all Osmaronites and brothers together, of a single galactic bond. This bond, in times of distress, crises and extreme danger, may pull us all together for the common good.*'

Then he floated back to his original position.

'*Friends, just as Andromeda is our sister galaxy, so has your world been made sister with the planet Caefon within Andromeda. This is a great honour for both human species and will allow you total freedom to visit and use Meron's home world and galaxy to your advantage. But this decree works both ways and also gives Meron's people the freedom to visit and exist on your world and galaxy. They can then assist you with whatever technologies you may require from his people for your mutual survival.*

'*The spectre of our enemies are already on the horizon. They will be on Caefon within the year. Therefore the remainder of his people, now some ten point six million, are to be evacuated in due course to the planet Mars. From there they are to locate other healthy settlement worlds within this galactic sector. This is because you will not be able to absorb their quantities within this world. However, with Meron and Lumak's assistance, you will soon have the necessary technologies to travel throughout the galaxy and become a great nation in your own right after the Javols are destroyed.*

'*Henceforth, all your deeds will be of significant importance to the Grand Lord and The Greater Purpose.*

'*In summation, your solar system is shortly to gain Class 5 status.*

'*Meron, Hamil and the elder Ancients will help design your new and advanced technologies, under Professor Longhurst's guidance.*

'*Jon and his young group will assist in your laboratories and educate your young in those technologies.*

'*When not occupied elsewhere, Lumak and Plato will help stair you in the correct direction in accordance with the master survival plan and enhance your own efficient survival goals.*

'*Although Earth and its population will be needed in future, they will not be directly involved in the rescue mission. That intricate task will be assigned to Meron's people, with the aid of certain technologies.*

'*However, they must first fit the Omegron Portal to a relevant stable point on Mars. That position has already been determined and must be made ready before the evacuation of the remaining survivors on Caefon may commence.*

'*In any event, this evacuation program will be of a purely temporary nature. After the Javols have been removed from the galaxies, many of you, including natives of this world, may wish to visit the freer and more sparsely populated galaxy of Andromeda, with an almost infinite scope for development. Since most of her resources are still in tact, any extinct life-forms can always be reintroduced or substituted, given the necessary ecological controls.*

'*The time period involved here is barely three hundred years. Even as I speak certain strategic plans have already been set in motion and civilizations made ready for the Final Battle of Andromeda.*

'*After the cleansing period and with the help of Osmaron and your Pleron friends, Andromeda will be slowly returned to normality.*

'*Any recovery will be slow at first, but may be attained within a period of about two hundred years, which is well within the natural lifetime of most of you here standing.*

'*During the period of reconstruction, the Omegron Portal will link both your systems together, in space and in time so your destinies from this moment on are implacably linked, as of one race and purpose. This is essential if you are to survive the Javols onslaught. By linking both worlds we also link both galaxies.*

'*The Javols cannot enter within the Omegron Portal and survive. Its energies are designed to neutralise their connecting bonds and on touching they will disintegrate. So even if they detect the link they cannot follow.*

'It is a long and dangerous road we travel. We shall meet many dangers on route, so we must not be complacent. Therefore we should be prepared for any eventuality in order to survive.'

Suddenly the sphere faded into a human-like form, with hands and feet, but also dressed in an ancient white robe. In his hands were the Great Book of light they called the Anachromagnon.

The figure walked towards Sintra and she went forward to show her respect to Lord Vektron and collect the great book. Then he disappeared through the wall as if it was not there.

Although many of Jerry's company were severely disturbed by what they saw and heard, they accepted the reality of it all. Even Jerry, the fearless president, suddenly realised his own galaxy was teaming with all forms of life, some of whom were completely beyond his comprehension and had acquired levels of technologies surpassing by far even his present company of Andromedans.

They were not to ask too many questions, but instead to get on with the job in hand. Namely: to save both galaxies and planets from the Javols with the aid of those more advanced intergalactic brothers and sisters, if indeed they could be so called.

Then Jerry took a somewhat disturbed Mickey apart for a more private discussion.

. 'We have so much work to do! This is a lot bigger than even the Apollo missions. I just hope we can handle it and convince the committee for more funding. What do you think, Mickey?' Jerry said, realizing the enormity of the problem.

'This is all too much for me to take in one gulp, Sir. I suppose we can do a lot with a few clever minds. There are still many rich organizations on our planet and some of them won't mind sinking some major bucks into any new projects that are guaranteed to be successful. We just have to convince them. Anyway, Professor Longhurst and his wife Sarah are about the richest people on the globe, so we don't have to go very far, do we?,' Michael Cockburn replied with sarcasm, presently recovering from the initial shock of Lord Vektron's untimely appearance.

'Do you think they can do it all by themselves? ... within the private sector?' Jerry inquired.

'That's the best way, Sir. That way we are not involved and it gives you plausible deny-ability. That way, there is also a much reduced possibility of leakage to the press and others, and we can always pass the buck,' Mickey replied, stressing his points.

'Don't be so darn cocky with me! You know, you always remind me of my older brother, George. You both could always find quick answers when it meant passing the buck and talk the hide off a buffalo. Anyway, the poor man lost his life at war in the middle east,' Jerry said, sadly.

'I am very sorry, Sir, for speaking out of turn,' Mickey replied, apologetically.

'Don't be! That happened quite a few decades ago. That was before I even dreamt of becoming president,' Jerry replied.

'Anyway, back to the original topic. In that case, we must immediately arrange a meeting with Professor Longhurst to discuss all those important matters, and try not to pass too many bucks,' Jerry said, giving a sarcastic smile.

'In that case, Sir, I shall call my good friend Harry to do us the honours. He is now a director in their organization,' Mickey replied. Harry was the first name of Professor Harry Lennox, who was one of Doctor Jeffery Longhurst's chief scientist.

After that meeting all of his country's economical problems suddenly appeared insignificant by comparison, but he still had to keep this new program a secret. If word of alien visitors and impending doom were to leak out he was not sure how the public would react, even when the danger was in the distant future and several generations away. Therefore, everyone in that room, even the air-force personnel outside, had to be completely screened and reassigned.

Anyway, he had the feeling most of his associates were extremely excited by this new opportunity of adventure. He was convinced they would go along with whatever he proposed, if there was the slightest chance of just coming along for the ride. But in this case they could always be assured of a bit of the action.

Further, many strings could be pulled in many directions, for he was well known globally and not the president of one of the greatest nations on Earth for nothing, and so he thought.

A quick decision

During the remainder of that evening Lumak had kept himself well away from Jerry and his most prominent associates and advisors. Although he had met Jerry once before as his other self, Doctor Jeffery Longhurst, he knew Mickey and some of the others quite well and did not in any way wish to jeopardize his present position and the progress made by Plato for his people. However he could always change from Lumak, the Shadite, back into the honourable Doctor Jeffery Longhurst on his arrival at his country manor. Failing his usual latex disguise, he could always use his cloak with one of the standard disguises in his implants. However too many disguises only confused everyone, including himself.

As Lumak, he appeared much younger than his more common identity, Doctor Longhurst, who was well known throughout many countries. That image had been created over the years beginning with a beard which was later discarded for an artificial attachment giving the same appearance. Since he could never age naturally he intended to modify his disguises every ten years or so to give that impression.

That facility significantly reduced any efforts on his part in the use of facial drugs or physical revectoring through The Mind. It was just a simple attachment that had been specifically designed for a single purpose and could be attached or removed in seconds. Thus making his character changes quick, constant and simple.

Obviously, the beard was a clandestine feature, and with the exception of his wife Sarah, her father Khan and a few close friends, no one knew of his disguises. Not even his wife Sarah knew he was a Shadite. Being well known, his disguise was assumed necessary for security reasons and many knew of that fact, although not of the true reason.

Nevertheless on this occasion he was to distant himself from certain people which included the president and his present company. It was therefore decided that Plato took the lead on any important questions while he, Lumak, remained in the background, incognito. Plato was the one to get Jerry's attention on the outer farm in the morning and appeared to have his full confidence and the present situation well under control.

Meron was also respected and admired by the president, but Lumak did not want their current venture to get too cosy. Security was of paramount importance and any disruption to their very delicate program could ensue if there was too much social interaction with Jerry and his associates at this stage in the master plan.

Despite their present achievements, there could still be unwarranted leaks to the press and from certain unscrupulous bodies. Any such leaks coming from presidential levels would not be ignored by the press and could lead to further complications. Lumak thought those matters out carefully before calling Plato for a quiet chat. After their discussion, Plato followed in the direction of Jerry, who was presently standing away from the others. He was looking out of the large window while admiring The Ship. Plato followed next to him with an extra drink.

'Would you like a ride in that strange buggy?' Plato asked, humorously. He turned his head and focussed on Plato, nervously.

'Where? I suppose to Andromeda and back?' Jerry appeared courageous.

'Even now, I still can't believe it's real... I mean, today's experience... and yet, here we are together, with all these extraterrestrial people that I almost know personally. All communicating together as if from a single race. I suppose in the back of my mind I always knew it would happen one day... I mean, a meeting with you visitors from another system, but never in my lifetime, and of all things, in my home? You are not even local to our galaxy, and yet, you are so similar to us!'

'Yes! Our universe is full of life, and most primal life is quite similar. If not in body, in mind,' Plato replied.

'When we started Ulysses, which was a follow on from the Apollo missions, but to visit Jupiter and it's moons. I, like most of my colleagues, assumed we would never visit the nearest stars for centuries. Now... you have changed all that by visiting us first.... and despite everything, we were not even aware of Lord Vektron and his kind... even though they shared the same galaxy with us. Perhaps to them we were just another basic life-form developing along some predetermined program....'

'We are all developing at different rates, some faster than others. Many are quite ancient.'

'I realize that, but some races are so darn clever, eh!' he replied, somewhat humbled by that fact.

'Lord Vektron and his race are devoted to helping all kinds of life throughout the Cosmos. They form the main trust of command from the Greater Purpose towards this dimension.'

'Then he must be a demigod or such like?'

'Well, he has existed for billions of years! They were once true mortals like us, but eventually grew out of their human bodies. They say, the human form hindered their true cosmic development. So now, they are truly immortal and can do almost anything because of knowledge gained throughout millennia by assisting others... but they can still use the human form when the need arise,' Plato said, defensively.

'If what you say is factual, they must be the true gods of the universe,' Jerry replied.

'There are others who are even more advanced and more powerful than the Plorans. Those had existed even before the beginning of our universe and will continue until the end. They are the Gohrans. Grand Lord Gerra is the one responsible for our part of the universe,' Plato said and Jerry was startled by that information.

'Oh my God! He could have been the one my friend, the previous president, met three years ago. He said he repaired his body in a flash. That one travelled like a bright star. I am truly humbled and amazed by that fact and cannot even consider those thoughts for now, not before getting used to the idea. Anyway, what about our trip to outer space and when shall we leave?' Jerry replied, changing the sensitive topic.

'For your first space journey... May I suggest a trip to observe all the local planets within this Solar System at close range and perhaps a visit to three more distant inhabited systems.'

'Inhabited?' queried Jerry.

'Yes, but not with very advanced life,' Plato replied, but continued.

'It will not be necessary to wear special environmental suits, so any observation may be carried out on board ship... unless of course we happen to arrive on a planet with a suitable atmosphere, plus or minus certain acceptable variations from our own. Nevertheless I am sure we can visit such worlds for brief periods.'

Jerry's eyes almost popped out in surprise and curiosity when he realized Plato was quite serious. He contemplated how costly such an interplanetary trip would be by Earth's standards and that journey was interstellar.

'You will make such a trip just because I ask?' Jerry inquired, excitedly.

'It is necessary for a man in your position to have a more realistic feel of the Greater Environment. It will allow you a broader view on cosmic life, which in turn will reflect in the way you think and make important decisions on Earth, and believe me, all of your future achievements will be a lot more prominent as a result.'

'You are so right!'

'Why don't we make it an interstellar vacation to remember. We can also take along some entertainment equipment. With refreshments at Mercury, Venus, Mars, et cetera and lunch on arrival at the first local system? Taking the remainder of the route more leisurely as we go. I'm afraid, there will be no golf on this trip though.'

'I can live with that!'

'We can include on board all necessary pre-cooked food and drink, with perhaps a small power generator for the microwave oven and any entertainment equipment we might need, with the exception of radio receivers. Unfortunately they will not work during our trip. However, any president of this great nation will be missed?' Plato replied, sarcastically.

'Don't you worry about my end, Sir!'

'Oh...?'

'Anything can be arranged with a little cunning, and my vice president is quite competent to take control in my absence,' Jerry said, unflinchingly.

'We are currently residing at Doctor Longhurst's country residence. Perhaps you could visit us officially for a short vacation, just two days might do to set our plan in motion.

'Our residence is fully secure; something to do with Doctor Longhurst's patented inventions and his critical attitude towards industrial espionage. He sometimes use the place to follow through some of his technical work and as you know, he is well known to all and sundry.'

'Yes, I met him a few times and know him by reputation. We once met in turkey while I was Ambassador there. He is the greatest, in my opinion!'

'Anyway, in my opinion, you should attempt to make the trip as soon as possible, especially before your important speech to congress. Before then, you might have a special announcement to make to the world,' Plato said.

Jerry was surprised by those last words.

'What do you know about my speech to congress and special announcements?' he inquired, with curiosity.

'Have you heard of project Zeus?' Plato inquired.

'No! I have not!'

'Well, that project was initiated by Doctor Longhurst about two years ago. It was fully agreed and funded by your people, but kept secret for obvious reasons. Anyway, it's in the private sector. It's purpose... to develop a new interstellar drive based on what we call... Linear Progressive Drive technology (LPD for short). Although it's not as advanced as the Infinite Probability Drive used by the ship outside, it's a lot more precise for interstellar journeys.'

'That's truly incredible, man! That means we have solved all our space travel problems. We can finally travel to the stars!'

'Well, Doctor Longhurst has been successful with that project and a practical working system is now available. Obviously it will have to be fitted to a ship, but that operation is merely incidental. We were hoping that... perhaps you would consider a demonstration after our space voyage to the stars... And by the way, would you consider naming a few planets when we get to the other systems. It will be considered a great honour.'

'Naming planets? ... Of course!'

'Anyway, what do you think would happen to your present political standing, if after your return from the stars, you offered your people three new solar-type systems, a brand new interstellar drive, a new type of super-clean transport that doesn't require fossil fuels, and mining concessions to the solar system,' Plato said. He was always expert at dangling the carrot and the president was biting.

Jerry was by now extremely excited in their new topic and signalled the waiter for more drinks.

'I don't know what you will do... but I will have the biggest party going and you will get my very first invite. I might even nominate you as my vice president and if that is not possible, because you say so, I shall nominate you as my blood brother. You know, that might even be a much better position than vice president. You are not kidding me, are you?' Jerry replied, not quite believing his luck. He was like a little kid with a new toy for play.

Plato spoke, this time with even more sincerity.

'No, Mister President. I am not kidding. It's just the way things have turned out. I want you to take full political advantage of present circumstances... and who knows, perhaps you might be able to do my people a good turn in the future. They have had a most terrible time in the past. That's all I ask,' he said, calmly and with sincerity.

Jerry was suddenly sympathetic.

'Yea, I can well imagine what it was like. You are never to worry about that aspect, my friend... I and my people will not get in your way either. If you require our assistance just shout and you will have the whole of this country to choose from... Further, don't worry about passports and other security documents for your people. You can consider those arrangements made. Anyway, who on Earth would believe you guys are from another galaxy,' Jerry replied, affectionately.

'Jerry, I think you should realize there are three habitable planets within fifty light years from Earth. This distance can be traversed by Doctor Longhurst's stellar drives in under four weeks... twenty-six days to be precise.'

Jerry by now had used up all his surprises.

'You mean... there are three populated planets within those systems?' He was absorbed with curiosity.

'Not populated by very advanced life, not even mammals. Only basic life-forms... even so, certain ecological rules should be upheld.'

'I agree!'

'After we land on those worlds you will understand my meaning. After all, we cannot trample on life just because we require resources for our own personal needs. We have to consider the needs of others within the greater ecology. However, that principle does not hinder our own development. In some cases it might strengthen them. As an example, consider Lord Vektron and his race, along with their very great achievements which has been earned by helping others.'

'Yea, I understand what you mean. We Earth humans have always behaved irresponsibly, like bulls in a china-shop. We have to change all that with space exploration. And I will ensure that is the case!' Jerry was insistent.

'There will be no recriminations. Nevertheless, despite the present over-population problems of this world, all life have adjusted and learned to live together for the common good. In the same way, if we are shortly to increase our sphere of influence, such good concepts of mutual survival must be upheld and followed throughout the Cosmos for the common good. Since we are supposed to be in charge, it's our responsibility to be their caretakers.'

'I cant fault that argument!' Jerry replied.

'Perhaps a universal survival book of rules might be more acceptable. The Great Book may already include such a system of co-habitable rules within its pages,' Plato said, while referring to the Anachromagnon.

Jerry gazed at Plato and realised that even with his strange qualities, he was a morally strong and law abiding individual. Perhaps even a member of some cosmic religion or special order. After all, what was a Shadite, but he did not wish to ask him about himself on this occasion and spoil the trend of their present conversation.

'I would like to make the trip as soon as possible. Perhaps we can leave with you tonight. It will make things a lot simpler and I shall have a lot less to explain to security.'

'Anytime you want!'

'I can leave a message for chief security and communicate with him again on my arrival at your place. I am afraid that I shall have to take along my two senior security men. Their presence will take the heat off my stay at your place. Thereafter, I can arrange for one of my doppelgangers to take my place. They are very good actors you know and can be made to impersonate and resemble me in every conceivable detail, with the exception of being unable to handle my office and the special security codes. Anyway, my security men are well known to Central and can always be made available after we make the switch,' Jerry said.

'Our ship is quite able to take a few more passengers and items. In that case, we can depart later tonight, after all your people have left,' Plato replied, in full agreement.

'Anyway, I am supposed to be on sick leave as recommended by my doctor and my Vice President is quite capable in my absence,' Jerry stressed.

Jerry's wife Sharon came along and handed them yet another drink and smiled at Plato. He returned her smile and walked away from the couple.

Plato kept Lumak up to date on all events that evening and Lumak was satisfied with their achievements. Even the young ones from Andromeda were enjoying themselves and had blended in well with the natives of their newly adopted world.

They were at last making new friends outside of their tight group and very soon would be independently exposed to everything, including the dangers. One or two might even die in the process, but that setback would only be temporary.

After what appeared to have been a very strange but socially enjoyable evening, the advisors and delegates departed. They were escorted by the air-force helicopters to some private location for debriefing and screening.

Jerry had decided to take along his two personal security men plus his chef and barman. The latter two, he thought, could assist in food preparations before their flight to the stars.

That evening The Ship was more than fully laden when it left Jerry's residence. Luckily for them, the journey was quite local and did not require interstellar transposition which was almost instant. Unlike atmospheric transposition, that process could only have been achieved with twelve human passengers.

Their voyage to the stars

They were awakened at first light. Lumak now in his disguise as Doctor Jeffery Longhurst had his own schedules to follow and left all other matters in the capable hands of Plato, the Shadite. After an early breakfast, Plato called the Andromedans together in a local room.

'We are to commence our interstellar journey today. Therefore those involved should be ready, for we depart in one hour. I have made a list to include only essential personnel for this trip. Those of you not selected this time can visit at a later date.'

'We are ready!' shouted and eager Jon.

'Since there are just 12 bunks for interstellar travel, The Ship is capable of carrying just twelve live passengers. Regrettably this somewhat restricts our numbers.' Plato appeared sympathetic. Nevertheless there were frowns on many faces.

Those included on the trip were; Meron, Hamil, Tomas, Jon, Merol, Ecrol, Plato, Lucia, Sintra, Lira, Jerry (the president) and his wife Sharon. They were all Andromedans with the exception of Jerry and his wife Sharon.

After they had finished their discussion with Plato, a small helicopter arrived carrying Doctor Longhurst and a colleague. Incidentally, his companion closely resembled Jerry, the president, and conveniently wore a facial disguise.

The switch with Jerry was subsequently made in one of the rooms in the manor. The real president left wearing the man's clothes and a different facial disguise, while the man wore Jerry's original clothes with a new facial disguise. The resemblance was so uncanny that no one knew by sight that he wasn't the real president.

Jerry was an active player in one of Washington DC's less prominent acting clubs so most of those actors were his close drinking friends. He had used such clandestine methods of disguise many times before while visiting friends and places incognito. That was when he needed a break from stressful duties of state. Those actors considered his impersonations a challenge and had bets to see who could pull them off with the least problems. They also relished the challenges of being the most powerful person on the planet for a short while.

The lookalike president soon made himself at home and began showing presidential initiative by asking his security men to check a blind spot he could plainly observe on the CCTV. The men soon realigned the equipment and apologised for the oversight.

During all this time, Jon, Merol and Ecrol assisted Tomas in loading The Ship with all necessary equipment and supplies for the journey.

The equipment included a chemically driven power generator, small refrigerator, microwave oven, video recording equipment, music player and transparent plastic containers held in a large rack. The last items were to store specimens from the worlds they visited and specially constructed and prepared for that purpose. All the loading was done before the arrival of Madeline and her young helpers.

All items were firmly held in place by cables anchored to powerful magnetic pads and clamps. Although strictly not essential, harnessing was a safety precaution in case of turbulence on route. Nevertheless, Jon and the young Andromedans were always thorough in their duties and responsibilities.

Those left behind were Merian, Julia and Petra. Although saddened they were not included, they realized there was little choice. Knowing they would be left behind initiated a few tears of sadness. So the other women went to console them.

'Don't you worry about a thing during our absence. We've been through much together so what is a little trip to some local systems? Anyway, I bet we'll be back within the week?' Lira said.

'Are you sure?' Petra asked.

'Yes, I'm!' Lira replied.

'I will miss you guys so much!' Merian said.

'You know it's very important for us to see the local worlds and plan for the urgent evacuation of our people from Caefon,' Lira said to Merian and she was calmed.

After Madeline's arrival Lumak decided to take her in his confidence. He began to explain to her that they were from another galaxy.

'You are not kidding me?'

'No. I am not! They are refugees in serious trouble, but very good people. So please keep it a secret between us for now.'

'I would never have known. They are so much like us.'

'Yes, they are just like us. No different!'

Soon after, Madeline (Mad) and her girls join the others to see them off.

After everything was ready, the twelve quietly said their temporary farewell and boarded ship. The others stood around to wave them off with more tears of sadness.

The ship viewed a ravaged and overpopulated Earth from space while Meron commented on the future effects of Global Warming and the dangers to all life on the planet should the process continue. He was a planetologists and knew the outcome from what he could observe.

'Our world went through a similar process about 5000 years ago. We lost most of the animals and our race almost became extinct during that period of extreme climate change.'

'How were you able to repair your world and survive?' Jerry inquired.

'We had assistance from our Supreme Lord, Grand Lord Gerron. My ancestor, King Melor, and his warriors were rescued by the Octans from our world and taken to this galaxy. The Octans thought them the ways to bring our world back from the brink and extended their lives for that great task. Luckily, the ancestors before Melor had placed several seeding Satellites in orbit and created an Oracle to advise the few survivors during their times of crisis,' Meron said.

'That was very thoughtful of them, and quite ingenious to have anticipated the future problems of their world,' Jerry replied.

'They may have considered worst case scenarios and gave it their best effort.'

'Do you think the same will happen to Earth?'

'I'm afraid so. You are following a similar path of over-population, indulgence and neglect. Within 200 years the water levels will rise to about 50 metres. Well before then your population would have grown to over 15 billion from its original 9 billion today. Sadly, during most of that period disease and other detrimental factors would have taken their tole on population growth. Along with pandemic diseases, there will also be extreme violence, riots, looting and such like, until food becomes quite scarce. Farmers cannot produce crops in unpredictable weather. This will be aided by floods, natural forest fires and desertification in times of drought leading to mass extinctions, further reducing food production and other ills in a downward spiral. Anyway, hungry people are seldom interested in growing crops. With desperate people food is always their main concern.' Jerry was shocked by that analysis.

'Your only solution is in drastic population control,' he said, but Jerry realized that population control was political suicide for any party in congress. How could any democratically elected government stipulate such controls on its people. He imagined telling his children they would never be allowed to bear offspring. Then he sighed and nodded his head a few times, wishing for another way out of that almost insurmountable problem.

MERCURY

The Ship was finally on its way to Mercury and followed an orbit that took them behind the Sun.

The large screen clearly displayed the solar disk with its many prominence and sun-spots. The image included a diagram of its atomic constituents and internal structure, highlighted in different colours.

The image soon changed to Mercury, showing an extremely hot and rugged world, but with an abundance of minerals and rear metals to be found on Earth only in extremely small quantities.

Although the planet was a miner's paradise, there still remained the problem of intense refrigeration, if humans were to survive sustained periods on its surface. But there were an abundance of solar energy which could quite easily have been harnessed for that purpose.

VENUS

A complete analysis was made and logged, and The Ship was soon on its way to Venus.

Meron observed the planet, with its dense clouds of carbon dioxide and other noxious gases, including its generally hostile environment and remarked to Jerry, now observing the smaller screen intently.

'That world is like the ideal neglected waste dump with every possible chemical action and reaction. This is what a dead but active world looks like, without the complex matrix of life.'

'It appears so!' Jerry replied.

'This is what can happen when a planet dies because pollution is allowed to accumulate uncontrollably. Although natural to this world, it can happen to any world, where environmental neglect and greed predominates. One should always treat a living world with love and care'

'This place must be a lot worse than hell!!'

'And hell it becomes when neglected by nature and life! Our world, Caefon, almost died because of such negligence. That was when we were like you on Earth, a self-indulgent people with little regard for other species. Under Lord Micol, we learnt the error of our ways and found a new and better way to live. That was before the arrival of the evil Javols. At that time the Octans thought us a new way of life.'

'I see! Perhaps you and your people can teach us your new way of life?'

'That we shall do after the evacuation of our remaining people from Caefon,' Meron replied.

'Thank you in advance for your assistance and call me if you should require our assistance,' Jerry said.

'Anyway, perhaps even this planet, Venus, can be made to

recover in time. But powerful machines and screened robots will be required initially to begin the process of terra-forming. Then with the introduction of suitable living strains of bio-engineered bacteria, the matrix of a living order may be induced to grow and start the slow process of reclamation. Once that process begins, the whole planet soon becomes a living entity in its own right and its Gaia will follow the path that confirms to Cosmic existence for mutual survival.'

'So living planets are alive?'

'In a sense, they are. I see them as a type of living order.'

'That's an incredible notion!'

'We once had a similar and seemingly hopeless project for conversion on Gyron II. The planet's atmosphere was first seeded with numerous quantities of chemically active crystals that was kept in place by large orbiting balloons. Afterwards we built large sealed domed cities on its surface for our mineral miners, which further assisted the process. Eventually special bio-engineered algae strains were introduced into the cleaner lakes. That way, the lakes were continually filtered and diluted of all acidic accumulations.'

'It must have taken a while?'

'It took us about three centuries, but the process of conversion was irreversible after that initial period of bio-distribution and cleansing. All manufacturing and engineering was subsequently banned and re-sited on Gyron III... which was then a completely dead world with little sustainable atmosphere. Manufacturing processes that produce pollution can be sited anywhere... and preferable well away from sensitively structured eco-systems.' Meron was enthusiastic while Jerry nodded his approval.

Jerry watched the screen while becoming overly concerned about the desolation implied by the detailed images of the planet's surface. Venus was incredibly hot and that heat tended to accelerate its crustal movements. Its planetary crust was much thinner than Earth's in many places due to those relatively extreme surface temperatures. As they watched they could observe many streams of flowing lava with frequent volcanic activity. All such activities being much more aggressive than on Earth. What if

Earth was triggered along a similar path with Global Warming? However he didn't wish to consider that parallel nightmare scenario if the Green House effect got out of hand.

Then Meron focussed the ship's telescope in Earth's direction to observe its blue-green disc and Jerry was relieved his planet was still there and in one piece.

Jerry believed in his privileged position with lingering doubt, for here he was, observing at close range and doing what some of his most experienced astronauts and scientists would have given their right arms for. And he was not wearing any special environmental suits or floating around weightlessly in zero gravity. To him, it was almost like watching a film on the topic of space exploration, but with the exception that he was one of the participants experiencing the real thing.

After they had seen enough of Venus, tea was served by Lucia and Jerry's wife, Sharon, assisted by Jon.

MARS and ASTEROIDS

They soon arrived above Mars. Once again Meron was at the viewing controls and decided to relay his views to Jerry and the others.

'Here too, is a recoverable planet. Venus could be robbed of some of its carbon dioxide by using large compressed storage tanks for delivery by robot controlled ships. In sufficient quantities, such gases could assist in the rejuvenation of the Martian atmosphere by increasing its surface temperature and regulating its turbulent weather patterns. Then after an appropriate time, solid hydrogen space-burgs could be toured across space from some of the smaller moons of Jupiter and Saturn for further replenishment. There is still much water on Mars to begin the process.

'Sound to me like an expensive operation?'

'This operation could be less lengthier than any Venusian recovery. Because of its lower temperature Mars will be more tolerable to human habitation. Environmental domes could be constructed to protect plants and animals during the initial period of conversion. Even anti-meteoric shielding could be included close to habitable areas. However, because of its smaller mass special Magnatron satellites will have to be constructed to create a strong magnetic field and control its atmosphere.'

'During that period could Mars be used to absorb some of Earths population?'

'Not in time, I'm afraid. With present technologies it will be a lengthy process, taking many generations.'

'That's disappointing!'

'Its central core is now almost a solid mass with a negligible magnetic field distribution, therefore using super-conductivity, several powerful orbiting magnatrons could be used to guide solar radiation towards artificially created poles as on Earth. This will prevent loss of atmosphere by the Solar Wind. Powerful ground stations could also assist in maintaining a correct ozone level in its upper atmosphere. This will reduce most of the deadly solar radiation until enough ozone is created.'

'There are so many dangers to life!' Jerry commented.

'Yes, but every problem can be solved in time. Mars to me is a better candidate for conversion, because its environment is a lot more chemically stable... and its atmosphere substantially more predictable than Venus... even water ice exist in reasonable quantities within its frozen surface,' he stressed.

Jerry nodded in agreement, with his limited knowledge on the intricacies of planetary bio-dynamics.

They soon approached the asteroid belt and once again Meron addressed Jerry and the crew.

'From observation and computer analysis, this orbit once contained two minor planets or planetoids. Perhaps a small one with an even smaller satellite... both almost equivalent in size to Mercury, although somewhat less dense. They could have included a much larger frozen area than Mars.'

Jerry observed the jagged planetoid called Ares, with its shattered surfaces and realized the universe was a very violent place.

'Although their orbits were initially quite stable, the extreme gravitational effects of Jupiter and Mars might have caused them to interact in a detrimental manner... Interaction between both bodies could have led to their eventual collision. By that time both planets were perhaps already shattered to their cores by strong tidal action due to Jupiter's gravity.'

'Wow! That violent collision would have been quite a spectacle!' Jerry replied.

'Luckily, both worlds were moving in near parallel orbits around the sun when they collided. This could account for the large remaining quantity of asteroids and smaller fragments, perhaps about 75 percent of their combined whole, but even so, some may in time get knocked out of their present orbits by comets or other wanderers. It is therefore necessary to build a sensitive protective screen to shield Earth from future encounters. Some of the larger bodies are rich in metals and may be mined with the correct equipment,' Meron again advised.

JUPITER

Jupiter was next on the screens and Meron commented on its satellites' usefulness as observation posts. They viewed the outer worlds, but Jupiter itself was unsuited for our biological type of evolving life and so was the other gas giants and their moons. All relevant data was logged by The Ship under Plato's guidance.

While assisted by Hamil, Plato was quite busy acquiring and analysing in detail all relevant planetary data. The collection of which was necessary for the future of human development within what he called, the New Solarian Sphere. Finally The Ship was out of the solar system. The sun appeared like another bright star on the large screen, with the planets only visible under intense image enhancement due to the significantly reduce reflected radiation.

Suddenly, the large screen changed to a new image, showing one of the galactic arms with a bluish dot. That dot indicated the position of the solar system within that arm, while three yellow dots marked the relative positions of the other local systems. They were within the same spiral arm, later to be called the Solarian

Arm of Osmaron.

The screen was once again dotted with hundreds, if not thousands of red specks and Jerry asked Meron for an explanation.

'The dots represent the location of sensitive observation and defensive stations. They have been specifically created by the Octans to defend and shield certain sensitive areas of our Osmaron galaxy from alien invasion,' he replied.

'You mean, our galaxy is ready for war with another... with the Javols?' Jerry asked, in utter astonishment.

'Yes, Jerry, I am afraid so, but we in Osmaron have a much more advanced technology than the others and they will be defeated in time. Even so, they are going to give us quite a fight for our money.'

'Wars! Always bloody wars!' The president Jerry complained.

'We are all involved you know. As Lord Vektron said: each of us in his or her own little way. Even so, most of us won't be in the front line,' Meron replied.

Jerry stared at Meron with sterner features as if aroused into a state of warlike fury.

'I will like to get a darn good shot at those nasty monsters, so you just tell me what I have to do to see a little action. Those darn Javols are not going to get away with anything in this galaxy of ours. You here me! Not one little thing!' Jerry snapped.

The Ship suddenly spoke to its crew:

'You may now resume a relaxed position within your bunks, ready to be transposed to Siron II.

'All causal matter must now be transposed.'

The warning sirens sounded.

CHAPTER 1

A beautiful planet called Eden

Having viewed all planets in the Solar System in great detail, the Andromedan ship was now on its way to the stars with its 12 keen passengers. They were to explore several new worlds for the possibility of human habitation and in the process experience and learn more about cosmic existence. Those worlds had been assigned to Solaria and Earth by the Grand Lord of our part of the universe.

It was the USA president's first journey into outer-space and he was excited in anticipation, but worried in case they became stranded in its black immensity.

The brave crew assisted each other into the twelve bunks, the canopies descended while The Ship began once more to vibrate. The vibration was followed by a bright light that tended to penetrate everything, even their bodies. After a short period, to be measured only in seconds, they found themselves in complete darkness and their canopies lifted.

To everyone's amazement the bluish disk of a most beautiful planet was displayed on the large screen in vivid detail. The complete planetary system was also displayed to one side. It comprised six planets of varying sizes and atmospheric constituents. The beautiful world they viewed had no satellite moons of its own. All its varying land masses were linked as one throughout the globe.

Although Siron II was slightly smaller than Earth, it boasted one super-continent, with many lakes and seas interspersed within that single land mass. Its oceans and seas were lesser than Earth's, making its fertile land masses much more extensive as a result. After a thorough analysis its surface environment appeared very similar to Earth. The planet was just at the correct distance from its parent star for the optimum survival of its many carbon-based life-forms. Although a little smaller, her star was slightly bluer and brighter than our sun, Sol.

Once again The Ship spoke to its crew:

'Siron II, Lori III, Colmi II and the Colmi III systems have been assigned to the Solarian System under treaty. Therefore you may land on these worlds without special permission from the Greater Purpose. However I strictly recommend the use of facial filters for our first visit. This precaution is because certain pollen strains may cause allergic reaction to those not used to this environment, even to a point of intoxication.'

'What's this you say? Facials for pollen!' Jerry shouted back boisterously, unconcernedly about The Ship's warning.

'I did not come all this way to be hindered by a few grains of pollen?'

He was adamant and fully intended to walk on this his first new world as Christopher Columbus had done with his America many centuries before. After all, it was the first living planet he had ever visited outside of Earth, so he wanted to feel and smell that brand new environment. Perhaps he might even rename it, Earth II, and so he thought.

The Ship soon landed at a selected spot close to the shores of an inland sea. That area bordered a large forest with many giant flowers in full bloom. They were nothing like he had ever seen before. They resembled the hibiscus variety, but were super giants by comparison that could automatically adjust their petals to sunlight. The perfume fragrance was intense and intoxicating.

At first sight the entire world appeared to be prehistoric, with forests of large green giant ferns, but there were also a wide variety of plants with numerous flowers of an enchanting nature. Those filled the air with a range of strong and sweet smelling fragrance.

Tiny fairylike creatures of every kind, with large butterfly-like wings could be observed sucking the nectar from those giant flowers. Those little angels completely ignored the visitors and carried on their collecting. They appeared to be essential in the pollination of those plants. Yet, there were no birds in its skies, insects or any other land animals and that fact worried Jerry.

'This is indeed a very strange place. It's so beautiful... it could well be Heaven, with its little angels and fairies everywhere,' Jerry commented.

'These conditions are perfect for evolution. However, it's still a young world, with life within its oceans and seas mainly predatory,' Meron said, while scanning the distant waves with binoculars.

'You think those predatory brutes will one day crawl out of the seas and take over the land?' he inquired somewhat worried.

'In a sense, we are those predatory brutes. However since we cannot hold back the natural process of evolution, that is a very strong possibility. But in this case it will take several hundred million years,' Meron replied and Jerry appeared unconcerned with such a long timescale.

The pollen acted on the travellers like a drug that enhanced their senses and emotions until they felt like gods.

Jerry thought that perhaps the world developed in a similar manner to Earth, but he soon changed his mind when he observed several variety of flying fish skimming the sea for smaller prey. It was indeed a strange world; for although the land creatures appeared to be some form of intelligent fairy-like insects, they were all noncarnivorous. Each going after the abundance of rich nectar oblivious to any natural predators, while the oceans and seas appeared to be filled with the most determined predators of every conceivable shape and size.

Jerry thought. 'Here is a big contrast in its different habitats. Perhaps no two living planets ever followed an exact course during their evolution. He search as hard as he could but could not find birds or even fruits anywhere. Then he realized the processes of life here were even more complex. As Meron had indicated, it was because that world was still quite young in its evolution. Either that, or it had taken a completely different route during that process.

Fruits were an enticement by plants to large animals and others like bats and birds. They were used as a vehicle to carry seeds in order to assist in the propagation of those plant species. Therefore, there would be little chance of such goodies in the absence of either kinds of animals. Nevertheless, other methods, even edible roots and bulbs could have existed in certain areas if worms or small creatures lived underground. Therefore some form of matured seeds would have been propagated for such life to continue. If indeed they ever existed.

Jerry and Meron followed the shoreline around a small enclosed bay, while observing some fish-like creatures. Many of them were similar to catfish and struggled to paddle their way towards the water's edge, but never too far away from their watery home. Those were learning to avoid predation in the waters and would soon adapt to living on land, where it was much safer for their kind.

'I see what you mean. These are already on their way to conquer the land,' Jerry said and Meron nodded in agreement.

'Here again there are differences between this and both our worlds. The first creatures that invaded land on Earth were crustaceans. Soon after those evolved into large insects. They had conquered the land well before types like dinosaurs took over.' Sharon interjected. She had studied earth's prehistory at university level.

'Although somewhat stranger, I think the processes here are very similar to the young Earth, although initially appearing to be quite different. You know, these fairylike creatures could well be the insect-like remnants of those first crustaceans. Further, Earth had taken many meteoric strikes and other setbacks during its life, which would have caused extensive changes in its biological selections at each upheaval. This world, on the other hand, most probably never had a major disaster in all its existence,' Meron said and Jerry was astonished.

'Wow! I fill like a kid again and so full of energy!' Jerry shouted and took a giant leap into the air.

As of yet, there was no observable survival struggle on land and that pleased Jerry. However he soon realized humans had a way of making things tidy like they did to their flower gardens, while mother nature was never tidy. Nevertheless he liked the idea of a peaceful and serene world that was uncontaminated by the presence of man and other unworthy predators. He swore that world would always remain that way.

At current progress it would have taken the sea creatures several million years to establish themselves on land, thus giving its present more natural occupants a long time to evolve and move on.

Jerry escorted Meron to a hilltop in order to view the distant shores of their newly found paradise. He inhaled the fresh and contaminated air with a long and steady breath that was filled with its inviting fragrance.

'Wow Pal! I would dearly love to retire to this world... perhaps introduce a few horses, cattle and some other herbivorous animal types... including some beautiful greens for my golf, providing it didn't create an ecological disaster,' Jerry said, happily.

'Me too! Let's take a few samples back with us for evaluation,' Meron replied, ecstatically.

'This is truly the most incredibly beautiful world. It's just like... It's just like Eden in the bible. That must have been just before man and woman came into existence to spoil it all,' Jerry said, while taking a leap over a small pile of rocks.

'It is very much like my own world before the Javols came,' Meron replied and Jerry suddenly became serious.

'You guys are looking for a new settlement world. Are you not? Well, you need look no further. This is it! Do you think you and your people can resettle here without detrimentally affecting the indigenous life?' he inquired of Meron.

'Yes, Jerry, I am sure we can! But this is your world?' he replied.

'No, Pal! This is our world! Don't forget, we are now twinned with Caefon as one people. The greedy and abusive population of Earth need never know of our future plans. Anyway, if our humans got to know of this beautiful world, very soon there would be nothing left of it. Once it got into the hands of Estate Agents, Road Builders and others. We must never mention a word about this paradise world to anyone outside of our group,' Jerry insisted and Meron suddenly became a very happy man, knowing that their search for a settlement world was finally at an end. In his excitement Jerry took another leap and twisted an ankle. They were surprised when it healed almost immediately.

'Jon!... Merol!... We need to take more specimen samples!' Meron shouted in ecstasy.

Soon they began collecting samples and specimens and had to go back several times for more containers. Meron wanted to make a thorough analysis of that world. When they were finished collecting, Jerry and Meron got the crew together.

'Guys, we have found our new Caefon. This is where we shall build our first city. However, this world will be called Eden and it must always be kept as the most beautiful paradise world in Osmaron. I know it will be a major project, but when we are finished, it will be a standard for every world in this galaxy to follow. So henceforth, we need only concern ourselves with the temporary evacuation to Mars,' Meron said and they were ecstatic with that knowledge. A heavy burden had been lifted off the shoulders of Jon, Lira and their other colleagues.

Although quite invigorated by the environment, the women took little notice of the pollen dust and started to prepare a hot picnic lunch at a selected spot just a few metres from The Ship.

Tomas and Hamil had assisted in mounting a small tent in that area near the ship, to which was added a plastic picnic table with unfolding stools. Amidst much joy and laughter, Tomas, Hamil, Sintra and others collected Video Cameras and went to take pictures of flora, fauna and whatever insects and fish they could find. They were strict vegetarians, so the idea of collecting animals on the new world, with its abundant marine life did not occur to them.

Since the planet had no moons of its own, waves appeared to be almost constant in frequency, giving a strange rippling pattern along its sandy shores. Although the weather appeared extremely stable, a pleasant breeze could be felt occasionally. After a while they returned to the tent for lunch.

Despite the variety and quantity of food displayed on the picnic table, there were no insects. Not even a single fly or mosquito to add the usual nuisance value to the picnic and the women were surprised.

'You know. This place with its lack of insects is so strange, but is ideal for the perfect picnic... with no unwanted bugs or flies to be a constant bother. Also, I can't see any litter anywhere. This must be the most enjoyable picnic of my life,' Jerry's wife, Sharon, said and they laughed.

'If it's so sterile, I wonder how it will affect our immune systems during any long term occupation,' Lira remarked.

'It can't be. There will always be waste recycling, or this world would not be so clean,' Merol interjected.

'We can always take along the common cold and a few other unfriendlier bugs from Earth, if you wish,' Jon commented and they had another good laugh.

After lunch, Plato made a list of the important aspects of their visit while the others went away to do some more collecting of specimens and samples. The more intelligent life-forms were not included on that list. However they were studied and recorded whenever possible.

Jerry had decided to rename the new planet Eden instead of Earth II. In his opinion that world was a real paradise. It was so unlike Earth, which was completely savage by comparison. He intended to make the whole world a garden park with no technologies or manufacturing allowed. It would be a world where only a few selected beautiful life-forms would be allowed to coexist in harmony with its indigenous populations. Nevertheless, Eden had more than enough of its own beautiful flowers, so only fruit trees and grass would be introduced in certain designated areas for human habitation. Green grass would be for his golf and the few grazing herbivores to be introduced later.

CHAPTER 2

Intelligent reptiles are discovered

Lori III was the next planet on their list to be visited. It was in the centre of a tri-planetary system. Her two distant neighbours being much too massive and extreme climatically to support normal biological life as we know it. One was slightly larger than Jupiter and the other like Saturn. Both displayed beautiful rings.

The main Earth-type planet was quite massive compared to Earth. Although about three times Earth's size, its density was somewhat less. It boasted two massive continents, one in the north and the other towards the south pole, with one very large ocean close to the equator. There were numerous seas, lakes and islands. Some islands even larger than the largest continents on Earth. There were extensive volcanic activity along one side of the continent which had a significant effect on the atmosphere of that world.

That planet appeared to be warmer than Earth and displayed a wide desert band along its equatorial region that almost encircled the planet. Its arctic and antarctic regions were green with little snow covering. Snow saturated the tops of its rugged mountain ranges in those regions.

Lori III had nine moons. The planet could be seen with several eclipses or dark spots moving over its daylight surface.

'What an incredible spectacle. How can anything live on such a massive world?' an ecstatic Jerry queried, while observing the expanse of blue, violet and green throughout the globe.

'Pal, you will be surprised what can happen in the course of evolution once life takes root. The survival urge within all living organisms can be very strong and given enough time, may adapt to even the most extreme conditions,' Meron replied.

'Then, you think life is ubiquitous throughout the Cosmos?' Jerry inquired.

'Pal, life is just another state of matter. Like water changing into ice, liquid or steam, when the conditions are right, molecules will become more complex, until a type of DNA is reached. Once that happens, the process of reproduction can start and rampant evolution ensues. Life is like a written code throughout the Cosmos. There is little random chance in the process,' Meron said and Jerry was aghast by that knowledge.

Jerry observed the screen and couldn't quite accept the strangeness of that massive world beneath them. Although it had so many moons, the three largest ones were spaced almost equidistantly in near identical orbits and were about the size of Mars, although with somewhat larger atmospheres.

Its gravitational pull and atmospheric pressure were several times that of Earth and its weather, although seemingly stable, could have been extremely turbulent judging from the greater volume. Because of those reasons, its skyline, moons and sunsets would have been quite stunning when viewed from its surface. Nevertheless on that day the cloud cover was sparse and formed wisps that floated mainly at high altitude.

While approaching, several large craters could be visibly observed along its equator, within the equatorial desert band.

'Large falling asteroids in geological times could have accounted for the great desert band that almost encircles this massive world,' Meron said and Jerry nodded positively.

Jerry, with Plato's advice, decided to land at the lower half of its northern region. They intended to pay that giant world a brief visit to recover some specimens and samples. This time they decided to wear facial filters, not knowing what dangers awaited them. However as always, their exploration would be with minimum technological assistance, since they wanted to feel the environment through their own natural senses.

Although the Shadite Plato knew everything was relatively safe, he allowed his crew much latitude in implementing their own choices. In his opinion, placing them in the deep end was an essential part of the survival equation. It was necessary for them to gain experience of other worlds, new survival scenarios and alien environments. Plato, The Shadite, had always been a great teacher and knew well the limits of his students.

The Ship set down in a seemingly peaceful and tranquil area close to the shores of a northern sea. The moment they landed the ship became neutral and they immediately became aware of a much greater change in their weight and atmospheric pressure. Although it was slightly uncomfortable at first, with parts of their bodies being pulled unevenly, they were quite fit and able to tolerate the experience of more extreme gravity.

When The Ship opened its entrance there was a sudden inward gush of methane loaded air. This time Jerry took the lead, moving slowly down the glittering staircase. He could observe trees everywhere, including a type of mauve grass, but the terrain consisted mainly of large earth mounds containing hundreds of holes. Each hole was perhaps half a metre in diameter. The area stank to high heavens and he wondered what caused the excessive generation of ammonia and methane gas, not to mention those strange looking mounds. He pondered those thoughts with trepidation and held firmly to his position on the stairway with no desire to place his feet on that planet; at least, not until he had some reassurance from Plato. That world was nothing like beautiful Eden.

It was then that he observed two large orange eyes peering out of a lower hole in one of the closer mounds. The creature's eyes were followed by a large head and an even larger body.

The strange life-form was even more frightened of him than he was of it. It had a medium length tail, was very quick and walked in an almost upright manner on two very powerful hind legs, perhaps gaining balance at speed with its powerful tail. But it could also have been used for defence.

The two much smaller front limbs were used as hands and appeared very similar to human hands ,with the same number of digits, but with sharp claws that were webbed for swimming, digging and hunting. To Jerry it resembled an illustration he once observed of a type of dinosaur called a Velociraptor. But this creature, although appearing reptilian, had a large head and rough scales throughout its tough body for protection. It was perhaps just two metres long from head to tail. He remembered the raptor was about the most dangerous of dinosaurs, so he retreated closer to the ship's entrance. The creature became fearful of him and ran off initially squeaking as it did, but stopped in its tracks and slowly returned to observe the strange craft and its visitor.

That life-form was very inquisitive, even showing signs of high intelligence, but did not appear to be ferocious or carnivorous, at least not towards them.

Soon after it began to make another loud squawking sound which changed in frequency, pitch and composition. Before long hundreds of little eyes were peering out of their holes.

The Ship very quickly analysed the creature's speech pattern and began to speak to them in their own tongue which when interpreted, meant:

'Do not be afraid. We are your friends from another great world in the skies.

'We are here to assess your world in order to assist your development at some later date.

'We have no intention of detrimentally disturbing your cultures or ways of living, now or in the foreseeable future.'

The creatures were astonished by the fluent use of their language and bowed to the visitors, who remained standing on the glittering stairway like glowing gods in their special shiny suits while in bright daylight. Then what appeared to be a blue crested male plucked the courage and stood up from among his group to speak, saying in his strange tongue.

'Dear masters of the skies, we are a peaceful race with little desires and welcome your presence in our humble domain. Do not be afraid of our appearance, we revere you and will not attempt to harm you, less the thunder and lightning may come and destroy us.' He moved his tail from side to side.

The Ship asked him his name and that of his tribe.

'I am Ooh-Kaa and my tribe is known to all as Hi-chie. Our tribal knowledge relate to a world in two halves but separated by a great desert called Mo-Lat. That desert is infested by deadly sand reptiles and serpents. We have never been able to cross its great expanse to visit the southern regions, which our ancestors say is ruled by large dragons, but I personally believe that place to be very similar to our own continent,' he replied calmly and this time with little tail movement.

Plato then spoke to the creature in its own tongue.

'Ooh-Kaa, we would like to collect some plants and other specimens to take back with us. Can you and your people assist us in this venture?' Once again the creature began to move his tail from side to side.

He explained the process to them and they joined the crew in the collection program.

When they were finished, Ooh-Kaa asked if they wanted to take one of his little children along. That one had recently hatched from one of the underground nests, but Plato said he couldn't take a child away from its home and family.

From information received, the creatures lived in large groups within the interiors of great dugout mounds. Those underground areas consisted of larger caves leading into specific areas for feeding, sleeping, playing and egg-laying. Their underground villages were guarded against intruders, who would sometimes rob the large eggs and infants. However there were no birds or indeed any flying creatures within the sky. Mammals were not even considered by the strange evolving order of that world.

Those creatures showed little inventiveness. There was virtually no technology of any kind. It was perhaps due to the nature of the planet and the sociological structure of the species involved; for even on Earth, creatures like alligators and crocodiles remained virtually unchanged for hundreds of millions of years. But this creature was different, with an intelligence perhaps equivalent to man and yet man had only learnt the use of tools quite recently in his evolution. Perhaps like mankind they had to be pushed along a specific survival path, whereby they could create a use for a need and vise versa along with the associated tools and weapons.

Although Jerry was still quite frightened by the little monsters, he kept a brave face with firm resolve and a hardy disposition. He could see much promise in that new life-form. Perhaps they could be trained to guard their planet in the name of Solaria... the new Solarian Government, he thought.

Lira took a sample of blood from one of the creatures for further analysis and realized it was as red as her own, then she glanced at Jon with surprise.

'They are not all green-blooded monsters, you know,' she said and he smiled. It was a known fact that most carbon-based life used iron to transfer oxygen, and all such were red blooded. That aspect caused many carbon based creatures in the universe to be similar.

They said their farewell and vanished like gods from the world of reptiles, leaving behind concepts of gods with invisible flying machines. Those incredible tales would live-on in the minds of their great reptilian patriarchs a long time in their future.

The Ship followed a path towards the southern region, but they decided to leave that world for now, as time was pressing.

CHAPTER 3

Opposite worlds

Barely ten Earth hours had passed when they arrived on Colmi II. That system was quite different from their two previous visits and consisted of seven planets, each retaining several satellite moons. The forth planet resembled Jupiter and boasted a beautiful display of multicolored rings. That world was much closer to its parent star than Jupiter was to our sun. The star appeared twice the size of Earth's star, Sol.

Colmi II and Colmi III were of similar mass. The former being the smaller of the two and a lot warmer. This was because of a thicker carbon dioxide layer and its closer proximity to the star. Both worlds appeared habitable and were spaced almost equidistantly within closed orbits around their parent star. Their near circular orbits were matched to such an extent that it was quite possible that the inhabitants of both worlds never knew of the other's existence. Since the companion followed a closely matched orbit it was always on the far side of the star at any given time when observed from the other.

'No two stellar systems can ever be the same. Each one being unique with its own identity. There were too many dynamic variables during their formation from the original accretion disc,' Meron said.

'Are these types of planetary formations always the same? I mean created from an accretion disk,' Jerry asked with curiosity.

'Almost always. Stellar systems behave more like an organ in a much larger body and will allow a set path in their growth that is quite akin to following some form of invisible DNA. That is mainly because stars are formed within stellar nurseries with the necessary ingredients. Because of certain types of interactions that type of order will control their formation to limit growth. Here, I am not thinking of the effects of gravity and such like. For instance, instead of having one massive planet, they will most likely grow several.'

'You mean... the evolution of a universe follows a set plan?'

'Yes! Universes may be considered a type of life at a higher dimension, with the ability to maintain their own survival causation. As such, they can procure new sibling universes. I like to think of universes like multi-dimensional trees, with galaxies like fruits and leaves on branches. Each spiral galaxy with a black hole nucleus ready to seed a new universe. After all, what is life? It's a process whereby matter is ordered in a specific way to reproduce its own kind, and is able to evolve in order to improve its survival causation. Life does not have to be biological. It could be Robotic, Silicon based, Crystal based, Electro-magnetic base, etc, etc. All it must do is reproduce it's own kind and evolve.'

'That's quite a revelation, and of all things I have the feeling you are right,' Jerry replied.

'You know, most of our universe is invisible to us, and there are many controlling mechanisms that make these complex structures as unique as living organisms,' Meron said and Jerry remained still for a while in deep contemplation.

'You are saying that universes could be living organisms in their own right and may be akin to whales swimming in their own invisible oceans of the Cosmos?' he said.

'Yes, I suppose so! But a better comparison is with trees. Even so, they will be infinitely more complex. You know, over 96 percent of our Universe is invisible to us,' he replied.

'Oh my God! If that's the case, a magnificent Creator must exist to control it all,' he said and Meron nodded in agreement.

'Strictly speaking a god is not necessary, since positive evolution takes place at all levels. As they say, what don't kill you makes you stronger, and the force of Chaos is always there to pull us down and make the survivors stronger,'

The first world to be visited was Colmi II. That planet was mostly desert. Nevertheless it was dotted with small seas and lakes throughout. The greatest diversity of life being predominant towards the northern and southern polar caps.

The antarctic region contained the largest of all seas. Large mountain ranges straddled the many wide bands of greenish vegetation. They decided to land within a region close to its largest sea.

Plato was first to walk on the planet, followed by Meron and Jerry. Facials were also included. Those measures made them more prepared for the occasional sandstorms. They worried about microbes, but Lumak had given them several medicines before they left Earth for that purpose. Nevertheless the planet's weather pattern appeared to be quite stable.

They continued to walk towards a small wooded area through a grasslike terrain. The trees and surface covering were not like anything they had seen on any of their previous planetary visits and distinctly resembled those found in tropical desert regions on Earth.

Signs of local animal life could not be seen anywhere so they decided to move closer to the woodlands straddling the shore.

Meron and Jerry were soon sweating from the high humidity and heat. Jerry was first to brake the silence.

'This is not like our Eden, but could make a great prison planet for our worst convicts.' Jerry felt utterly disgusted.

'You know. Jerry... this could have been a most beautiful planet once. I mean, some time in the distant past... but I get the distinct impression it follows this current disastrous path because of a previous period of excessive abuse and pollution. This abuse could have gone on for many centuries... Perhaps by a very advanced civilisation... the evidence is everywhere, despite the lack of ruins and other telltale signs... Anyway, all relics of that bygone past could have been dissolved away into the raw chemistry of the planet by now. Either that, or corroded by the frequent sand storms over a timescale of several hundred thousand years. There could even have been some type of global thermonuclear warfare, but there are little signs of the resultant radiation or indeed any massive craters to substantiate that theory. A previous advanced civilization, not necessarily like us, could have existed here.'

'In that case, this must be a very old world,' Jerry replied.

'Not necessarily. I think what we see here is the result of induced environmental pollution caused by a very advanced technology. That stage of development could have been reached more than a million years ago and all that is left remaining could be the residual life after the planet's most final and desperate attempt of recovery. The survivors could have left for another world.'

'Not Earth, I hope?'

'It's difficult to say. You could even be the descendants of those ancient survivors. As much as we Andromedans will soon settle in this galaxy and bring new life to a new world.'

'Wow! You are so right!'

'This world must be at least 3 billion years older than Earth and is now approaching old age. I think Earth will be very much like this one in about the same time period. However even such worlds may be revitalized with the necessary terra forming technologies. From observation, its star is still active and might have another 3 to 4 billion years left with a stable output.'

'What a complex universe in which we live!' Jerry said.

'A world can be considered a giant organism... With love and attention it may live forever and flourish, but with neglect, it may become just like this one,' Meron further advised.

Jerry looked towards the distant deserts and couldn't even consider the remote possibility of planet Earth ever becoming like their present hostile one. Suddenly he became aware of Earth's status in the scheme of things and was more concerned for her future existence.

'We always tend to take our homes for granted until they begin to fall on top of us.'

'Yes Pal, this is indeed a good reminder of what can go wrong when greed, self-indulgence and selfishness predominates within any advanced civilization. And I am afraid, Earth is currently following a similar path, to ultimate destruction and death,' Meron replied.

'I see what you mean!'

'We had been through a similar period ourselves and will never forget the lessons learned,' Meron said.

It was now around midday on the planet and small clouds could be clearly seen forming against its horizon. They waited for while, but there was no sign of life, even of birds or insects, neither was there any flowers. Just thorny bushes and plants with long sharp spines. Most of which closely resembled the Cacti variety. Yet, the planet was not all dead. Barely one hundred metres away a strange crab-like creature clawed its way out of the sand. It was completely black in colour and was neither insect, reptile nor mammal.

On closer observation it appeared to be a large crab-like scorpion with telescopic eyes, several large pincers for claws and a smaller stinging tail.

It was exceedingly large for a crab, being about forty centimetres across its almost circular body.

It observed them closely but showed little concern and popped its eyes back within its scaly lids, to dive once more into its sandy environment.

It was then that Meron and his gang decided to move away from the sandy areas for greater safety. Under closer observation those areas appeared to contain a greenish insect that fed on a type of moss. They soon realized that there was some form of food chain in operation and the world was evolving new life and recovering once more.

Meron wondered what other secrets that harsh world concealed from them; for he sensed a lot more within its surface.

They would have liked to carry out a more extensive investigation, but time pressing, decided against such dangerous activities. After collecting more biological samples they went back into the much cooler ship for a second lunch.

Finally they decided to pay a brief visit to the other planet, Colmi III, before returning to Earth.

Jerry had felt very uneasy on Colmi II. Despite its sticky and un-welcoming heat, it reminded him of an experience he once had in the Arizona Desert. During that time he barely survived two days and nights without food or water. On that occasion he and others of his regiment were on a tough survival course and missed the rendezvous point, having taken the wrong direction with his faulty compass.

Luckily for him he had taken along some flares and was eventually rescued by an army helicopter. That experience had always remained with him, and that planet brought back those memories most vividly. For some odd reason that place gave him the willies, but perhaps he was jumping to conclusions too prematurely. He had always believed in fair play, which meant giving everyone a fair chance, but even so, that planet was definitely the most disappointing.

'My God! This place is so harsh, it could make the ideal penal colony for our worst criminals! Luckily, no flies or mosquitoes!' Jerry commented, with sweat pouring from his body. He tried drying himself with his handkerchief but it was soaking and had little effect.

'I don't know much about you, but I would rather be executed than spend a year wandering in this petrified and humid wilderness. Nevertheless, it serves a good lesson to us all... of what things can become through our own negligent hands,' Meron replied.

They arrived on Colmi III soon afterwards, but this time landed on a semi fertile area at its equatorial region. Although the world was much colder, it was a little larger than its sister and compensated for its reduced stellar radiation by a much denser atmosphere.

There were more ice and water on Colmi III than on any of the other worlds visited, even during monsoon on Earth. It was pouring during their arrival and continued even after then. Plato insisted on visiting to collect specimens and samples, so they used whatever covering they could find. Nevertheless they decided to mount the picnic tent close to the ship.

The near tropical planet was teaming with insects, small reptiles and plants of every variety imaginable, including several varieties of flowers. They soon discovered an assortment of small reptilian creatures resembling lizards. They could change their colours at will to match those of the flowers, making them virtually invisible to their predators. However all those creatures had four legs and two small hands. Some would climb the flowering plants with suction feet and patiently wait for flying insects with their long retractable folded tongue.

Birds and mammals could not be seen anywhere and all life very small by comparison. The main difference of that world was its constant chorus of song. Like crickets on Earth, all those insects were constantly communicating with each other.

'Although of similar age to the previous world, this planet is either younger or a late starter. Either way, it's much younger than Earth. Perhaps even at an age corresponding to just before the first dinosaurs existed and began to take over the land. So this world holds many questions and could make an ideal laboratory for our geneticist,' Meron said and Jerry nodded, while brushing a persistent insect from buzzing too close to his nose.

The planet's atmosphere was extremely turbulent and stormy, while its weather pattern showed little sign of predictability, so they decided to collect as many samples and specimens as they could before departing.

Jerry was very disappointed with his visits to the Colmi worlds, but thought they were habitable by mankind with little adjustment to their respective environments. Yet those Colmi worlds showed the two extremes of planetary evolution. In any case, they were all living worlds and hence, much better for re-settlement than a dead world like Mars. Even so, with the exception of Earth, Mars was in his opinion the most suited of all planets within the solar system for human settlement, but could not compare with any living world. Therefore, this evaluation trip could never be considered a wasted effort.

'Of those four worlds I definitely prefer Eden. But Lori III, despite its more extreme gravity is also quite suitable for human settlement. I am sure our bodies would adapt to such worlds in time,' Jerry said.

'Perhaps, but I think this one is better left to its beautiful multicoloured reptiles for now,' Meron replied.

Despite the apparent harshness of some of those worlds, they were obviously full of natural resources, and humans could always import some of their own plants and seeds, providing they had negligible effect on the indigenous ecological systems.

Jerry realized how critical the introduction of alien life could be for any naturally evolving system. They were all so precisely balanced that even a simple virus like the common cold could cause irreparable damage.

Animals from other local worlds would be kept well away initially until a more thorough analysis could be made by the terra forming scientists. If such a detailed analysis was not completed before any human settlement and relevant measures taken, it could have led to major problems for the indigenous life in such precisely balanced ecosystems. Nevertheless there was always the option of isolation dome habitats.

Jerry soon realized how diverse the Cosmos was and soon came to the conclusion that no two planets ever underwent the same processes during its evolution. They were individuals and like mothers, nurtured their own types of children. He also realized that he could never in all his short remaining life ever allow self-indulgent mankind to settle on any of those worlds. Not even in the hot and uncomfortable deserts of Colmi II.

CHAPTER 4

War between worlds

Finally, they were on their way home, or so they thought, until The Ship spoke to them in its usual polite and diplomatic manner:

'May I suggest a slight diversion on our way? We are to visit the Polokan system. That visit is very important and is within a local spiral arm of our galaxy.'

This time a new image was displayed on the screen, showing the relative positions of the stellar systems to Earth within the spiral arms of Osmaron. Our galaxy was shown to comprise of just three major indistinct arms which spiralled out of its nucleus quite symmetrically. Their new destination was dotted in red. That system was in another arm of the galaxy.

They realized they had to agree with the ship and once more took their places within their bunks. Before long the whole ship and its crew were transposed to the new system.

That galactic arm was much denser with stars than our own. Towards its centre were two systems about three light years apart.

Once again the screen changed to display all relevant parameters, with yellow dots representing their destination worlds and numerous red dots indicating concealed Octan bases that were only detectable by the most advanced Class 5 civilizations with special equipment. Although those bases existed, they were Virtual Massless Bases that did not affect the system. However, they could be transposed into our reality when needed. Such were the advanced technologies of the Octans.

As they approached Polok II they could observe several large base stations and ships orbiting the planet. Judging from their size and make, they were obviously constructed for waging a sustained war, but where were they from?

Occasionally a missile would be ejected from the planet's surface only to be countered by several missiles and hot plasma beams from the orbiting ships and spheres.

The larger ships apparently knew that they had already won the war and were only returning fire at just the correct levels necessary to neutralise the mobile missile stations on the planet's surface, or so it appeared.

They observed the situation for a while and to their further surprise several of the larger vessels were under attack by smaller ships coming from the planet's surface. Those small fighters did not show on their screens until The Ship utilized its more sensitive detectors.

The small fighters were obviously concealing themselves from the larger orbiting vessels and spheres by some new and unknown method of shielding.

Several missiles were fired from the invisibly cloaked fighters. When a missile hit its preselected target it vaporized in one massive nuclear explosion. The sight was foreboding to watch and disturbing. Jerry and the Andromedans were always against the use of nuclear weapons, even in space, but the other side appeared to be fighting for their very survival.

It was not long before all the larger orbiting stations on the viewer was destroyed, with the exception of a larger and more specialised enemy sphere that had been ignored for a specific purpose.

'This is a real war we've found ourselves in and a nuclear one at that. Don't these fools realize their callous actions can lead to further escalation,' Meron complained.

'My brother, judging from the looks of their world, I don't think they have anything left to lose, do you?' Plato commented. While they observed the pitted and cratered world.

'I think that attack was for revenge and could also be a cry for help,' Jerry said.

'Jerry, you are very perceptive. We must help them, if we can,' Plato replied.

The Ship suddenly spoke to its crew:

'This situation you now observe is the continuation of an

interstellar war between separate species in local stellar systems.

'The two races involved are the Polokans, who live within the cratered world you now observe. They are under constant siege by their enemy, the Lodorians.

'By comparison, the Polokans are very much like you, but with a more advanced technology than on Earth, while the Lodorians come from the more distant system of Lodor III, here shown circled.

'The Lodorians are the more advanced of both species, who have conquered and ruled over Polok since the beginning of the bombardment.

'Lodorians are not human by nature and are a more ancient race.

'The present war has continued for more than one hundred years. During that time the few remaining Polokans found ways to survive on their battered world. They are not the type to give up or surrender. Now they require our assistance to bring lasting peace to both systems,'

'I like their guts! After all, it's their damn world! I would never give my Earth up to anyone, for anything! One hundred years? How could anyone exist in those conditions for that long?' Jerry exclaimed.

Jerry could not believe his eyes, for most of the once beautiful planet's surface was cratered and lay in utter waste. All major centres of civilization had been obliterated. Overgrown and ruined cities could be observed everywhere, but there were still a few fertile areas remaining. Those were mainly in the mountainous regions.

Human life could not be observed anywhere so it was thought incendiaries and other forms of biological weapons had destroyed most animal life during the initial phase of destruction. However there was still some opposition and that meant there were survivors.

Still observing the almost unbelievable desolation, Jerry spoke out again.

'How can anyone still exist on such a barren and ruined world, never mind to plan the most effective attack we've just observed?' he commented with astonishment.

The Ship replied:

'They went underground.

'Their enemies are not yet aware of that fact, because they have not been able to land since the initial phase of bombardment, to make the necessary observations. However, Polok is now ready to strike back, and as you have just seen, they require your assistance.'

Jerry turned his head around to observe the others, but with utter surprise.

'What do you mean...my assistance?'

'Yes! Your assistance!' Plato replied with a broad smile and Meron nodded his head.

'You mean to say... after all this time, we were on an interstellar diplomatic mission?' he inquired.

The cunning Ship replied:

'You may call it that, if you wish!'

Jerry turned around to Plato for an answer.

'I don't mind a little action, but this will be without any knowledge, preparation or planning on my part. What if I broke some of their customs and rules?' Jerry hesitated.

'Don't worry about such matters. After all, I am Shadite and may lead you in such matters,' Plato said, and Jerry calmed himself.

'I suppose that's what I get paid for, so let's get on with business, then! Anyone in that situation can do with a little help. Do I wear my diplomatic gear?' he asked, dubiously.

'Yes, Jerry, you must look the part. After all, it is the first time Solaria is being represented politically in another advanced system. We should all be ambassadors during this mission,' Plato replied, smiling.

They made themselves ready while wearing their best. Meron was in his special robe, including dangling scabbard and sword.

Jerry was spectacularly dressed in his grey suit with white shirt and bold red tie. Plato had insisted everyone took such special attire on board before leaving Earth.

Despite those measures, they had to enter their bunks for a vectored transposition to the underground city. During that process The Ship was capable of altering its material structure somewhat different to normally vectored matter. This process was better known as Vectoring and caused the ship to move through solid and dense matter as if through water much like a submarine. This time it had no intentions of concealing itself from the underworld people involved.

The Ship landed within one of the larger underground city complexes. When it materialised most of the local people ran for their lives. It was not long before the narrow streets were clear of traffic. Soon to follow were a small mobile military unit carrying what appeared to be a laser weapon that also discharged missiles.

The Ship communicated with the senior officer in charge of the mobile unit:

'We are visitors from another stellar system several thousand light years away and have come in peace!

'We represent Solaria, and as you can see, are not of a similar construction to those of your enemies. Neither are we armed with weapons of any description.'

The officer was by now utterly dumbfounded and frightened by the strange aberration. Nor could he believe in the existence of such a massive object speaking to him in his own tongue and in such an intelligible manner. He and his gunner remained confused for a while.

'How can anyone from beyond the stars know of our language? Not unless it's our enemies, the Lodorians... the large object has no doors or entrances... and has been thoroughly investigated by sensitive scanners... with no results,' the captain thought. Nevertheless he held his aim until he gained permission from his superiors.

Using his small communicator he relayed all information received from the strange craft to his senior officers, but held his position.

'Captain! What shall we do! What shall we do!' he shouted impatiently and in utter fright.

'Don't do anything. Just observe the object while I contact Command,' he responded in the loud communicator.

Before long that same information was received by their chief, Malik, who had suddenly become anxious for the safety of his people.

'What if this thing is some type of doomsday weapon, to be triggered by the slightest military intervention. It could be another one of their clever invented deceptions, you know. But how could they have known about our concealed underground cities and are able to get here in such a manner, using some previously unknown technology... To pass undetected through solid matter? Even if they knew of our present operations, it would have taken them a day at least to plan counter measures, and we would have known their intentions through our spies, Darling!' his wife Mira responded.

'If what I think is correct, they must also have spies within our midst. If that is the case we are already doomed. For they will shortly be arriving to drop penetration incendiaries that can reach even our lowest cities,' Malik said, despondently.

'But, my darling, what if they are an even more advanced civilization that have really come from some other more distant system?'

'You think?'

'What if they were to get through our enemies' screens and visit us without even their slightest knowledge.' Mira was sympathetic, while trying to calm him down.

'Can you remember what your father told you once about advance life-forms, like the friend he met... who could walk through walls? What if they are from such an advanced civilization?'

He turned around and glanced at his perceptive wife in utter astonishment.

'I know you are very intuitive, but that is not possible. How do you know that the object is a ship that could do such things?'

'It's the most likely conclusion!'

'A ship that can speak in our own language?'

'Yes! Why not? Lumak, the friend of your father spoke in our language!' she advised.

'Even if what you say is true. They couldn't have chosen a more inappropriate time for their visit; right in the middle of our greatest military operations!'

Malik knew his wife well and was aware of her special intuitive powers, so he knelt before her and kissed her hand before departing, still contemplating the presence of the strange object.

Having thoroughly considered the tricky situation from all angles, he came to the conclusion that the object was not sent by the Lodorians, but would have to see it himself and establish communication.

He gave the necessary orders via his communicator and a small ship arrived with two military escorts. They were to accompany him to where the object stood.

Malik was very tall and rough looking, but handsome in a tough and abrasive manner. As a guerilla fighter he wore a black leathery suit with many pieces of electronic equipment and weapons on belts, hand and arm bracelets. On his head was a small helmet with 3D stereo attachments in a retractable visor.

His whole body was itself a master computer and telecommunications station that linked to a central control system.

Although human, no one knew exactly to what degree, because many of his vital organs could have been replaced by more efficient and longer lasting synthetic parts that were renewable. As a guerilla fighter he had been damaged by war over a period of many decades. So far he was over 100 years old, but still resembled a 40 year old Earth human.

The small craft soon arrived, so he climbed out while accompanied by two female escorts. On his world both sexes were equal in all things. Bravely and slowly he moved towards The Ship while followed by his two female escorts and attempted communication. The other military troops stationed themselves close by and took aim.

'You say that you are from another... more distant system?' Malik inquired, nervously.

The Ship soon responded:

'Please wait and do not be afraid! My passengers will be with you shortly!'

The side of the ship suddenly melted into a stairway, throwing Malik back in surprise and scaring the remaining soldiers into a more protective stance about their leader. All weapons were aimed towards the now opening entrance. There they waited in silence, not knowing what to expect.

Malik moved his large arms slowly upwards with fingers outstretched, signalling to his men to remain calm. The entrance dissolved and to his further surprise a human figure showed his face, to be followed by several others, slowly walking down the glittering stairway.

Malik slowly approached Jerry, now wearing a grey suit. He was followed by Meron, wearing his special robe with sword and jewelled scabbard dangling at his side. Plato wore his Black Shadite's Cloak with the insignia on his lapel. He was also involved in the intricate plan.

Malik hesitated for a moment before taking Jerry's hand. In detail he observed his veins and eyes for any telltale signs that indicated he was android. Once satisfied that Jerry was not an enemy, he apologised in a tongue that Jerry could not understand, but Plato soon translated.

'I am very sorry, but I had to thoroughly check you out. Our enemies are quite capable of constructing look-a-likes like you. Fortunately for us and yourselves, they are not yet able in constructing types with real flesh and blood,' Malik said, smiling.

Malik then fell into laughter and embraced Jerry. Then he turned his attention to Plato, with his black Shadite's cloak and couldn't take his eyes away from his insignia; for he also wore an identical one. It was the one he had removed from the decaying hand of his dead father and had always kept pinned to his jacket for good luck.

'My late father... the great King Olav, God bless his soul... Anyway, he was once a great warrior that fought with his mercenaries for a powerful emperor within the Sheol Nebula. On his return, he told us of his incredible adventures, which included several stories of that great war.' Plato and the others nodded.

'He died during the first phase of the siege of our planet. God, bless his soul.... I, for one, thought he was immortal... for he had survived so many past battles.'

'Your father was a very great person,' Plato replied.

'Indeed he was! Anyway, he frequently talked about a great human emissary that looked very much like me. He also wore a black cloak like yours with a winged crest also similar to yours, but his name was Lumak, the Sha... dite or some such word.'

'Yes, indeed!'

'My father was forever indebted to him for having saved his life during an attack on one of the hostile planets, somewhere or the other... the name of the place is not too important. We have survived to this day because of certain underworld plans given to my father by this incredible person.'

'I see!'

'Because of that great Sha...dite, we now live! Do you know of this person?' Malik inquired, with a tear of sadness and utter gratitude rolling down his cheeks.

Plato closely observed the insignia Lumak had given his father, Olav and the fact that Malik still wore the item above his left breast for luck.

'What an incredible coincidence? He is also my close friend and now lives within Solaria, the fifth sector arm. The one you call Beyond-Fille.'

'Really? This is truly incredible!'

'His name is Lumak, the Shadite, and I am Plato, the Shadite,' Plato replied.

Suddenly the communicator came alive and Malik turned it on.

'Sire, Polax system. All now in place,' the voice said.

'Lorie, keep me up to date on all future developments or change in status. It's nice to hear your voice. Goodbye!' he replied, nervously.

He broke off the communication and continued his conversation with Plato.

'You say Beyond-Fille, but that is uncharted territory, filled with asteroids and dead zones.'

'It is, indeed!'

'Did you travel through it?'

'In much the same way as we travelled through your planet's surface to this place,' Plato replied, calmly.

'You obviously utilise some form of inter-dimensional transposition... that is well beyond our technological capabilities at this time, but we know at least of its possibility and that is usually enough for our capable scientists,' Malik said, humorously.

'You can have such technologies in the future with little effort, after we have organized some trade agreements, but that aspect should be discussed with Jerry, the Solarian diplomat,' Plato replied with confidence.

Malik smiled.

'But as you can see, we have little to offer you at this time. We are in a stalemate situation here, perhaps even defeated... although we have not yet been told of that fact by our supposed rulers.' Malik was convinced of defeat.

'If you knew all the facts you would consider yourself to be in a much stronger position,' Plato replied.

Malik changed the worrying topic.

'Are you Shadite people truly immortal?'

'Yes, we are!'

'After my father met Lumak his whole attitude towards fighting changed and he became more concerned for the good of all things. I sometimes think his soft attitude towards his political opposition and the Lodorians may have led to the invasion. However, it was his idea to build the underground cities using his own wealth. Without your blueprints and their construction, we would surely be dead by now. Anyway, let bygones be bygones. I have always respected him too much to speak ill, because he was a very great man.'

'I understand!'

'So much for the past, and now I find myself indebted to you in order to fulfil my father's wishes. Therefore, after we have been cleansed, I shall consider it a great honour if you and your friends will be my guests during your brief stay in this makeshift place.'

'May I, on behalf of my colleagues, thank you in advance for your kind hospitality?' Plato said.

'Think nothing of it! You bring us hope and a ray of light in our darkest hour!' Despite our very rough-looking exteriors, we are inherently a peaceful race, believing in the mutual coexistence of all, including the lower species. I suppose my father is mainly to blame for those altruistic concepts. But sometimes we are unable to attain those higher goals and become fully occupied with just basic day to day survival through no fault of our own.'

'Yes! Survival should always take precedence!'

'We must however visit the main hospital centre to cleanse ourselves free of any dangerous organisms that may have accompanied you across space. This area, including your ship must also be disinfected. These precautions are absolutely necessary if we are to survive within this confined underground facility, with limited medical supplies and resources. Further, in such a closed space any type of viral epidemic could spread uncontrollably among our people with disastrous consequences.'

Plato fully understood Malik's concerns and translated all of their previous conversation to Jerry and the others.

Malik soon called Central and before long the soldiers began to leave the area of The Ship. Then a larger mobile craft appeared to take them to the hospital for cleansing.

The whole decontamination process was quick and efficient. Their medical technology was very advanced. Certain sensitive devices could even sniff out the existence of foreign bodies. They simply scanned their clothes with a device that sucked in all substances and gave a full analysis. It was similar to a dog's nose, but many times more sensitive. By simply smelling an individual it could give a complete printout of their ailments and infections. They were not infected by any dangerous organisms and were soon given the all-clear.

While in constant communication with his military, Malik took them to his residence situated at the very top of one of the largest underground buildings.

The Ship was not so lucky. He was given a proper rub down with soapy sponge and very soon had a powerful hose turned in his direction. Although self-cleaning he had little choice in the matter.

CHAPTER 5

Another underground city

Malik's underworld was designed in such a manner as to minimise the use of all types of time and space consuming operations including transportation. For convenience, main pedestrian walkways were sited outside central squares. Those led into inter-building passages and more narrow walkways. Since they utilized powerful fusion generators, everywhere were brilliantly lit. That aspect made the enclosed environment more livable as would have been on the surface.

All other conveyancing were by means of small space craft that roamed the near conical canopy while guided by laser beams, thus forming highways in the sky to speedily transport people and supplies to different stations at different levels. Since those crafts were only on the ground for short periods, while taking on or delivering passengers, this aspect further minimized space.

When not in use, they were parked at the highest levels and used in much the same way as small flying craft like helicopters on Earth, although with much more precision in a more confined environment. All such devices and forms of transport were controlled by a master computer. They did not utilise any type of jet propulsion and were almost completely silent except for the slight pulsating and throbbing felt by their passengers. They were obviously driven by some kind of LPD drive in miniature.

Jon, Merol and Lira were interested in the expansive underworld that stretched as far as the eye could see. One that was even larger than Lower Cantor, and was one of many within that part of the planet.

They tried to find parallels between both underground environments, but little similarity could be found. Both places had been designed and constructed for completely different reasons. Further, there was a lacking of green vegetation, while the beautiful projected canopy with a brilliant artificial sun had not been considered.

Since the Polokans could still freely visit the surface to farm their hidden and screened agricultural fields, such costly additions were not necessary. In the case of Lower Cantor, its population had to be completely contained and remain isolated from the surface for several thousand years. In this case, its occupants resisted too much comfort in isolation.

They were greeted by several dog-like pets, which jumped all over them with excitement. The animals were soon called for food and disappeared.

'This place is truly incredible and well contained from the surface, but it's so different from Lower Cantor,' Lira commented and Jon nodded in agreement.

He found the technological scene most incredible, but that was not all. He realized the universality of the Cosmos and how alien races unknowingly assisted each other through the Greater Mind. Despite the fact that Lower Cantor was all the way over in Andromeda, these people had received its plans, which they modified to their own designs. That knowledge had allowed them to build this place and save themselves. Yet, all that happened because they came in contact with a Shadite.

'Those guys deserve a lot of respect?' he thought. Then he considered Seno's ancient historical records and the Shadite Siit who had assisted Micol and others to repair his own world and wondered where Siit would be at this time.

'Thank God, you guys are immortal!' he said aloud and Lira turned about in curiosity.

'I was just thinking deep thoughts,' he replied and she giggled.

Then he realized the importance of meeting other civilizations, the cross-fertilization of ideas and general transference of knowledge for the common good; for all cosmic life depended on each other and were like one in all things.

When they arrived at Malik's house Jon asked Malik, through Plato, for the local library of information. He was always interested in learning about new cultures and civilizations. He wanted to find out more about the technology used for flying their craft. Although he had heard about LPD drives, his more recent people on Caefon were Class 2 and used jet propulsion and a powerful type of ion drive they called a Space Drive.

The history of Polok was of greater interest to Lira, who wanted to learn about Malik's family, his system and their continuing struggle for survival since the beginning of their conflict.

Malik took them to a large console in an adjacent room which he called his Information and Educational Centre. The console included a large circular desk with three helmets that were positioned equidistantly.

'Here again, there is a parallel in evolution,' Jon thought, but this time it was with the Ancients and their use of helmets. Although Jon and Merol had realised a similarity between Malik's language and sunolingua, he could only have understood some of the basic word structures. Without the use of brain implants that information was not enough for even basic interpretation. He required some other appropriate means for better translation. It was then that he realized Malik's people were in all probability from ancient stock that had settled in that system from some other part of Galaxy Osmaron.

Malik took them to a local panel with several plastic-like draws, from one of them he recovered a broad belt with a very large buckle. He unplugged the buckle from the belt and inserted it into a panel on the console. Then placed a helmet on Jon's head and asked him, through Plato, to name all objects in the room. This he did eagerly for a while until Malik was satisfied with the amount of variation in his choices. Finally, Malik removed the buckle and plugged it back into the belt. He asked Jon to fix the belt about his waist and to speak naturally, which he did.

As he spoke, the unit translated almost every sentence into the language of his host and vice versa. It functioned like a translator and learned new words at the same time until it became one with its host. It did not just learn words like a computer, but intelligently linked words to objects and their actions, colours and textures. Malik clipped a small device behind Jon's ear. It was probably a microphone with an inbuilt transmitter.

Both could not speak at once. He had to allow the buckle time to translate after each sentence. In much the same way as you would with a human interpreter. New words like nouns, once given an equivalent comparison, were added to the buckle's vocabulary. It learnt concepts in much the same way as an infant, both visually and through other senses.

The helmet may have acted as the buckle's eyes initially, while recovering visual information from Jon's optic nerves or other relevant centres of his brain.

Plato was very pleased by the introduction of this novel device. He was not a keen interpreter and didn't like the idea of translating for everyone and sundry as and when required.

'You know, Jon, it is much more natural to use a brain implant. Such an operation, although permanent, is quite simple and will eliminate the nuisance value of the Voice Belt. Also, important time is wasted by the duplication of speech. All such processes can be computed in an unobtrusive and silent manner directly and more efficiently through the mind.'

Jon listened patiently but was not keen when it involved anyone tampering with his brain.

'Sorry, not interested!'

'Some species like the Lodorians are very good at those functions, being highly conceptual. Apparently, us humans relate to the universe in a more visual manner. We have not fully devised the necessary neurons, there being no survival requirements for them. However, this apparatus, although of a makeshift nature, will augment the understanding process, and hopefully quickly assist you in the learning of our language,' Malik further advised.

Jon and the others did not like the idea of brain implants and quickly declined Malik's offer and decided in favour of the more cumbersome belts.

Malik carried out the same process on the others. Very soon they were wearing large belts that enabled them to communicate verbally with Polokans, but in an irregular manner and less precise.

Jon, Merol and Lira were taken into the adjacent teaching room and there they learnt the history of Malik's world and the nearby systems, including those of their enemies on Lodor III. Most information was received via the information helmets and other displays which they soon learned to operate once given the necessary instructions.

They were now able to tap into a wealth of data from the main control computer which stored enormous amounts of information covering numerous generations, including historical data of all systems within that region of the galaxy.

They were very quick learners and soon able to transcribe the data in their own language, which was Sunolingua at that time.

As they had deduced, Malik's species were not indigenous to that part of the galaxy and had travelled from another distant world many millennia before. Since there was not many similar types of animals on that relatively young world, the animals that remained were those they brought with them during that exodus. The Hegris and Phanto were domesticated and still used as pets. They were akin to our dogs and cats and were usually harnessed and kennelled while in the underworld.

That world had evolved marine animal life and a wide variety of trees, but its sea life hadn't yet made the move to dry land. It was probably because competition in the seas and oceans were still quite tolerable.

Unlike the Polokans, the Lodorians in the local system were not human, but a truly ancient race that were responsible in the past for most of their technologies. Lodorians were not indigenous to their current world and relied heavily on the Polokans for their mining and raw materials.

Before the wars, both species were linked together for mutual survival. However the clever Lodorians did not accept reliance on the relatively unstable human Polokans, so they invaded their systems, captured their mines and put the human captives to work within those mines as slaves.

After they had won the war it was decided to remove all life from the main world, Polok. Soon that task was accomplished. They assumed the Polokan's longing for their home-world would diminish, but many Polokans had survived. Malik's father anticipated their actions and completed the building of several under-worlds. When the war started several millions of his people were evacuated to those underground cities without the knowledge of the Lodorians or their spies.

CHAPTER 6

The surprise invasion

According to historical records, the great war between Polok II and Lodor III had continued for just over one hundred years. The Polokans were a young human-like species who were miners and explorers. Through their efforts they had retained large quantities of essential fossil fuels, metals and other types of natural resources.

They mined worlds within the stellar systems of an old local constellation. The few stellar systems involved were ancient, so most of those older planetary environments had become too harsh for any permanent human settlement. Nevertheless fossil fuels were in abundance and virtually untouched by whatever previous indigenous life that had existed billions of years before. Presently mining enclosures and equipment could be observed strewn over most of their barren surfaces.

The Lodorians, being a much older civilisation, had exhausted almost all their natural resources and relied heavily on the Polokans for those requirements, almost to a point of dependency. For those essentials and the benefit of good relations, they supplied some of their advanced technologies to the Polokans.

Despite their dilemma, the Lodorians were a very independent species and not in the habit of relying on anyone for anything. Least of all on young juvenile species like the Polokan humans. They had seen so many such civilisations come and go over the ages and considered the Polokans a week link in their survival. Because of the frequent political turmoil on Polok, they could no more rely on that system for their supplies and decided to take their mining systems by force, using Polokans as their mining slaves. However they had to first subdue the Polokans.

They called a meeting of their Supreme Council of elders and during that time voted unanimously to prepare for a planned strategic war.

'My lords, we are well behind on recent deliveries. Their new political system fails to keep their promises and schedules, and are even more erratic than their predecessors, making endless excuses. At least, we always had our deliveries on time when they were under King Olav.'

'Yes' I realize the many shortfalls in our current deliveries,' Karon interjected.

'Those upstarts also want us to assist them politically, by encouraging our Polokan workers here to take sides. Who do they think they are?' Bailor barked.

'My lords, I'm afraid the present situation is unsustainable. Our peoples survival on this world can only be sustained if the Polokans are defeated and used as our mining slaves,' Volt advised.

'This can only be accomplished by a well-planned invasion. We have not fought in such a manner since the Nemeans,' Karon interjected.

'Yes, but they were not land dwellers. Surface cities can easily be destroyed if we take them by surprise,' Volt said.

'My Lords, I realize the problems, but we are now much more advanced. Our strategic war computers are presently quite capable of completing the task on their own,' Bailor advised.

'In that case, we must put this matter to the vote,' Karon said and all hands went up.

'This vote is unanimous and carried. Therefore, we must initiate plans for war against the Polokans,' Karon added.

During that time they would take control of Polok and all its systems and resources.

Their plan was to take over the main planet of Polok II in one fell swoop, thereby giving its inhabitants little time to launch their war machinery and respond militarily against them.

When the war began it took the Polokans by surprise. At that time most of their surface defences had been sabotaged either by their own traitors or Lodorian lookalike androids. Those androids and devices had been secretly planted in key positions well before the initiation of war. Not knowing of the Lodorian plans, all the Polokan major cities were exposed to enemy attack and as a result were completely destroyed during the initial onslaught.

Nevertheless a few important Polokans, including Malik's father, King Olav, knew of their vulnerability. They had planned for such a crisis over the years by secretly building large underground cities to which they could evacuate most of their essential personnel at the start of war.

When their enemies attacked Polok, King Olav and his loyal people were already fully prepared for evacuation. All their most essential personnel were soon dispatched to those underground cities. By that time all important installations were already in operation several hundred metres below surface, within their shielded underground facilities.

Once the lengthy evacuation was completed, all underground facilities were sealed from the surface. Those measures prevented any traitors returning to the surface to escape and warn their masters. During the intervening weeks all traitors were detected and terminated.

King Olav did not mind sacrificing a few surface cities and their populations if it meant saving their fight for another day and to thus deceive the clever Lodorians into thinking his people had been defeated. To them, that was a much better option than the plight of permanent slavery within some out-world mine at the hands of android masters.

Shortly after their apparent conquest, android troops landed on Polok II and began to take control of the planet. At that time almost all remaining human survivors were herded like cattle and loaded onto large passenger liners for the mining colonies within relevant stellar systems.

As far as the Lodorians were concerned, they had taken the Polokans by surprise, won the war and claimed the spoils. Their conquest was swift and complete, and they were now masters of all the local systems including Polok II.

Despite the Lodorians apparently strong position, the Polokans were able to manufacture some of their own android spies which they planted among the Lodorians in many of their cities. There were also numerous Polokans on Lodor. Those worked in their factories and did most of the menial tasks.

It was known that many Lodorians were sympathetic to their cause. They liked the Polokans and did not agree with their government's strongarmed measures. Generally speaking, the Lodorians were a very peaceful people and the war was all about greed and resources, so their sympathisers recruited many Lodorians to form their own secret underground organisation. Those assisted in acquiring more rights and better living conditions for the human slaves and also played a major role in their extensive propaganda campaigns. However since there were always spies within all such sympathetic groups on Lodor, they could not be made aware of the underworld survivors on Polok until the time was right.

After their conquest of Polok, the Lodorians landed in droves to take control of the world, but King Olav and his Polokans had sabotaged their world by placing large tanks of poisonous gas beneath the surface.

When retribution came it was sudden and swift. The Polokans had sealed off all their underground cities from the surface air and ignited those pre-positioned canisters containing deadly virus and rotting chemical agents. Such poisons were lethal to the Lodorians. Their androids containing highly sensitive and intricate life support systems, fell in their droves while their occupants suffocated.

As the massive undersurface tanks exploded, so also did all Lodorian life on the occupied planet of Polok II cease to exist. They assumed the planet was previously mined by the Polokans and placed on a timed fuse for the later suicidal destruction of all remaining surface life on that world.

With the exception of a few human survivors, who had developed a resistance to the virus, the planet in their opinion was dead and would remain that way for centuries to come. They were of the opinion that the virus couldn't be stopped by any means short of sterilising the complete world.

It was soon agreed that such an extensive cleansing project would be a further waste of scarce resources. Polok II was not very rich in essential resources and even after the completion of such an expensive program they could not be sure that every microbe had been removed.

Despite those factors, they were aware of a few surviving Polokans on the surface. In their opinion, it would have taken those few survivors many centuries to have grown in significant numbers. By their reckoning they could never again be considered a serious threat on such a polluted and damaged world.

The Lodorians soon turned their attention elsewhere, towards the richer planets within the group and ignored Polok II completely. However they left behind a few satellite ships programmed to observe all future developments on the world. They would target any large constructions and missile bunkers, many of which had been missed during the wars and were still active.

Although the Bio-engineered virus was not contagious among the few indigenous human populations living on the surface, it was still dangerous to those living in the underground cities. Therefore no one visited the surface without the use of special vaccines and facial filters. Every journey to the surface was thoroughly screened and special suits worn, even during brief visits.

The Polokans living below in their underground cities were in no great hurry to return to that battered and cratered surface and visited only when it was necessary to fight the enemy, service their concealed bases, barter with the few surface renegades or plant and harvest their few hidden crops. Anyway, they had everything they needed within their underworld, even animals and plants, and an abundance of nuclear energy. They were probably the best miners in the galaxy, with the most advanced drilling equipment. Therefore, they continued their excavation and constructed even larger underground cities with every conceivable facility.

The Polokan's war of attrition had begun in earnest after their first strike, by poisoning their enemies on the surface. Soon after, secret and coded lines of communications were opened with other worlds within the conquered territories. Then their retaliatory plans were to be enacted.

Brave King Olav died during the initial phase of the war. After his death his son, Captain Malik, was voted in as War Chief Councillor. Malik was well trained by his father in all needed guerilla tactics and activities. During the intervening years he learnt about the weakness of his enemy and fought them relentlessly.

Malik's family, although from previously exiled royal stock, had a good reputation and was well respected by his people for his relentless effort against the enemy. He was a devious planner, tactician and strategist, and manifested a persistent attitude and patience in seeing his plans through to the bitter end.

He had planned his Great Surprise, as he called it, over several decades and the day of the Visitor's arrival (The Ship and its crew) was the start of its enactment. His plan was to initially cut off all normal communication links between Lodor and their local command centre, which relayed data from most of the local colonies. All such information would be replaced by their own propaganda program. Because of those reasons, they had to acquire the main satellite base station in orbit above Polok II.

After that task had been accomplished, along with the immediate and complete destruction of their enemies' robot ships, the space would be freed for their main fighter squadrons to depart to the other worlds. At that time their many sympathizers would have created numerous disturbances and unrest within the Lodorian Empire and her colonies by sabotaging essential installations.

During that time of turmoil, the Polokans' fleet, previously concealed in vast underground reenforced bunkers, would take up position for the main battle and final assault. The ships were shielded by a new type of cloaking device not easily detected by the Lodorians.

Their plan was based on the element of surprise. Even so, all operations had to be timed and synchronized precisely to coincide with others on distant planets, cities and mines.

In the mean time, their fleets remained concealed from the massive observation and defensive stations still orbiting above several worlds. Then there were the most protected of all; their enemies home world, Lodor III.

Initially, all orbiting stations were to be vaporized by nuclear missiles. That operation would be instantaneous, giving them time to carry out other timed operations and manoeuvres in sequence. Thus allowing their enemy little time to communicate and plan any retaliatory actions.

The Lodorian fleet was enormous and virtually untouched by war, so a maned assault had little chance of success against such a force once aroused into action. As always, it took time to configure such large fleets for war. So that delay would allow the Polokan pilots a short window in which to do their worst. First of all, the main ships of the fleet had to be staffed by suitable Lodorian personnel and new resources added. Then weapons had to be serviced, refilled and primed for any type of sustained warfare. Malik took all those factors into consideration.

Malik's fighters arrived in the vicinity of Lodor III and there patiently awaited the final command. They realised they were taking an enormous risk and prayed none of their cloaking devices failed before the final command was given. But there was no other way to defeat a resourceful enemy. They remained hidden for several days before the others were in place and orders given.

'Go! Go! Go!' Malik shouted over their communicators and the second war had begun. This time the other side was taken by complete surprise, as nuclear explosions turned the large arrays of the Lodorian fleet into cosmic dust. However they never used nuclear weapons on the planet's surface.

'Khal, get your squadrons in place ready to do their thing!... Now!' Malik ordered.

'Yes Sir! Squads you heard our commander, it's time for some real payback! You know your jobs! And try to keep away from rogue fighters! Apparently, all enemy fighters are presently on our side!' he commanded and his fighters were curious as to how it was possible, but always followed command.

Khal was Malik's eldest son and always as determined as his father in defeating the enemy. His responsibility was in taking over the Lodorian's main world, with all its defensive installations. It was a truly enormous task, but he was aided by a large part of the Lodorian's own fleet. They were tricked by one of the Lodorian's own war computers. It was a computer virus that Jon and Lira had designed specifically for that purpose.

During that time, Meron, Jerry and the others were advising on military strategy. Lord Meron was a genius at such planning. With Andromedan assistance they were soon ahead of their enemies, even without the super-intelligent war computers of the Lodorians.

CHAPTER 7

Lodorians and Androids

At that time the Lodorians were not prepared for war. Neither did they expect a defeated and almost extinct race of humans to retaliate in such a manner. Despite that knowledge, they were highly technological and could readily adapt to almost any eventuality or emergency. The situation had taken them completely by surprise, not having planned. Nor were they prepared for a sustained war. They were unable to retaliate immediately, thus giving the Polokans time to infiltrate and take up strategic positions above their most sensitive installation and defensive stations.

'Who are these invaders and what is our fleet doing to remove them from our system!' chief councillor Henol barked. He was presently head of their governing council. Bailor was currently in one of his underworld tanks relaxing when he received the news and could not respond immediately.

'Volt, quickly check our military status and give me an update and estimate of our present capabilities and response time against their fleet!' he said and Volt soon replied.

'Sire, many of our main computers are down and most of our defence stations are being attacked. They know precisely where and when to hit and they hit with powerful explosive weapons. I am afraid, we can do very little during the present onslaught,' Volt replied and Bailor was dismayed by that knowledge.

'In that case we must open a channel to negociate terms before we lose more of our facilities. Do it urgently!' Bailor commanded. Volt tried to make contact, but all the relevant installations had already been destroyed.

'My lord, the defence of our world is presently out of our hands. We cannot even communicate with the enemy for peace. All our important installations are down. I had always warned the Council about the importance of maintaining our fleets in a state of prepared readiness. However, I was always opposed by you and your councillors because of the extra resources needed. Now we are all to pay for such negligence,' Volt complained to Henol and Henol realized his days as ruler was over.

THE LODORIANS

Lodor was an ancient world that had been specifically adapted to the needs of the Lodorians. It was not a living planet in the truest sense and its atmosphere was poisonous to most life, including Lodorians, so they existed within their own sealed watery enclosures. Most of their people lived beneath their covered world, with its many installations, including storage and other major processing facilities. Large structures had covered most of their world's surface for many millennia.

Their numerous hydroponic gardens needed sunlight and those grew in large transparent domes. Most of such operations were run by their master computers that controlled low-level androids. Those intelligent computers were probably among the most advanced in Osmaron. As far as Lodorians were concerned, they were completely isolated from the atmosphere of their world and preferred an existence within their watery environment.

Their population, having reached its optimum sustainable level, was presently under strict control. New members could only be conceived by a unique cloning process. When it was absolutely necessary for a new member or a substitution, due to illness or old age, a newly cloned infant would be allowed to take the place of a previous important member.

No one really died on Lodor. The more technological parts of their brains carried information specific to each individual. That part was removed after death and stored in cryo while awaiting the individual's rebirth. At the appropriate time that part would be implanted into the newly cloned infant. By so doing, the new being could acquire almost all the qualities and experiences of the original, including its identity and personality. All personal experiences being downloaded into the new brain.

In this manner most Lodorians could almost live forever, receiving a completely new brain and body at each rebirth cycle, but with the added advantage of being able to fulfil other ambitions besides the one held in a previous existence.

Most aspects of memory, including their past experiences, were usually stored within their Personal Mind Libraries. Those storage systems could be quite extensive. All or part of that information was always ready for download; to become a part of their memory and previous experiences. Stored information was added to their minds through brain implants and other outside means of communication. All such information could be retrieved or removed invisibly from their minds as and when required and in any desired quantity. That way, their minds were kept uncluttered and always contained relevant information for the task in hand.

In form, the Lodorians resembled a large light-grey fishy multi-leg slug with no skeletal bones. I suppose they could have evolved from a creature similar to a squid or octopus on our world. That aspect gave them the ability to change form and colour to mislead their prey. Perhaps a better description of their present forms could be a cross between an electric eel, octopus and giant slug. Along with small dorsal fins were two long extendible tentacles for holding on to objects. They also had a pair of small webbed hands with sharp claws that assisted them on land and for catching prey in water. Lodorians had evolved within the oceans of their home-world and had become thinkers because of their type of culture and unique wanting for knowledge. But they also took pleasure in fashioning tools to make their lives easier.

Being an aquatic species they had devised many methods to deceive others. One of their best was the ability to change form and colour to mimic most prey of an equivalent size. Nevertheless they had always been top of the food chain on their home world and with a clever mind could always devise methods to catch and subdue their prey.

During that process they had evolved a comparatively large brain and telescopic eyes. They had also evolved powerful electrics for shocking their prey and communicating with others throughout their world. With a highly developed sense of smell and the abilities of sensing weak electric fields, they were formidable predators in water. While on land, they were assisted by connected memory banks and computers in miniature. For protection they mostly occupied lookalike androids many times their size, which although independent in operation, could be utilised by them as vehicles and be placed under their own personal control.

All such androids were built with internal chambers for housing Lodorians. They included a small tank and relevant life support systems for one or more of their kind. They were a very versatile race and could duplicate the life cycles of most other species, including humans, with the use of such specially designed androids.

In the beginning their small bodies were obviously a hindrance to them on land. Along with a relatively small pair of hands, it also included small extendable limbs which were frequently used to rap around distant objects like twigs on a bank. They would aid their movement by awkwardly pulling their bodies along the bank at a snail's crawl. Such extendable limbs being mostly used when migrating to different areas near land or catching distant prey.

On land, without protective androids, they were just a large brain with basic protection against the environment. Then their weapons would be just limited to their powerful electric fields and the warnings given. During that time even the largest predators would stay well away.

Once they had become technological, the whole process of their survival and dependency on the natural order changed. They began to utilized machines and devices for virtually every operation possible. They, like most other intelligent species with advanced technologies, soon began to exist within their own Virtual Worlds and by so doing could create virtually any artificial environment to their liking and for any purpose.

For those and other reasons of self-esteem, they relied heavily on android technology. Such technological devices had opened up a new universe to them and significantly enhanced their potentials and mobility to almost any degree.

THE POLOKANS

By comparison, the Polokans were a completely different species. They were land dwellers, almost 100 percent human in form, but included a certain amount of bio-engineering, which made them a lot more efficient with a significantly increased lifespan.

They had over several centuries supplied essential resources to the Lodorians in exchange for advanced technologies and products, and were now almost equal to them in science, with the exception of certain specific types of advanced technologies. Those were types the Lodorians thought unnecessary for their natural development. The Lodorians were also afraid they might use their own technologies against them in the future.

Since many Lodorian factories on Lodor were manned by Polokans, the Polokans had placed spies in almost every level of Lodor. That way Polok were constantly kept informed of all new developments on that world. Therefore it was quite usual for the Polokans to find out about very useful and confidential information, including the invasion plans of their enemy well before the initial attack. That was one of the reasons why they decided to evacuate all necessary surface personnel just before the Lodorians' invasion 100 years before.

Finally and without warning, the day of payback had arrived for Lodor and its unsuspecting populations. Polokan ships appeared from nowhere and remained poised above all relevant planets and most sensitive installations.

'Commander! All Wasps in systems 1, 2 and 5... now in position and ready to strike,' group captain Lorie said.

'Good! Hold your position!'

Malik was ready and waiting to give command to initiate hostilities.

'Commander! Systems 3 and 4 almost ready. Now aligning on

targets,' she said.

'Sontral give the order to prime weapons for attack and release screens on my order!' Malik yelled.

It was not long before Malik received another message to say all ships were in final position. Then they received a string of codes transmitted on a tight beam from the orbiting station to his control centre. It was on a frequency seldom used by the Lodorian fleet, but carried a batch of identification codes with which they could deceive the enemy. By so doing, the Lodorians could be fooled into considering their enemies' ships as their own. At the correct moment Malik gave instructions and the codes were programmed into their ships.

Polokan ships were now identifiable by the super-intelligent war computers within the Lodorian systems as their own. Their ships were to all intents and purpose Lodorian military ships. The virus had also infected most of their systems, so they were unable to respond in an appropriate manner. Even the Lodorian fighters had been misled and presently fighting on the side of the enemy.

There was however just one remaining problem. It was to do with the main Lodorian defence computer. That intelligent computer was well shielded from all types of threats. It could during statistical analysis, deduce a higher than normal number of military vessels within a given volume of space and take relevant measures. However in view of the speed of their surprise attack, Malik decided it was a risk worth taking.

With little time to waste, the captains of those fighters programmed and set instruments to their relevant coordinates before pressing their overdrive buttons for quick and precise positioning. As they approached their destinations, which was still a risky effort, they fired their missiles towards preselected targets. Viable targets included satellite stations and ground bases. All those soon vaporized into cosmic dust.

After the first phase of the battle the Lodorian worlds including Lodor III were completely exposed to further attacks. However Malik was only after their launching stations and high energy screens, and most of those had disappeared into cosmic dust during the initial stage of conflict.

Many of their communication satellites were also destroyed, leaving them the use of the less effective ground-based communication systems.

Their ground stations were put on alert and secondary screens went up, but screens could only stop the less effective electromagnetic beam weapons. All other fast moving missiles could only be stopped by intercepting missiles and beam weapons from the ground and most of those were already destroyed.

Malik gave orders to release plasma beams, which they did. Those beams consisted of magnetically held hot plasma, hundreds of millions of degrees centigrade. Once ejected, they travelled very close to the speed of light.

It was quite a sight to watch, as they tore their way through Lodor's dense atmosphere to vaporize screens and missile launching stations. Those powerful beams of matter and energy could not be stopped by missiles, lasers or screens and left devastation in their wake. However Malik did not intend to destroy the great monster; just wound him a little to place him in shackles.

Having taken a great beating that day, the Lodorians were finally defeated, with the loss of countless ships, stations and installations.

Polok's fleets took up positions throughout their many mining colonies and destroyed all relevant military installations that posed a threat. Soon they were landing their squadrons in droves and recovering all their planets from the Lodorians, while freeing their joyful natives from the burden of prolonged slavery on those harsh mining worlds.

At long last there was freedom for the numerous slaves from their cruel, oppressive and uncompromising android masters and most importantly, the inhabitants of Polok II from their enclosed and restraining under-worlds. However in Lodor's case any freedom for Lodorians would be a matter for future consideration.

The Great Battle had only taken five days from its initiation to its completion. During that time, Jerry, Meron, Plato and the other visitors were advising Malik on strategy while taking an active and constructive part as his assistants. Although Lumak was not there in person, it was as if his spirit was alongside the spirit of his dear friend, King Olav, to guide his son, Malik, in winning the war.

When the war was over, Malik gave a considerable sigh of relief and found himself even more indebted to his great brothers from Solaria, without whose effort he would doubtfully have won such a precisely timed battle against such a well equipped and powerful foe. They had appeared just when they were needed, like gods from the sky and in the name of his father.

'Oh my God! I don't believe we've really won! We've really won and our people are free! Everyone is free at last... After such a long, long time!' he shouted emotionally and with utter exuberance, while taking hold of his wife, Mira, and embracing her. Then he turned his attention to Meron, Jerry and others.

'My glorious victory this day is mainly to do with my most beloved friends from Solaria. I will always have a place in my heart for you, along with father and mother,' he said, sadly but with extreme gratitude.

He suddenly realised his father's spirit was still alive and at long last his greatest wish had come true. He had finally claimed recompense for the death of his parents by the defeat of their mutual enemies.

He said a long prayer for his father and mother, and gave orders to his command centre to stop all hostilities. Then he rejoined his guests and friends for celebration and rejoicing.

Even at that moment of victory, little did he know of certain future events that would make him part of a much larger system and that Solaria was already at the hub of their civilisation.

CHAPTER 8

Red Alert!

The Gohrans, as they were usually called, neither were composed of solid matter nor were they of any form of energy known to our present universe. They had evolved into inter-dimensional beings that could utilize the raw substance of any dimension for their own purpose and by so doing had become the all-powerful Supreme Beings of the known universe. There were seven such brothers and they ruled over the seven sister-universes within our plain of universes or multiverse. One of those universes happened to be Claron, which is known as Seth to others. That one also happens to be ours, which includes our galaxy, Osmaron.

Some said they came into existence during the initial phase of creation, tens of billions of years ago. That was during one of the initial and highly explosive periodic phases of our universe. They were probably formed from massive pre matter clouds the size of complete stellar systems. That was well before the evolution of causal matter as we know it. During that period time was in its infancy.

Others say they came into our dimension from another and others, that they themselves are a different type of universe that exist to protect the others: a kind of anti-body among universal cells. The truth of the matter is that no one really knew who or what they were or from whence they came. But it is a known fact that they have the mass and size of a stellar system and can shrink and shield their immense energies and gravitational fields by their own internal screening methods while vectoring,

In our reality, they appear to be just over a metre across when travelling in their partially phased physical mode. At that time their intense starlike form would light up complete continents. That form was used whenever they wanted to make their presence felt, by causing their subjects to become fearfully aware. However such an energetic aberration was extremely rear for the rulers of the known universe. Their most frequent and preferred type of travel being instant and inter-dimensional and in a form more suited to their recipient subjects.

Being extremely ancient in origin, but young at heart, they preferred to live among the lower life-forms and would select a new home-world every thousand cyclons (1600 years). That change of residence was usually just after their heptarchal nexus reunion for their millennial conference at the innermost plane of Goh.

On their newly adopted world they would build a beautiful palace or monumental structure to be awed by everyone, and take the form of one of the previous native subjects.

At that moment in galactic history, the Gohran, Grand Lord Gerra had chosen the beautiful world of Kanaefon within a close globular cluster called Kalboron. It was just within the periphery of Osmaron (our Milky Way Galaxy). That world also happened to be Lumak's home world.

Although his master plan was being enacted as he had predicted, he sometimes had to give a little push or impetus at certain critical stages. The present great battle between Polok and Lodor, and its aftermath required his presence. Among all the other Gohran Supreme Beings he was the only one that was free to interact directly with his lower subjects. Those steps had been taken since the creation of the Javols; for they were created in his part of the universe, making him directly responsible for all primal life through the Greater Purpose.

Being quite capable of a bit of harmless fun, he sometimes enjoyed seeing his subjects in fearful demeanor. They were always more easily conditioned and receptive to his advice during that state of mind. Also, such diversions temporarily released him from his other burdens and more serious matters.

Grand Lord Gerra, known to the Andromedans as Grand Lord Gerron, had observed the situation from afar and for some unknown reason knew of its unsatisfactory outcome without his intervention. Therefore he commanded The Ship to visit the planet

Polok II, knowing that Meron, Jerry, Plato and others would help swing the balance in favour of a military success for Polok.

Although he disliked interference in the affairs of evolving species, the services of those species were required within the Greater Purpose in Osmaron, and just that fact alone outweighed any of his own personal considerations.

His complex causal mesh of civilization was slowly knitting into place. Strong unity was essential among all advanced species, if they were to win the considerable more difficult conflict against the Javols.

His form of order propagated all things and affected even the lowliest life-forms while his Shadites and Plorans were just the instruments used to carry and promote that most important of all orders.

It was late evening on Polok II so Malik decided to visit the planet's surface with Plato, Meron and jerry. He wanted to greet the many faithful surface chieftains who had assisted in the long drawn out war and together say a prayer to their love-ones now departed. In his case, he would say a prayer on his parent's grave to God and his brave ancestors, but most of all his parents, while giving thanks for a successful victory. Then they would watch a long awaited clear sunset together before the celebrations began.

When Malik arrived he was hailed by many of the surface people and proceeded to introduce his Solarian friends to those hardened war veterans. They had learned to survive on the harsh surface of Polok during the turmoil and lost many of their own family members and close friends at the hands of occupying Lodorian guards.

'We have won! Comrades we have won with the help of our Solarian friends! The war is over. Now we can get on with our lives after repairing our damaged world!' Malik yelled across the crowds and they yelled back.

'Long live Polok! Long live King Malik!'

After greeting the crowds, he and his company visited a large concealed building that had been mostly overgrown by creeping vine. That building had large transparent windows and was kept in reasonable condition for just such an occasion. They went to its uppermost floor and decided to view the surrounding area towards the distant horizon, when he was aroused by an urgent communication.

'Your excellence, sorry for this intrusion... One of our remote command posts have sighted a very brilliant starlike object moving from the west under its own power. An attempt was made to analyse the object, but we were unable to fully ascertain its composition and purpose. From the little data received, it is not constructed of any known materials, neither of stable elements known to us outside nuclear furnaces and stars. Its brilliance is so great that special goggles have to be worn by observers. The object is also visible on our electromagnetic and infrared displays.'

'So it's not an enemy ship?'

'Can't be, Commander. From visual and other analysis, its composition appears to be that of a small super-hot star. Yet, it is able to propel itself at great speed through our planet's atmosphere, unperturbed by anyone or anything and its destination appears to be close to your complex.'

'Really?'

'Yes, Commander! We need your urgent advice, Sire!'

Instead of watching a beautiful sunset, they were presently observing the strange blueish brilliance of a small star coming from that same position to eclipse their own star setting in the horizon.

'My God! What can it be?' a worried Malik commented. While the others remained numbed by its brilliance and progress.

Malik observed the brilliant object but could not understand its true nature and decided to place the whole system on red alert.

The powerful observation beams went on, but were completely useless against the much more brilliant sphere which appeared to light up continents at a time and outshone every conceivable thing.

Fighters left their bunkers and became airborne from the large concealed base stations. They were soon pointing their plasma nozzles in the direction of the bright light. However close observation indicated the object's temperature to be hotter than any other type of plasma. Making their weapons ineffective and useless. Nevertheless every weapon was primed and waiting the order to fire. Malik held that order and waited for more objects, in case of an invasion, but no others appeared.

As the object approached their building it was escorted by several fighters. Then it unexpectedly changed direction downwards, as if to land and the fighters could not follow. Finally it went directly for Malik's building. He could observe its journey through his visual communicator. He realised it was too late to fire their weapons, since any missile would equally have damaged their building at such close range, so he prayed and waited.

The space about his building became under incredible tension while its walls began to glow. Then there was a static build up followed by lightening discharges everywhere. Even Plato looked apprehensive, not quite knowing what to expect.

The starlike object went directly through the building's walls as if they were not there and hovered in front of Malik and his companions. There it remained for a brief moment while shielding itself from the easily damaged humans.

There was a sudden flash as if by lightning and in front of them stood a godlike human figure, still in his youth but wearing a white robe.

The glowing figure was the size of a giant about twelve feet tall and overshadowed Meron who was the tallest member of the group. Never in Malik's wildest dreams had he experienced such an occurrence. He knew of the existence of superior beings throughout the universe and also knew they could only be observed if they wished it that way. But never before had he met one and now, here was a great human form standing in front of him not very unlike his own young father and the complete transformation had occurred as if by magic.

Malik and the others hair stood on end and were very disturbed. They began to stare at the brilliant figure while frozen in their present positions. The figure studied the individuals for a while as if to extract information from their minds. Then he turned his head towards Malik and smiled.

CHAPTER 9

Lord of Lords

A powerful voice resounded through their minds and in all life within their vicinity.

'Ah Malik, I see you have on this glorious day won a great victory over your enemies, the Lodorians? For that incredible feat I must pay you my sincere congratulations. I am also pleased to have at last met you, Meron, and, Jerry, from Earth and Solaria.'

Malik plucked up just enough courage to speak with a deep swallow.

'Please forgive me for asking, my lord... but who are you?' he replied, still shivering in his bones.

Grand Lord Gerra did not hesitate to reply:

'My name is unimportant, but to you, I am Grand Lord Gerra, Lord of the Grand Council of Universes and of the seventh part of all seven universes, including our present one.

'I am personally responsible for this region of galaxies, but alas, I try not to interfere too much with your personal development, unless of course there is an overriding reason. Even then, I try to be as tactful and discrete as possible, despite my present activities in visiting your world.

'Nevertheless, the time has come for you to become an important part of the much larger whole. This is because significant dangers abound that in time will affect your civilization even more detrimentally than the Lodorians.

'Those dangers I speak of are from far beyond this galaxy. In due course I am sure Meron and Plato will brief you on those matters, because they have been personally affected.

'Henceforth, your people and those of Lodor must end your conflict and work together towards the common-good. Such wars serve little purpose other than to accelerate with greater wastage your already dwindling resources.

'In future, Solaria will become your third partner in all your endeavours. They will guide your respective races in a more democratic manner to attain your respective goals.

'They will show you the way and guide your hands to take a more practical and efficient course in future events for your mutual safety and protection. Trade routes will soon be operational between your worlds, Polok, Lodor, Solaria and other remote systems within Osmaron, and believe me, there is more than enough resources for all.

'My Son, we need your present enemy, the Lodorians, because they form part of the complex matrix of events. You have doubtlessly realised that they depend almost entirely on your civilization for most of their essential resources and therein lies their Achilles heel. So please let bygones be bygones and try not to unduly humiliate a proud and ancient civilization.

'Therefore it is imperative that you and your representatives, including Jerry from Solaria, pay an urgent visit to Lodor in order to sign your relevant treaties, which you should draft immediately. They will now be receptive to all your proposals. These agreements will ensure your mutual coexistence and maintain free trade between your three systems.

'Malik, in your case the future will be a grand one. It is your destiny to assist in all aspects of the future development of all three systems, by manufacturing new and faster ships and by giving aid whenever necessary with your type of technology.

'They, on the other hand, will do likewise and Solaria will supply you with your microid parts and other advanced technologies.

'However, for those efforts to move smoothly, you must sign the necessary trade agreements and treaties among yourselves. Those measures will prevent any misunderstandings in future.

'It is destined that your separate species, including Meron's, augment each other through trade, sports and the arts. For it is *through these creative activities that your relationships and cultures will gain focus and flourish, and Solaria has much to offer in those areas.*

'Your initial task will be to build advanced ships for your newly formed federation. They will guard your shipping lanes and maintain peace and order throughout this region of Osmaron, and later within the much greater Osmaron Empire.'

The Grand Lord removed a small container from under his gown, but continued:

'These are the specifications of your first assignment. These two ships will be assigned to Solaria. Others will be manned by your people and some of Lodor's. They will contain Class Seven technologies. They are of Octan design and will include the latest Infinite Probability Drive systems unheard of in your technology.

'Despite their great size and mass, they are capable of traversing Osmaron within minutes and other galaxies in days and weeks.'

He handed the sealed container to Malik who hesitantly went forward to collect it.

'Thank you, My Lord!' he said, while kneeling and bowing his head.

Then the white and glowing figure simply disappeared from sight, leaving behind the fragile humans with their hairs standing on end from more static electricity while heavy currents of air almost knocked them off their feet. Within seconds everything in their vicinity was back to normal.

'My God of all Gods! That was our true God of many names!' Meron exclaimed, and kneeled to say a prayer, while the others still tried to gain their composure.

'Sire, is everyone in your area ok?' came a nervous voice on the communicator.

'Yes, Sontral! We had a close shave, but everything is ok now!' Malik replied, still shaking.

Although Malik and his company were disturbed by those proceedings, they were hard military men and therefore able to contain themselves in the midst of difficult and dangerous situations.

Malik did not wish to show any weakness among his comrades, so he shrugged his shoulders and gave another order through his communicator.

'Cancel red alert!'

Then he commanded several of his most senior officers to visit him immediately in the surface building. Many of them formed part of the Provisional War Council.

Seven of his most senior officers entered the unused surface building and sat on makeshift stools in the beautifully decorated room. He waved his companions to join them and went to look out of the tinted window towards the distant horizon. Although the sun had recently set beyond the horizon, he stared at that position in an attempt to gather his thoughts. He expected to see another strange glowing visitor, but nothing happened. Soon he returned and started to introduce his companions to his officers. Some had already met at the Control Centre during the Great Battle. Then he showed them a replay of their meeting with Grand Lord Gerra. After the recording was played he removed the special container from his pocket.

'This he gave me, Gentlemen & Ladies, and he was absolutely correct in his assessment of our current situation here and of our enemies on Lodor. He further mentioned that we faced a much greater threat from outside our galaxy and about our future friendship with Solaria in particular,' Malik said, enthusiastically.

Plato stood up and taking the little black box from his pocket began to project the destruction of Caefon on a nearby wall.

'Oh my God!' Malik exclaimed. The others sympathised with Meron for his great loss.

After viewing the terrible images, questions were raised about the nature of their mutual enemy and they were brought up to date.

'What do you think, Comrades, and members of our Provisional Council?' Malik asked.

A young officer raised her right hand and began to speak.

'Don't you think, Sire, that this whole incredible situation could be a propaganda tool, engineered by the Lodorians to gain our trust? Perhaps a form of distraction while they prepare to mount a prolonged attack against our bases here? Surely by now they could have repaired their damaged installations and reassembled many of their scattered fleets from most of their shielded hideouts. I think we could now be even more vulnerable to a prolonged attack than before,' she replied, aggressively.

'Given our current knowledge of the strength of the enemy, both militarily and politically, and the technical assessment of the entity, not being of a solid form, do you think it possible for the Lodorians to have engineered such a form of deceit? Further, our Solarian friends are not from Lodor and neither are the dangerous Javols,' Malik replied, defensively.

There was no response and he continued.

'If when we analyse the data held in this container, we should find the drive system to be of a superior alien design. That would be proof enough of the Grand Lord's true existence and good intentions. Would it not, comrades?'

'Yes, Commander!' she replied.

'Why should the Lodorians freely give us such advanced technologies... that will allow our ships to visit their worlds in minutes, if not seconds. Would they not have found some other simpler method... not in anyway detrimental to their own future survival?'

His officers agreed with his explanation and turning to his chief technical officer he handed him the small container.

'Carefully analyse every aspect of this data, Sontral. Enter all information into our central computer under special security coding for a thorough analysis.'

'Yes, Commander!'

'You may use whatever trusted personnel and equipment necessary to get this job done urgently!' he stressed.

The meeting was subsequently terminated and he and his companions returned to the underworld for more victory celebrations.

CHAPTER 10

Two great ships

The highly intelligent master computer had received the information in a form suitable for analysis and soon began to produce the required data. As a result, what unfolded was a truly incredible design.

The vessel so formed would itself be a conscious living entity with the capability of altering its form and structure, including its decor to the needs and benefit of its passengers and crew. It was not a war machine in any sense, although weapons could be mounted on certain external platforms. It was a passenger liner for luxurious interstellar and intergalactic cruises and contained all the necessary recreation and entertainment facilities for the mutual benefit of its fifty thousand human and other passengers. The present design could quite easily be scaled up and down in size or modified for a different purpose.

The drive system was equally alien. It was indeed a strange concept that they could not have imagined at their present levels of technology. The ship could easily attain speeds well in excess of several thousand times their swiftest star fighters. But the strangest thing of all were its modes of construction. Although the major parts of its drive systems and internal coatings were engineered in the usual manner, large moulds had to be constructed and later filled with a special metallic dust. That basic microid dust would be subsequently transformed in moulds to form the relevant parts of the ship's structure. It could only be used in conjunction with certain Constructor Microids. Those special microids and other relevant control modules could only be acquired from Solaria.

Each ship required a precise amount of the Constructor Microids to trigger the process of their formation and become part of the ship.

The design of the two ships were in such a manner as to make virtually impossible their use without the stellar drives, their controlling minds and other essential items that were to be supplied by the Lodorians. It was truly a ship of partnership, peace and leisure; for it brought all three civilizations of the federation together in several unexpected ways.

Another meeting was called the following day. During that time the federation charter and treaties were to be eagerly drafted by Jon and his friends.

'Comrades,' Malik said. *'I have given serious consideration to everything in this matter and have decided to follow Grand Lord Gerra's advice in taking the lead in peaceful negotiation. Because it makes sense and incidently, so does the special ships. They were designed specifically for peace.*

'We should realise, however, that even if we built the largest fleet and completely obliterated our enemies from the galactic map, those drastic measures would have only allowed our worlds more security for a short while, and at a very high price. During the process we would have used up most of our rear metals and chemicals for our war machinery, including the enormous wastage of our already scarce resources. However, given the correct level of diplomacy and safeguards, I am sure the Lodorians will accept a mutually agreed formula for our coexistence, with the inclusion of our friends from Solaria.

'Anyway, the Lodorians were our neighbours for countless generations and have been peaceful until they became unsure of their energy and other essential supplies. That was mainly because of the unpredictability of our political system at that time. In future, it could be a lot more desirable if we worked together as one race and shared the resources together.

'I now think there is more than enough resources for all our races if we put our minds together to create the necessary technologies to extract them. Therefore, I have decided, with your vote of course, to form a diplomatic envoy for an immediate visit to Lodor III.

'This group will also include our diplomats from Solaria, who are also included in our charters and treaties. I shall however like

to receive a unanimous agreement on all matters here discussed.

'*Just a simple show of hands will do. Any questions?*' he said.

His group of senior officers, who were also his governing council remained silent for a minute while considering and weighing their options.

There were no questions. The defeated Lodorians had not responded in any way and were presently awaiting an initiative from Polok.

ON LODOR

'A few Polokan spies have been captured, Sire. They were responsible for sabotaging our bases. We are interrogating them at present,' the Lodorian Kol said.

'So what you are saying is... Polokans were behind the invasion? The one they called Malik must have survived our bombardments and the deadly contamination... He must be a very clever planner to have lived so long and instigated such a successful coupe d'etat,' Bailor commented.

'My lord, we of the grand council have decided to vote you in as Chief Councillor and Chancellor,' Volt said and Bailor smiled in his own strange manner.

'I hope I don't become another sacrificial Goof for the slaughter, if things go wrong under my rule,' Bailor replied, but accepted the post all the same.

'Why have they stopped their bombardment?' Bailor inquired of Volt, now his second in command.

'They are human children and think they have caused us enough damage for today,' Volt replied, sarcastically.

'They may be considered by you and council as human children, but they have kicked our butts this day. In future we shall have little choice but to treat them as our equals. After all, they have earned it and gained my respect.'

'My lord, that's assuming we have a future,' Volt said, reminding Bailor of urgent business.

'Get a communication to Polok immediately. Offer our

unconditional surrender!' Bailor barked and Volt was surprised but got on the task.

Malik continued to explain matters to his group of councillors.

'My beloved friends, we have been through much together over the years, so take it from me when I say, the Great Ships are practical. Their incredible designs are not from Lodor and those magnificent friends from Solaria did assist us in the success of a great war. Therefore, those in favour of the diplomatic mission just described... and those against?'

Almost all voted for diplomacy.

'Those in favour of building the special ships, and also in taking our places within the greater Osmaron Empire with the benefits and powers gained by so doing... and those against?' Malik continued.

All hands went up.

In all cases the vote was unanimous and with a unequivocal yes. The meeting was adjourned until after their return from Lodor III.

'This is truly a fantastic outcome! All we must wait for is the Lodorians willingness to partake in our mutual goals,' a worried Malik said.

They were soon to form an envoy to visit Lodor and the very advanced ships would be built to assist in the greater war effort against their common alien enemy, the Javols.

CHAPTER 11

Charters and Treaties

Beautiful Lira stood in her blue military outfit and passionately viewed the strange looking flying machine. It was shaped like a wasp and called by the same name when translated through her voice-belt. That notorious fighting machine was meant for two trained operators and included two stereoscopic helmets for Virtual Operations. Those special tasks could be accomplished many times faster than was possible with normal methods. There it proudly stood missing its payload of bombs and other deadlier missiles. Nevertheless it still displayed its powerful plasma projectors. The large one stood out boldly from its nose with two smaller ones on the extremities of its sloping and curved wings.

She pressed several buttons on her hand-held keypad and a stepped ramp dropped, while the side door lifted to reveal the illuminated cockpit and all other relevant controls. Normally the versatile craft could be operated in both manual and implant modes, with inbuilt auto pilot. All Polokan pilots and navigators had brain implants fitted, which eliminated the need for cumbersome keypads and the like. Even so, physical controls were always present in the main control cabin in case of damage to their communication systems and pilot.

'Darling, this is truly a fascinating craft!' Lira exclaimed, while glancing at Jon for approval. So he came forward to observe.

'She is a most beautiful design. Everything is automatic and she utilizes the latest LPDs with integral cloaking.'

'He does? It's nice to know!'

'Shall we take her for a spin?' Jon said.

'To discover his potentials!' Lira replied.

'It's a female. So I've been told by Sontral. Lira moved her head, meaning for him to be her navigator on their first maiden flight. She assumed the most spectacular fighting ship was a he, but Jon saw it as a she. The complete opposite of each sex.

'How different the sexes were in admiring the things they appreciated and loved,' she thought. Nevertheless, before they could climb the steps Meron halted their progress.

'My children, why don't you go for your spin later! We have very important work to do, and it's urgent. The war might be over, but not so is politics. I would like you, Jon, to assemble your group and draft a treaty to include Polok, Lodor and Solaria as main partners in trade. Since you are young, I would like it to be youthful in context, practical, and yet broad in its stipulations. And don't worry, I shall be available should you require my assistance,' Meron said.

'Ok dad, we are on it!' A responsible Jon replied and they left to find the others. Since Jon realized Meron was his genetic father he always called him, Dad. Anyway, he never knew his true surrogate parents and both got on well together as father and son.

The charter would deal mainly with the legal structure of the federation and the treaties specific to trade, visiting rights, stable prices and so on. However, each system would remain isolated from its co-members politically. Anyway, most species did not wish to have outsiders interfering and meddling in their internal affairs and politics.

Jon and his remaining group of six, presently just Jon, Merol, Ecrol and Lira - the others being left behind on Earth - were ideal for that task. They were young, neutral in such matters, and could judge all situations objectively, with no axes to grind, so to speak. Anyway, they were the future of the Solarian Federation

Initially they wanted to write the document on specially prepared paper, but that material was not available on Polok, so they finally decided on a type of noninflammable synthetic material that resembled and felt very much like paper. Those sheets could be obtained in almost any length. Therefore beautiful scrolls were devised and marked with their relevant crests and colours.

Both respective civilisations were not familiar with the art of paper writing. Although used in ancient times, they had lost the necessary abilities, tools and art in forming letters on paper. Those skills had been neglected with the advent of miniaturization of computers and more advanced communication systems. At present levels of technology, Malik and his people could always place implants directly into areas of their brain for virtually any purpose. Such implants were ideal for storing and translating thoughts, which could be carried out invisibly within minds. Further, they utilized a very advanced network of information, similar to our Internet, with its Email and Voice Com systems, but in a virtual space.

The Lodorians, on the other hand, could never have developed such a method of communication like writing. They were mainly aquatic and always had a strong sense of smell to an almost visual level. Their heads included sensitive telescopic antennae as part of their eyes. Those super sensitive organs could detect electromagnetic and other radio type signals anywhere on their world. So they could observe their 3D universe in many ways other than the visual and mostly virtual space.

Their electrically generating tail organs were almost like those of an electric eel's, and although mainly used to stun small sea creatures before swallowing them, could also be used to transmit modulated information at almost any required frequency throughout their planet. Carrier frequencies could be altered in sympathy with their body colours. A specific carrier frequency being related to their genetic groupings.

Malik liked the scroll-and-ink idea for its authenticity and originality, and also agreed on the sunolingua language in written form. That language was meant to be the common trading language of the federation, later to be extended throughout Osmaron. After Malik was satisfied with progress, he decided to alert the Lodorians of his future intentions to visit their world.

He was to broadcast instructions of their intended visit from several locations towards the main planet of Lodor III. This was to ensure the signals were quickly intercepted. Further, being still not sure of the Lodorians' intentions, they ensured the transmissions could not be traced back to any single source. A positive reply and invitation was soon in coming. The visual message under coded seal was taken to Malik.

The screened information read:

'Most honourable and esteemed Councillor Malik, we urgently await your visit to discuss war reparations, the resumption of trade between our two worlds and any other matters you may wish to discuss, in order to reestablish our past friendship.

'We and our people look forward to your urgent visit to our humbled system.'

Malik read the information with surprise and screened its contents for Jerry, Plato, Meron and others to read.

'I think it's a surrender! What do you think, Mister Solarian Ambassador?' Malik said, handing the communication over to Jerry.

'They are a proud race with their face in the dirt. I don't think you will get anything better from them. At least, we have peace and with this we can mend fences and move forward,' Jerry said.

'I read our new treaty, it was properly constructed and tackles all important points quite thoroughly. All thanks to Jon, Lira and Ecrol,' Meron said and Malik agreed.

CHAPTER 12

Their visit to Lodor III

Although the Lodorian skies were filled with Polokan ships, all fighting had ceased short of destroying their large enclosed cities and essential storage installations.

Malik's fighters had only targeted military bases and other installations necessary for their retaliation. Presently the Lodorians were like sitting ducts with little means to defend themselves.

Also, since there were many Lodorian sympathisers and Polokan slaves on Lodor, further bombardment of that world could lead to innocent loss of life.

Bailor and his Grand Council soon realised that the Polokans did not intend to destroy them and had immediately stopped further hostilities while waiting for them to make their first diplomatic move.

The Andromedan Ship was made ready and the chosen ones left for Lodor the following morning.

The Ship's company included Malik, with two of his female officer companions, Jerry, Plato, Meron, Jon, Lira, Merol, Tomas and others. Mira, Malik's wife, remained at Malik's underworld to take over in his absence. She was also to prepare and organize the forthcoming victory celebrations.

Further, work had to be done in preparing the underworld people for surface life once evacuated to that part of the planet. That program would include vaccinations and special medication necessary for survival on the surface.

All that information had to be programmed and made ready and available before the mass repatriation of so many enslaved families from the mining colonies on distant worlds. All such work broke with tradition during such an overwhelming victory and everyone tended to partake in the ongoing victory celebrations at the exclusion of all other types of important work.

Malik and his two companions were indeed surprised when the ship melted into its stairway and entrance, and when they entered, by the lack of instrument panels on board. They were then asked to enter their bunks for transposition.

Within what appeared to be seconds, they had arrived on Lodor III. They abruptly materialised in the middle of the largest enclosed surface city called by the same name. It was also their seat of power.

On the correct signal several of the Polokan ships landed and soldiers took up position around The Ship to protect its occupants against snipers and hostile demonstrators, but that area was completely clear of such threats. Also the strange ship's appearance scared all life away.

After a while the Lodorians began to appear, still keeping well away from the Andromedan ship.

Malik was the first to descend amid shouts of: "thank you!" and "we love you!".

In their own way they were thanking him for not having inflicted greater carnage and for having stopped short of destroying their world. He waved to the different android figures, most of whom resembled human forms and many waved back.

A large surface vehicle soon arrived to take them away to an unknown destination. It had a large symbol on each of its four visible sides and utilised traction instead of wheels. The vehicle was apparently not driven by anyone, since there were no front or rear compartments for that purpose. The passenger's compartment appeared to be just a box with uncomfortable seats that were not upholstered. It was assumed that since such vehicles were only used by androids, decoration, and texture were non-essential parameters in their designs. Lodorians were always quite conscious of efficiency and wastage. That was most likely due to their lack of essential resources and their dependency on others for such materials, so they recycled everything that was recyclable.

Their society appeared to consist only of bare essentials. Visual beauty was not apparent anywhere. Everything on that world was designed solely and efficiently for a specific purpose or task and all unnecessary shapes were boxlike. Within their basic cities were no advertising signs, shops, restaurants or indeed any human-like activity or building. They were indeed a very different life-form and could doubtless have learnt a lot from humans.

Everything about Lodor was large and that also included its buildings, but by some strange quirk of nature the Lodorians were very small by comparison, being barely thirty centimetres long from head to tail, excluding flexible appendages. Their small size and cumbersome form might have given them an inferiority complex and hence the reason for their much larger adopted android vehicular forms. Despite that fact, their androids were not plain statues, but contained an intricate nervous system which when properly connected would fuse with the personality of its primary occupant. Such androids could be engineered to duplicate almost anyone and to any degree of precision visually, with the exception of living tissue.

They mimicked many life-forms, but mostly humans and bipeds of great historical standing. In particular, of those ancient people and species now dead or extinct. In their society it was honourable to respect great leaders and famous individuals in that manner.

Some important Lodorians utilised more than one android in much the same way as a human would wear different clothes on different occasions. But even those personal androids could themselves wear different clothes, so there was much flexibility within their unique society.

Occasionally they would free themselves of those physical contraptions and visit their sealed underground tanks for a relaxing swim within its warm waters and to sometimes take a live meal. Their main food however was a specially prepared protein gel. That type of processed food was free of germs and toxins when extracted from certain plants, including a variety of marine life.

Not all Lodorians possessed androids. That freedom had to be earned and many remained within their watery enclosures in meditation and learning, until they were required for some special purpose or mission. Nevertheless they had access to a wealth of information within their massive Virtual Libraries, which was another Virtual World that spanned many millennia.

They could never allow themselves to be seen by outsiders in their basic form, as it would be considered sacrilege and a great insult to their kind. The shock of that knowledge could cause them psychological harm. Yet, they were able to mimic and simulate the emotions and muscular activity of most forms and to all intents and purpose, became the true nature of their android's original. Being quite strange to us humans, next to octans, they were probably one of the most advanced life-forms in Osmaron.

Their form was probably one of the end products of evolution for Octopus and Squids, who were another intelligent and successful species throughout the universe.

Although quite complex, their senses were in many dimensions and unique, and with such varied abilities could observe the 3D+4D+5D universe in many different ways other than just the visual. That gave them a much greater scope in acquiring knowledge on many topics that were currently invisible to humans with just five basic senses.

CHAPTER 13

Lodor's official welcome

The transporter went into a very plain square building and all four walls, including the top of the vehicle, began to unfold into a platform, leaving its occupants sitting on a slightly elevated stage and exposed on all sides. Since most of those areas were used by human slaves, oxygen was always present in correct quantities.

In front of them stood three tall figures. The most central and more dignified occupied a Pharaoh-like android, with radiant metallic headgear. He soon came forward to greet them and introduced himself to Malik.

'I am Bailor, present chancellor of our Grand Council. On my left is Lord Stradon and on my right Lord Volt,' he said, without emotion.

Malik was abruptly taken back by the figure of Stradon. He bore such close resemblance to his father, King Olav, and Volt resembled one of his ancient ancestors. They would have thought both men to be great leaders to have created such senior android figures in their likeness and honour, he thought.

Malik introduced them to his companions starting with Plato, the Shadite.

'My Siend, Bailor, may I take this pleasure in introducing an important person from the galaxy Andromeda and the imperial ambassador of Solaria,' Malik said and they were astounded. He continued to introduce each in turn.

Bailor and his colleagues gave the expression of utter surprised and excitement when those from Solaria and Andromeda were introduced, with an aspect of curiosity as to their almost instantaneous mode of travel over such great intergalactic distances.

They were a very inquisitive race and considered their whole purpose of existence to broaden their knowledge of science and the universe. Because of those reasons they were also extremely interested in the inter-dimensional ship from Andromeda.

After a small ceremony, with many senior subjects in attendance, they were taken into another smaller but specially prepared room for the occasion.

They sat together and began to discuss matters of state. After they had expressed their needs and concerns, the scrolls were read out and relevant copies signed and stamped with their approval. All the scrolls were written in triplicate and suitably inscribed by each of the three relevant presiding members, including Jerry for Solaria.

The previously tense Lodorians were suddenly quite happy and pleased by the way things had turned out. Feeling in the company of revered friends, they decided to have some of their greenish and pink jelly-like substances, which they sucked into their mouths through small circular tubes like straws.

Their human friends helped themselves to drinks which had been acquired for that special occasion.

Officially, trade had been initiated between all three civilizations and the Lodorians accepted the idea that they had in the process acquired new friends and a new human species from Solaria. A complete new civilization from Beyond-Fille to further add to their pool of knowledge and scientific benefit. There was nothing to be gained through mutual extinction.

'Do you think they will ever learn to party on this drab world,' Lira commented.

'They will first have to build a few clubs and learn a few steps,' Ecrol replied and Jon smiled.

'It might appear quite funny to you guys, but I suppose it must be difficult for any intelligent marine species to adopt an acceptable way of life on land. Assuming they are capable of learning human ways. we must be the ones to teach them,' Jon said. Lira was intrigued by that answer. Nevertheless Lira could see an impossible task ahead of them in every respect.

After discussion, it was agreed that a formal democratic parliament be created between both local civilizations. That was a new concept of democracy Jerry had introduced and everyone accepted the idea. It would handle all political affairs within their vicinity. Malik was unanimously chosen as president of both systems and temporarily represented Solaria during their absence in any matters that concerned their interests in that part of the galaxy.

After those matters were fully discussed and finalized, Plato showed them the images of the Javols invasion of Caefon and explained the nature of their real enemy. When he was finished, they were shocked and worried by that knowledge. Then Malik went on to explain the appearance of Grand Lord Gerra and showed visual information of his appearance on Polok II. They were not aware of such a Supreme Being in all their existence and were seriously disturbed by what they heard, so Malik stood up and began to explain his experiences.

'Honourable members, I fully understand your doubts and concerns in this matter. I went through a similar questioning process myself... after those experiences just described and it took me many hours to overcome my fears and trepidations.... We even thought it was caused by you.'

He gazed at the three excited Lodorians sucking at their tubes and continued.

'With some new and previously unknown propaganda technology. But on analysis it could not have been you, because we knew each other too well. So I followed Grand Lord Gerra's suggestions, albeit hesitantly at first. I soon came to the conclusion that our Grand Lord was correct in his assertions and our presence here have proved those methods to be correct. This is because we have now communicated with each other and signed agreements which have given us even more powers than before.'

Malik paused for a brief moment to clear his throat, but continued.

'There is one more thing that proves his existence and those are the blueprints of the great inter-dimensional ship that he gave me... for us to build and use together.'

It was like the greatest bombshell had been dropped. Bailor and his other two companions stopped immediately at their sucking, removed their feeding tubes, and gazed at each other in utter astonishment.

'This godlike being gave you the drawings of a super ship?' Bailor asked, in utter surprise.

'Yes! With speed enough to get us even to the most distant galaxies within weeks and in minutes within the furthest reaches of our own galaxy,' Malik replied, showing little surprise.

Bailor stuttered slightly.

'You... you have those schematics here?'

'Yes! I have also taken a copy along for you,' Malik replied.

It was almost as if Bailor's life dream had been finally realised. He put his hands forward and waited patiently for those drawings. Jon retrieved a container and handed a disk and drawings to him. He immediately removed its cover and carefully emptied its contents. He briefly observed the sheets and then passed them over to Volt who handed them to Stradon. Bailor then placed his right hand over his forehead and stared at Malik, then he lowered them.

'What an incredible surprise you have brought us today and also what a great treasure you have delivered to us. For now, we find ourselves even within a much greater conflict, partaking almost in the presence of a great universal god and with the knowledge of the existence of a Great Solarian Empire.' He glanced at the documents again.

'We thought we were dead from true spiritual life and from real science, but now, you have brought our whole civilization back to life once more from the abyss, to strive creatively towards a common greater purpose. For that much greater freedom you have shown us today, we shall be forever indebted to you and all your peoples, wherever they may be.'

Volt was trying to decipher the complex jigsaw of blueprints and showed overwhelming surprise.

'Let us in future strive for the common good of civilization and for our newly formed federation of worlds... to assist and help our weaker neighbours, wherever and whenever possible, to thus ensure their freedoms within that greater purpose,' Bailor continued with commitment in his manner.

Once again Malik stood up to thank Bailor and his companions.

He got on his communicator and gave the necessary orders for his people to resume normal activities within their systems. Bailor had also given orders that all slaves be made free men under their new constitution.

Most Polokan ships would remain on Lodor to assist wherever possible. Then they would find a suitable sight for an operational base and embassy for all humans there. However, as agreed, the Lodorians would also build a similar complex on Polok for the benefit of their own kind. It was time both separate species learned to live together in peace and on equal terms.

Malik showed Bailor, Stradon and Volt the Andromedan ship and explained as best he could its mode of operation and they could not believe in its reality, for it was so unique in every sense.

They said their farewell and The Ship reformed itself and simply disappeared while they were still watching.

Jon and Lira found that world to be the most boring and uninteresting place they had ever seen.

'Jon, if I live for 100 more years, I can guarantee you I shall make it one of the most important projects of my life in giving this whole planet a face-over. One of these days I must have a serious chat with Bailor on that matter.'

'And I will wage you 100 dollars that he will have little choice in the matter once you made up your mind,' a happy Jon replied and she firmly agreed and defiantly walked away.

Malik and his companions soon returned to their underworld. They were very pleased with the day's outcome and the signing of those very important documents. He suddenly felt a sense of utter freedom within his being. It was like a giant weight had been lifted after so many years of struggle.

As they walked down the glittering staircase from The Ship, they were initially greeted by their families and friends and then by numerous bystanders. They had all heard the news and were out to greet their leader and his important friends from Solaria.

Banners were up everywhere within the underworld. As far as eyes could see, people were celebrating the end of a long and devastating war. Finally, their people were free everywhere and the planet's surface free of bombardment by satellites. It was finally ready for clearing, rebuilding and resettlement of countless millions after more than one hundred years of isolation, war and decay.

They could now bathe in their native sunlight and its almost forgotten oceans and seas. Yes, finally they were truly free from their underground tombs and hoped it would remain that way forever.

Malik was to give a speech to his people that same evening. During that time he introduced his friends from Solaria in person to the special cameras.

Later on that evening he discussed the future program and the construction of the two special ships with Jerry and others. It was subsequently agreed that Jon and others of his young group of six would return to assist in the ships' construction, with all the necessary microids and control equipment.

Jerry and his company decided to leave early the following day, so he informed Malik of their future plans. Malik was saddened, but knew their departure was only temporary. It would be until The Ship returned again with Jon, his friends and the special microid supplies.

His wife Mira exchanged photographs and other items with Jerry's wife, Sharon, and the others. The Visitors gave what they could find, including a spare video camera and several entertainment videos and music disks.

In most human aspects, both races were quite similar, with the exception that Malik's one was much more technologically advanced than Earth's. Perhaps as a result of the influence of the more brilliant minds on Lodor III. However, despite that fact, many things like music, art, fashion and cinematography were unknown to their culture and in such Earth was always worlds ahead. Not to mention the numerous recreational games like Football, Baseball, Cricket and Golf.

CHAPTER 14

Orban, the glorious world

The Ship spoke:

'We are now to visit Orban, the home world of the Octans. This will not take long and is very important for Lord Meron and his family. Octans are similar to the Lodorians. They are another advanced race that had evolved within the oceans of their world. It was they who saved Lord Meron's world and its people in ancient times. That was in the days of great king Micol, Seno, Sefran, Melor and others. That was several thousand years before the existence of the Javols.

'This planet is one of the most beautiful in Osmaron and has always been a holy world for followers of Lord Seno and his worshippers, as was written in the holy books. While there, you will experience the greatest surprises of your lives.

'You may now enter your bunks ready to be transposed to Orban. All life must now be transposed,' he said and the sirens sounded.

'Oh, Great Lord Gerron! I always wanted to visit that incredible world!' Meron exclaimed and immediately reclined in his bunk.

There was a bright flash of light. Then they found themselves in a strange constellation with many beautiful gaseous nebulae of every conceivable colour and form. There were red specks everywhere on the large screen and Jerry became curious.

'This place is truly beautiful! It's like looking unto the face of God!' Meron exclaimed, awed by the enormity of it all and Jerry was speechless. He had seen such beautiful images in pictures taken by the large orbiting telescopes, but never anything like this.

Then The Ship began to speak:

'This place is at the furthest reaches of Osmaron and also the greatest distance from Earth. It will be the first to be invaded by Javols, so there are many more important defensive installations

in this part of the galaxy.

'At this time the small galaxy of Balion is colliding with Osmaron. Even so, only rarely will their systems be in any danger of collision.

'Balion is the home galaxy of the Plorans and is now part of a greater Osmaron. Lord Faemon, the Ploran, is responsible for Balion and this part of Osmaron.

'I must now make contact with Orban for landing.'

However, search as they could through the ship's telescope, they were unable to find any worlds or indeed any satellites in that part of space.

While their eyes were on the screen wisps of clouds began to form against a starry background. Within the cloud a massive doorway opened in space.

Jerry was amazed by it all, but still could not fathom the enormous tasks of any single individual responsible for a small galaxy. Then he realized the Plorans were like gods and Lord Faemon was most probably like Lord Vektron. Perhaps they were even brothers.

Suddenly the whole world appeared with its three moons. Powerful satellites had enclosed their world in a shroud of invisibility. Their technologies were also capable of taking their world away from its present location and replacing it with an uninhabited one of the same mass and motion.

Jerry and the others assumed the Octans were an ancient race, but were surprised when they learned their world was billions of years younger than Earth and they were millions of years more advanced. That was because their world had evolved in a less dangerous part of the galaxy. Further, marine life tended to be a lot more resilient to mass extinctions than land animals and most creatures learned and evolved at different rates. Octans being faster learners than most. That was probably because they seldom fought wars and used everything they couldn't understand as a challenge and riddle to solve.

Once again Jerry and other members of their Solarian group were dressed in their best. The ship was parked on a large orbiting station. Finally they were engulfed by a beam and found themselves in one of their large auditoriums on the surface. Standing ahead of them was a Shadite. He calmly walked towards them and introduced himself to Plato.

'I am Siit,' he said and showed reverence by Shadite salutation. Then he went to shake Jerry's hand, then Meron's.

'Were you the great one in black who knew our Saint Seno and King Micol?' Meron asked.

'The very same!' he replied and Meron was speechless. Then as if from nowhere, Octans began to appear. They silently floated in the air as if they were swimming in water. They were semi invisible, but with the usual abilities to change colour. In that mode they were able to do everything their normal bodies could but were unaffected by the matter in our universe.

'Greetings, to all my friends!' Halban said, waving his tentacles while moving closer to them and the group replied in similar vane.

'Greetings, Lord Halban!' they replied.

'They wear the badges of Senots! This is truly incredible!' Meron commented.

'Yes! These days all Octans are Senots and Lord Seno is their accepted saint,' Siit said and they were utterly surprised.

For some strange reason they knew their names and felt at one with their hosts in all things. Not only had their bodies been transposed; their minds had also been updated in the process. Such were the technologies of the Octans.

The Octans had become so advanced in the millennia since Micol's death that presently they had no further need of our material universe; with its catastrophic randomness and pain. They had moved well beyond the natural order and were now in a most magnificent realm of their own creation in a world of Virtual Reality. One where even food, water and oxygen was not required for their survival but used all the same.

They could channel their beings into that Virtual Multiverse, where they could become Virtual Gods of their own Virtual Universes. Yet, the process was as real as any other universe to its players, based on their intentions and experiences. They could also link their Virtual Universes to the plenum of Gohenna for further experiences in that realm of all possibilities.

It is said that the ultimate evolution of all evolving species that survive extinction is to find God by their own hands and so had the Octans. Nevertheless they always retained strong links with their original home-world and galaxy.

Presently they were much more advanced than the Lodorians and could create virtually any item within our universe for any purpose whatsoever.

Siit and Halban took the group outside, towards the monument. It was built by King Melor, Lord Seno and others to thank the Octans for their assistance in saving his troupes and their world.

When they entered the beautiful park they could observe Meron's Ancients everywhere. They were all Senots. It was as if Orban was another Caefon, during his time, 3000 years before. They were all going about their business as on his ancient Caefon before the Javols came.

'Like you, they are King Micol and Lady Sefran's descendants, but that is not all. Please follow me to the Admin Block,' Siit said.

They entered another building of human design and in a flash found themselves in a large area with many computers and operators. Then they were taken to its governing chambers where several mixed humans were debating certain issues in a diplomatic matter. They stopped the moment Lord Halban entered and bowed.

'Let me introduce you to some great people,' Halban said.

'This is the one known as King Micol, the great, next to him is Lady Sefran. Then Lord Seno, our ancient profit, doctor and priest, beloved by us all... then King Melor, King Micol's father. Lord Hale his brother...,' he went on to introduce all twenty people that stood around the great table.

'All you guys are back with us from the dead?' Meron inquired, surprised but excited.

'Yes son, we have been brought back by our God to assist in the Javol's defeat. We are to defend this part of Osmaron during the initial stages of battle. Then Meron unclipped the scabbard with sword and handed it to King Melor. King Melor took the item, removed its blade and observed the alloy for a while, then he handed it back to Meron.

'It is not my sword anymore,' he said. Then he handed it to King Micol, who did likewise and passed it on to one called Lord Mond, then to Meron's own father, Lord Meran.

'It now belongs to you, my son,' he said and handed the item back to Meron. All Meron's ancestors were among them, even his father and he couldn't hold back a tear.

That day even Jerry could not believe what he observed. They had all been resurrected by the Grand Lord to partake in the destruction of the Javols, who were the greatest threat to all life in the universe. Even so, how was it possible to bring back the dead after so many years. Then he realized virtually anything was possible with their brand of technology.

Meron was probably the happiest person in the galaxy when he realized they were alive and he could visit them on special occasions.

After having spent three days on that world they decided it was time to return home. They said their sad farewells and were transposed to their ship still in orbit.

CHAPTER 15

They return via Tarran

After travelling within the Orban's system for a while, they took a final look at the distant worlds on the large viewer to say a final farewell.

Jerry reflected on the interstellar battle and contrasted those civilizations with the incredible technologies of the Octans and wondered what new surprises the ship had in store for them.

He was worried that his trip might take longer than planned, with his look-a-like on Earth being discovered with all the ensuing problems with press and media. Nevertheless his new experiences were well worth the risks. With the help of Plato and others he could always rustle up a plausible excuse or find some palatable tale to tell.

He also considered the oneness of the Cosmos and the hospitality of some great people, not too unlike his own friends on Earth.

The ship gave its usual orders for them to enter their bunks, and continued:

'We have successfully completed our immediate assignments and are now on our way back to Earth. However, may I suggest a different route this time. One by way of Tarran, the planet of cats.

'It's a system within another spiral arm. That one is situated at the rear of our Solarian Arm as seen on my screen and is almost on the opposite side of Osmaron when viewed from this position. We shall not visit for long, just a quick call to meet a chosen one.'

Jerry and the others agreed. Anyway, they realized they couldn't contravene The Ship's schedules.

They thought their visit to that distant world would have been previously scheduled and very important to the Grand Lord. Further, The Ship appeared to be in his employ and obeyed his commands above all others. Yet, what could be so important?

Within a flash they had arrived within the system. The large screen displayed a massive boiling star with a smaller companion orbiting just outside the orbits of three inner-planetary worlds. Jon and his young companions gazed at the massive impetuous boiling star with dread and dismay. Then they glanced at the brownish world below. It was almost void of green and blue.

'How can anyone live on this desert planet, with such an unstable star!' Jon exclaimed.

'Perhaps it wasn't always desert and primals have a unique way of adapting to change,' Lira replied.

The Ship soon landed on that barren world, with deserts where oceans should be. That planetary system included several satellite moons and rotated about a single erratic star which formed the major part of the binary system. The other small companion star being positioned well beyond the primary system with a long elliptical orbit. Even so, the weather pattern on those worlds might have been extremely unstable to say the least. Not to mention gravitational effects due to tidal action, and yet here was life. Several large castle-like structures could be clearly observed within the greener and yellower areas close to a small sea in the middle of what appeared to be the largest desert.

The Ship observed the terrain for a while and landed close to one of the more fertile regions. Then it opened its stairway and Plato, Jerry and Meron walked out wearing facial filters. They were immediate hit by the repressive heat and returned close to the ship.

A strange figure stood barely one hundred metres away. She stood close to a mound of stones and appeared to be admiring the beautiful sunset. Two suns, including one that was fainter were setting amidst orange and red, but no one could see the person's face. She had her back to them and did not yet know of their presence. When she turned around, she realised she had strange alien company and jumped backwards to save herself.

Jerry was startled, for her face was not human, but catlike, almost completely covered with fine facial hair that formed a pattern of different shades of brown, grey and black, with two long curly whiskers.

He thought her human-like features so ferocious. Yet, her face was so much like that of a domestic cat's, although much larger but with humanlike expression.

Her hands were slightly webbed, while fingers included long sharp retractable claws. Using his Black Shadite's Cloak, Plato changed his visual form into her type and went forward to greet her.

'Bawaki, I have something for you from our Grand Lord!' Plato shouted, in her catlike language.

Then he withdrew a small tunic and a head band with a beautiful crystal insert at its centre. The items matched her large golden hunting bow and buckle. Bawaki gave the appearance of a great hunter and warrior in the diminishing light.

She came forward to collect the items and thanked him in her own language with a bow and broad smile. Then she walked back to the mound and bowed in prayer, still looking at the distant horizon with her back to them and with little fear of anyone.

They left her there and went back to the ship.

Jerry and Meron did not know the significance of their experience, so they asked Plato for an answer, but The Ship replied instead:

'She is from a catlike race, for this planet is called Tarran, the planet of cats.

'She has been chosen to become a disciple of The Greater Purpose, but she still has some way to go before she may become a Shadite. I am sure you will see her again, if not in her present form.'

Not too far away they could observe a monster pulling itself out of the sand and Jon could hardly believe his eyes. It was the size and colour of a black dragon with a reddish tongue. It smelled the vicinity for a while with its mobile tongue.

'This must also be the planet of largest monsters!' he exclaimed as Lira watched the giant monster dive back into the sands. As they adjusted the screen, they could observe flying creatures like giant bats and gargoyles. They could easily lift a full grown human in the air. Despite the harshness of that world, they soon realized the powers of evolution in moulding her children to fit virtually any environment.

While he sweated from the extreme heat, Jerry viewed the strange horizon, with its two suns and could not stop his innermost spiritual feelings from surfacing. Here he was on a remote and hostile world observing a strange and almost human form. She stood on two human-like legs while wearing strange leathery clothes and she looked so feminine from behind, but from her front she was so catlike. He wondered whether the large cats on his world could evolve in a similar manner if humans were not around.

How strange the universe was, for it showed two faces; the familiar and the unexpected and unfamiliar, and yet, both blended into a unique oneness of purpose through knowledge, wisdom and intelligence.

The Grand Lord within his greatness must have observed those spiritual concepts in much greater detail and depth. The meshing-in of such dissimilar life-forms, each speaking a different language for a common and greater purpose.

It must take a unique mind to visualize the Cosmos in such vivid detail and the Shadites must be the beginnings of that type of clarity. Although coming out of darkness, they must be the true disciples of eternal light.

CHAPTER 16

Back on Earth

The Ship had no more surprises for its crew and landed on Earth almost ten days after it had departed.

Lumak, in the form of Doctor Jeffery Longhurst knew in advance of the late arrival of The Ship. Therefore he and Jerry's lookalike made the usual excuses to the press, and other relevant foreign diplomats and organizations regarding the presidents continued illness.

Doctor Longhurst was a well known and respected person, so when he told them that Jerry had a further relapse of the flue and needed more rest before resuming his normal schedule, they did not press him further for explanations. Anyway his lookalike was always at hand to show his face to the cameras while pretending his severe illness. They also accepted the fact that his wife and friends were conveniently on holiday, incognito.

When Jeffery knew The Ship was on its way he arranged two cars to be present at a concealed location not far from their residence. The moment The Ship landed they entered the cars and drove home, leaving The Ship to complete the trip to the small hanger on its own and invisibly.

Jerry, the real president, was soon driving one of the cars and once again wearing his bearded disguise. On arrival, the bearded man went in to see the lookalike president. Another switch was made and the real president was finally back within his own shoes, so to speak, with his security men none the wiser.

He wrote his lookalike friend a large cheque to cover the extra time and thanked him for his efforts.

'Pal, this should cover it. See you at our next reunion for panto,' he said.

'Thanks Jerry! See you soon! That's more than enough for a great party and I have some bets to collect,' he replied and left quietly.

The young ones and others had lots to talk about, so after the initial excitement had died, they went into an unused room to exchange presents and watch the videos of their adventures and of the great war between Polok and Lodor.

'Did you guys see the Tarranian?' Lira said. She was just like Tiger, our cat, but with the size of a human and standing on two strong legs.'

Really?' Petra inquired, doubtfully.

'Yea! She looked completely human from the rear but the moment she turned around, was all cat. I tell you, her face looked exactly like our little Tiger,' Merol said and they were awed by that revelation. The others that were left behind were soon listening to the strange adventures of their friends, and soon exchanged experiences and presents. Even Madeline joined in. Then they listened patiently to their adventures on Orban and was told that Lord Seno and others of the great Ancients were alive. They were amazed by it all.

Doctor Jeffery Longhurst soon disappeared and Lumak reappeared in his place to discuss matters relating to their memorable trip.

'People, we are all children of our universe. There are many strange worlds out there with many strange life-forms. It's our duty to bring order in all that strangeness. Don't forget, they also see us in the same light as strangers. It's our duty to assist all life when we can, so that we may all have a common voice within The Greater Purpose,' he said. They remained silent and listened carefully to his words.

'One more thing, People. A few words please! You guys have many important projects and adventures for the future, so henceforth, you must be fully focussed. There is a good bit of news however, which is to do with the Omegron Portal. It has now been installed within the underground city of Lower Cantor. Within a week the other one will be fitted on Mars. From that moment on the evacuation of our people on Caefon will commence, so what do you say!' he said. They cheered and couldn't stop dancing around the room in happiness.

'This is fantastic news!' Jon and his group exclaimed.

'There is more! Bawaki the cat woman you are so interested in, will be joining us soon in human form. Nevertheless we have Constructor Microids to manufacture if we are to build the great ships, so very soon your education will begin in the new field of Micro-Robotics, known to those on Earth as a branch of Nano Technology,' he added and they cheered again.

'Finally, but not least, we have decided to form the new Solarian Empire. That great empire will eventually expand throughout this complete galactic region, finally to engulf the complete Osmaron galaxy. This is necessary if we are to work together with one voice and win our battles against the evil Javols.' This time they remained silent and in awe of such an empire, but in anticipation of much worse to come with the Javols invasion.

Since Jerry's trip to the stars he had become a changed person and so did all his companions. He had returned to his original job as president of the USA in much the same way as he had left and the anticlimactic shock of normality was almost too much to bear. Despite his interstellar adventure, where he gained a somewhat heightened level of insight and attitude, with much spiritual enlightenment and broader horizon, he was finally brought down to earth with a bump and facing many painful political decisions in government and elsewhere.

The country was still in deep recession and people were beginning to take the law into their own hands. Drug addiction was endemic and that sole factor alone accounted for most lawless behaviour. There were mass redundancies, even from unexpected large OEM companies. Every stratum of society had been affected one way or another and most of that happened a relatively short time during his absence.

There was also the more serious problem of a trade embargo with the European government over the breaking of certain rules of equal trading. To add more salt to his wounds, a few foreign enemy cells keen on destruction were threatening massive explosions if their important prisoners were not released.

Public unrest and mass demonstrations were constant reminders in Washington DC and other major cities. To top it all, several pockets of violent street rioting and looting had occurred, requiring the National Guard.

He was an unhappy man. Things were a lot worse than when he left, barely two weeks ago.

Although the businessmen and farmers were a resilient lot, with a strong entrepreneurial drive, their fighting spirit was down to barest bones and only a miracle could prevent further unrest in that sector. Those problems were not only in North America; the whole planet was infected and undeniably in the grips of major recession and turmoil. He knew most of it was related to dwindling oil reserves and food shortages due to fires and desertification, partly because of Global Warming. Producing oil fields were constantly being sabotaged by extremist, further compounding the problems.

He prayed for something positive to happen and then an idea came into his head.

'Perhaps I should make a statement to that effect... Tell the world of my interstellar adventure and of the agreements...' and then he thought again of its consequences to society.

'Such knowledge could give the world a false sense of hope. They might not receive benefits from those projects within their lifetimes and the majority needed help right now,' and he thought again.

'But if I mentioned about the special interstellar drives and the possibility of opening up the solar system to exploration... and the three local systems... perhaps two, excluding our beautiful Eden...?' He was set on that idea.

'Plato was correct, after all, in me giving an important speech on my return.' He phoned his chief advisor, then Plato, Meron and finally Jon for relevant video recordings of their trip.

The meeting was arranged for the following day in his country house. During that time Doctor Longhurst (Lumak) was nominated as his new chief scientific advisor, with Professor John Laroche as his second, in charge of all those new technologies. Lumak in turn nominated Meron as chief scientist, to take charge of the special interstellar drives.

Meron couldn't be more pleased with his new assignment. He always wanted to be more directly involved. Knowing that many of his Ancients had survived the Javols and were living on Orban gave him and the others hope for the future. They were also overwhelmed by emotion when they were told that Lord Seno, King Melor, King Micol and others of that time were alive and immortal. Therefore they were even keener in taking Earth back from the brink.

Some relevant information discs were played to a group of specially chosen scientists. Those currently assisted Doctor Longhurst on his ME and Zeus projects. ME was the acronym for Microid Engineering.

They observed the videos, but could not seriously believe in their content and implications. Then Jerry produced a few live alien specimens that were kept in special containers and other technical bits of equipment he had acquired from Polok and Lodor, including a translation belt. They were soon convinced and became like pet dogs, wagging their tails for more. At that time they would have accepted almost any task he offered; for they had the promise of an incredible and exciting future, with a range of technologies the likes of which they had never seen before.

They were excited and impressed, and decided to go along with future plans under the guidance of Doctor Longhurst.

After further consideration, they agreed the samples were too incredible to exhibit in public. They were concerned such knowledge would create more harm than good by way of confusion and incredulity among the general public.

Jerry also explained the manufacture of special intergalactic ships that were very much larger than the one he had used to travel to the furthest galactic arm within seconds. By that time the scientists were almost in the same mental state as Bailor, the Lodorian, and excited for an adventurous future with a great purpose. However, Jerry did not mention anything about the ship being from Andromeda. They assumed Doctor Longhurst had completed the special drives and had taken the first prototype for a test drive.

Finally, he discussed the preliminary forming of Solaria and the signing of the treaty with Polok and Lodor and they were further impressed.

Earth hadn't yet realized that her local system had become part of a much greater whole in which she now represented the seat of power, but as destiny would have it, that power would shift to an almost unknown world within the group of four local systems. One that was destined to become the head of a much greater federation of planets and even those facts were not yet known to any human on Earth. Whatever little was known would never get to the people of Earth within their lifetimes.

And the worst was yet to come, for while Earth continued along its self-indulgent path, plans were being put in motion for the final termination of more than 95 percent of her human population.

Finally, Jerry decided to take things in small steps, beginning with a preliminary speech to the people about the new interstellar drives and the opening up of the solar system. All other relevant matters would be taken up by a special Solarian body which included present company and the Andromedan visitors. During all that time the people on Earth were ignorant of the Andromedan visitors or indeed of any alien technologies, with the exception of a few scientists.

Earth would be kept out of the more distant systems for now until the time was right. They agreed to visit the Project Zeus laboratories the following day and the meeting was adjourned.

As they left Jerry's residence that evening, he handed Plato a small pile of passports and other documents for him and his people.

Once again Lumak got the Andromedan group together in the dining room for a general discussion.

'As promised, Jerry has arranged all our papers for us. At this moment in time, we are citizens of the USA!' They cheered. Then Plato began to hand the large envelopes around.

The Andromedans were now legitimate nationals and registered scientists, working for the government under special license.

The President subsequently called his publicity people together and after much discussion with his advisors, told them when he wanted to make the necessary arrangement for his special speech to the nation.

'So be it! Call the studio, Larry, and arrange it! Make it urgent for the agreed time!' Jerry snapped.
'Yes, Mister President! Consider the deed done!' he replied.
The Television broadcast was set for Tuesday the fifth, in just two days. That was a day before his budget speech to the house.
He thought, 'by coincidence, things couldn't be better timed.'

CHAPTER 17

Dr Hal Seaton, the perfect Phantom

Dr Hal Seaton was 25 and not happy with the way irresponsible mankind were slowly destroying his planet, Earth. As far as he was concerned the majority of mankind were like parasites, with little intelligence to take his world further. He hoped those would become extinct through wars and plagues, and give their places to those more deserving. As far as he was concerned, over 95% of the population were surplus to requirement. They were little more than flies in the ointment that needed fumigation at the quickest possible time.

They were like filthy breeding pigs having children even less intelligent than their useless parents. They brought new life into the world only because they were programmed genetically by past evolution and would continue that way until the planet destroyed itself. They could never see the stupidity of their actions and would always pass that irresponsible culture on to their future generations. After all, they were not clever enough to find better ways to exist without children.

Currently in the year 2042 the planet's population was just over 9 billion and rising, when it should be 750 million with current resources. That was about 12 times more than was sustainable.

Dr Seaton was furious, but could do little, short of designing some type of bio weapon to cause a pandemic. He realized any such weapon would kill randomly and take the good as well as the bad. He needed another method. If only people were interested in long term survival? He knew the latest President was interested, but realized it was political suicide. No one was brave enough to fight his corner. Nevertheless, Jerry had removed most guns from the streets. A good move, but sadly not one for reducing human population.

'Lennox told me there was a program, but where is it. I can't see any signs of any program to save the world or anyone,' He

continued reading the newspaper then turn to a page. It read:
 '100 more Elephants killed with gas for their precious horns. It is thought that the Snow Leopard is now extinct along with Rhinos in the wild. Extra care is given to those held in zoos. A plan is currently in action to increase breeding in captivity, but it is thought their days are numbered...' And so it went on.

Hal kept reading the papers until his rage peaked and he threw it away in disgust.

'How can any human species be so bloody useless and stupid. Tiger flesh and bones for medicine. How bloody ridiculous. Has the whole world gone mad?' Hal was not a happy man.

Although an Olympian with one Gold and two silvers, he was also prolific in the Martial Arts with two Black Belts. He had studied Buddhism to its finest points and tried living by those rules, but realized he was changing into a more reckless and cruel persona. That was probably due to his basic nature while driven by irresponsible humanity. He could be the only proper force left for good among a planet of idiots.

That day in the Gym he was not his usual self and went at his student with full vigour. He had lost most of his patience and rules were blurred. All he could see were human pests going home to breed some more.

After Gym he decided to walk home and do a little jogging to clear his mind from the disappointments of that day. While on route a poor girl was being molested by a hooded man. The man took her handbag and decided to run, but their paths crossed. Hal was merciless. The man drew a knife, but with an Olympian movement the knife had changed hands to end in the shoulder of the hand with the bag. The man was lifted into the air and then dropped and crushed like a bag of potatoes.

The frightened woman soon came forward to claim her handbag.

'You broke his neck!'

'I know! And his back! He wont be bothering you again!'

'You are not worried about the Police?'

'No! They are all dumb bastards and I have ways to remove my DNA profile from their primitive database!'

'You have?' she asked looking most apprehensive.

'Can I trust you? Or shall I kill you here and now?'

'No, please! I have not seen or heard anything!' she replied and he let her on her way.

A few days later while in his office his secretary handed him a note, which he carefully read. He was to take on a new project.

'Doctor, Harry would like you to join him in private!' His secretary Sandra said, while dropping a pile of large sealed envelopes on her desk for scanning.

'Any idea what it's about?'

'No! I think its for your ears only!' she replied.

'In that case I must see the dreaded man!' he said, sarcastically and left.

'Hal, come in! Have a seat! Sandra, espresso please!'

'What's this about?'

'It's to do with your favourite subject!'

'What subject is that?'

'It's about the culling of humanity!'

'Thank goodness, someone is seeing the light!' Hal replied with a half smile.

'The Boss is also worried for humanity and our world. So you got the job. Give it your best shot. Anyway, the Boss has done most of the major work. All you have to do is put it together. These are some of his notes and a small capsule of stuff you should inhale. Apparently it increases brain power.'

'Nano-bots. I don't like bloody nano-bots. They will destroy us all one of these days. I hate the bloody stuff!' He collected the notes and disks, but threw the small vial of dust across the room and walked out in utter rage.

As he scanned through the information that day he was surprised by it's complexity, but realized he could do that task with his eyes shut. As a Grade One PHD from Oxford, England, he had engineered similar cell structures in the past with timed viruses, and that was without the use of nano-bots.

After just two weeks the bacteria plus virus was engineered and laboratory tested. Hal was ecstatic in the knowledge that he was the best, with extraordinary abilities in the field of bio-engineering. It was a pity he would not receive a Nobel Prise for his great feats. Anyway, any idiot was excepted for that particular prize and his face would probably end up on television, which was not where he wanted to be. He had been a bad boy too many times of late and many could recognise him. Anyway, he was now working on his own genetic code. Soon many would not recognize him.

Having tested the product for another week, another meeting was arranged with Lennox.

'Please enter, Doctor!' Lennox yelled with respect.

'Hello, Harry!' He greeted.

'I read your report and watched the device in virtual simulations. As far as I am concerned, it works to spec,' Lennox said.

'Of course it works, and without nano-bots. However, we need a few human guinea pigs. May I suggest Africa. We can choose a poor isolated village for that purpose. We can repay them with a school, hospital and a few of our research people here. I was thinking of a few of my laboratory assistants?'

'Sounds a good idea. I shall mention it to the Boss. The older ones wont be losing anything other than their abilities to have kids. The young ones can be given the antidote and closely watched over the next few years, with incentives,' Lennox replied.

'Incentives?'

'I was thinking of a good university education and such like, so we can also be loved in their community. Then later they might allow us access for medical purposes, in case we have long-term problems. We never know what might happen twenty years down the line?' Lennox said.

'I see what you mean. We should also educate them with more anti-poaching literature and build more protective domes.'

'I told you, we have a program for saving all endangered species. Between you and I, some are being taken in the dead of night to an alien world very much like Earth. We now have the technology to travel to the nearest stars. I have been told, we can now travel within a 50 lightyear radius from Earth. So Pal, don't worry. We are going places fast,' Lennox said while touching his nose to stress the secrecy of their present conversation and Hal was numbed by that knowledge.

'Ok! If you say so!'

'By the way, I think you are a dam good doctor. At this rate the Boss will soon be admiring your work. If you make him happy, he might even promote you above me, which is never a good idea! Any way, you have got a raise to double your present salary,' Lennox handed him an envelope and a cheque.

'I love you!' he shouted, kissing the bonus cheque and was soon out of the office in ecstasy.

CHAPTER 18

Meteor strike

As the Comet Solo approached the Solar System with an elliptical orbit towards the Sun. Many scientist and astronomers speculated as to whether it would crash into the solar corona or dissolve in the solar atmosphere. Others thought it would break into multiple pieces and continue its journey. Nevertheless they were more interested in its constituents, in particular carbon based molecules that could lead to the creation of life in planetary systems. With over 20 billion Earth-type worlds in our galaxy alone, it was a question due for an answer.

Nevertheless, if life was ubiquitous and similar to those within the jungles of Earth we would not have expected alien visitors for sometime. If that was the case, were we "The Chosen Ones"?

It was thought, that only a very few life-forms would have developed like mankind, with an overwhelming need and desire for tools and technology. Further, since the majority of universes cycled like trees, during which time they expanded and contracted, it was thought life would begin about four billion years after the beginning of each expansion. That was within the first quarter of each expansion. It was also thought new galaxies began at the start of each expansion and continued their expansion even during the stages of local contraction. That way, new universes that formed in their black-hole nucleuses continued towards their own space-times. Therefore most spiral galaxies seeded primal life along with new universes at their nucleus during universal expansion.

Anyway, at the start many massive stars exploded to form the heavier inter-stellar elements and particles which subsequently formed nucleic acids; the foundation of life. However most of this debris went on to form the denser worlds like Earth.

A complete universe being seen as a living tree, albeit in a higher dimension, with branches of galaxies more like leaves and fruits on those branches. The Oort Cloud was formed about the same time as our Solar System, but was composed mainly of distant comets. Once in a while comets like Solo moved away from the cloud and were accelerated towards the Sun.

As Solo approached the Sun it broke into several large pieces which took different paths through the solar system. One solid part about 100 metres in diameter was on course for Earth. Since it travelled close to 50 thousand miles per hour a disaster was imminent.

Hal read the daily news and was disturbed by implications.

'Dam bloody idiots! Sometimes I wish I was never born human. I wish I could leave this primitive world here and now. Any halfwit species would by now have built at least six defensive platforms around this planet with penetration missiles for taking out such objects. For Heavens sake, we have had over ten close misses over the past hundred years, one was going to hit sooner or later. Thank goodness that one will target Antarctica. It should speed up Global Warming and Ocean Spread. Now, all our coastal cities should be under water much sooner than expected. Thank goodness that object was not on coarse for a populated area.' Hal could not believe in the negligence and uselessness of humanity and its senseless politicians.

'Come in, Doctor!' Lennox shouted.

'Good day, Harry! It's about the comet fragment!' A worried Hal greeted.

'You mean, Little Solo? What about it?'

'Will it really hit Antarctica? I can't trust any of these idiot scientists anymore. It might hit the middle of New York for all I know!'

'It will! We are evacuating penguins while we talk. They are also a very important species. Thank goodness their numbers have dropped significantly. Most are taken to a floating dome in the Arctic region,' Lennox replied.

'How so precise? I mean the area of collision. It's the cleanest spot on Earth!'

'Don't worry, Pal. We have seen to it! We have the technology to destroy the little rock, but we must keep a low profile. If it suddenly disappeared or exploded people would ask too many questions. Anyway, the Boss wants to speed up Global Warming, so it's an opportunity he couldn't miss!'

'You are telling me, our organization can weald that much power? The power to move comets?'

'Yes, Pal. And a lot more besides! So don't worry about a thing!' Lennox said while an unsatisfied Hal left his office.

When Hal got home that day he was handed a letter by security. It was hand delivered by special courier.

'What can it be?' he muttered. He opened the envelope and began to read the single sheet of special paper. Then pocketed the travel tickets and credit card. His name was imprinted on the card to show he was important.

'Visit us at the Metropol tomorrow the 13th at 1 pm. Don't be late! We would like you to become a member since our last death. This letter will dissolve while exposed to the atmosphere.
The Power of Thirteen.'

The letter began to dissolve in his hand, so he dropped it and rubbed his shoes into it, until it became a liquid.

'Who the hell is The Power of Thirteen? Thank goodness I don't have the police after me since my last caper. No street cameras in that area, I suppose. That criminal idiot deserved what he got and I'll do it again to save someone. Dam it, I hate New York. No one can catch a cab these days, and by 1 pm. I have to start packing now and inform Harry first thing.'

Despite the short notice and inconvenience, Hal had to visit that hotel and see what they were all about.

He caught the morning flight to New York and push through the crowded shoppers. When he arrived he was tired and sweating.

'Dr. Seaton? You are expected! Please follow me!' The

red-haired receptionist greeted.

There were twelve old men sat about a large table. The one in command sat at the top with the bottom chair vacant.

'You are on time! Please seat, Dr. Seaton!' he stood and pointed while observing the large clock on the wall.

'Thanks! Why am I here?'

'We have been observing your efforts for a while. We need new blood in our group. Particularly young aggressive blood to take a stand against crime and all the ills of stupid humanity at this time. We think humanity is going down the pan and would like to save something before the final hour.' Okeke said.

'So where do I fit in?'

'Just come to our meetings at the 13th of each month at 1 pm. You will be rewarded generously for your participation. During that time you may advise us on any unusual changes you may have observed. You are young, very clever and with your hands on the pulse, so to speak. We think there are many strange things going on. Things we cannot explain by natural progression.' Okeke said.

'I shall try to find what I can, if we survive the collision!' Hal said in jest.

'You think it might hit us, here in New York?' One of the group inquired.

'My first good bit of information to my group of thirteen, is that Little Solo has been guided to a spot in Antarctica. So we are all safe for now,' he said.

'How do you know that?'

'Gentlemen! Please don't ask too many questions. Let's say, I have friends in very high places. Little Solo hits in three days. That will tell you if I am right or wrong.'

'We shall wait and see. From this I take it, you are now one of us?' Okeke inquired.

'You may take it as such, Gentlemen.'

'Congratulations!' They cheered.

'You are number 13. Secured membership information will be kept in your bank vault from now. Relevant codes will be sent to your address by special courier. Memorise them for future use.' Okeke advised.

As predicted, in three days Little Solo crashed into Antarctica and created a whole new set of consequences for the planet, including a few unwanted tsunamis. However the damage was not as extreme as were expected. Nevertheless most of the ice in that part of the world began to melt at a much accelerated rate. Even so, countries 5000 miles away would not experience detrimental effects for several months.

Nevertheless, since most of the worlds ice was held in that part of the world, it was the worst place to hit for long-term survival. It would eventual lead to a change in climate with accelerated Global Warming. As the ice melted so would oceans rise leading to serious flooding. All coastal cities would soon be at the mercy of the rising waves.

CHAPTER 19

Project Zeus

All of Project Zeus's tests and experiments were conducted within an underground military bunker some twenty miles from Doctor Longhurst's residence. That laboratory was situated within the state of North Dakota. Those bunkers were probably utilised in the past for intercontinental ballistic missiles (ICBMs). But had since been cleared of all such devastating weapons along with their installations after the ratification of relevant treaties. Thus leading to the subsequent reduction in the proliferation of such weapons. This process was completed towards the end of the 20th century. After signing the relevant disarmament treaties, that base was one of the first to be decommissioned and went into disrepair soon after.

When Lumak (Doctor Jeffery Longhurst) arrived in North America, he searched within the area and accepted two possible sites for the development and production of his special projects. At that time both sites were bought from the government for a song. During that period the previous president and his scientific advisor, Professor Harry Lennox, assisted in the release of those properties to the civilian sector so that Lumak could begin his projects immediately. Harry Lennox had since left his job with the previous president and was presently professor in charge of all Lumak's bio-engineering experiments in that division. Dr. Hal Seaton was in charge of the Bio-Engineer section dealing with preventative diseases and viruses. His department was under Lennox.

Lumak (Doctor Longhurst) soon had those areas repaired, refitted and staffed with some of his own people. Most of them were his original devoted students from Turkey. Many lived locally within the original military barracks, which had been renovated and refitted with the most luxurious decor and appliances. However his students also spent time with him and his guests at the Manor.

He believed in sharing all profits from their projects and they earned comparatively high salaries and bonuses for their enthusiasm and effort. They were considered his most loyal family members and would kiss the very ground on which he stood. Many still addressed him as My Lord.

There was also a local runway that was built specifically for military jet aircraft. Despite a current need for resurfacing, it was still utilised by small propeller aircraft, gliders and helicopters.

On the special day of the demonstration, Jerry visited the site by military helicopter. Doctor Longhurst, Plato, Meron and others joined him in two limousines. Several guards took their places in their prearranged manner and Jerry climbed out of the helicopter, followed by his wife, Sharon, and some of his close associates and senators. Then he entered a large limousine and followed the other cars into the highly secured installation with thick metal doors.

Jerry was impressed by the high level of security associated with the project, which was considered a private venture. They entered a large personnel elevator and were at the relevant level in seconds. On arrival, he was greeted by Professor George Strongman and others of his British crew. He and his team had since joined Doctor Longhurst's staff and were from England. The intrepid reporter, Michael Cockburn, was also there. He used to be a fledgeling reporter for The Times and later became one of Jerry's scientific advisors. He was presently with Doctor Longhurst team and assisted him as project manager of the new LPD department, under Meron. There were also a few other familiar faces working within the laboratory. Jerry was amused by the sight of so many faces he knew personally and realized almost half his previous staff were currently on Doctor Longhurst's payroll.

They continued towards the rear of the building to observe the device in operation.

Despite the fact he had been with the company for almost six months Dr. Hal Seaton had never met his Boss. Well, not until the

President's visit to the LPD plant for the demonstration.

'Please to meet you, Dr Seaton! And thanks for some great work!' Dr. Longhurst greeted.

'Thank you, Sir!' he replied, not knowing who he was.

'Please join us for the demonstration!' Dr. Longhurst said and he followed with the group of observers.

'That was our Boss. He always like to be incognito, so consider his words a very great compliment,' Lennox advised.

'He is the great man, himself?' Hal was pleased, but intrigued..

'Yep, so watch your step!' Lennox was stern, but curious in anticipation.

At the distant corner they could observe a long small-gauge railway with an integral cart containing a type of cradle. Hanging from the ceiling was a large block of metal, held in position by four very thin nylon cords. The weight of the block was clearly shown on a local indicator as ten point zero metric tons.

On each of the six faces of the block were fitted small black modules, just three inches in cross section. Those units were apparently stuck unto the large block by a type of strong adhesive and could well have been battery operated.

Michael Cockburn, known personally to the president as Mickey, soon came forward to introduce his team.

'Mickey! So this is where you hide from me these days,' Jerry said in jest.

'He made me an offer I couldn't refuse, Sir,' Mickey replied.

'I think I might have to give up my job at the White House, if Doctor Longhurst will have me,' he said and they smiled at his humour.

Then Mickey retrieved a similar small block from his desk and handed it to Jerry.

'Mister President, this is the Excitor Module. Even such a small size is capable of shifting a mass the size of a small house outside of Earth's atmosphere. It can drive a ten-ton mass at a linear acceleration of eighty-five metres per second, doubling each second.'

'That much?'

'Sir, it's incredible! Let's say we are travelling at eighty-five in deep space, after the first second that speed will double to one hundred and seventy and after the same time again about forty-three kilometres per second and so on; forty-five thousand kilometres per second after twenty seconds and about one-point-five million kilometres per second after about twenty-five seconds.'

'Truly incredible!' the president was intrigued.

'The technology in use is not dependant on any given mass. As a result, acceleration continues on to an almost infinite level, limited only by the ship's composition, its reaction to sustained acceleration and other external factors. There is also a critical limit, when the inertial frame becomes unstable due to gravitational side-lobes, but in theory that limit is never reached and it can be reduced by inertial dampers and stabilizers.'

'Really? This is truly incredible!'

'Sir, you can therefore see the potential of such a system, because it beats all forms of trust propulsion which incur expensive and heavy fuel payloads and works on the principle of equal and opposite reaction. All we need to sustain the process is a small supply of compressed hydrogen within the Excitor fusion chamber to supply the required energy.'

'And so efficient?'

'Absolutely, Sir! This method is purely linear and there is no opposite reaction to the forward forces involved. In other words, there is no equal and opposite reaction as would be required in Newtonian physics. Hence, its name Linear Progressive Drive or LPD for short,' Mickey was overwhelmed by enthusiasm.

'One question please!'

'Yes?'

'Let me get this right. You are telling me that normal humans have discovered a method to take us to the stars. And that method was given to us by aliens? Is that what you are saying?' Hal interjected as the President turned around.

'Sorry Mister President, but this whole cock and bull affair is too ridiculous to be believable!' Hal apologised and Jerry smiled.

'But it works!' Jerry said.

Jerry was taken back by that knowledge but appeared utterly confused as much as Hal was.

'You mean to say it defeats our basic laws of Newtonian physics and of motion being due to the result of equals and opposites?' he replied, inquisitively.

'Not quite,' responded Mickey. 'It's like the difference between ac and dc current. Dc doesn't obey ac rules, yet it's all electricity. Further, it utilizes frames of reference which has very little to do with equals and opposites,'

'How will its crew withstand such extreme acceleration and what will you do about the negligible gravity problem during long journeys?' Hal asked with curiosity.

'There are two different devices for that purpose. They are based on a similar principle. One we call the Linear Excitor, for stimulating atomic mass in synchronism with the LPD's. This device reduces almost all internal effects due to high acceleration within specified limits. Then there is the Central Attractor, which accelerates all matter towards a preselected point or centre of gravity within or outside the vessel. Call it an imaginary point of gravity if you wish, at a rate of almost ten metres per second squared, effectively the same as Earth's gravity. All these devices are powered by the same hydrogen energy cells using a type of fusion reactor.'

'You are telling me that someone has found a way at sub-atomic levels to utilize Dark Matter and Energy?' Hal interjected again.

'Seems that way, Doctor! The basic principle is simple; each new velocity is treated as its original frame of reference and all matter is excited in the same linear mode, but with the added bonus of its previous frame of reference set to zero. It's almost as if the ship remains within its original position in space, while all space is pushed behind it at enormous speed. Also, with this method the mass of the ship is completely neutralized, so no light speed limitations.'

'Oh my god!' Jerry responded.

'The whole thing is incredibly simple, but its concepts... darn difficult for any human to grasp... almost like pealing an onion, sometimes also from the inside and tweaking each peal in a different way each time to cause movement in just one direction... Like getting rid of all other negative reactions once ignited above fusion thresholds, and the whole thing is constantly active. That operation is done at the microcosmic or sub atomic levels on nuclear forces and fields. They act on sub-space in a manner that causes such displacement in space, but not in time. There is almost no time dilation.'

'What do you mean,' Jerry interrupted.

'If we left Earth and travelled to the nearest star in a single week close to light speed, when we returned the people on Earth would just be two weeks older and not 50 years or so as would be expected by Eienstein's special theory of relativity,' he replied.

'So because it functions in sub-space the effects of relativity is nullified?' Jerry inquired.

'Yes Sir! I prefer to think of this device as a motion diode, causing motion in just one singular and concentrated direction, in much the same way as an electronic diode which separates randomness by causing ac electric current to flow in just one direction to make it dc... and the theory of relativity doesn't come into the picture, as the ship is always within its own frame of reference within hyperspace.... I suppose it happens in much the same way...'

'I see!'

'As you may appreciate, we are presently travelling away from the most distant galaxies at close to the speed of light and other universes and dimensions are supposedly moving well beyond light speeds away from us relativistically speaking, if we can visualise things in such a simplistic manner. That is because universes are supposed to be a type of Super-String in hyperspace. Since there is no Space-Time in 5D, such structures are smaller than an atom. Therefore we should be able to jump across a universe in seconds if we were in 5th. While because of 4D, just ordinary Euclidean and Einsteinian spaces exists within universes. Further, each universe will contain a different light speed with different relativistic parameters. Some may even be at different time periods.'

'I think you lost me! This is all too much above me, remember, I am but a simple human!' Jerry said.

'Mister President, all I can say is... the person who designed this thing must have been some alien genius; for it quickly breaks even the light barrier... so special dynamic three-dimensional maps have to be used during transit until the ship's computers become fully acquainted with those routes. However we have to be careful of asteroids and other sizable objects on route. We are currently developing super-sensitive detectors and screens, coupled with super-fast forward looking computers that can divert the ship away from such objects. Obviously once standard routes are explored those problems will be considerably reduced,' Mickey replied.

He selected one of several remote control units from his desk which appeared very similar to a television remote control keypad. He dialled a code on its panel and pointed the control towards a large suspended block. The block immediately moved forward as far as it could go while restrained by the thin nylon cords.

The three large indicators displayed a change in mass and the leftmost one showed a linear force component in the forward direction of twenty-five metric tons. The vertical component due to gravity was still showing on the most central indicator as a little under ten metric tons.

He excited several faces of the block. Each time the block was only held in position by the restraining nylon cords. In the vertical direction the force was much less when the effects of gravity was taken into account.

Then he took the small module from Jerry and fitted it into a specially reenforced cradle and again selected codes on his remote control unit.

'As you know, we use the old Newtonian concepts of motion, which relates to equals and opposites, but the alien designer and his race visualised the universe in a completely different way... perhaps more like a clever fish within its watery habitat would see it.'

'I see!'

'They thought of movement in terms of positive and negative

motion. In the case of jet propulsion, they would consider the hot moving jet particles and gases as negative and the ship's more stable forward motion as positive. They would also think of motion as composed of fluidic waves within the ether... and the ether as a kind of ocean media that carried many things, visible and invisible. A sort of quantum sea saturated with energy, in much the same way as an ocean is saturated with water of a given density. Today we consider this great cosmic ocean to be also composed of dark matter and energy, but there is much, much more that is hidden from us.'

'Really?'

'Yes! Furthermore, they considered the original universe to be a two dimensional structure, but stretched under tension, as if with infinite and invisible elastic lines... to form the forth-dimensional universe with the added effects of time. But time is not the only factor that cause our universe to look and feel as it does in giving us the illusion of 3D. Many do not realize our perceived 3D universe is created solely by our brain, since over 80% of that information is already in our head.'

'What a strange concept!'

'Space, or the ether, they considered to be the invisible elastic bands which were to them a special type of cosmic substance. The modules, in their concepts, reduced the elastic tension and untangled the bands in a given direction, thus reducing the distance between the ship and its destination.'

'I see!'

'The Theory of Relativity still applies within a given plane and frame of reference. However, in our analogy the ac movement is both negative and positive. Therefore, when the negative velocity aspect is removed, the equations will have a limit to infinity and not the speed of light. This is quite unlike what we have always believed to be the case, because the theoretical observer is not within the universal frame of the ship during transit, perhaps left behind in one of the previous frames of reference,' Mickey said.

With the small block fitted, the railway cart and cradle began to move silently and accelerated along the narrow railway line towards a distant reenforced barrier. When it crashed into the buffers, its final impact velocity and inertia along with other parameters were displayed on a large computer screen. The railway cart then returned to its previous position.

Jerry was impressed by such a thorough and intelligible demonstration. The project was so unique and devices so small. There were negligible fuel costs involved other than the electrical energy required to maintain its excitations within its highly efficient miniaturized nuclear generated fields. The tiny nuclear core would last for many years and be re-primed or replaced as many times as necessary with new supplies of hydrogen. He thought of its impact on the present motorcar-based society.

This new nuclear driven device could be the death of all such outmoded chemical engines, based on the inefficient use of rare fossil fuels. At last, environmental pollution could be significantly reduced. Yet, the use of petrol-driven vehicles was reducing due to exorbitant fuel costs as that resource was inexorably depleted and the surge of electric vehicles, despite limitations of their current electrical power distribution systems.

After the demonstration was concluded, Jerry visited Lumak's house for lunch and was escorted by many people and reporters. During lunch they further discussed the project and some of their future programmes.

Jerry was a much happier person when he left the Doctor's manor that day. He also realized Earth would soon be in the grip of change that were beyond his abilities to control.

'So you guys have met advanced aliens? I still can't believe that, but the product seems to work. If it does what it's supposed to, some motorcar manufacturers and oil moguls will become severely pissed!' Hal said while chewing on a crab's claw. He was no vegetarian. Everyone, including Meron remained silent.

Jerry couldn't believe in Hal's doubting attitude. He wondered why he was such a skeptic and realized he knew very little about the Andromedan visitors or their recent visit to the stars.

'Where are these aliens? Please take me to your leader! I want to join!' he exclaimed in jest.

CHAPTER 20

Microid Plant explosion

Hal heard about the new microid factory being built and was not pleased. He realized there could be great problems faced if things went wrong and could imagine little nano-bot robots eating into everything. He had seen films of what could happen if things went wrong. After all, those tiny bugs could become a plague that was exceedingly difficult to eradicate. As far as he was concerned, they were contrary to nature and all its natural processes. He did not realize that Dr. Longhurst's microids were of a well-proven design. Neither did he know of the Andromedans or of the alien Lumak, now living as Dr. Jeffery Longhurst. However, despite those factors, being a member of the thirteen, it was his duty to take action against all unnatural processes.

That day he was more worried than normal, so he visited Lennox's office. His boss Lennox seemed to be informed about everything.

'Come in, Doctor!' Lennox shouted at the smoky glass door. Hal was tall so Lennox could always tell.

'Hi, Harry! Are we doing nano-bots?' Hal inquired.

'Yea, I think so! A new production plant was recently built but not yet producing. I think it's in Sector One, you know, the ex-military warehouse place. I don't think it's ready yet. They are awaiting some special deliveries.' Lennox said.

'They will be the death of us all!' Hal stormed out of the office somewhat upset. He was concerned that it was an area of technology better left alone and never to be touched. Now of all things, his company was taking a lead in such deadly products.

'My God, I must move on this. I know a member of the Thirteen with friends in bad places. Someone of my student past. I must give him a call!' He muttered. Hal soon made the call.

'Hi, Powell, sorry for calling this late!'

'I know that voice from way back!'

'Hal Seaton. Now Dr. Hal Seaton!'

'What's up, Hal? I remember you from MIT. You had some great ideas in bio.'

'Yep! I did my thesis in gene-splicing. Now, I am one of the best in that field!'

'Nice one! How can I be of assistance?'

'My company has decided to do nano-bots. Those things pose a great risk to all life. I hate that bloody stuff. It gives me nightmares just thinking about it. Can we do something about that production plant. I don't want to kill anyone in the process. I don't like killing the innocent!'

'I would use a small bomb and blow the dam place to smithereens. The job can be done at night after everyone has gone,' Powell replied.

'Who can we use for the job?'

'Don't worry, I have contacts. They can plant a few micro bombs on their next delivery. They wont detect a thing. But they can build another factory somewhere else!'

'So we'll do it again and again, until they get the message. Next time we kill a few in broad daylight. That would make the point!' Hal said.

'Shall I leave it in your capable hands, number Nine?'

'You may. Don't worry about costs. Our group is quite wealthy and well respected. All expenses will be covered!'

'Thanks! I will upload all relevant info by secured email!'

'See you at our next meeting, number Thirteen!' Powell said and hung up.

Lumak (Dr Jeffery Longhurst) had decided to build a new microid plant solely for producing the Constructor Microids for the large Solarian ships. Crates of that material were to be delivered to Malik on Polok II by Jon and some of his young companions. However he awaited materials from another robot-controlled plant. That plant was hidden underground because of certain types of radiation dangerous to living organisms. Although that material was slightly radioactive with a short half-life, that sludge was not very dangerous, so it could be delivered by road transport. Therefore, it was not difficult to tape some micro bombs unto a few containers. Those would include micro receivers with a tail antenna. They were not timed and could be triggered remotely anytime, day or night. The small trigger device could be operated through satellite from virtually anywhere on the planet.

Hal received a call late at night. It was one he was waiting for.

'Hal, everything is in place. An item has been sent to you by secured courier. Now it's in your hands, so good luck in your efforts,' Powell said.

'Thanks for that. Now I owe you one!'

'No prob, see you at our next meet!'

'Thanks again!' Hal said and disconnected.

Hal had a small long-zoom camera fitted locally to watch the plant, so could observe traffic in and out of that area. When he was satisfied the plant was fully operational and final deliveries made, it was time to take action.

It was late at night when the place went up. Although a grand spectacle on camera, the damage was superficial. The radioactive sludge was sealed in anti-collision units and were not affected by the explosion. Therefore those materials were not lost to future production. Only the sampling and testing equipment were destroyed. Nevertheless there was much damage, with water everywhere.

Lord Meron was first on the scene and couldn't believe the sight he beheld. Because of the position and construction of that building the explosion was contained. He soon contacted Lumak, now Dr. Jeffery Longhurst.

'Jeff, we have a major problem at the new plant. Someone decided to take it out with a small bomb. Police are everywhere!'

'Let them do their job! Is anything recoverable?'

'The containers are untouched, but the place is a complete wreck, with water everywhere!'

'Thank goodness, no fire! Don't worry, it will be rebuilt in a week. I think someone doesn't like our microid program. He or she has been watching too many old movies. We can continue in our old place for now. It has everything we require and no one knows of its location,' Lumak replied.

'Once we are on target for our first deliveries?'

'We are, but just in case we should step up security in that area. I shall have words with Dad!'

'Yes! Ben will not be pleased with this situation.'

'I shall have to calm him. Very soon all such production will be sited on a distant world, so it's only a temporary setback,' Lumak replied and Meron was satisfied.

'Do you think it could be one of our Turkish students or people from back there?'

'No! I think it's from someone more local. Could be from one of our other factories. The explosion was at night with no one about. That tells me he or she only wanted to target the plant after completion. I have known our students too long. They are like family!'

'Ok! At least no one was injured or killed this time!'

'Thank God for that! By the way, please don't mention a word on this topic to anyone. I don't want Jon and his group to get worried for no reason!' Lumak replied.

'I understand!'

As far as Hal was concerned, his bomb had done its job. Nevertheless he would leave the small surveillance camera in place to monitor future changes. Lumak's decision was to rebuild that plant and use it for another product, so Hal had done very little to stem the flow of those Microids.

CHAPTER 21

Within the Microid Factory

After the destruction of the new microid plant, Lumak became more conscious of security, so all production plants were placed on high alert. He realized lives could be in jeopardy. The person or persons unknown were still at large and posed a great threat. Despite their intensive efforts the police were non the wiser. Their forensic department had found nothing. Micro bombs never left behind tell tale signs of their sources. So everyone was in the dark as regards the antagonist. Anyway, Lumak expected the occasional setback. To him it was the way of chaos and order could only work through chaos.

The following morning Lumak (Doctor Jeffery Longhurst) read out a list of names which included the young six and some elder Andromedan members.

'Today we begin our training in micro-robotics and other essential topics of education. From this moment on, those of you on my special list should always carry your passports and other documents of identification. They will be required for verification by my security officers and the local police.'

'Will there be a genetic check?' Lira inquired.

'Don't worry! That will be taken care of!'

'Goody!'

'Since you have been selected as my personal scientists your new positions will also give you the benefit of a generous salary. This should be reward enough for your tireless efforts during your interesting work for our organization.'

That's truly fantastic!' Jon was overwhelmed, while the others cheered.

'Your salaries are yours, to do with as you wish. Therefore, from this moment you will be free as when you were on Caefon, with only minor restrictions for security reasons and personal safety.

Even I, am not as free as I would like. Can anyone be truly free of all responsibilities? However, the lack of ultimate freedom doesn't mean that I am not satisfied with my existence.'

'We understand!' Merol said.

'Maturity is like the learning of a fine wine, with the added appreciation gained by an acquired taste. After all, we never like the same things in exactly the same way too many times, do we? Anyway, those measures are only for your own protection, until you have gained more experience in living among the natives of this world.'

'Yes! We shall always remain together!' Jon insisted.

'Take my advice and always remain close together, because you are a lot stronger and more efficient that way and we have much work to cover.'

He handed each a folder containing their agreements and time tables.

'I shall introduce you to the Microid factory this morning, so get ready before the hour strikes.'

They collected their folders with written documents and went away to get ready.

The microid assembly plant and various laboratories were situated about forty miles from the doctor's home and in the same direction as the special-drives laboratory, although a little more distant.

The area covered many acres of scrubland. That place was originally used by the army for storage of small firearms and nonperishable supplies. It included several prefabricated buildings, many of which had since been adapted for office and staff accommodation. Once again the complete area was being expansively developed. Large diggers, lorries and gigantic cranes could be observed everywhere.

Towards the centre of the large complex was a more secured and fenced-off area that contained three buildings. As they approached the electrically operated gates, a guard released it and they drove through towards a small makeshift hut.

There were several guards positioned throughout the compound.

'Please follow!' growled their chief officer. He was African-American, tough and more than two metres tall. He was not scared of anyone.

'I am Captain Errol Barclay. I have been expecting your company. Sheila will check your identities.' He handed them over to a female guard.

Errol Barclay was ex military in charge of all security matters within that complex and was well respected by Lumak.

'Please follow me this way, Doctor!' the guard said politely, showing him even greater respect than her superior. They always called Lumak, Doctor, in those facilities. Lumak had always maintained his security independent of himself and his other projects. That way everyone was treated in exactly the same manner and no one was allowed to be above the law. That level of security warranted that type of scrutiny.

'Don't worry about certain peculiarities, genetically. I can personally vouch for them,' Lumak said while being scanned..

'No problem, Doctor!' she replied.

The female guard closely observed their documents parrot fashion, making patient comparison with data on the local monitor. Then she took them into a darkened recess and asked them to place their fingers and thumbs on a square translucent surface to be scanned by laser. Then she took a retinal scan, which she considered to be quite strange for Earth's humans. However she realized the doctor worked on many new and advanced projects, so those close looking humans could well have been a new type of android or genetic clone. Her job was never in asking too many delicate questions. Yet, they were so real in appearance and deeds. After she was satisfied they were not imposters, she called one of the local guards and asked him to accompany them to the doctor's building.

Lumak's personal laboratory building was the third on the right and part of a group of three buildings. Towards the left was the three-storeyed administration block and in the centre, the much larger prefab production unit which although expansive, was on a single floor. Lumak's own building was the mirror image of the administration block.

As they entered the guard left them and the Doctor went directly to his secretary's desk. He told her he didn't wish to be disturbed for the next hour. They followed towards his local office on the same floor. They were subsequently taken around the building and introduced to several of the most prominent of his local employees. Then he showed them upstairs to their respective offices with each of their names meticulously inscribed on each office door panel. Finally they were brought back downstairs into his office as morning coffee was served by his secretary.

The phone rang and his secretary insisted that his impatient wife was on the line, so he immediately took the receiver.

'Hello, Love.... When did you say?... I shall come personally to collect you both... Everything ok in your stretch of the woods?.... In that case, see you soon!' he said, smiling and placed the phone on-hook while glancing nervously at Jon and the others.

'It's my wife, Sarah. She is on her way home. Her arrival should make our lives even livelier at the manor.' He appeared much happier. They were surprised but quite eager in meeting the famous Sarah. They had seen her photograph so many times in magazines and newspapers, but never in the flesh.

At the rear of his office was a large vault where he kept his special developments with their respective documents and schematics. There was a large safe within the vault for even more important items.

As they entered through its large metallic door, he gave a voice command and the central section of the floor parted to reveal an almost vertical stairway. He guided them downwards into what appeared to be the basement of the building. That area was truly extensive and at several levels the full width of the building.

'I had this area excavated and constructed to my specifications. It is completely bomb proof and controlled by a security computer. Don't worry, your bodies have already been thoroughly scanned by our AI system. She knows virtually everything there is to know about you, including your genetics. She can also update the master computer used at the gate. Anyway, I use this concealed area as my own personal laboratory for special prototypes. This place is very quiet and free of all distractions. However, for security reasons I have arranged another such place for you on the topmost floor of this building.'

'I see what you mean! This place could not be more secure!' Lira said.

'I shall arrange for you, Jon, to have the special codes for this place. This is in case you need to work here after hours. But you must keep its location between yourselves. No one knows of its existence except you and I. You may also use it for your own private projects. As you see, there's lots of space in here and the concealed tunnel over there leads directly to a local car park.'

'Very nice!' Jon replied.

'One more thing... this small cubicle over there is a portal. That one links this place with the basement in our house. Since this technology is well beyond anything used on Earth, only use it in an emergency.'

Jon took a deep breath and swallowed, remembering the strange technologies of the Octans.

'Wow! How bloody Incredible!'

'We'll need to take some of these more advanced control modules with us,' Lumak said.

They collected the special items as requested and took the small elevator to the uppermost floor. After having delivered the items and taking a quick look around, he decided to show them the other two neighbouring buildings.

When they entered the large factory unit they were surprised by the many scientists and engineers, with assisting robots of all shapes and sizes. Those advanced AI robots were themselves constructing other even more advanced robots. The place was filled with all the latest robotic technologies.

They could recognise several of the scientists on many different projects. Some had been present at their first dinner with the president. They soon came forward to greet the new arrivals. Everyone was excited and pleased when they realized they were also joining the team.

The young Andromedans could observe crystal containers everywhere, but the technology they observed was somewhat different to that at Lower Cantor. Even so, the place brought back memories and made them feel even more at home.

He took them into his local office within that building. They sat around a table containing several samples of the Microid powder and other equipment. Then he showed them a bluish dust that was kept in a sealed transparent container.

'What do you guys know about Micro Robotics?'

'Only that it's a small branch of Microid Engineering, more commonly known as Nano-technology on Earth,' Jon replied.

'Well, let me explain the basics. Just as we are able to modify and link molecules to create Polymers, Plastics and such like, which are unnatural substances, not common to nature. So are we able to go a step further and modify atomic structures to create molecular systems with diverse characteristics, from Memory Modules to a type of living organism. The basic building blocks of all such substances I call Microids. Others call them Nano-cells. A Micro-robot or Nano-bot may contain several Microids or Nano-cells to perform specific functions under some form of external control. However, like biological cells they can be designed with their own internal controls.'

'Truly un-imaginary!' Ecrol said

'To give you an idea of scale, if a three bedroom house was an average biological cell, then an average Microid would be the size of this pencil. They are so small that a complete human brain, with all its neurons could be the size of a pinhead and retain all its original functions. This can be done using quantum engineering.'

'So small!' Jon exclaimed.

'Further, biological cells are relatively loosely bound. This aspect makes them prone to environmental factors like changes in temperature, infection, external forces and such like. Although such changes in adaptation is essential for natural evolution, it weakens the structure concerned. Our Microids are Cross-linked, so they cannot be affected by even the most violent chemical explosions. Anyway, if in the unlikely event they are damaged by hot plasma, they will simply repair or discard the damaged area and adapt. This is akin to the healing of a wound, however all such repairs will be carried out in millionths of a second as opposed to days in our case, without technological assistance.'

'The stuff bad Javols are made of!' Lira exclaimed and became concerned.

'Yes! I'm afraid so. We have to be so careful with whatever steps we take. However this is a well proven method and much more advanced. This is the main reason why Brain Implants the size of a pinhead can be designed to extend our minds some tenfold, and contain several pre-programmed doctors in the process.'

'This is so incredible! Perhaps one day we'll use such methods to defeat the Javols,' Merol commented.

'We have better weapons to fight Javols. By the way, you guys should seriously consider the addition of Brain Implants.' Lira became more troubled.

'Is the process an easy one. I mean the operation... and learning to use it,' Merol asked.

'It's not even what I would call an operation. The devices are simply inserted with a small needle. The process is quite painless and is no different from the first test you underwent in Lower Cantor. Anyway, please consider what I've said. With brain implants, you could learn everything about Micro Robots in seconds instead of weeks,' Lumak said.

'Wow!' Lira yelled with disdain.

'This Microid powder is the one used for your special ships. It is the Constructor Microids and you will require approximately one microgram of this material to every kilogram of the Medium Microid powder. Obviously, the reaction can be accelerated by adding more or less to delay the process. Too many of the Constructors, however, can cause bonding errors during construction... because the computer can be overloaded if there are too many instruction pathways at once.

'Bonding errors can cause weakness in the structure so formed, leading to errors while revectoring and during mass transformation. These devices here on this shelf can test for such errors during construction. Obviously, a two-day growth factor is quite adequate for a ship of the type and body mass described. Therefore a one microgram ratio is quite substantial.

'I see!' Jon said, while lifting a small container to carefully observe its powdery contents, but nothing moved.

'This value will give you an error ratio of one part per ten to the power of one hundred million microid parts, but even that very small error level can be reduced by replenishment of the molecular bonds during the construction phase. However, after that phase has been completed, it is then too late to further improve the structure. In some extreme cases, one might have to give dissolve commands and start the process all over again from scratch. However, if most of the structure was initially contaminated, that process will not work... You see, the dissolve command in its purest form will not work on randomly contaminated structures. Therefore you have to use this special equipment over here... called the Random Dissolver Unit. It will scan through all possible combinations of the Dissolve Commands in a more efficient and random manner, until it keys into a set of random groups. When it hits the correct frequency, the bond will brake. Then the structure will collapse into more Medium Microids.

'All Constructor Microids become Medium Microids during the construction phase, hence a new set of Constructor Microids will always be required at the start of each forming or reforming process.

'Moulds are useful because the same Medium Microid material can be used time and time again for a particular shape, but Constructor Microids are difficult and expensive to produce here on Earth. Some of the metals used... like platinum and osmium ... are quite rear. Anyway, you get less contamination from foreign bodies when moulds are constructed for that purpose.

'This microid substance is nontoxic. Small quantities of this powder is in no way dangerous to animals or plants. It will readily dissolve in the body in a useful manner. You know, even sand in enough quantities can kill, and numerous people live in deserts. The Medium Microids can easily be manufactured by you on Polok II, but nothing can be done without the relatively smaller amounts of the Constructor Microids. That key material can only be acquired from Earth or Solaria,' Lumak said.

'Why Sire?' Jon inquired.

'It's purely for political reasons. It's to give us greater leverage over the Federation! Our Grand Lord planned it that way and he is always right!'

'I see!'

They remained silent while listening intently to every word Lumak uttered. When he was finished, he took them back to his part of the building and introduced them to his computer library which was situated on the topmost floor. That library contained scientific data on all his advanced projects. The information was either written in sunolingua or in coded form to be interpreted by his most senior and trusted people. Those were mostly his students and the Andromedans. Only the less sensitive information would be cleared before being passed to scientists and engineers at lower levels.

CHAPTER 22

The President's speech

Jerry sat at the studio desk, papers in hand and ready. The studio cameras were given the signal to start and he was introduced.

'Ladies and gentlemen, the President of our nation!' At first he began to speak in a low key.

'My dear people and friends, over here and abroad. I am to announce to you and all nations of the world, great future possibilities due to a recent... very important discovery. It is so important to us at this crucial time in our history, that it will doubtless affect all our lives in a positive and extremely productive manner... from this moment and well into the distant future.

'This extremely important discovery was achieved with the aid of our best scientists and most advanced computers since the initiation of that special project several years ago.

'You all know that one of our main problems and limitations in the past was due to the high cost of energy and as a direct result, the use of fossil fuels... which incidentally has since been significantly depleted.

'This and other factors had placed limits on our space exploration program. Mainly because of the high fuel costs with heavy payloads and other aspects relating to the construction of those very massive and inefficient spacecraft... even when constructed in orbit. Other systems like the Ion and Plasma drives not being suitable as interstellar drives. Furthermore, the time involved while travelling even to the nearest star by such methods would have taken us several centuries, making it virtually impossible for us to visit other inhabited stellar systems in our short lifetimes... Thereby making us permanent prisoners within our solar system.

'The second problem that concerned us was, how to reduce the

use of our dwindling fossil fuels and at the same time minimise the resultant pollution from vehicle exhaust and other combustion processes as we used more coal.

'We also thought... that is, until very recent discoveries, that there was no life in our Osmaron... I mean Milky Way Galaxy. But I am pleased to announce, that it is now positively verified that the whole galaxy is teaming with life, much more even than our tropical rain forests, and intelligent life including human types are no exception. Although it has been found that most of those life-forms are varied and not highly intelligent by human standards.

'Anyway, to get back to our discovery. I am to announce that at ten-fifty a.m., American Standard Time... Our scientists, working under the leadership of Lord Meron... tested a new device called a Linear Progressive Accelerator or LPD for short.

'When fitted to a vehicle or machine it will deliver zero pollution. When fitted to a ship the size of a large passenger liner... it is capable of travelling to a local stellar system... some eleven light years away in just three point five weeks, and that is not all. It is of an extremely small size, requires little energy and can be fitted to virtually any object... Since it uses a fusion process at the sub-atomic level, there is virtually zero pollution generated while in use. I have also been advised that our present design can be improved some twenty times.

'This new form of interstellar travel will open up new frontiers to humanity and shrink the distances between our planets and local stellar systems.... Can you see its potentials?... for exploration, mining, trading, resettlement, and so on. But we must also be aware of our ecological responsibilities to other life-forms, as we now do on Earth. You must consider them to be part of our galaxy and hence part of an even larger ecosystem. Because of those important reasons a system of basic rules are being drafted. They are for your optimum survival and the benefit of other less fortunate life-forms within those systems.

'In the mean time, we have decided to use Mars as our first step on that very tall ladder of exploration. As a result, several large sealed environmental domes will be installed on that planet to

accommodate those first explorers and scientists. That is, before it is made generally available for mining and other relevant uses...

'Remember, I speak of the whole world in this matter; because no single country has any personal claims on space...' The president appeared nervous.

There was a barrage of hands in the audience as every reporter wanted to ask their questions.

'Yes, Pamela. Let's have your question first!' Jerry shouted above the voices.

'Sir, is space really worth the effort... while people are starving here on Earth?'

'Yes, I'm afraid so. We have survived in the past only because we were not afraid in facing new challenges and those gains are reflected in our technologies, which are presently used to heal cancer patients and improve our current way of life. Without new discoveries, which is due mainly to such exploration, we could soon become a useless species with extinction in the horizon. By facing new challenges and meeting new civilizations we can learn new technologies and by so doing learn new and more efficient ways of solving our survival problems.'

Many more questions were asked and answers given, but the audience were never close to the real questions and answers behind the new space drive.

Jerry had dropped the biggest bombshell of his political career. Viewers were stunned and couldn't believe what they were hearing. International and national telephone lines, even satellite systems were jammed with traffic.

The news media everywhere were buzzing for headlines on this controversial speech. Had Jerry of the United States of America gone stark raving bonkers or even flipped his lid? Who was this scientist called Lord Meron? He must be a bloody clever Britisher to have come up with such an incredible invention. Was he another Brit like the famous Professor Jeffery Longhurst.

We must urgently interview this Lord Meron guy if we are to get to the bottom of this story. We must know if this speech is for real before we go to print... and so it went on. Reporters were now like bloodhounds, searching for the story of their lives. That evening there were headlines that read: *'Meron's New Remarkable Space-drive.'* Others read: *'And Now The Galaxy!'*, *'Science Fiction Becomes A Reality'* and so on.

They had used sections of the president's speech, and still hadn't the real story.

When Jerry finally concluded his speech that day, which also included the present state of the economy and other matters about patience and hard work, he had to be taken out of the studio via the roof of the building within a crowd of security men and into a waiting helicopter to the security of the White House.

He soon realised the effectiveness of his speech, so before things became seriously out of control he called everyone concerned at a secret location for discussing this new crisis.

They were soon fully briefed. Lord Meron was given the task to speak to the press on Jerry's behalf. He and others were given slightly different identity papers in case their past histories on Earth were scrutinized by the press. After all, Meron and his people were Andromedans.

Meron called a press conference for the following morning and arranged for Jeffery Longhurst and some of his other assistants to be present. They took along a makeshift remote controlled demonstration model that resembled a small shuttle craft for his doubtful politicians and press to observe.

CHAPTER 23

The Conference

As usual the first reporter to speak was a very nervous young woman called Pamela. She was always the most noticeable of reporters and fought her place well. While standing at the rear of her over-enthusiastic group of noisy reporters.

'Mr... I mean... Lord Meron. In your opinion, will we find other humans out there in space... I mean, like our type?' she inquired, using all her endearing powers to make her head visible above the noisy front row.

'That's a difficult question to answer, since Mother Nature is not always able to create from scratch virtually any type of human or other preferred forms to specification. Furthermore, what will be the big difference between look-a-likes here on Earth and those elsewhere in the universe. Anyway, I always thought variety was the spice of life. I suppose, since we tend to see alien monsters in our dreams, that aspect of our perception does not also apply to diverse forms.'

'What do you mean.... lord?'

'Will one's form and position in time and space make a big difference? What if that world had a most deplorable alien culture, but looked exactly like us? What makes a civilization is not form, but how they think and relate with each other. Whether they have love and compassion for their kind and others or are just prejudiced, self-interested and self-indulgent savages. When it is possible to create all forms with intelligence and incredible attributes... would form itself be relevant?'

'I see what you mean!'

'To be more specific, there are many beautiful species including human forms throughout this Osmaron Galaxy of ours and some of them are very advanced technologically. Our drives will get us to those worlds eventually. However, I am not sure the time is yet right for us in such a venture. We must first be ready to accept all forms as our friends,' he replied.

Dr. Hal Seaton, while pretending to be a reporter raised his hand and began to speak.

'Lord Meron. You speak with an air of confidence and authority on such matters, as if you have been to some of those worlds. Have you, yourself, visited any of those alien worlds?'

'Yes, I have visited several of those so-called alien worlds within this galaxy, in particular, the civilization of Polok II. Incidently, that one happens to be human. That civilization is within a forward galactic arm some five thousand or more light years from our system. Visiting is not a problem, it's living together in peace and harmony.'

'I shall need some proof!'

'That you can have, Sir!' Meron replied and Hal remained silent in anticipation.

'You are kidding us, Sir! No one can travel that distance... not even in a thousand years!' Pamela shouted and Meron waved his hand to bring the crowd of reporters under control.

'You are right! No one can travel those distances with Earth's present antiquated technologies. I am afraid, my technologies are much more advanced.' Pamela's appetite for more knowledge was un-quenched and further aroused.

Meron removed a translation buckle and began to show them the strange technology.

'This translation belt was given to me as a present from the ruler of Polok II. As you may observe, my friends, such advanced technologies do not yet exist on earth or you would have used such devices to overcome the language barrier when interviewing those with a different language.' He showed the object around their fleeting cameras.

The reporters were amazed by his answers, and at the same time extremely excited by his manner and knowledge. He held back very little from them. Meron was also enjoying his new profession and gave them what they wanted for their respective publishers, no holes barred. Even so, he was careful in not being too specific.

Another male reporter asked a probing question.

'Lord Meron, regarding your model ship. When will you be able to take normal passengers like myself on a day trip to Mars, for instance?'

'I have yet to meet a normal passenger, but if you mean the average person? All our future ships will have normal simulated gravity and atmosphere, so problems relating to space, weightlessness, G-forces, atmospheric pressure and such factors will not exist on my trips,' he replied with certainty.

Then Meron decided to stare the questions away from space exploration and aliens.

'Shall we continue with questions relating to the drive system, if you will? Perhaps we should reserve stellar navigation and other questions relating to interstellar life for another such conference.'

Yet, Pamela posed another question. This time she realized it was not the right time to pursue her more probing questions and changed the topic.

'How efficient and large are these devices, Sir.'

'I think it is time for us to show you our laboratory model. It is just to explain the basic drives and how they may be used.'

Meron turned his gaze to Strongman, Mickey and one of his other assistants, who immediately went into another room and began to push what appeared to be a miniature shuttle craft. It was the size of a small two-seater motor car that they moved towards the audience.

Meron stood tall and erect among his assistants with golden hair and piercing sea blue eyes. He wore a creamy milk suit with gloves to match.

He had the appearance of a human god, just more than two metres tall. They wondered whether he was really who he said he was. He could equally have been from another human world, if indeed such places really existed. They reasoned that he could equally have been human in the truest sense of the word, but of the more eccentric type. He exuded much poise and magnetism, with a most charming and sincere personality. They also liked the way he answered their question, with a tinge of sarcasm and humour.

Nevertheless, how could he have travelled to distant worlds with his new invention without the knowledge of the mass media. How long was he involved with designing those incredible interstellar ships? Could all those UFO sightings be attributed to his interstellar experiments?

Although the reporters had turned their attention to the demonstration model, several questions still remained unanswered.

The model was placed in front of the rostrum. Using a remote control unit he dialled codes and the ship silently lifted into the air just above their heads. The reporters quickly moved away from the silently hovering object. Only Pamela remained. She slowly passed her fingers along the side of the ship as if to convince herself that the object was real. Meron had never seen such a persistent person in all his existence, other than his wife Lucia.

'What is your name?' he inquired.

'My name, Sir! I am Pamela!' she replied, still observing the small craft.

'Well Pamela, if you insist on holding up our demonstration, you may visit my home in the near future for a proper interview.' She immediately handed him a piece of paper with her phone number and other essentials for arranging the appointment.

The demonstration model hovered for a while, then hopped and flipped over on one side. It silently and quickly rotated through all possible angles, immediately stopping in mid air and once again began to hover in its original spot.

He asked one of the younger assistants to hold on to the small ship. He was lifted into the air with his feet just above the floor.

Cameras flashed while video cameras recorded every image in detail.

After they had asked all their questions and Meron was satisfied that he had given them what was required for now, he ended the conference.

The only problem with that demonstration was that he could not show the speed of the craft in such a confined space.

Dr Hal Seaton carefully observed the model's demonstration and was soon convinced of the technology. Although sceptical at first, he realized Meron had discovered a new method of space travel.

If that was the case, he now had an opportunity to travel to other worlds and perhaps meet some more intelligent people for a change, albeit alien in origin. He was intrigued by it all.

Nevertheless, he would wait a while and bide his time until the technology had progressed into something more substantial. To him that meant the production of more commercialised models.

CHAPTER 24

The reunion, Sarah's return

That day Lumak was up early, being more excited than usual about the arrival of his wife, Sarah, and father-in-law, Ben. He began to reorganise and move furniture and other items about the house to Sarah's preference. Then he prepared to collect her and her father from the local airstrip while the phone rang.

'Darling, we are on our way and will arrive within the hour,' Sarah said.

'Love, I am on my way,' he replied.

'By the way, did you listen to our President's speech. He must have been intoxicated or on drugs. I've never seen Jerry in such a sorry state before,' she informed, worriedly.

'I know. The poor man has many problems at this time. He also has sensitive fingers on the pulse of our nation. I think he acted the part well, don't you?'

'He acted?'

'Well, he is a professional actor. I suppose that way he can convince the people of the new technology and gain their sympathy at the same time, as he had obviously succeeded with you,' Lumak replied.

'As usual, Darling, you are always right,' she said.

It was then that Sarah realized the whole performance had been staged by an accomplished actor. Nevertheless, she had no idea about the Andromedans arrival on Earth or of Jerry's interstellar trip to the stars.

'Darling, with all that's going on, we must invite him and Sharon for dinner soon. It's time I met some old friends,' she said.

'Don't worry, we have lots of them and some new ones besides,' Lumak replied.

'What are you saying? What do you mean?'

'See for yourself when you get home.'

If everything went to schedule, they would arrive at eleven a.m. Lumak wanted to be there on time. He also wanted some company on the way to the airstrip. At that time Jon and Lira just happened to be the most available and felt like a ride; with the sun shining brightly at the onset of a most beautiful and romantic day.

On arrival they didn't have to wait long. They saw the small twin engine aeroplane approach.

It landed and taxied towards a small checkout point. The two local officers knew of the doctor's reputation, so they declined to search her luggage for drugs or other contraband, knowing their resentful attitude for such toxic substances. Anyway, they were the wealthiest people on the planet.

The moment Sarah observed Lumak, she ran forward ecstatically to greet him, leaving her father Ben and his guys to collect and haul the luggage.

It was a very affectionate reunion, as they remained tightly poised in each others arms, while viewed almost to embarrassment by Jon and Lira.

Like most hard and conscientious workers, beautiful Sarah walked dignified in the bright sunlight. She was wearing a tight fitting pair of blue jeans and leather jacket with comfortable running shoes. She was about five feet eight inches tall and her father just over six. He was wearing a grey suit with white shirt and matching grey tie. As usual, he used his walking cane for effect with six of his special Oriental ninja guards following behind wearing dark shades.

Bengizara Khan usually known as Ben by his friends, tried his best to follow them to the car while struggling with two very large stubborn suitcases on worn wheels. Two of his guards soon came to his rescue. They ditched the cases into the back of the second limousine and left with Ben for the Manor. They always took a small propellor plane from the main airport, where they left their personal intercontinental jet. The helicopter was only used for more local flights.

Some say Ben, Sarah's father, was distantly related to the great Moguls, but there was little real evidence to substantiate that rumour. Lumak waved to Ben as he left and pulled Sarah along to meet his two friends now standing close by the car.

As always Sarah could read Lumak like a book and had known intuitively that he was up to something in her absence, although she couldn't yet figure out its modus operandi.

'My love, meet Jon and his close friend, Lira. They and their respective families are spending some time with us at the house. They are scientists helping me with a new project.'

She gazed into their large brown eyes with curiosity and individually shook their hands.

'Jon... Lira... I am pleased to meet you both. You appear too young to be scientists. You must be protégées. Are you married?' She glanced at their fingers for telltale signs.

They got into the car and both gazed at each other momentarily and began to blush.

'No! We are not!' Jon replied, in a most defiant manner.

'I can see you two love each other, but there is no need to hurry. You are both still quite young.' Both remained silent.

'You must be very sure and serious about each other before you make that decision. So many people get divorced these days... even some of my oldest and dearest friends,' she added, turning to Lira.

She glanced at Lumak and continued.

'We are from an old-fashioned family that believe in marriage as a lifelong commitment.'

She gently smacked her husband on his wrist. By now he was driving out of the entrance.

'Has my husband been tending to your needs?

'Yes!' Lira replied.

'Jeff sometimes get rapped up in his work and when that happens he ignores everyone ond everything, including myself,' she said. She always called Lumak, Jeff, which was short for Jeffery.

'Yes, Sarah, we are very thankful for his kind hospitality and have everything we need. Thank you both for everything,' Jon replied.

About half an hour later they drove into the entrance of the large manor. As they approached Sarah was surprised when greeted by so many people and reporters at the entrance.

There were eleven people standing close to the house. Those she presumed were Jeff's guests, who were accompanied by her two domestic helpers, Jackie and Clara. Ana, the eldest and her mother, Madeline, were nowhere to be found. They were all waiting close to the front door for her arrival, while several photographers and reporters were ready with cameras. She felt like a queen returning from some overseas visit, to be greeted on return by her fanatic subjects.

As they got out of the car Lumak told her to ignore the reporters and photographers, but she showed them several poses which they could not ignore. He took her and Ben towards the house to be introduced to his guests.

While moving towards Meron she remembered seeing his face in the newspapers. She knew he was the famous Lord Meron and also the great inventor of the space ship with its peculiar non-combustible drive. She gave a slight curtsy and firmly shook his gloved hands and he smiled in return.

Finally the photographers asked her to move closer to her husband for a together shot and she bravely hugged and kissed him.

'Was that one good enough for you guys?' she asked with a sensuous pose. Sarah always felt secure with a multitude around her. She enjoyed being in the limelight. At that moment she was not sure to where it all led and neither had she been briefed about her present very famous guests or of the ensuing publicity. Sarah was very photogenic and the devoted wife of a very famous person; so she was going to get the most out of the situation and grab as much of the limelight as possible while it was still there for the taking.

They went into the dining room for an early lunch. As always, she was the only mistress of the house and made that fact known by ticking off Ana for a small indiscretion. She was also the life of the party and tended to bring the best out of people in the worst of circumstances. Nevertheless she had her quiet moments, when she could be a good listener and advisor.

Madeline (Mad) and her family, including the two domestic helpers began to smile again, despite their increased workload and duties, which they accepted without a single mourn. It was not long before many presents were handed around to Madeline and her family. Despite the fact they had been severely reprimanded for their negligence during her absence. In a short time the Andromedans grew to love and respect her and she was soon accepted as a senior member of their extended family.

After breakfast the following morning Jeffery (Lumak) called her to his study.

'Darling, I have an important matter to discuss with you and it can't wait, I'm afraid!'

'That important, eh!' she responded.

'Please follow me!' he insisted.

She followed him to a room on the uppermost floor and there they joined Meron, Plato, Jon, Lira, Hamil and Lucia.

He sat her down and made her comfortable.

'I know you believe in life on other worlds, because we have discussed the matter on several occasions, but the reality of that belief is now with us in the form of our present guests.'

'What exactly do you mean?'

'Lord Meron, his family and friends are from Andromeda, our neighbouring galaxy. The complete galaxy is now in dire trouble. Most life there face extinction. That dire problem will eventually get to us here in the not too distant future. If we are not well prepared.'

She turned her head to observe them a second time, not quite knowing how to face that new brand of reality.

'Are you... sure... Darling. They look just like us?' she was confused.

Meron pulled off both his gloves to reveal six fingers and two thumbs. Hamil and Lucia did likewise, but she still couldn't believe in such a ridiculous story. She had on occasion seen humans with extra fingers on each hand due to a genetic disorder. If nature made extras she could also make fewer. Then Plato stood up in his Black Shadite's Cloak and like a shadow faded into the air until he disappeared. Then faded back into his normal form.

She could not accept what she saw any more than she could, of demons and devils. To her way of thinking such technologies defied the very laws of nature and her concepts of the solidity of things. But as they shattered, one by one, her deep-rooted concepts gradually began letting go. Her very firm beliefs and religious faith gave way to another form of reality. In her case the conversion was a slow and difficult one.

She tried to compose herself but could not.

'You are then... from a very advanced human civilization?' She inquired with difficulty.

'Yes Sarah, we are, but we need your help and wish to know if we can rely on your assistance in this matter. Jeffery has given us his full cooperation in our current operations here on Earth,' Meron replied.

'Whatever... I can do with my husband's assistance to help,' she said in bewilderment.

She was still dazed by the whole affair. Lumak (Jeffery) realised she needed a little more time to get used to the idea, so he quickly changed the topic.

'So that's it for now... Love. I have arranged a picnic for today near your favourite spot on Little River close to Beavers Bank. We can do a little bird watching and also catch some fish... I've promised Jon and Lira. We should get ready now because I leave in half an hour,' he insisted, while viewing his time piece.

Sarah, still stunned by the strange experienced quietly went off to prepare.

After arrival at the picnic sight Lumak took Sarah away from the others to a lonely spot to talk privately. It was one of those lovely late spring afternoons, several trees were flowering and there was a most desirable fragrance in the air.

'You know, my love, I missed you a lot while you were away. I wanted to visit you several times but was a bit tied up here with one thing or another. I also thought my presence might have hindered your progress. You know what we are like when we are close together? Anyway, I would like to make up for my gross negligence by remaining a lot closer to you from now on. So no more long separations for a while, please... I believe we need a little time together and you know our guests could never come between us. Anyway, you have done more than enough field work for now. Your organization is quite capable of doing the work themselves without you being constantly at their beck and call.'

 She gazed at him intently as if searching deeply for his innermost thoughts.

 'Do you seriously mean that, Darling? I have been feeling so lonely and insecure lately. It felt like my old solid world had begun to erode and crumble. I know you always mean well, but I can't help the way I feel and these... guests... from Andromeda. They were the last straw. Are they for real?' she inquired as if needing reassurance.

 'Yes, my love, they are very real and there is a lot more besides. But I want you to overcome this initial shock before I give you another. You know, you are the most dearest thing in this universe to me and I want you to start thinking about things on a more cosmic scale. I know you have the mind and potential for it, so I shall try my best to help you along. If there is anything you wish to know in the mean time, you must ask me. Do we have a deal?'

 'Yes, Darling. You know I always trust you and I am always on your side,' she said, affectionately.

 'They came with an advanced ship. It's still parked on one of the helicopter pads at the rear of the house.'

 'Does Madeline and the girls know?'

 'Mad knows. Only Mad! No others know except Jerry, Sharon and a few of his special people. They all have high-level security clearance.'

 'How long did it take them to get here? I mean to Earth?'

 'They said they took about a day. Apparently it also travels through dimensions and can go anywhere almost instantly.'

 'If what you say is true, and you haven't lied to me yet... we have to help them as best we can... I know that story back at the house was a little too much for me to swallow in one gulp at the time, but I am getting used to the idea... I mean, of a more cosmic existence when you put it in such a reasonable manner... So don't you worry too much about me from now in that respect.'

'That's fantastic!'

He embraced her and they kissed while in each other's arms. Suddenly her insecurity and worries had vanished into thin air. Her man was in her arms and she wouldn't be disturbed, even if the whole universe was to collapse around them; for she was now in the universe she preferred, the one of deep affection and everlasting love.

After a while they returned to their friends and continued the fishing competition while attempting to catch the biggest fish. They were not allowed to use fish hooks. Those were considered unkind to the fish. Special bated nets with long handles were used and the fishes were selected by length. That way, the fish was seldom touched by human hands and gained a free meal in the process. They could be automatically weighed while in the net. Each time they said farewell to their catch as it was returned safely to its watery habitat.

Finally lunch was served. During that time they freely discussed everything, including the problems in Andromeda in Sarah's presence.

After arriving home that evening she watched the films of Caefon being destroyed by the Javols. Then there was the information relating to their more recent visit to the three local systems. The war between Polok and Lodor, with the resulting peace after a hundred years of hostility. The new formation of a Solarian Empire. Finally she was shown images of the world of the Octans and cat-people of Tarran.

Suddenly she felt a new kind of energy surge within her person. She now had a much greater task ahead of her, in helping every down trodden species throughout the universe. She realized her modest efforts on Earth was just a stepping stone for the stars.

Jon and Lira showed her their initial drafts of Jerry's proposals for the mutual survival of all cosmic life. When she read it she glanced at Jon in disgust.

'Our President's proposal is far too biassed in favour of humans and other superior life-forms. We need a charter that is a lot more impartial!'

'Ok!'

'Sintra, can you find us a practical compromise through the Great Book, with Merian, Tomas and Hamil's assistance? Then we can draft a new proposal, president or no president!' she blared.

'It's fine time this universe was made a little fairer... far too many advanced species think they own the place!' she barked.

Sarah was aroused by an unknown force and suddenly became a changed woman. She felt invulnerable to anyone and everything, and that she was.

She was soon nominated to lead the group, being even more dominant than Lucia and Lira. Then she began to restructure their efforts in a more humane manner towards the common good of all life.

She placed the local ecological problems in the hands of her father Ben and other keen and responsible deputies. Thus releasing her more precious time for handling her greater responsibilities, and to form a closer and stronger relationship with her husband, Lumak.

She had now set her aims towards a much higher goal. Therefore a lot more time would be required in the pursuance of that new and much higher ambition, and so she thought.

CHAPTER 25

Microid samples in production

THE PRESIDENT

After the initial turmoil caused by Jerry's speech had subsided, both Meron and Jerry became the best known and most wanted individuals on the planet. The many departments within the Pentagon and elsewhere had to take on extra staff to cope with the demands from many enthusiastic foreign countries.

The conferences given by Lord Meron and his associates regarding the new interstellar drives had substantiated Jerry's speech. The world was convinced of the new invention and of Lord Meron's surreptitious trial voyages to distant worlds.

Enthusiasm grew at highest levels within the larger companies and financial institutions. Their many scientists, would-be space explorers and miners, with previously ill-considered ridiculous projects for the moon and beyond, were coming forward in droves. Many saw this new invention as an alternative to fossil fuels in most areas of travel.

During this time Jerry spent most of his time interviewing and entertaining the many foreign diplomats and delegates. Then there were his own senators and governors. Each fighting for their home industries and wanting a small slice of the cake.

The motorcar manufacturers, chemical and fuel industries were doubly worried about the future of their respective waning industries. They had plowed much of their remaining funds in other alternative types of renewable energy, including solar, wind, ethanol and safe hydrogen fuel cells. Those companies would surely sink if this new LPD device became popular. Therefore Jerry had to do his best to pacify and resolve those worries.

His original idea was to make them co-manufacturers and suppliers of the units, but he was not sure whether Doctor Longhurst and Meron would agree in releasing their products to those highly commercial organizations, on the meagre legal grounds of compensation for their reduced production. Anyway, the drive modules were in the hands of the private sector and he would never use pressure from his office on his friends to prop up a pollution generating and now waning industry.

He believed in the natural evolution of systems and if it was their time to go, like the dodo or dinosaur they should lie down and become extinct with the others.

If they wanted a deal, they would have to negotiate it themselves through their own efforts. Even so, he told them he would try his best and talk to Lord Meron about the matter. At least, that was always his most natural response to those wanting special favours.

MICROID PRODUCTION

Jon and his young group of six were actively engaged in the production of Constructor Microids. They had a special laboratory built in the large factory, within that isolated area they fitted all the necessary production gear.

Among other things, were computers, microscopes, lasers, masers, ultrasonics, spectrum analysers, controller modules, magnetometers, and a range of other equipment yet unheard of on Earth. Those devices were required for the production of the Constructor Microids to be used in the construction of the large space ships. They were all within Class 5 technological level.

Several chemical and other processes were initially carried out on the relevant samples within processing plants elsewhere before delivery to the factory.

After its arrival the crude material was slightly radioactive and resembled a greyish sludge. As a result of which certain precautions had to be taken by the human scientists against contamination and over exposure to radiation. However that particular type of radiation was relatively short lived and not a major problem during production.

The liquid sludge was made to flow down a near-vacuum sterilized chute into an ultrasonic bath where its fine molecules were agitated for a predetermined period. It was then fed into another much larger unit called the Primary Excitor, were pulses of intense radiation were scanned through the material under the Microscopic Guidance Computer, MGC for short. When that process was completed, the MGC had a detailed knowledge of the molecular structure. During that process every complex molecule was precisely scanned. The sample was then in a stable semi-solid state and kept in balance by gravity neutralizers. Without such neutralizers, the process could only be carried out under zero gravity in space.

No external forces were present during this period. Soon after, several intricate and precisely aligned high energy lasers began targeting the semi transparent sample scanning and firing at precise points under computer control.

After another process of intense magnetic orientation, the sample was finally passed for primary testing. As it passed through the unit and the anti gravitational forces released, it collapsed into the blue microid dust. The material still had to undergo a final and even more intricate process, where another even more complex molecular structure was added with more ultrasonic stimulation.

The equipment that produced the blue substance was extremely complex and precise. Even the microscope used could very easily resolve images down to the smallest molecular level and with the Statistical Predictor the same equipment could observe the atom, its associated electrons with constituent fields and forces.

Once they were acquainted with the equipment and processes, Jon and his companions began to produce the microids in earnest under the guidance of Doctor Longhurst, who insisted he be called Jeff by all. The complete process was subsequently automated.

It took them another three weeks to manufacture enough of the Constructor Microids. Nevertheless a small quantity of Medium Microid dust was required for the construction of the two great ships. The latter quantities of Medium Microid being used only for sample verification purposes.

By that time they had completed the paperwork and blueprints for two new microid production plants. One was to be constructed close to the present factory and another sited on the recently discovered planet called Polion II. Relevant blueprints for the production of Medium Microids being presented to Malik on Polok II after delivery of the first batch.

The new Microid factory unit on Earth would be constructed to function under robot control and able to supply large quantities of the Constructor Microid material on a twenty-four hour basis. It would remain functional until a new site was found on some dead, but environmentally suitable planet like Polion II. The main production of the Medium Microids being of much greater quantities, would be sited on Malik's world or within one of his systems. Since the bulk material were Medium Microids there were no security risks involved at Malik's end.

From henceforth, the whole production and storage areas on Earth would be kept under the highest security levels needed to protect Solaria's richest resource from any possible attack, either from within or without.

GRAND LORD GERRA

The Gohran Supreme Being, Grand Lord Gerra, having taken stock of the seventh part of our universe had a much clearer picture of the development of Osmaron over the next thousand years or so. He visualised our galaxy as the hub of power within the seventh region. His conceptual equations introduced Solaria as the new pivot of power within Osmaron and that fact surprised even him. Then an intense pulse appeared in his conceptual charts that signified the existence of immense powers on Earth that could be used to counteract the Javols.

That pulse stretched almost to infinity, but had little width and arose out of such a small adjustment factor, that somehow became amplified by other major events within the causal matrix. Then all catastrophic and chaotic nodes had to be subsequently adjusted within the equation to align with the greater order that included the Javols destruction within a shorter time frame within that continuum. When that happened, Earth and Solaria became the most significant of all worlds and systems that were affected.

He had little choice in the matter, for he was also part of certain causal events, and a major player. Therefore Earth or one of its local systems had to become his future residence for the next thousand cyclons (1600 years). That was until his next stocktaking and reassessment of procedures within the seventh part of the seventh universe, just before the next meeting of their Heptarchal Nexus with his other six Gohran brothers.

Because of those and other findings, he had to visit Solaria and make his presence felt, but this particular visit would be different, for he intended to take the Plorans, Lord Vektron and Lord Patron along to make a complete assessment of Planet Earth and the other relevant systems.

CHAPTER 26

Earth in motion

LPD PRODUCTION

Within an orbit about Earth, two prototype ships with the special drives were being constructed for their first maiden voyage to Mars. Many smaller craft were also being fabricated for local planetary requirements.

That mission to Mars would take several weeks to finalise. The large shuttle was able to carry many scientists, engineers and industrialists for making a more thorough assessment of the planet's environment. They were to select a suitable route for a fleet of such interplanetary shuttles. Professor Strongman was in charge of locating and clearing a suitable path for the route to Mars. The orbits of local asteroids and other perspective dangers were to be recorded and three-dimensional space maps compiled for the chosen space corridor or Spaceway as it was later called.

Lumak and Meron always represented Solaria when visiting the president of the USA to discuss extraterrestrial matters. Their company, under the auspices of Solarian Banking, was subsequently allowed sole rights for manufacturing their range of products within the United States. That was providing they supplied relevant products through local distributors and they agreed to his terms. However to remove their commercial links with Earth, they intended to move the bulk of production to Mars and other local worlds and systems. Lumak was never interested in commerce. His whole purpose on Earth was to improve its technologies so that they could fight the Javols. The new Solarian Empire would not be based on capitalism or commercial ventures for the benefit of a few large greedy organizations. He was also concerned about pollution. Siting all such dirty production plants on dead and uninhabited worlds would eliminate any further pollution or dangers from those sources.

Many of the larger companies had already started on their space-car prototypes. International systems and controls were being evaluated and standardised. His more advanced robots were available for constructing such devices, so human workers were only needed in the more technical and scientific areas.

Finally, they decided to use Doctor Longhurst and Meron's proposals for highways in the skies above Earth at different levels of the stratosphere. Each lane being controlled by scanning laser satellites which were to be positioned further into space and linked with associated ground-based laser beacons. Those were to be used for the guidance of vehicles along predetermined corridors.

Unlike radio waves, scanning lasers could carry control and other types of digital information relevant to a particular highway. Certain dead zone tubes or spirals as they were called, would exist for the purpose of changing routes or landing. Each Spiral terminated with a ground station.

This new endeavour for travel would transform the atmosphere of Earth into a massive 3D super-highway, with virtually no pollution to the atmosphere and near perfect safety.

After the original prototype tests, many such ground stations and space-car parks were built, placing civilians through major upheaval and inconvenience. Governments invested enormous sums to make those systems work and many looked forward to the benefits of this new global form of transport. After all, it was quick, clean and almost perfect for the future of space exploration. That was providing they always had a generous supply of LPDs for such ships.

At long last the planet was coming out of the depression as their respective leaders saw a new horizon in sight. Furthermore everyone was keen to work towards that new and exciting future. Planet Earth began to move once more into a new period of wealth and prosperity, but this time with significantly reduced pollution and a much higher awareness of the needs of lesser life-forms and their responsibilities towards them.

SARAH AND HER GROUP

Sarah and her other Andromedan friends were fighting for all life throughout the universe and did not want mankind and other advanced species to trample on other so-called lesser life in the process of mining and resettlement, so they were constantly planning and lobbying all important persons concerned.

Lucia and the other Andromedans, being Senots, assisted her enthusiastically in those endeavours. Having read Seno's ancient books, Sarah soon realized it was the most suitable religion for life and the caring for life. Even Jon and his young group of six had adopted that ancient religion.

Their Solarian order was gathering momentum and power to such an extent that very soon the President and others of global importance had to meet them to ask for a compromise. Sarah was at that time in charge of BioLive, the largest charitable organization on the planet. She was also in charge of Solarian Banking, the largest and wealthiest bank on Earth.

At that very meeting they discussed all important issues regarding their new and most powerful organization. An organization that had become the wealthiest on the planet.

They insisted on being a separate entity from Earth and its erratic short-term governments. Therefore certain concessions were made regarding Solarians being treated as foreign diplomats, with all the necessary freedoms including diplomatic immunity. This treaty with the USA made all Solarian Banking establishments protected embassies and places for Senots. Later other countries followed.

Nevertheless, Jerry decided that he would not mention anything about the three local stellar systems they had discovered, provided he and his wife were allowed to visit Eden from time to time and live out the rest of their days there after retirement. In return for that minor concession, he would ensure Earth only remained involved in the solar system during his reign of office.

In any case, no one knew of the exact location of worlds like Eden or the other two systems in question. It was estimated that it would have taken Earth another fifty years of technological advancement and searching before they were found. This gave the new Solarian Empire enough time to establish itself and construct a more acceptable structure to deal with the other two members of the federation, namely Polok and Lodor. The Octans were not yet part of their Federation.

Therefore, Jerry, the president of the USA, left the new Solarian Empire to develop in the hands of Lumak, Plato and his colleagues, fully trusting in their good intentions. He and others agreed to Sarah's new proposals on "The Rules for Mutual Coexistence of Stellar Life" within all populated systems. He had always been on their side and they knew it.

Sarah had suddenly become one of the most important individuals in the galaxy, although she was not yet fully aware of her unique position and capabilities. Nevertheless she held the purse strings of all the major charities on Earth, being president of the Solarian Banking organization, who was the wealthiest and presently had branches in all countries throughout the planet. Currently, that bank was used to finance their many dome-habitats, charities and other building projects. They also assisted in giving aid, education and medical assistance to the poorer countries.

POLOK AND LODOR

Normal trading had resumed between Polok and Lodor and both worlds were now building on each others soil. They were getting their technologies ready for the construction of the two great ships. Bailor and his people were keen in following their new path for the Greater Purpose. Many Lodorians were released from their tanks for new duties elsewhere. Since meeting Jerry and the Andromedans, who were a very jovial and happy lot, Lodorians like Bailor began seeing a completely new age of enlightening and renaissance for his people.

Malik and his people were awaiting the return of Jon and his friends from Earth to commence the production program. They had finished constructing the large moulds required for the purpose of building the great ships.

Malik and Bailor had decided to select the uninhabited planet of Safon for spaceship production. The almost habitable world was being completely restructured with space docks and every conceivable technology. Those installations would eventually cover a large surface area, with the exception of what was considered possible fertile areas close to its seas. Safon was within the Polokan system and similar to Mars in many respects although with a somewhat denser atmosphere.

Malik and his wife, Mira, were looking forward to their first trip to Earth in one of the great ships that were to be built for Solaria. They wished to see their old friends, particularly Lumak, and perhaps learn some native culture in the process.

The Universe was unfolding before them in a completely new and unimagined way and they were caught up in its firm and compelling grip.

CHAPTER 27

Solaria - Beyond Fille

Jon and his young Andromedan companions were presently under Sarah's wing. Being the one and only child of her parents, she considered them her younger brothers and sisters, although their relationship was more of a parental nature. She took on the responsibilities of ensuring they had a normal family upbringing with the usual social graces expected in North America at the time. Neither did she like them to consider their other close companions as brothers and sisters, so there was always a certain element of matchmaking from their eldest sister and guardian. Apparently, the six young Andromedans, being genetically engineered, were already in matched pairs. Nevertheless they knew her game and accepted all the fun and embarrassment it sometimes brought. Anyway, they knew they had been cloned from the Ancients, but whether they accepted such unnatural pairing was going to be another matter that only the future could tell.

Although they were very similar to their older and more ancient biological parents, they were much younger and as a result very modern in their attitudes and fashion. Sarah, with her much rougher edges, reminded them more of their surrogate parents, who had brought them up from birth. She was even stricter than they were in some ways but compensated in other ways by having lots more fun with them.

Presently they were happier than they had ever been and at long last finding their places and niches in the scheme of things. Despite the nagging thoughts of their family and friends still stranded on Caefon, more than two million light years away, they followed their mission with enthusiasm and gusto, while placing their faith in Lumak and Plato. Those two Shadites were the main ones concerned with their program and education.

The young six, the Ancients and Sarah now felt they could take on the entire universe and win, and could with Lumak's brand of new technologies. Presently they were on a healthy diet planned by Lumak's own dietary consultants. With the introduction of certain microids, they could learn virtually any language and profession in days instead of years, and that was without the use of his special brain implants.

THE BOOK OF RULES

A program was engendered for the production and delivery of relevant microid parts, materials and other products that were considered essential for trade within the Solarian System and other co-members of The Federation of Worlds. Because of the depletion of inhabited worlds by long term seepage of essential resources and materials, it was essential that some form of strict accounting be made during transfer of such materials to different worlds.

By their deductions, life-forms, items of art and culture, including antiques and paintings, were not to be allowed for trading purposes, unless similar artifacts were exchanged. However an occasional exchange of such items of equivalence would be tolerated by important representatives and diplomats. Nevertheless there was an annual limit on all products that were to be adjusted by customs and excise at a later date.

Rear elements like gold and others would remain rear, because if they became commonplace the financial consequences on Earth could have been disastrous, leading to destabilisation of many political systems and financial institutions. Many still invested heavily in such rear metals. So there was a permanent ban on the importation of such materials, in particular metals and stones that were considered precious on Earth. Nevertheless mining for all such substances within uninhabited worlds would be permitted and products placed in storage. Raw materials and chemicals were in abundance on moons and uninhabited worlds within most stellar systems.

Furthermore, trading in essential life sustaining materials and elements like water, air, relevant metals, primal biological structures, plants and all other forms of primal life, other than those carried by official travellers and their restricted pets, were positively not allowed.

They argued that if poorer worlds were free to take such materials from richer and more fertile ones containing highly tuned ecosystems, that within a short period of time to be measured in centuries, even the rich and fertile worlds would become deserts to the detriment of their ecosystems and other dependant life-forms. However certain allowances would be made for transferring endangered species to other habitable worlds for their own safety and survival, providing there were no detrimental after effects.

Those rules also prevented the richer worlds from further depleting the poorer ones, with even more disastrous consequences. Trading worlds were listed into two categories, namely: Donor Worlds, which were net exporters and Acceptor Worlds, being net importers.

All trading elements other than those collected from asteroids and uninhabited worlds, would be replaced in identical amounts within a fixed period of time to be entered on each shipping contract. Therefore, all items for interplanetary export would be listed with mass and chemical constituents, to be clearly stated on all relevant documents and packaging.

Another method had to be negotiated for life-forms, but that one was more complicated because it related to the place of birth, period of settlement, times travelled, destinations, place and time of death, and more.

Random travellers were also a problem, but they were considered in the minority and could be ignored for now. Even so, after death all body elements being mostly water, were to be returned to their Donor Planet, wherever and whenever possible. The transfer could be made immediately after death or some equivalent compensation made. This however did not apply to immortals.

Inhabited planets were to be considered living organisms in their own right. Therefore the balance of elements were essential for their healthy existence. Identity cards that could be directly read by computers during transit could resolve most of those minor problems, if indeed there was really a problem that couldn't be solved by resourceful accounting technology.

Sarah, Lumak, Meron and the others did not wish to create a cold and uncompromising computer-based society. It was also essential that all life benefited from the resources of the Solarian System and not just the wealthy, powerful and most intelligent. Therefore all items and materials for trade would be put into standard crates, suitably stamped and tagged with all parameters to be retrieved at a later date through their accounting systems. By so doing, it was deemed illegal to transport items to other worlds without customs' permission. Nevertheless, visitors were exempt initially for small items like presents.

The book of rules included many pages of such interplanetary transactions. It was hoped that book of rules would be accepted as the standard for trading throughout the galaxy. Copies of which were drafted with the help of Sintra and The Great Book, the Anachromagnon. Several copies were made for distribution among all members of the federation. Those books were written in Sunolingua, the ancient trading language. The only English copy was the one given to Jerry, the President of the USA.

Sarah had designed the new federation insignia almost identical to the Shadite's one, with the exception of its inner blue circle. Her insignia included three colours instead of just one. The three equal segments were blue, green and orange. When asked about their significance, she quickly replied:

'Blue is for the living oceans, waters and air, green is for the fertile areas of land, and orange for the living deserts. These three colours represent primal cosmic life in all its varied habitats and will constantly remind us of our duty to assist and maintain all such life within the universe.' She realized there could be many other types of life other than those that evolved like primals (naturally evolving animals) within planets.

She suggested the formation of a special body of planetary scientists or planetologist, as she preferred to call them. Those scientists would consist of biologists, ecologists and geologists. A true planetologist mastered all three subjects and more.

It was intended that such scientists investigate all worlds within the federation and pass them as either Active or Inactive.

Dead worlds with no signs of living organisms were considered Inactive and hence released for general exploration, mining and resettlement. Active worlds were in three classes. In some rear cases class three worlds, which were deemed to contain basic cellular organisms with no intelligence, could be released in a limited way for exploration, mining and resettlement. However only very old and dying worlds of that type were released. All young and living worlds were to be protected and left to evolve and develop on their own without any intervention from outside intelligence.

It was subsequently decided that the new interstellar planetologists consist mainly of the few Ancients, including those left on Caefon. Other nonhuman alien refugees like bird people from Coln would be added to the group at an appropriate time.

The remaining Ancients were to be given the freedom of Eden under Lord Meron and build a new society there. They were to consider Andromeda a free-for-all galaxy for those wishing to return and settle there including humans from Earth. Even so, the standard trading and ecological rules still applied.

After due consideration by their new council, Solaria had the right to promote or demote worlds within the classified structure with powers under the new Solarian Council, headed by Sarah, to either permit or prevent manufacturing or mining and resettlement on Class 3 worlds. This type of classification was not the same as the one given to technological advancement to a particular civilization and was based on the worlds planetary suitability for manufacturing, mining and resettlement. Nevertheless planetary exploration by neutral unmanned probes would be tolerated for knowledge gathering purposes.

A brand new order of interstellar existence was on the way and would quickly grow to engulf all civilizations within the Osmaron Galaxy.

COOPERATION BETWEEN PARTNERS

The Ship was adapted by Plato to take the extra load of microid crates. Several passenger cubicles had been removed for that purpose. Being of a microid designed all such changes could be made by a simple change in shape.

It was decided that Jon and his five young companions visit Polok II, where they would assist in the building of the two great ships. There they would remain until that task was completed. Afterwards, they would hand over all production procedures and processes to Malik and Bailor. They would continue the building program to the mutual benefit of all. Any additional supplies being sent via one or both of the two great ships after they had been commissioned. That method of transportation was the only type available at the time, since long-range interstellar portals had not yet been installed.

Solaria had supplied her investment in the form of the blue Constructor Microids, some Medium Microid samples and relevant equipment needed to manufacture the Medium Microids. Polok gave their labours and Lodor their superior brains and technologies. That way there would be minimal funding involved. Therefore each co-member would owe each other very little at the end of each project. However the first two ships belonged to Solaria. After their completion they would each have been allowed to build two ships for their own purpose. All ships other than those used by the new Federation Navy would be at a 30 percent profit to Solaria. Most of the raw materials were plentiful on Mars, Mercury and in other stellar systems.

EVACUATION OF ANDROMEDANS

The evacuation plans were finally drafted. The intention was to take most of the refugees from Mars to specified areas on Eden and eventually to other less hostile worlds within local systems. First of all a system of environmental domes would be build on Mars for the temporary containment of over 10 million evacuees.

It was not intended to involve the inhabitants of Earth in any way. Therefore Earth was not made aware of that critical operation. That was in case they felt threatened by their numbers.

The two great ships, once built, would be used for that purpose. They would contain the latest inter-dimensional drives and could ferry many passengers.

The planned program was finally completed. It was just the small matter of mounting the Omegron Portal on Mars and building the necessary structures to accommodate the many intergalactic refugees. After that task had been completed, preparation for the real wars against the Javols could commence.

Sarah had a clear view of the future of Solaria and everyone agreed with that picture. Therefore she planned for everyone in that future empire. Each of her new councillors were given a task and each had to earn their keep in her greater scheme of things.

CHAPTER 28

Young Andromedans return to Polok II

The day of their departure to Polok had finally arrived. After loading and securing the crates there was just enough space left for eight passengers. Since Merol, Petra and Julia were not included in the previous interstellar mission, they looked forward to that new alien adventure.

'It's sad we are not visiting Eden at this time. I would have liked to visit our new home for the first time,' Merol said. Jon turned his head around, ignoring him.

'Pass me that small crate over there!' he shouted and Merol complied.

'I am tired of hearing that same tune sung, time and time again. You guys will see beautiful Eden soon enough. Now, we have important work to do, so let's get on with it!' Jon rebuked and their faces sank.

'Master Jon, it's on the way. If you wish, we can spend a brief moment on that world, before arriving on Polok II,' the Ship said and even Jon's face lit up.

'Ok... you heard The Ship. I'm sure a few minutes on Eden wont hurt.' Lira went closer and kissed him on the cheek.

The young six Andromedans said their emotional farewell to Sarah and others, but had a strong resolve in their objectives. Sarah was saddened by their departure but knew they would soon be back. Anyway, everyone within the new Solarian Empire had to take risks for the common good and the benefit of the greater whole. Sarah embraced each in turn and finally Jon.

'You take good care of my family for me and don't you take any undue risks on anyone's behalf,' she commanded, with a few tears running down her cheeks. At that poignant moment she couldn't help herself and knew not when she would see them again.

'Don't worry, Sarah, everything will be ok,' Jon stressed. She knew he was always capable of fulfilling his important missions.

Jon was given responsibility over his companions, the consignment and project, and was well chosen for the task in hand.

Once on board, the ship absorbed its stairs, closed its entrance and disappeared from its pad at the rear of the house. Although Sarah found it hard to believe in such advanced technology, she now accepted such possibilities. Madeline's girls were also suspicious about The Ship and other strange occurrences about the house, particularly with Plato and Lumak. Nevertheless they put all such strange occurrences to a few clever scientist using advanced technologies and never to aliens from distant worlds.

As The Ship rose out of Earth's atmosphere the six watched its beautiful globe for a brief moment on the large screen and sadly waved goodbye to distant friends.

For the benefit of Merol, Petra and Julia, the ship followed a course through the Solar System and immediately transposed to Eden. Suddenly the beautiful disk of Eden was displayed on the screen. They observed the image of their future home world for a while, but could see no similar features to Caefon. The planet was like a single continent with seas interspersed, giving about two thirds land. Then The Ship transposed to the exact position of its previous landing on the surface.

'Wow! This is some paradise! It's beyond imagination!' Merol yelled.

'That's not all. The fragrance intoxicates with healing powers, almost turning us into gods. At least we'll feel that way. It even has powers to rejuvenate our bodies,' Jon said and they were amazed.

'I was told by Jerry that we might be able to take Horses and other herbivores later,' Lira said and they became even more ecstatic.

They remained on the paradise world for a while, but Jon knew the score and insisted they left before becoming too intoxicated.

The Ship then spoke to them:

'I am required to take a slight diversion to Tarran and receive a passenger called Bawaki. She is a chosen one and must visit Kanaefon for her conversion.

'After our arrival on Polok II, I am to continue to that world and onwards to Caefon.

'You may deliver a message to your parents via Bawaki, if you wish. She will accompany me later to Caefon.

'Then I am to return to Earth directly from Caefon, but also with Merian, Plato's past assistant. She is also required in the master plan. We shall meet again when you return to Earth after your current mission. At that time I shall be assigned to Councillor Sarah and the Solarian Council, so God speed.

'You may now return to your bunks in order to be transposed to Tarran!

'Please return to your bunks. All matter must now be transposed!'

The warning sirens sounded and the ship transposed and re-materialised at its predetermined location on Tarran. Its entrance opened and a catlike figure hesitantly entered its strange environment.

The young ones were wearing their translation belts in anticipation of their arrival on Polok, but had also brought it along for any communication difficulties they may have encountered on-route. They realized The Ship sometimes visited places not on their schedule. Nevertheless, the belt could only translate to Polokan.

Bawaki's figure was larger than life and appeared like a great warrior. As she entered, she glanced at their communications belts, then stared directly into Jon's eyes and spoke in a catlike fashion.

'No need for those inadequate means of communication. My special headband makes me understand and speak your tongue.'

They stood as she entered in her catlike form.

'Let me introduce myself to you. I am Princess Bawaki of the esteemed Marawi clan. We are one of the strongest clans on our world, Tarran,' she said, proudly.

They remained still but with outstretched arms. All intending to shake her paws, but she declined. Her powerful arms resembled those of an athletic human, but contained very sharp menacing black claws with slightly webbed fingers. She smelled like a large cat and wore strange leather-like sandals with thick sleeves.

She glanced at the others and sighed with disappointment.

'Perhaps I shall transform to your form after I am Shadite. Then I can join your clans on Solaria; for I sometimes think my form to be a menacing one. I have learnt many new things about your world, Earth, and its people from my headband and the little black box given to me by Siend Plato.'

'Have you really?' Lira replied.

'Yes! Once I am like you, I can concentrate all my efforts against our mutual enemies and help my still primitive people to gain status and become a member of your esteemed federation.'

Jon and the others were surprised by the deep quality of her mind in such a ferociously vicious body. Although a most vicious looking cat that walked on two legs without a tail, she was very human in her mannerisms.

'Bawaki, we'll be very pleased to have another member in our most esteemed family,' Jon replied.

She was even more surprised by that statement from a male. On her world the males were inferior little creatures and only assisted in domestic duties, leaving all the fighting, collecting and hunting to the females. Here, she found the males to be larger and more boisterous than the females. Yet, she realized the possibilities of anything on her special journeys.

'I may take you up on your offer when I am ready. Now, is there anything I can do for you by way of my journey to Caefon?' she inquired.

They were somehow aware that she could almost read their thoughts or perhaps she clearly anticipated their actions as would any supremely capable hunter on an extremely hostile world like

Tarran.

They suddenly remembered about their surrogate families on Caefon and thought of written notes, but their parents couldn't read or write in the normal sense. That was not part of their computerised culture. Finally they decided to send any small items or mementoes they could find. Those were tagged with their personal hieroglyphic codes that their parents could understand. The items were handed to Bawaki and put into a small leather pouch which was held in a secured place near her belt.

The Ship landed on Polok II and materialised on the surface close to Malik's administrative building. The one used by him on the previous occasion when the Grand Lord appeared. As Jon and the others disembarked they could see construction cranes and machines everywhere. Most of the workers appeared to be robots controlled by a master Lodorian computer. The whole process stretched out in all directions as far as the eye could see.

Malik was still using the surface building as his headquarters and received communication of their arrival. He knew exactly what that implied and immediately communicated to his wife, Mira, telling her the good news.

Several of his senior officers went along to help retrieve the large crates from The Ship. They placed them into the building using small traction trucks. When they had finished, Jon and the others waved goodbye to The Ship and it simply vanished from sight.

Jon followed Malik into his office and handed him other files and blueprints for the microid factory.

'These are the instructions for the manufacture of Medium Microids. I have also taken along a small amount of sample material. While we are here, we can assist you to set up your production units and help in areas where needed. This material will form the bulk of the ship, but we require extremely large amounts.'

Malik called one of his senior officers and handed him the instructions.

'This is very urgent... for the manufacture of the large ships... keep me informed of progress!' he ordered.

Malik had almost completed a full set of moulds, some were tens of metres in cross section. Just one more week was needed before completion. Even so, work could be done with those already constructed once they had been checked and scanned for flaws.

Each mould could be used to produce hundreds of the large microid blocks required on each ship and could continue for thousands of runs. The process was similar to building a house with standard bricks until one reached an odd shape, then the few special moulds would be introduced.

Once mounted close together, the blocks' geometry caused all those in contact to form a solid structure and that shape was finally fused molecularly by a process of ultrasonic excitation, from hull to stern.

The whole place was still a disaster zone since the war. Despite all those efficient Lodorian robots and androids, Malik needed several weeks to complete other essential areas of the project.

Despite those problems he was much happier and in no great hurry to begin the production program until the microid materials and other equipment from Lodor had been delivered, so a couple of well-earned holidays wouldn't go amiss.

'Your new city of Miran will be most beautiful on completion?' Lira said while observing the expansive construction.

'I have decided to use New York as its main template. Images were on one of the video disk you gave me,' Malik replied.

'That's fantastic!' Jon exclaimed, realizing a direct link to Earth.

Malik subsequently excused himself from the council, saying he had to check out a few things regarding microid production and immediately took Jon and the others to his home to meet his wife, Mira.

'You may completely forget about work while you are here. We are capable of doing all this work by ourselves. While on this world you will always be our guests,' he insisted. Then a large truck on traction arrived to take them away.

It was incredible how similar human types were throughout the universe. Apparently, among all primal life-forms, only certain very rear types became highly intelligent and technological.

The process could be considered in the abstract sense to breaking the mind barrier, and once that barrier was broken it opened up new strata of infinite possibilities.

For some unknown reason, human types had that original format, which like that particular model of jet plane - not the propeller variety that was limited only to a relatively dense atmosphere - could be pushed even further up the ladder of evolution. Once they had attained a certain level they could leap to those much greater heights of previously unknown realms by creating specific tools in the form of advanced technology.

But that type of creature, call it Homo-Sapiens, Ape, Gondril, Tarranian Cat, Octan or whatever, had existed with those inclinations and potentials from the start. Such technologically evolving life-forms could only have moved in one singular direction, or they would very soon have become extinct along the way. That was one of the main reasons why their specific tendencies were so similar.

There were obviously genetic variation in colour, size, looks, etcetera, depending on environment, but those factors were merely incidental when one considered the similarity of emotions like love, joy, happiness, jealousy, hate, insecurity, boredom, and all the rest, which were considered human qualities.

Even so, such powerful and sometimes hated negative qualities, were really what humanity was all about and most probably the driving force behind their efficient survival. They were neither prey nor predator, but something in between and could be either when the time arose. But humans were not only derived from Homo-Sapiens. They could evolved from any of the basic types, including mammals like Apes, Cats, Horses, Cows and such like. While the oceans gave us Octopuses and others. Given enough time to evolve by themselves. Then there was the wider groups like Reptiles, Crustaceans, Molluscs, Insects and others. Those also led eventually to their own types of humans like Semonites, Lodorians and Octans.

They had to use specialised tools in order to survive their harsh environments. Many hadn't stings in their tails, hard protective shells or sharp claws. Their bodies and minds were easily damaged by the harsh external universe. So they had to use protective means like clothes and invent their much more efficient stings and claws by way of technology in order to create their own universe of survival.

But once they learnt the book of survival, nothing could ever stand in their way, for they knew it by heart.

Malik still lived within the underworld while his beautiful palatial home was reconstructed on the surface. Therefore he took them back to the underworld via one of the previously concealed surface elevators.

On arrival Jon handed Malik and Mira a present in an ornately designed wooden box. When she opened the box she removed an astoundingly beautifully painted antique vase.

'This we call a vase. It is sometimes used for holding flowers like your Chortah in the garden outside. Such ornamental items are considered a very important part of interior decoration, even more so than electronic equipment. This is because of their aesthetic beauty... to some it's almost spiritual, like you, Mira, and Malik... full of memories and thoughts,' Jon said, attempting with some difficulty to explain a new concept to their different culture.

She gazed at Malik who was happily smiling out of curiosity and embraced the item as if trying to collect some of its memories, then she replied, never taking her eyes off Malik.

'Jon, I know what you mean. Our ancient peoples used to think in a similar romantic fashion generations ago, but my husband's computers and wars eventually turned us into technological savages. Hopefully, with your assistance, I am sure we'll once again be able to relearn the art of appreciating art and real beauty.' Malik was also eager to learn this new concept.

Finally Jon handed the computer book of rules and more information to Malik.

'All these items, including the vase are from Chief Councillor Sarah, who has been nominated Chief Councillor and Coordinator of Solaria,' Jon said, proudly.

'And how is President Jerry... Plato and Shadite Lumak?' Malik inquired with curiosity.

'Jerry is still the great diplomat and president of his territories on Earth, but he is very busy at this time... there is also much reconstruction on Earth, although not as extensive as here. They are due mainly to timely technological improvements. Anyway, when you visit us you will see for yourself and spend time with Jerry on Earth. Councillor Sarah wants you to read the relevant books and note any comments you might have, changes you would like to make or chapters you wish to add. And here is her picture,' Jon replied.

John showed them Sarah's photograph and Malik was surprised by the close resemblance of her to his departed mother. That was when he was a young boy and his father was away fighting.

'My God! She must be a very great woman as she is beautiful!' Malik said.

'She is great in many ways and we love her dearly,' Jon replied.

Malik observed Jon's sincere expression of loyalty.

'She must truly be the greatest woman in your empire as my mother was in ours, even like a queen. We may even learn a few important lessons from her as we have from Jerry, Meron, Plato, you and others.'

They sat for lunch, but Malik was still over excited by their presence.

'I have decided for us to have a short holiday on the surface from tomorrow. That is after I have taken you around the production plant and shown you our progress.'

'You have already built the plant?' Jon exclaimed.

'Yes! It was completed two days ago and is now ready for the supplies.'

'By goodness! You guys are so great!'

'Time waits for no one. Anyway, The surface environment will not affect you, because Earth humans are immune to that type of virus and Mira, myself and most of the surface military are vaccinated against it... But I am afraid, most of my underworld people will require more than one type of vaccination before they can resume normal living on the surface. They have been isolated in this bubble of an underground city for far too long. Their immune systems might need a kick start before they can resume normal life on the surface. Because of those reasons, we are to erect large concealed enclosures currently under construction by robots and androids....

'By the way, Jon, the first moulds will be checked tomorrow and the day after, so that gives us a little time to play before the really hard work begins.'

CHAPTER 29

A strange design

The next morning Jon and his group followed Malik to the local microid production and moulding plants. Those buildings were truly massive by Earth's standards and contained many robots, androids and cranes. They were the first to be constructed on the surface using robots.

'Lodor has began to construct similar facilities on Safon, one of our local worlds. We intend to use that planet for the specific purpose of building ships for the federation.'

'Absolutely Fantastic!' Jon replied.

'Several of the moulds you see here can be used to produce large parts of the ships repeatedly. As can be observed, all instructions relating to production have already been programmed into the master computer. So there is little need for you to be involved in this most basic and repetitive process.'

Jon and the others were astonished by what they saw. The progress was truly the most ingenious in automation. All their anticipated hard toil were already efficiently carried out at great speed by specialized robots and androids. Those intelligent automatons operated about 20 times faster than any human.

'After construction both ships will be one-point-eight kilometres long, point eight at their widest, horizontally. Both front and rear tapers to a small hemisphere.'

'That's truly gigantic!' Lira exclaimed.

'They will be the greatest! Our main concern is in building the last stages of such massive structures here on our world. This process is so much easier in space, well away from the influence of gravity. However we are also learning a lot from this construction method, the knowledge of which may further assist us in the future when constructing such gigantic forms.'

'Yes, all such working methods are important! It makes the process more repetitive,' Jon said.

'These robot-controlled cranes and other machinery you see here, despite their enormous size, can be controlled to well below the nearest point one mil. This is achieved by the use of special lasers and other precise means of alignment. According to my information, several of the blocks are moulded first before being transported to the assembly site just outside the old city. On arrival, they are fitted unto the larger units.'

Jon stared profusely at the enormity and quantity of equipment in disbelief, wondering how Malik and his people could have gone that far in such a relatively short time.

'My friends, it would have been a lot easier on Safon, because it's a much smaller world and additionally we have our hands tied with the construction and evacuation programs here, as you see. Constructing such structures is not a major problem for us planetary miners, since we can utilise many more capable robots, androids and computers.'

'You guys are truly ingenious!'

'I must show you one more thing before we leave for our holidays.'

He took them to a smaller and more secured building and they followed him to a storage room.

'We received these two items recently from Lodor. They are supposed to be the ship's minds, made to the instructions given us by the Grand Lord. They were unable to properly test the units. For some strange reason they can become alive only when accurately positioned within their relevant places on each ship. Therefore we are not sure whether they will function correctly in service. Apparently these computer minds use a very strange form of alien symmetry in their design; something even the Lodorians could not quite come to terms with and have had great problems duplicating.'

'Wow! Minds of opposite symmetries in multi-dimensions!' Lira interjected.

'Each one seems to be of a one-off nature and the surprising thing is, once the first one was constructed the second could not be assembled in exactly the same way. It's almost as if some of its symmetry got reversed in the process due to the presence of the first. Something to do with parallel universes and dimensions. Despite those unsolvable problems, the Lodorians are quite a resourceful race and only the portals remain to be built.'

'What are these special Portals?' Jon inquired.

'Because of the enormous size of those ships, it will be necessary to move passengers very quickly from point to point over great distances. The Portals, when fitted to main doors and corridors, will automatically transfer passengers to their destinations almost instantly in time. It links two separate points in space together at virtually the same relative time, and that's another alien science, perhaps even capable of transferring us bodily across the galaxy,' Malik replied, dreading the concept.

'The Omegron Portal!' Jon mumbled to himself. Suddenly realizing the similar methods used for that type of inter-dimensional travel.

'What did you say?' Malik inquired.

'I was just thinking aloud.'

'But, Volt, Bailors technical advisor, was so excited with this new technology that he mentioned those facts to me, albeit in confidence. You know, the Lodorians can be rather tight-lipped when it comes to talking about technology, in particular very advanced ones. But they no longer think of us as little babies. I suppose now more like little brothers and sisters. Bailor also wants to visit Earth, by the way,' Malik said.

'Yes! That is no problem. I would also like to hand him Sarah's gift. However she insisted I saw him in person out of respect. Can you arrange a meeting?' Jon said.

'He visits here in just one week and three days to evaluate progress, so why not have a celebration then. I need a house warming party anyway. You guys can supply the music and mix the drinks, while Mira and I prepare the food. My sons and their wives can also assist. You can leave the strange Lodorian menu to me,' Malik replied, sarcastically.

They left the sight by traction car to a relatively beautiful spot some fifteen miles away.

Malik's family still owned the very large and almost completely demolished stately mansion or palace with a large fief. It was in a valley below twin peaks. Its surrounding fertile lands were situated near a small lake with a cascading waterfall between the mountains. Presently the whole area was overgrown with green everywhere. In that respect Polok II was very much like Earth.

Since the beginning of the great war and the resulting mass evacuation to the underworld, the place had fallen into disrepair. That was a century ago and all those areas were free of human intervention since that time. Out of a population of several billions only about five million survived the bombardment. Some survived in the underworld cities while another million or so were captured and used as slaves within the mines and on Lodor. Malik preferred the natural look of his family place and decided to build around it. He also wanted to build a monument in memory of his parents.

His father used the palace during the initial period of the war, but it took a direct hit when targeted by satellite stations. During that bombardment both his parents lost their lives. They had become one of the first casualties of a lengthy war. Since that time the place had remained uncultivated and unused, but there were still fish in the lake. He enjoyed the larger crustaceans when prepared in a particular way by his wife.

The once beautiful palace was presently being reconstructed to its former glory. There were robots, androids and building equipment everywhere. It would have taken a few more days before the builders completed its interior and fitted all the electronics and furniture in place. The large service house close by, originally used for storage, was cleared and refitted for use as temporary surface accommodation. He wanted his palace completed before Bailor and Volt arrived to assess the great ships.

For the first time in over 100 years he got hold of an old fishing line, baited the hook and through it into the small lake. He was surprised with the quantity and variety of fish in the water.

'You know, Malik, we never eat fish on Earth. Although we catch and weigh them, we always return them to the water,' Merol said and he was surprised by that method. Jon soon adapted some equipment for the task of fun-fishing and Malik got much more enjoyment from the competition and fun involved.

'Sorry, Pal, but I think we really need some more games on this world, so from now I'm going to take some notes,' Julia said, while Malik listened. He realized many changes were afoot, but those were fun changes which he had began to enjoy.

Although the local fishing was not as varied and plentiful as on Earth, they had lots of fun. The young ones always saw the happier side of almost everything and were a joy to be with.

For the first time in his life, Malik began questioning his own technological culture. He felt a yearning for the more basic, natural and truer side of life. He was having a second refreshing taste with his youthful friends from Earth who had brought back all those exciting memories with his mother and friends when his world was paradise and he was young. It was then that he remembered his best friends Ramm and Safa. He had lost them both about fifty years after the start of war by enemy incendiaries.

His idea of an ideal society was quickly changing. He suddenly realised that he wanted a different order from the original plans he had for his wife and remaining family. That order was to include his already fully grown-up sons now serving in the military. It would be something closer to the simpler things in life, like fishing, visiting friends, reading books and poetry, even watching and listening to those Earth videos and music disks as they were called. He hoped their new city of Miran, named after his wife, Mira, would contain most of Earths venues and products.

Solaria definitely had something more of the human side of things to offer. Even Bailor and his Lodorians were infected by such progress. He had only recently met these humans and their influence was so pervasive. Just by a brief encounter he had suddenly won a one-hundred-year-old war, there was lasting peace between Polok and Lodor and he was finally at his ancient family's home, thinking those incredible thoughts. The whole thing was almost like a dream and the dream was not yet at an end.

After their brief holiday, they decided to remain on the surface, so the small house was quickly redecorated and made more comfortable for Jon and his companions.

Malik and his wife began to transfer furniture and other items from the underworld to the palace as each room was completed.

They were finally at work and although it took a little while to synchronize their efforts with the more efficient robots and androids, the program was moving a lot faster than predicted.

Almost a week had passed by and the grey Medium Microid powder was finally being manufactured in great quantity. Malik's palace had been completed. He insisted that Jon and his friends shared the large house with him and his wife. So they moved into the larger palace and more comfortable building.

They had at their disposal more technology by way of games, Earth videos and music disks, although having probably viewed them a thousand times. The only thing that was missing was a com-call to Sarah and members of their family and friends back home. That interstellar communication link was not yet available and would require H-Wave technology.

At long last a few more human faces other than the military could be seen with their families on the planet's surface. Their eyes turned away from the bright sunlight. Many wore dark eye-shades to shield their sensitive eyes from the surface brilliance. The majority used facial filters to further prevent contamination. Resettlement was at last in progress on the surface.

The massive ships were taking shape while constructed in two large hangers. Within their respective enclosures were every conceivable crane, scaffold, numerous elevators to carry materials while transportation crafts constantly moved in all directions.

The blocks were slid in place and every type of robot and android involved in the construction process. Like ants in a nest, each following precise instructions from some master Lodorian computer.

Soon the hulls of both ships were completed. Then the robots and androids began working internally, fitting special surfaces, furniture, utilities, control lines, local control modules, power systems, portals, safety devices and finally the unique computer minds. The inter-dimensional drives which consisted of a large spherical unit was to be located at the very centre of each ship.

After everything was fitted in place and inspected by a separate team of androids, they left and both ships were sealed and made ready for the Structural Molecular Conversion phase.

During that period there was much tension in case of contamination or misplaced components during assembly, causing the conversion process to go irretrievably wrong. If such a disaster occurred they would have to dissolve both massive ships and begin the complete rebuilding process all over again from scratch. That would have been a daunting task and one requiring a fresh quantity of Constructor Microids from Solaria. They had just enough of the rear and expensive substance for two ships and all had been used.

Molecular Conversion could only be initiated with a special type of ultrasonic generator which they brought from Earth. That item was to be placed at a predetermined point at the stern of each ship in turn.

That position coincided with the centre of the large federation insignia where the three colours met in the centre of the circle.

Jon was given that most important but difficult task and ascended the high position on a makeshift elevator. He was accompanied by two androids in case he needed assistance. All such androids were considered expendable.

'I am now in position. Device display has been reset to zero and ultrasonic energiser initiated... still showing zero. Now placing gun over the cross-hairs on the hull,' he said, while Malik and his scientists listened patiently. They wanted no mistakes on that final operation.

Jon was little afraid of heights, even when it was about two hundred metres above ground level. His main concern was being blamed if the process was unsuccessful. He plugged the unit in and cautiously dialled some buttons. While muttering a personal prayer, he pressed a large red button. Then patiently observed another piece of equipment which displayed a reading of just over one hundred and his eyes lit with pleasure. That figure represented the saturation levels due to multiple boundary reflections. The equipment received its data from the original unit by the same ultrasonic process.

He waited patiently. Half hour later the reading gradually dropped from its original figure to zero point three five which was below the required value of zero point five, the maximum acceptable level. He gave it a little longer for certainty and unplugged the equipment to repeat the same process on the other ship.

When he was finally on the ground they patiently waited for some response from the ship's computer minds, but nothing happened.

They were not happy on their final day of testing. Being of microid design, the ships were completely sealed molecularly. Therefore it was not possible for anyone to enter and carry out repairs or make fine adjustments.

After waiting several more hours they decided to call it a day and continue observing the ships' birth process early the following day. Nevertheless android observers would remain posted and on guard to instantly report any changes in the ships' birth process.

CHAPTER 30

An unexpected awakening

Hopefully, both ships were now completed and programmed to Grand Lord Gerra's instructions. It was based on a complex mathematical structure that was unheard of before. Its inter-dimensional subtleties were incomprehensible even to the Lodorians with their advanced knowledge.

After the conversion was completed, the program began to grow, slowly at first, but not too unlike the beginnings of an inquiring mind within an enormous brain. By using Lumak's special microids, which could be compared to living cells in a large body, the whole ship could become a living entity. It soon created its own types of arteries and veins for servicing those microids, using a type of self replenishing metallic fluid for blood. Thus, it was able to create all required materials for its strange metabolism from its own Quantum Matter Convertors and those in turn were controlled by its powerful mind.

It was not long before they became self-aware and conscious of their existence and structure. It took almost a complete day before they learnt the nature of our material universe in which they were now living members. It took them a little longer to observe the local occupants and learn about their constituents, respective languages, cultures and technologies through their newly connected senses.

Although twins, both ships had completely different personalities and could sense every nut and bolt within their own structures. Each viewed their living bodies in the same way as a human brain in its own body, but with greater powers in combination with their incredible size. To all intents and purpose the ships were superior living entities in their own right.

While Malik and the others waited, they felt a slight tremor and as if by yawning, some sentences were uttered from the closest ship in a feminine but booming voice.

'Where am I?... Ah... You have followed instructions well... I see that you have made some slight changes... here and there to the original plan... I shall have those repaired and updated as and when necessary... otherwise I feel fully operational.

'I have been given the name Venusa and my sister Martia, from the worlds Venus and Mars within Earth's system in Solaria,' the ship said.

'Can you hear me, Venusa?' Malik asked, now in quite a very nervous disposition.

'Of course I can hear you. I have scanned your body parts and observed that you are quite different to myself. You are primal and carbon-based... but for some extra technologies which I have just analysed in detail.

'My sister and I are on a special mission for our Lord, but you are also important to us because our Lord respects and loves you,' Venusa replied.

Malik was bemused, but equally confused by the strange ordeal he found himself in. He thought the visitor's ship was strange enough, but here he was with two massive female types having names and they were talking to him in his own tongue and quite fluently.

'The Grand Lord must have a very marked sense of humour. And what if Bailor or Volt was here today. What would they think?' he muttered.

He spoke again to Venusa's ship.

'Your sister, Martia... Will she be awake soon?... and will you take us for a test flight through this system to show us your abilities?' he inquired.

'Yes, Captain Malik, she is also awake and in answer to your second question, only if it pleases you and your friends,' Venusa replied.

Jon and his group couldn't stop their sarcastic smiles and some of the girls had to try hard to hold back their giggling.

Malik thought, despite their strange abilities, his labours would be successful if they performed satisfactorily during their test flights. There was also the possibility of improvement when they learnt more about their environment and its civilized cultures. After all, they were supposed to be self-repairing.

However he was not too exuberant with the outcome and wondered whether Volt and his scientists had followed the Lord's instructions to the letter.

Even so, he could not have made a proper judgment until he had assessed their performance in full.

CHAPTER 31

Earth and Mars in progress

Just two Earth weeks had passed since her young friends had left with The Ship for Polok II and Sarah missed them. She wondered whether they had arrived safely at their remote destination within the vastness of space.

She had since acquired a twelve-inch reflector telescope which she had fitted in the loft with Lumak's assistance. Despite the interfering lights from the local town and some tall encroaching trees, she had spent many a restful evening viewing the heavens and gaining an appreciation of its immense vastness and depth. In all her existence never before had she such a propensity for the greater ecology and that type of outlet tended to bring her closer to her vision. It was so strong in her that it was like a voice calling.

Although she was still quite busy attending meetings and official visits for Solarian business affairs and her many charities, she was also very competent at delegating and could always find time for weekend picnics and evening viewing sessions at her telescope. That was when she was not entertaining or visiting friends and colleagues socially.

Having recently acquired planning permission for a similar but separate building in the same grounds, the builders were everywhere. The large manor was also being redecorated with a constant mess everywhere. She always hated chaos which disturbed her and made her irritated for no reason.

The adjacent house was to be built just a few metres away with a connecting walkway. Hopefully it would be ready for the young ones on their return. She intended it as a surprise and saw it as their future home for when they were ready to settle with their own families. That was assuming they decided to remain on Earth.

She considered them responsible enough adults to use the place sensibly after their return if they so desired. The Ancients and other more senior members could remain with her and her husband in the old house. If necessary it could be further extended.

While viewing through the telescope one evening and watching one of the larger craters on the moon, she became curious when the sharp image seen through the telescope became blurred. All details had disappeared but its large disc still remained. Thinking it to be a fault in the telescope she took the viewing binoculars and decided to observe the image through the large loft window, but to her even greater surprise the lunar disk still remained blurred.

She wondered what strange occurrence ensued and went over to the vertical side window to observe the local area. As she did she was engulfed by a tension in the air which made her hair stand on end and gave her goose pimples. To her further astonishment The Ship suddenly materialised at its usual place at the rear of the house. The moment that happened there was an almighty bang. One of Lumak's large empty oil cans had fallen from its unstable perch on one of the storage shelves.

Nervously, she observed The Ship's outline and took the binoculars for a second look at the moon but the blurring had gone and the image back to normal. She wondered what strange effect The Ship had on light and space during its transposition, then it suddenly dawned on her that more extraterrestrial visitors had arrived. She quickly dumped the binoculars to one side and ran downstairs expecting to see the young ones saunter down its glittering stairway, but instead two new visitors in the form of rather tall women clambered down with large containers.

Merian was the first off The Ship to be followed by a female Shadite in her black hooded cloak.

At that time the other occupants and helpers were away from the house and no one was around to assist should there be an emergency. Sarah was quite apprehensive at first, even when she could contact her husband with her security bracelet. She soon realised her nervousness was unfounded and fought it vigorously. She took a firm hold of her emotions and literally dragged herself forward to her unsuspecting guests. Merian put out her hand forward in friendship.

'Lady Sarah, I presume? I am Merian, Doctor Plato's assistant and my Shadite companion is Bawaki from the world of Tarran!'

Bawaki soon folded her hood back over her neck to reveal a most beautiful and perfect human form. Then she came forward and likewise offered her hand in greetings.

'Lady Sarah, I am to be assigned to you as your personal guard and assistant... I am also under training in the clan of Shaditry.'

'I see?... are you both hungry after your long trip? Please follow me and perhaps we can have some dinner together. Then you can tell me all about your trip before my husband arrives.

'Thank you!' Merian said. She resembled Petra of the young six Andromedans closely , except for her sea-blue eyes, pinkish complexion and six fingers.

'The others including my two helpers have accompanied Meron to an art conference in the city, so I was left here all on my own. That is, until your arrival,' Sarah replied.

She took them into her large modern kitchen-diner and without the use of robots or automatic food dispensers, began to remove pre-cooked meals from one of the large refrigerators. Some she placed within a large Microwave oven. Suddenly Bawaki stood up, assuming it was her duty to assist. After all, her lady Sarah must be the most superior female of the human clan, she thought.

Sarah indulged her for a while and they both got on very well together while preparing the food. They were soon eating the vegetarian meals, which although enjoyable, was quite unusual to both her visitors. For Merian it was a desirable change from the unvaried meals served at Lower Cantor.

'You both speak such perfect English?' Sarah inquired.

'Madam Sarah, we were given special implants and training before we left,' replied Bawaki.

'Have you any knowledge of Jon and his companions?' Sarah inquired.

'Yes! Madam Sarah. They collected me from my home planet, Tarran. I saw them arrive safely on Polok II. They also gave me a few gifts for their parents in the Lower Cantor City on Caefon.... But I have not seen them since I left Polok II,' Bawaki replied, politely.

'I suppose they must be all right. Perhaps I am just the worrying type,' she said, showing motherly concern.

When they had finished their meal she took them to the two remaining small rooms on the first floor.

'When the house next door is finished, we'll have lots more space and you can both have larger and more comfortable rooms. In the mean while, I am afraid, these are all that's left,' she said, apologetically.

She showed them both rooms, drawing the curtains as she did.

'Make yourselves at home and should you need anything, please do not hesitate to ask me or one of my helpers. There is an additional large wardrobe in the corridor... have a look through it and select whatever clothes you require. When we visit the shops tomorrow we can get some more to your liking, if you wish.'

The two women viewed the rooms and couldn't believe their fortunes. Although those rooms appeared small to Sarah, they thought they were large and the best ever viewed. They were very comfortable and everything within was so neatly arranged.

Bawaki thought she was in the paradise of which she and her people had always dreamt and Merian, of freedom from the technological prison of Lower Cantor with the ever present threat of the Javols. Completely overwhelmed by emotions they both went down on their knees in front of Sarah and couldn't stop kissing her hands. At that time she appeared to be the focus of their deliverance.

Although Sarah felt slightly embarrassed by the ordeal, she accepted their gesture of respect, but quickly assisted them to their feet before going downstairs to await her husband's arrival.

GHOSTS FROM THE PAST

After the Ancients arrival from the art conference that evening, they were introduced to Merian and Bawaki. Merian explained who she was. Her ancient ancestor also named Merian came forward to observe her descendant in detail.

'Did you know...You are my grand daughter, over one hundred generations removed and called by my very own name. What a great honour this is, my child,' she said.

Merian soon realised the older woman was truly her ancient ancestor. She had observed her on many occasions in the crypt in Lower Cantor and realized she had been dead for more than three-thousand years. How could she be here if she was over there and had departed this life so many years ago. She thought for a moment, 'I must also be dead, for so also are all my ancient ancestors. This must be the place we call Gohenna, where everything is possible and every thought realized. I was thinking of them just before we left for Osmaron.'

She couldn't accept what she saw. She slowly turned away and left the room. Then ran to her room screaming and in tears. Plato understood the problem and followed her upstairs to calm her down and supply a plausible explanation.

'They are so real! So real! How can that be?' she exclaimed, still confused.

'Come here my love. You know of the technologies to bring us back using the Megotron and Psyrotron? Well, think of those technologies taken a step further. What you saw in Lower Cantor was just their previous bodies. Like old clothes, those can always be cast off for the newer and better designs,' Plato said, almost jokingly.

Plato patiently described the advanced technology used and the real existence of the City of Goh and the variability of other planes within the Cosmos. He also told her that the bodies in the crypt were like the serpents skin that had been shed and left behind on the way to a more glorious future. Merian accepted his explanation and was soon to rejoin them. She apologised for her very immature behaviour. Then they sat down and had a drink together.

Although Merian Senior had missed her husband, Ranul and other family members, she realize she still had a very important task to do and the possibilities existed for their resurrection in the future, after the demise of the Javols.

CHAPTER 32

Technological progress on Earth

Under the assistance of Lumak (Doctor Jeffery Longhurst) and Meron, LPD and robotic technology were being adapted almost everywhere on Earth. Very soon their demands far outstripped production and planetary requirements became too great for both men to handle. Even with a highly competent team of several thousand humans while assisted by numerous advanced robots and androids, demand far outstripped the processes involved and the needed resources.

Virtually every large hospital on the planet wanted their own operating robots, with added features like Microid Sprays and Nasal Inhalers. Once these microscopic Microids entered the human body they could repair virtually any organ or type of tissue, even regrow limbs from the patient's genetic code. The latter could only be done by the introduction of a protein gel and certain footprint drugs to enhance the growth process. That was not all, those robots could operate twenty times faster than any surgeon and were much more accurate, leaving patients with less trauma and quicker recovery.

The Solarians under Sarah, had to quickly find a much larger production location on another world. Although Mars was a likely candidate, it was too close to Earth and they didn't want to pollute Earth's sister world with the promise of humanity's first planetary adventure. Neither did they wish to pollute one of their most loved planets, namely Earth. They had to move production to a dead world where robots could run all such production with minimum human intervention.

The first LPD shuttle test flight was made to Mars under Meron's supervision and was an overwhelming success. It was Professor Strongman's first space flight. He became a changed individual as a result of that incredible experience. Lumak had promised him adventure, but he never realized, not even in his wildest dreams, that he would have come this far so quickly. As a result several larger LPD shuttles and satellite stations were scheduled for construction. Many large voyagers were at that time being constructed in Earth's orbit for use as passenger and cargo ferries between the two worlds.

The first shuttle craft was subsequently donated to Meron for further experiments and flight demonstrations to the Moon. He soon had the large ship modified and fitted with robots for the transportation of building materials and technical supplies to Mars, in anticipation of the evacuation program. Such materials would be used in building the first dome environments.

The original two weeks and three days taken for a one-way trip to Mars was soon reduced to three weeks in both directions, with room for improvement if things were not moving to schedule. Therefore all that remained was the fitting of the Omegron Portal on Mars.

Presently, Lumak's advanced robots and superior computers were being used extensively in our planet's hospitals, industries and construction program. Earth was progressing in leaps and bounds. All those incredible machines could change in form and create virtually any tools for the task in hand. They were precise and could complete their tasks twenty times faster than any human.

In a very short time the Solarian Organization headed by Sarah would be one of the most revered and loved.

President Gerald Fraser and most of the other world leaders had accepted Sarah's book of rules in principle. It was hoped that the flow of goods between Mars and Earth would be listed and controlled as Mars became more populated. This was necessary when Mars became habitable. However since there were no detectible life on its surface, that world was currently considered dead. Therefore its category would be changed from inhabitable to habitable before its listing was changed. Those rules would become established with the first inhabited dome environments. In the interim period it could be used for exploration and mining.

With all those changes due to new technologies and improvements, many wealthy organisations felt left out, while others began asking questions.

'A rich senator I know is not happy with the present LPD situation. His business did not receive concessions during the last symposium. Also, he things the guy Meron to be an imposter. He could even be an alien. He thinks he is a lot stranger than human.'

'Why do you say that?' Hal inquired.

'He is too dam clever for a human. Try to get us a DNA sample. While you are at it, get us samples of all important people in your organization. You can do some checks for us, if you like,' Powell said.

'Ok, but is he a good or bad alien? I like good aliens!'

'We can never know the difference. They might be too clever for us,' Powell replied.

'You think there could be a populated world out there?'

'There could be a complete empire out there for all we know, watching us and getting ready to take us over!'

'You sound really worried!'

'I am! Anyway, for Meron and your Boss, we don't mind paying one million dollars for their charts!'

'I better get busy then! Give me a few weeks!' Hal replied.

'Ok! I'll be waiting!'

Within two weeks Hal had all the DNA information necessary and was intrigued by Meron's chart. The charts for Dr Jeffery Longhurst and Professor Lennox were normal and so were everyone else in his company. He was not able to check the other Andromedans. They were seldom around and some always wore gloves. Meron's DNA was collected from saliva left on a drinking glass. He soon passed the information over to Professor Powell and was one million dollars richer.

Despite all their endeavours, they had enemies in the form of a few powerful organization with money enough to buy senators, so it was no surprise when they received a warning.

The phone rang and Meron answered.

'Hello Jerry!' Meron greeted the president.

'I thought you should know. I've recently heard on the grape vine that one of my Texan senators, no names mentioned, have completed a thorough search on you. I don't know what he found, but he is well in with the FBI. I shall try to put one of my security men on it, but I can't guarantee much. I think he became curious after the public demonstration you gave.'

'This is very worrying! I shall pass it on!'

'He could be financed by a few multinationals and others who were left out of our list for LPD concessions. Some of these people are notorious criminals so you should watch your back. They are not interested in the others yet, but they could start snooping around any time now.' Jerry continued.

'I could be their prime target, being responsible for the special drive!' Meron responded.

'Anyway, I've got to go!' Jerry, the president, said and hung up.

CHAPTER 33

Sarah's first outer-space journey

The Ancients had lived for five months on Earth. They had arrived about two years after Lumak's landing in the remotest hills in Turkey. At that time he took on the guise of one Doctor Jeffery Longhurst. After that time he had created a highly advanced technological infrastructure in principle, with his brand of Class 5 technologies. Like a bomb those changes were just waiting to be lit at the correct moment. Once initiated all those changes would be made without the general knowledge of Earth's human population.

It was necessary to advance all of Earth's technologies and improve on the planet's environments and ecosystems, if they were to win the war against the rapacious Javols. Those dreaded Nano-bots were currently on their way to our galaxy to destroy all naturally evolving life and were an uncompromising and completely alien species.

They saw all primal life like us as mere nutrients in their complex metabolic processes. So the bringing together of all advanced civilizations within the local galaxies were essential for our long-term survival. Therefore Lumak had chosen Earth as his first port of call during this great mission of his.

Like an unstoppable virus his technologies took over and contaminated everywhere and everything, assisted by large robots that were themselves constructed from microids. Such efficient and precise automatons could change their structures at will into any conceivable shape or form for the task in hand. They were so good at their task, that very soon human workers realized they were completely useless by comparison.

Nevertheless, the power over all such technologies always remained in the hands of mankind and all such intelligent devices realized that mankind, being Primal, was their creators and therefore their masters. In any event, Lumak had included many safety devices like computer viruses that could be initiated by a simple signal. Once initiated all such computer-based systems would stop functioning and robots crumble into dust.

Once his robot factories had begun to mass-produce those devices, with their incredible efficiencies for virtually any type of operation, every government, manufacturer and business wanted them to enhance their economies. During that period the economies of Earth soared.

Just three months after the Ancient's arrival, Laser Highways had been already installed in the sky and were in use, while normal jet planes and petrol driven motor vehicles were being turned into scrap metal for recycling.

During this period of furious expansion, large sealed domes were constructed on Mars by similar robots for Solaria and several other large mining consortiums. Even then, careful count of materials including oxygen and other gases were noted by Solarian Banking. This was an organisation formed previously by Lumak and Sarah to handle such records and finances. By so doing, all of Earth's materials could be returned in the course of time.

After the great Martian domes were completed, the enclosures with their strange brand of technology were ready to accept the Omegron Portal. It was time for this device to be installed in place within the most distant dome above its anti gravitational clamps. That was when Lumak and most of the others decided to take a short break on Mars to assist in adding the human touch to many of the domes' environments. Sealed environmental suits were subsequently added to The Ship's cargo, just in case they had to visit the planet's surface.

Those unique suits were constructed not only for Mars, but could equally have been used in almost any type of hostile environment. Alien suits being constructed in a similar manner once the relevant measurements and chemistry of its occupants were known.

Sarah also fancied a first-time space trip, so she organized the general program to include her at the helm, and was prepared to assist in anyway necessary. Lumak decided they journeyed together in The Ship in order to introduce her slowly to those new environments.

When the day of their Martian trip finally arrived, Sarah, Marian, Bawaki and others went along, with the exception of Meron and Lucia, who were then occupied on Earth with more demonstrations and conferences. Lumak was too busy at that time, so decided to remain on Earth.

Sarah and the others intended to visit the planet Mars for just one week and had taken onboard just enough rations for that period.

While they boarded, Sarah nervously walked up the glittering staircase. She soon entered The Ship's interior and began to observe one that had been described to her so many times before. In all the time since its stay at the rear of her house she had never once plucked the courage to enter into that strange environment. Presently she stood in amazement while viewing every inch of its confined spaces, observing the several large bunks, central table and large display screen. Then the smaller screen with its single helmet. No instruments or displays were visible and she assumed there was some other cabin area for driving the ship. Despite everything, The Ship's interior was quite a comfortable environment.

She had memories of shuttle pilots floating about in confined spaces, sucking their meagre daily rations out of tubes and living in complete weightless conditions. She thought she had an idea of the difficulties involved, having watched so many movies on the topic. But The Ship had no such embellishments and was purpose-built to take its passengers from one point to another in the quickest possible time, and technologically speaking, there were no difficulties in that process.

Its living quarters were more like the interior of a house, but for the closely spaced bunks and the large viewing screen. She thought the bunks were large enough to change her clothes but not wide enough for a sharing couple.

When The Ship transposed, she felt no side effects and was soon told that they had arrived within the Admin Dome enclosure on Mars. She couldn't believe the short time taken for the journey, but sighed with relief when she and everyone had arrived safely.

'The powers of advanced technology,' she muttered.

She was the last to leave the ship and while disembarking, marvelled at that miracle of science and gently tapped its hull.

'Thank you very much, for a most comfortable and safe trip, marvellous spaceship,' she said.

But to her surprise it replied:

'You are welcomed, chief councillor of Solaria!'

She was surprised by those words and quickly followed down the stairs and off The Ship. She was greeted by a pinkish Martian sky that was clearly visible through the massive transparent dome.

While inside the protective dome, they walked unto the surface of the rough and hostile planet and could observe many robots at work building more domes. She wondered how beneficial robots were in such hostile environments. They were not affected by almost any degree of heat or cold, the absence of air and sunlight, and was able to handle materials that were poisonous or hazardous to most living organisms.

'Us poor humans have wasted our time over so many millennia, constantly struggling to bring up our families. What a wasteful culture. If only we had known and could realize the uselessness of such efforts in the wake of true advancement, we could have used such machines and trained our minds for more cosmic endeavours,' she thought.

Although the ship had materialised directly within the sealed dome, there were many sealed pressurised entrances, exits and docks that gave full access to the external Martian landscape and future planetary ferries.

Once again The Ship spoke to them:

'I have been assigned to serve the chief councillor of Solaria and henceforth, I am to obey members of that council.

'My insignia will now change to the Federation's colours.'

While they listened and watched, the insignias visibly melted and changed into the new ones of the Federation.

'My first task is to install the Omegron Portal at its prescribed location.
'Merian can activate it remotely at the appropriate time.'

The Ship disappeared but reappeared a moment later at the remotest dome several hundred metres away. They could observe an eerie pulsating light coming from within that area. After a short time The Ship reappeared in front of them:

'The Omegron Portal is now in place. It has been prepared and made ready for the moment of linkage.'

In only one week most local domes and facilities were ready, but the accommodation and other materials were still being ferried from Earth on the modified LPD shuttle.

The Omegron Portal was at last floating in its dome and they were very happy, because the main evacuation program was on schedule and the Martian part of the process was almost ready. Soon, the large inter-dimensional ships would arrive to ferry the evacuees to the planet Eden, but even if they did not arrive on time, more of the less advanced LPD ships could be constructed and even those could be used to ferry people as far as Planet Eden.

CHAPTER 34

Kidnapped

Jerry called Meron's office in late afternoon that day.

'Pal, I recently heard on the grape vine that some people have completed a full search on your background and were not satisfied with the results. Suddenly a few in high places have developed an interest in you and your LPD drives. The people involved could be well in with a few foreign multinationals and others who were left out of LPD concessions. Some of these people are hardened criminals with contacts in high places, so you must watch your back. They are not interested in the others yet, but could start snooping around any time now,' Jerry said and Meron was worried.

'Ahhh! That dangerous, eh?' Meron was not pleased.

'They think you are the main scientist responsible for the LPDs. We must let them continue thinking that way. The less you say on the topic the better it will be for all concerned,' Jerry continued.

'I see your point! I shall pass the word!'

'If we give enough rope they might hang themself. I have a few cages to rattle. Let's see what jumps out. I think from now you should always wear a well hidden locator, just in case!' Jerry said.

'In that case, I shall take the necessary precautions and my lips are sealed, Mister President,' Meron replied.

When Lumak arrived home that day Meron told him what the president said.

'Pal, I think we have outstayed our welcome on this world.' The other Ancients were curious and realized something was sadly amiss. Never before had they seen Meron in such a nervous state.

'I knew it was going to happen sooner or later, but not this soon. Such computer files can never be perfectly hatched and the present-day FBI have many ways of tracing anyone's background or the lack of one. They can use some of the best technologies to find out what they wish to know about virtually any individual on this planet. Anyway, I wouldn't worry too much if I was you. We move to Eden after the evacuation and no one in their right mind will make an attempt on you while in this place, with our tight security. I think you should quickly finish off your present commitments and remain close to the Manor from now on,' Lumak advised.

'What about you? Aren't you worried?' Meron inquired.

'My credentials are impeccable. They belong to someone who died years ago. So my time-line can be traced all the way back,' he said and Meron was surprised.

'Like your brother, Plato, I am Shadite. And a Grade 1 at that. So don't you worry too much about such matters. Anyway, if they shoot you we can always bring you back to life again,' Lumak said with a grin and Meron did not relish that possibility.

'Pal, something you must always remember is that we Solarians are fearless and can do almost anything. I could easily send one of my new Primorphs into any of those buildings and when he came out it would be just a pile of rubble. We have the technologies and potentials to do virtually anything, but brute force is never the answer and is always a last resort. We have also to consider innocent lives in all this,' Lumak said.

Although Meron tried his best to keep a low profile, there were a few prearranged commitments he had to finish.

At that time Sarah and others had already left for Mars. Anyway, Lumak always preferred to handle such situations with minimal assistance. Therefore he called Plato and discussed the matter with him.

Meron's kidnapping was easy enough. Someone came up behind him as he was entering his car in one of those multilevel car parks.

'Don't make a sound. Any resistance will be futile. Just follow us,' he said in a mild voice.

Then he was taken to their car and driven to a secret location. He did not put up a struggle. Neither did he ask where he was being taken. He realized such a scenario was inevitable and expected the incident almost as if he had already visualized a replay of the complete process in his mind's eye. They quickly searched him for weapons and forced him into the back seat.

'Boss, we've got the package!' the driver said and they sped away from the underground car park.

When they were not looking in his direction he pressed his insignia which he always used as a tie clip. No one was suspicious of its use as a communicator. From that moment his movements could be traced and the group identified.

Lumak realized the kidnappers were small fry and most probably working for someone who took his orders from another even higher individual. His plan was in getting to the root of the tree to remove the pest once and for all time.

That evening he brought everyone together at the manor and told them of the incident. Meron's wife Lucia was distressed, but soon realized the situation needed planned positive actions. Lumak preferred everyone didn't become too involved to further complicate matters.

He also realized that Meron was too important as a scientist for just ransom. Neither would they kill him while the opportunity existed to make him one of theirs. That way it was going to be a lot more economical for them to use him in one of their remote laboratories. However that didn't exclude them asking for a large ransom just to muddy the waters and add a little salt to the wound. They probably needed finance to pay off a few in their criminal organization.

Lumak soon contacted Jerry on their personal line and explained the situation to him.

'I cannot trust the FBI and other military organizations in this matter. I don't yet know who is involved. It could go all the way up to senator level. Can you help?'

'Thank goodness you don't think the ladder extends to me,' Jerry, the President, said in jest.

'No! You are now one of us,' Lumak replied.

'Well, I know a good captain who is the most trustworthy with some of his men. Perhaps we could arrange a quiet meeting at my country residence. I shall arrange a time. That way no one will get suspicious. Then you can explain the matter to Mallory,' Jerry said and hung up. Lumak realized he had heard that name before but never met the individual.

Meron was taken to an old unused factory outside town where he was to be held for a while before being transferred elsewhere.

No one of his kidnappers gave their names. They were dressed in blue overalls. Their heads were covered and they held latex masks over their faces. Only their boss communicated with Meron, and he did it through a flat screen on the wall. That face was just a 3D graphics image with lip sink. They were quite clever in their planning. That way no individual could be easily identified.

Meron was soon searched again and given a package. Then he was ordered to wear the blue overall over his clothes. When they were not looking he hid the small insignia in one of his jacket inner pockets. Although it was unable to relay images, sound and position was more than enough for Lumak to retain his trace.

The flat screen on the wall came to life and a face appeared. It was graphically generated and moved in sync with the voice of the real person in another room. He tended to talk a lot, as if liking to hear his own voice and that further annoyed and irritated Meron.

'I am pleased to meet the eminent Lord Meron from England... If that's where you are from. I was the one who collected and analysed some of your DNA. A few of your chromosomes were intriguing to say the least. I expected 23 pairs but got 47 instead, with a lot more besides, with different sides, no pun intended.

'Really! You must have a vivid imagination!'

'Nano-tec and Robots are outside of my interests for now. I am convinced you and the one called Doctor Longhurst are not of this world and I can prove it. I know you are an alien human, so why don't you admit it. I did the same tests on your friend Longhurst a year ago with a drinking glass, but he appeared ok, with normal human fingerprints. However, I am convinced he is another human alien that is too clever for us to identify this way.'

'You are wasting your time! Your equipment could be faulty!'

Meron complained.

'No! We double checked!'

'I wonder how many aliens like you are presently on Earth and for what purpose. For all I know, you people could be here to plant some dangerous bug in the waters. At the very worst, you might even have one of those doomsday weapons, with the sole intention of putting us out of our misery!'

'That's utter nonsense! You must have quite an imagination!''

'Anyway, your little secret is safe for now. None of my idiotic colleagues will ever believe in such a ridiculously strange tale, about alien humans taking over the Earth. Not even if I showed them your DNA charts. I might end up looking like an ace nutter and that will do me no good. Anyway, what do I care. This planet is being irretrievably ruined by its billions of pathetic morons, anyway. You guys can have it all... for all I care.'

'That's encouraging!' Meron replied with a degree of sarcasm.

'By the way, that's another important point, I might want a way out of this planet later. Perhaps we can do a little deal for a ride out of this place. As for now, they want me to get answers from you and I must oblige.'

'No alien ships, I'm afraid, but ask me your question!'

'Nothing has yet been recorded, but when I start I would like the real questions answered, plus a few agreed favours, off the record, before we can leave this place. As for now, you may collect your thoughts and carefully prepare your answers regarding LPD technology,' the voice said and the screen went dead.

Meron had followed the presidents advice, to keep his lips zipped, but was willing to talk as much irrelevant nonsense as possible. However he realized that they would soon want answers, so his next plan was to construct a plausible story in his mind. Even so, he wanted to find out more about those involved and the real reasons behind his kidnapping

There was a clunk and a click and the thick metallic door slid open. A large woman walked in with a tray. She was also wearing a blue overall and male face mask. She placed the tray of burger and fries on a small side table and went forward to release his hand restraints. His feet was still chained but he could walk about slowly.

'Enjoy!' she said and left.

It was now late afternoon and once again the screen came on with the same boring voice.

'You know, they want you purely for your knowledge of LPDs. They hope your efforts will give them an edge over their competitors. However, I believe the real mind behind all your inventions is Longhurst. He is the one the idiots should have kidnapped, but he is always much too slippery for anyone to gain a firm handhold.'

'I did tell them! They got the wrong person!' Meron replied.

'You know, this is all set up as a proper kidnapping, because we need some ransom as well. The money will serve as finance for our new laboratory and other accrued expenses.'

'I don't have any money!'

'I am told your organization has lots!'

'Which organization is that?'

'Solarian Banking of course! I had to do some digging to find that out. By the way, I've drafted the letter with a demand for 500 million dollars. That should be enough to get us started and I'm sure if you don't, our beloved president will consider that sum petty cash for getting you back. You can give this great nation of ours a lot more, if we released you to complete your projects. Which we are not going to do.' The voice continued.

'You ask for a lot!'

'Just what we need! Anyway, what have you to say for yourself? I want answers now!' he yelled and the screen went blank. Meron remained silent. From now his plan was to keep his mouth shut until the time was right.

With his hands free, Meron was able to scan the room with his insignia device. Then it suddenly came alive.

'Place this device close to your air,' the voice said and the volume reduced.

'We have located all the ring leaders, but have no real evidence to convict them, so we shall replace the one in your place with an android. The others in your area will be tranquillised and stored for now. He is the only one that communicates with the others. Prepare for a few military freaks in fifteen minutes and keep a low profile until the job is done,' Lumak said and Meron smiled.

'They are planning to move me soon.'

'We have them all under constant surveillance. Therefore we can locate them even if they were in the deepest cave on Earth,' Lumak informed and the device went dead.

After breakfast that morning two people entered the room and took Meron to a smaller one with a swivel chair. They sat him down and connected his chains to metallic rings on the floor. Then his hands were tied to the chair handles. Near by was a small table with drug vials, injection needles and scalpels. He observed the equipment and swallowed hard.

The screen on the wall soon came alive and the same irritating face appeared.

'Good morning, Lord Meron. I trust you had a most enjoyable and relaxing sleep. This chair is more comfortable, I suppose. Sorry about the chains, but we have too much to lose if you escape from us at this time.'

'What do you want from me today!' an agitated Meron asked.

'Only a little chat!'

'Well, you've been doing lots of that recently!'

'My friend, since we leave this place tomorrow, today we talk serious business. In case you decide to keep your lips sealed, we have a range of drugs guaranteed to make you chat like a parrot. But that's going to be a last resort, isn't it?' he said.

'Ok if you insist, I will tell you everything you wish to know about the design,' Meron replied.

'That's good! When can you get started?'

'This place is really not suitable. First of all I need a computer terminal and a large writing board to structure and check my equations, before entering them in the computer,' he said and the person was agreeable to arrange all Meron's needs.

CHAPTER 35

Covert operations

The rescue meeting was held in the evening at Jerry's residence in Wisconsin and Mallory Colman brought along his most trusted lieutenants.

'What ever transpires in this place can never be discussed among outsiders. This includes spouses, family members and friends. This will be considered a top secret covert operation, and a lot is at stake. During this time, I will be your only chief of command. That way, we can have no leaks to the FBI and other relevant departments. Is that clear!' Jerry (the President) said.

'We signed the papers, Sir!' Chad barked, while remaining at attention. He was one of Mallory's most trusted lieutenants and his second in command.

'I understand, Mister President. I can personally vouch for all my guys!' Mallory replied. Then Jerry turned his gaze in the direction of one of the doors.

'Mickey! You can show us the stuff now!' he shouted. Michael Cockburn soon entered the room pushing a large casket on wheels and stopped the container in the centre of the room. He pressed a small remote key and the hydraulically operated cover lifted to reveal an assortment of weapons, body armour, surveillance devices and other gadgets.

'Guys, I don't have to remind you, all this is next generation. It's all top secret and designed specifically for covert operations. However, in this case their field use is limited to just three weeks. After that time their internal components will begin to fail. Once that happens they become useless,' he said.

'For just three weeks? No warrantee, I suppose!' Chad commented.

'Ummmm! Built in obsolescence. Lets hope this mission don't last any longer,' Mallory commented and Chad couldn't hold back a broad smile.

Mickey leant over and retrieved a very small weapon. It was shaped like a small gun, but more streamlined and designed to fit in the palm of the hand. It was kept in place by a small elastic strap.

'Don't give me those disappointing looks. Large doesn't necessary mean better and palms are seldom noticed during active duty. In this particular case, this little Twisting Viper is deadlier than any snake on the planet. It fires tiny needles which are virtually untraceable. The needles are made from Nano-bots. Each small capsule contains over 10,000 of them. Each needle has a range of 50 metres. Once you select a target, the needle will home in and find it all on its own even if the weapon is pointing in the opposite direction. So you may aim, select on cross-hairs and turn your weapon in almost any direction before firing. It will always hit the target.'

'Silent needles with in-built love. That's a new one on me!' Carl interjected.

'One more thing. This weapon is unforgiving. Once a needle enters a human body it begins a chain reaction that literally tears the body apart from inside out. You have just a minute before it blows. It's perfectly silent and cannot be felt until the damage is done,' he said and they were awed.

'Must be quite messy!' Mallory replied.

Chad quickly passed the weapon over to Mickey who placed it back in its case.

'For this mission we want no deaths, so the capsules included are just tranquillisers. They will keep the target in a dormant state for about 15 minutes. During that time they are able to speak under interrogation. If you need them to stay under longer, you simply give them another jab. There are no side effects and the target will resume normal functions afterwards,' Mickey said.

Then Mickey retrieved a black metallic suit interweaved with some form of strange flexible fibres. It covered the complete body and included integral heads-up displays and controls.

'This one is called the Devils Jacket, but it's really a suit that completely encases the body. There are numerous micro vents to regulate circulation, so it's designed to keep the body warm in winter and cool in summer. Sweat is absorbed by the Nano fibres. It is powered by a small hydrogen fuel cell coupled to a micro fusion generator. The belt carries a dozen cells and each cell will last about a week under active usage.'

Wow! And quite fashionable! I must get me one of those!' Carl commented. He was another one of Mallory's capable lieutenants, but with a love for whiskey.

'The head gear contains the usual night vision and a range of filters to locate the target. Your weapons automatically aligns to the cross hairs in your heads-up display, so all you do is move your head and fire where the crosshairs meet. It's really designed for people with Brain Implants. In your case, use voice commands. They will not be audible through the head gear. Anyway, you don't have to worry. Daisy has full control of your suits and other equipment,' he said.

'Who is Daisy?' Carl inquired.

'Daisy is short for, Digital Assistant Instrument for Searching and Your protection. She is feminine, quite beautiful and knows virtually everything about everyone on this planet,' Mickey said.

'You don't mean some bloody super intelligent female computer,' Carl commented.

'Yes, I mean exactly that. And you guys better treat her with love and respect. Don't forget, your lives may be in her hands,' Mickey said and Carl swallowed hard.

'Now carrying on... the body pads are thick and can stop sniper bullets on their own. However, it also includes a field generator that can neutralize any object that touches the field. It will stop the fastest missile. Once they touch the field all their energy will be neutralized and they will fall harmlessly at your feet under gravity.

'What if we are on top of a high building?' Chad asked.

'If the missile falls from a great height it might still go off, but that's a better risk than the other option of blowing you up,' Mickey replied with sarcasm, but continued.

'This also has a stealth mode. This will render you and all that you carry invisible. I don't mean those crude devices that bend light. This one really makes you invisible. As a matter of fact, while in this mode you can walk through walls and solid structures, even super hot furnaces. It time-phases you almost completely out of the present into a neutral space occupied by you and only you. During that mode however you cannot communicate or meet any of your colleagues. You are simply on your own and in your own little universe. You will have to spend a little while familiarising yourselves with the different aspects of this suit. Daisy will help, just call her name when you have a problem and she will advise.'

'Wow! This stuff is so out of this world! This is almost like Christmas! Without Santa Claus!' Mallory yelled.

'There are quite a lot more devices for the field, but I think I'm going to show you the last in the list. Any others can be advised on a need to know basis,' he said.

Then he retrieved a much larger item from the container.

'Yea! Now you talking!' Carl said while taking the weapon from Mickey.

'This I call the Mega-Blaster. It's a weapon of last resort and packs three different punches.'

'It's not exactly what I would call stealthy,' Mallory commented.

'No. I am afraid not. It's main purpose is to cover up when things go badly wrong. It contains a Maser weapon. This is like a microwave laser that packs quite a punch. The weapon utilizes a hydrogen cell to fuel a fusion reactor that can generate several terra joules of energy. During scan mode it is capable of taking out a crowd of a thousand people in less than a single second. The second weapon is a small missile with a warhead capable of levelling a city block. However, the size of the explosion can be adjusted.

'Further, when the missile goes off, the EMP generated is enough to neutralize all computer systems and other sensitive electronics within a radius of five miles. So it's also a communications killer.' Mickey said and they could hardly believe in the potency of such a relatively small weapon.

'I wouldn't like to see the real big ones,' Chad commented.

'No you wouldn't. We have weapons that can destroy a planet like Earth from way out in space,' Mickey replied and they were numbed by that knowledge.

'What? Bloody Hell!' Carl screamed.

'I suppose I better brief you on the purpose of your mission.
'Lord Meron has been kidnapped. Therefore use whatever means necessary to get him back. I would also like to know who is behind this farce. If any of my senators are involved I want them taken down.. you hear! There could be some hard and heavy players in this game, so be extra careful.' Jerry was firm.
'We will, Sir! We have the right tools.'
'Doctor Longhurst will update you on the location of the target and other information. He will also keep us informed with new information through Daisy, as and when it becomes available. Now, good day gentlemen!' Jerry said and dismissed the meeting.

A middle-aged bearded man soon came forward to introduce himself. It was Lumak in disguise.
'I am Jeffery Longhurst. Please to meet you Mallory. This small package will keep you up to date on progress. You should however connect it to your main computer system in an unknown location,' he said and Mickey handed him the package.
'During this operation I would like no killing. Everyone concerned must be captured and placed before our courts for a fair trial. Even if you are fired upon, your suits will protect you one hundred percent, so use your discretion in all things,' Lumak stressed.
Mallory and his group soon left the building and took a local flight to Washington DC. He rented a small apartment in one of the hotels he knew. Then he fitted a small satellite transceiver on the roof for all his outside communications. Finally he borrowed two female operatives from one of his friends in security.
'This is going to be your base for a few weeks. It's all top secret, so I want no slip-ups. Roseanne, you will be in charge during our absence, so everything comes down to you,' he said.
'On it, Boss!' she replied.
Mallory left them to man the temporary information centre.

CHAPTER 36

Surveillance and rescue

Lumak listened intently to the voice and realized it was from a person he once met in a TV studio about a year before.

'So my old friend Powell is back. I hope he is not in league with the Turkish bad guys? I thought he was in jail?' he murmured to himself.

'Clair, please run some checks for me on this guy?'

'Yes, Jeffery, I am on it... I have found all relevant links and dates.'

In a short time the information was downloaded into Lumak's brain implants.

He ran some further checks and found Powell had been recently released from prison. Lumak realized he used to be an eminent professor in genetics, with many contacts in high places, including one Senator Murray. Both were jailed about a year ago for embezzlement and other criminal offences. Murray was still incarcerated with no firm date for release. Powell had good lawyers and were released on appeal. However no one knew he was a member of the Gang of Thirteen or his associations with Dr. Hal Seaton, also a member of that organization.

'He must be quite desperate to add kidnapping to his list of crimes. Perhaps he just wanted revenge against my organization for his previous downfall. Depriving me of Meron was one of the best ways to accomplish his aims. Nevertheless, he must have other collaborators to finance this operation,' Lumak thought.

Then he realized one Senator Cleary had pushed his release and was a known associate. Then after further checks, he found the senator was in league with a large foreign oil consortium who had their head office in North Africa.

At that time several foreign countries realized their black gold was drawing thin from the well. The new LPD technology could put a stop to their dwindling revenues. Therefore drastic actions had to be taken to redress the balance in their favour. If they could get Meron to create their own drives for them, they could compete once more. What they didn't realize was that LPD technology was Class 5 and well beyond even Meron's capabilities to develop. Only Lumak, the Shadite, had the keys for that particular project. Therefore Meron's best option was to keep his mouth shut and delay them as long as he could before help arrived. So he had to pretend he was the real inventor, otherwise they would have had no further use for him.

'Hi guys,' the female said through their 3D displays and they were astounded.

'Who is this? Don't tell me... its Daisy? But you are almost real and so damn beautiful!' Mallory exclaimed. Carl and Chad couldn't help but admire the holographic female in her tight fitting outfit.

'Daisy, I didn't realize you were such a sexy female blonde with such beautiful curves,' Chad said and Carl began to sing.

'Daisy, Daisy, give me your answer do. I'll go crazy...!'

'Cut it out guys! I think Daisy wants to tell us something about our mission,' Mallory said and they stopped their play.

'Anyway, Daisy, you look good,' he said.

'Thanks guys! I always aim to please!' she replied with a sexy wiggle and they smiled.

'I thought it was time I introduced myself and brought you up to date on the mission. All the offenders have been located. However, it is essential that we find evidence, so I have concocted a plan. For it to work you will have to neutralize all the kidnappers, by putting them to sleep.'

'No problem!' Mallory said.

'Replace the one called Powell with one of our best androids. No one will know the difference. The android is being program as we speak, with Powell's basic characteristics. Lets hope his colleagues don't dig too deeply into his past while talking to him. He has been programmed with just basic records. Anyway, he is like the real Powell and waffles a lot, so he will be able to get away with virtually anything.'

'That's neat!'

'After Meron's rescue, you will go undercover as part of a criminal gang from England with some LPD blueprints to sell to the highest bidder. This will flush them out of the woodwork and give us enough information to convict them. Powell is small fry and can be securely stored and ignored for now.'

'That should shut him up for a while!'

'You guys are required at Meron's location in one hour. Here is all the information you require for this mission, including the images of Powell and his collaborators,' she said. The information was downloaded into their systems.

They were at their destination within the hour. It was in an old factory close to the docks. That area was air marked for demolition. They simply spouted nitric acid into the locks and were soon inside the building from three different points. Every operation was silent and didn't require the stealth facilities in their suits. The first one down was a male guard close to the main door. Then they entered a small room where the nurse was getting ready to give Meron his first injection. On the table were several vials of drugs and a few syringes. There were also a couple of scalpels. Mallory fired twice at her neck and she slumped.

'Thank goodness you guys are here!' Meron exclaimed.

'Just in the nick of time, are we? Keep still for a while, I have to blow your chains,' Mallory said and Meron was even more worried.

He placed a small thermic device on the metallic bangles and in a second they melted. Then Mallory removed Meron's chains.

'Captain, we found Powell. He has been replace and I turned it on, but it won't stop talking,' Chad said through his communicator.

'That's quite normal for the windbag, Powell! Get the real one down here and assist us with these bodies to the van. Roseanne and her friends can sweep this place and do some forensics for a change,' Mallory said.

Although Powell had written the blackmail demand, he hadn't

time to post the letter, so Mallory did a preliminary sweep of the area to remove any trace of their presence and collected all the incriminating evidence before the official sweepers entered the building. Anyway, the gang would get suspicious if the letter was not sent on schedule.

The information about the stolen papers were soon circulated about the criminal grape vine. Further, Lumak created a set of dud blueprints with manuals and placed a substantial ransom of 10 million US dollars for their immediate return.

For that part of their mission Mallory would take the persona of an English gangster with the documents in question. His credentials were altered to match his new criminal identity. It didn't matter too much about his lieutenants. They were playing the part of muscle for Mallory's protection.

Once the criminal gangs knew certain high level brass were involved in the LPD papers they realized the stakes were too high and the job was better left well alone.

Mallory contacted a few anonymous negotiators and settled for 50 million US dollars. The senator involved kept well out of the picture and considered himself too important to be involved in the nitty-gritty, so he employed a criminal gang to negociate on his behalf.

To guarantee his safety, Mallory agreed he would deliver the blueprints first for 20 million dollars, which was still higher than the reward. That gave them time to check the papers authenticity. If they were happy, then the Service Manuals would cost a further 30 million dollars. Anyway, he knew no one other than Doctor Longhurst could have verified those documents. They were far too complex even for Meron to decipher.

Since they assumed Meron was the inventor, he was the one chosen for the task of authenticating the documents. Therefore some of the information was downloaded to the kidnappers hideout. They Emailed parts of the blueprints to the android Powell and he took copies to Meron.

'Yea... Yea... That's definitely my work. Where did you find my papers! Even the signature is mine!' Meron shouted, acting his part to the full and they were convinced.

'You are not to worry about that for now. Not while the boss is listening to your stupid gripe.' Powell's android reprimanded.

'Ok! I'm easy!' Meron said.

'Boss, our guy checked the papers and reckons it's all his work. I must say, the signature in the bottom square is definitely his,' Powell's android replacement said. Senator Cleary couldn't hold back a grin of satisfaction. He took the papers and placed them in his wall safe, behind a large oil painting.

During all this time Senator Cleary didn't realize he was constantly being scanned by miniature bugs. They were the size of small flies and almost invisible to the naked eye. They were nano-bot bugs that could relay visual, audio and other information from the senators office. They only stopped transmitting when he placed the documents in the safe. They were so good that even the combination of the safe was recorded and downloaded to the local surveillance vehicle.

Even then the job was not done, Mallory had to complete the second delivery and the real Powell reinstated in their hideout before the troupes went in to make the arrests.

That day Mallory made sure his company wore their special protective suits with visible machine guns. He knew such criminals never gave money up lightly, not 30 million US dollars.

Once his lieutenants showed their willingness to use their weapons everyone was calm.

'Let's complete the deal as agreed. I'm sure you guys don't want any bloodshed in a public place for a measly 30 mil,' he said. The short stubby member of the gang came forward with the case of money. Mallory decided to count the bills and took his leisurely time doing so. When he was satisfied, he nodded to a distant colleague and a large case was retrieved from the trunk of their car.

His two lieutenants, Chad and Carl took the real Powell back to his hideout and collected the android replacement. Then Meron allowed himself to be chained once more to the chair. Powell had been drugged and was not himself when placed into his office. All the other staff were in the small tea room, also tranquillised. Then calls were made to the FBI and local police regarding suspicious characters in the neighbourhood. The drug was timed to bring them out at the time of the police arrival.

'Oh my God, What's happening to me?' A drowsy Powell exclaimed.

'You have been a naughty boy and is being arrested for kidnapping. Someone, please read the windbag his rights!' Mallory shouted.

'No! You got it completely wrong. I was also kidnapped by them and forced to do what I did!' Powell continued, pleading his innocence.

Mallory passed some of the surveillance information to a security chief he knew and soon the senator was being paid a visit.

'Senator Cleary, we have a search-warrant for these premises,' the officer said and he was numbed.

'I am your senator... and find this intrusion in my affairs completely unwarranted and will take it up with my lawyers. When I am through... you guys wont find work in Timbuktu,' he complained. Then Mallory came forward and showed him his special presidential badge.

'Now Cleary, I need you to open your safe. Yes, the one behind the picture on the wall over there. We have been observing you for a while and know of your involvement with Powell and others in the kidnapping of Lord Meron,' he said and Cleary was silent while opening the safe.

'You will not get away with this!' he later complained.

'Senator Cleary, it's quite strange we are able to find these top secret documents in your highly secured safe, when they were reported as stolen?' Mallory said and he was arrested and handcuffed. Soon all the others were arrested and confined for trial.

'You guys must have put it there to frame me!' he complained while being dragged away under handcuff.

The mobile phone rang and Mallory answered.

'You guys have completed your mission most satisfactorily, so the boss sends his thanks for a job well done. But I'm afraid the money and equipment must be returned forthwith. Anyway, the president has been advised to use you in future as his own independent security team, with my assistance of course and he has agreed. This will almost double your current salaries.'

'He decided? Ehhh!' Mallory replied.

'You are to deliver the equipment and Lord Meron to the manor,' Daisy said, showing her beautiful and most sexy outline on the small screen.

'That's nice. It means we are going to see your beautiful face again,' Mallory said, but Daisy did not answer.

THE REUNION

Once they were told of Meron's timely rescue, everyone waited outside the manor for his arrival. When the car arrived in the front of the house they chaired and Meron slowly inched his way out of his seat.

'The great man has arrived!' Tomas shouted and Lucia went forward to give him a hand.

'Are you ok, Darling?' she inquired.

'I have a couple cramps and muscle aches, but otherwise I feel great,' he replied. Then Lumak went forward to greet Mallory and his lieutenants.

'You guys were truly awesome. You carried out a most brilliant operation, with no lives lost.'

'Well, Sir, we had help from Daisy. Anyway, we always work great as a team,' Mallory replied.

'You guys must remain with us for a while and have lunch. We have so much to talk about,' Lumak said and they agreed.

During lunch they were a happy bunch and Mallory was surprised by Meron's colleagues. They all had penetrating sea-blue eyes and the most likeable features he had ever encountered in a human.

'I didn't tell you guys, but my wife, Sarah, was kidnapped by Columbian guerrillas a few months ago. Her father, Ben, went in and took them all out. So our organization is quite capable of taking care of its own, with a little help from Jerry, Mallory and other friends. For their services to our organization, we shall always be indebted.

'If we can help, we shall!' Mallory said.

'From this moment on, Meron may consider himself a real veteran in the services of our esteemed nation,' Lumak said and Mallory and the others cheered.

'Further, from this moment on, Jerry should be considered to be one of us, with the same privileges. Under his command, Mallory and his team will now be available for covert ops. Don't worry guys, you will always have the best equipment for the job,' Lumak said and they were satisfied.

When Sarah and the others returned after their Martian trip, they found those incidences difficult to believe.

'I want our complete security system revised and updated. Only those living at the manor must be allowed entry in future,' she insisted.

'It was all taken care of in your absence. The new Macron, Clair, is presently quite capable of handling all the manor's security from now,' he said.

Then a hologram of another beautiful woman suddenly appeared on the table close to them.

'Please to meet you, Mam. I'm Clair,' she said and Sarah almost choked on her tea.

'I am Daisy! Responsible for external security and Ops!'

'Thank you ladies for your kind assistance in those matters!' Sarah replied to both holographic computer images.

'I trust I can also assist in the evacuation program from now,' a worried Meron interrupted.

'I should hope so, after what you've been through. I want no one in this house to visit anywhere without a strong security escort from now,' she insisted and they agreed.

CHAPTER 37

Two great ships

At about 1.8 kilometres long and 0.8 kilometres at their widest cross section, they were truly monster ships and could easily contain the population of a small city.

The two great ships, Venusa and Martia, were living entities that existed on a much higher level than primal life-forms. Perhaps they could be considered dual-dimensional, with the ability to exist within several virtual dimensions at once. That was one of the peculiar qualities of the original mind seed that had grown to encompass each ship in its entirety. They had the ability to create many different worlds of Virtual Reality and learn from the interplay of such experiences. Therefore, our universe was just another in their list of possible scenarios of existence.

In conceptual terms they were at a much higher level than mere primals, including humans. If a comparison could be made by reducing humans to insects, then they could be judged human, and that comparison was not just one of form. Their minds possessed enormous depth.

Their uppermost decks were arranged in two unequal sections. The forward parts occupied almost two thirds of the volume of those enclosed sections. It was thought all inaccessible areas were reserved for alien passengers of the non-human variety.

Their forward sections were designed specifically for humans and included every Earth-type venue and facility, including schools, colleges, religious temples and churches, hospitals, recreation, games, and entertainment. Towards the rear of that section were the development and production areas which included everything required for extended tours or prolonged assignments to undeveloped or uninhabited worlds. They could equally have been used as luxurious space cruisers, battle ships or cargo transporters.

Being of a microid design their internal surfaces had a warm velvety appearance and texture that could be altered to almost any colour or pattern under computer control.

Most areas of the ships included more subtler types of microid engineering, to a greater or lesser degree. Those parts would automatically change form and texture for comfort or flexibility. They were truly unique, with numerous androids supplying the more personal touch, prevalent behind bars, at restaurants or used in an official capacity to assist and advise passengers at any time and in any situation.

The androids, unlike the robots, appeared totally human and it was not possible to tell the difference by looks alone. The ships' main goal was towards the pleasure and comfort of their numerous passengers and to maintain a safe and exciting trip towards their respective destinations.

Their controlling minds occupied the highest decks towards the front and close to their strange original mind-seeds, which since their expansion had created what they called their Mind Rooms.

Within that large area they could create any conceptual form at will for their own learning and experimental requirements, but also used a smaller area for entertaining their special guests.

Unlike the little ship, they did not melt into a stairway, but instead had many large ramps that could be released underneath or from their sides while on land or in space. Those could be utilised as small space ports or for vehicular transport.

There were many large tubular transparent elevators which descended from the ships' underbelly towards the surface. Those tubes contained many portals and were not used to physically lift the passengers to a higher deck bodily. Instead, they constantly rotated inter-dimensionally into the ships' main hallway. From there passengers could enter other portals for other destinations. That was with the exception of certain sealed areas on its uppermost deck that were inaccessible to normal passengers in transit.

Portals could be operated by keypad, voice commands or identification cards. Their internal inertial frames were in constant rotation. All identification cards were automatically scanned and read in transit, even without the knowledge of their holder. Most hallways and passages included such portals. By entering a simple code one could visibly see the passageway change into that of their new destination. However, one could not simply walk through a portal. They had to first enter an almost sealed area from where they could be physically rotated inter-dimensionally.

When the rotation was complete, they simply found themselves leaving a similar portal at their new destination. The larger portals could quite easily handle one hundred humans at a time, but the smallest could just carry three.

BAILOR'S VISIT, IN PREPARATION

Android crews had been programmed and placed on board both ships, either to operate under their own volition or their ships' overriding control.

The time had arrived for Bailor's visit, during the later part of the morning. He had decided to make the trip to Polok using his personal flagship and many awaited his arrival. Through Jon and Lira's prompting, red carpets and ramps were laid. Groups of soldiers stood on parade in their best military outfits while awaiting the arrival of a great Lodorian leader.

Their first trial run of the ships was set for that day. Jon and his companions, Malik, Bailor and Volt decided to travel with the Venusa ship. The other company would travel on Martia's ship.

Martia's ship had been previously given instructions from Jon via the master computers to take on extra provisions, building equipment and robots, for its visit to planet Eden. That visit was scheduled immediately after their first test flight. It was considered part of the greater test to assess the ships' potentials in creating a human environment on a previously alien world.

Surreptitiously, that task was really for the purpose of building a small city at a predetermined location for the evacuees from Caefon and was to include many dwellings and facilities. All necessary items were taken on board the previous day. Many were allowed on temporary loan from Malik and would be returned or replaced afterwards.

Jon had expected Eden to contain most of the essential raw chemicals necessary in processing glass, iron, bricks and other relevant building materials. Therefore, only the essential construction, production and mining equipment was loaded. They were to be operated by the extra numbers of skilled preprogrammed robots and androids. Anyway the great ships had been specifically designed for such tasks.

Malik did not know the exact reason of Jon's request for such building equipment and neither did he inquire. He simply gave the orders and it was done. There were already a surplus of such materials and heavy equipment on his world and the building program on Polok II would soon be at an end. When that happened all such equipment was useful for export and he mentioned his thoughts on that matter to Jon.

Before their departure, they had agreed that Malik and his wife, Mira, Bailor and others visit Solaria in a few months. Their visit was timed to coincide with the return of Martia's ship with the next batch of microid supplies. Malik and his wife ecstatically agreed for their extended invitation to Earth and elsewhere.

CHAPTER 38

Ships, Venusa and Martia

The Lodorians Bailor and Volt soon arrived in their small military spacecraft and were greeted by many. Malik, Jon and the others patiently stood on the makeshift platform prepared for the launching ceremony.

Jon had briefed Malik on whatever protocols he had learnt from Meron regarding the launching of spaceships but the breaking of champagne bottles were not included. Nevertheless, Malik was ceremoniously dressed in the type of attire used by his ancestors on such auspicious occasions. Jon and his companions wore well-cut grey uniforms with federation insignias just below their left shoulders. The men had broad rimmed hats and the ladies high caps, again with similar insignias in front.

Bailor and Volt were bedazzled by the beautiful rows of soldiers all standing at attention with the stately laid carpets and he was awed by it all. They walked up the ramp and were saluted by the soldiers. Then they shook hands with the group. After the initial introduction, Jon went over to the rostrum to give his introductory speech on unity, peace, love and prosperity. After he had finish the short speech, he unfolded the launching scroll and read its contents directly to the two ships, then he bowed in the Shadite's way, with his right fist on his heart.

Finally he said: 'Do you agree to these rules and obligations?'.

At that moment both ships replied in sympathy:

'I shall!'

The ceremony was complete.

Although Bailor and Volt were surprised by the talking ships, they had an inkling that something was amiss in their design from the start. After all, large parts of the instructions had been followed parrot fashion; not quite knowing the underlying principles involved. Perhaps a few mistakes lay in the construction of their intricate minds. But if they did what they were supposed to do, which was carrying passengers and materials from point A to point B, things would be ok. Anyway, why worry about possible defects in self-repairing entities. Even so, both felt slightly embarrassed.

Despite everything, Bailor thought the whole ceremony superbly done and all proceedings historically pleasant. He, of all Lodorians, enjoyed pageantry, pomp and ceremony and wondered why his race had never thought of such a unique concept before. He was soon taken around to observe and inspect the warriors and their seniors.

Jon considered playing a Solarian Anthem at the next ceremony with a Solarian band of musicians, but they still had much to learn of Earth's culture before that aspect was adopted, and a suitable anthem had to be composed for the task.

Soon after, Volt joined Jon and his colleagues in one of the large traction trucks. Bailor joined Malik in another similar vehicle. Then they rode up the large ramps into the ships. Jon, volt and company went into Venusa's ship and the others into Martia's ship.

Volt, was overwhelmed by their size and couldn't stop nodding his head in admiration as he viewed her immensity, beauty and technology.

A pleasant and most tranquil feminine voice soon spoke to them:

'You are invited for entertainment and discourse at my Mind Room.
'Please enter the nearest portal for that purpose.'

They left the truck and moved towards a large portal through a circular door. The surface rotated them around and when it stopped the door opened into a dimly lit room with a greenish glow. There were several red and white spots of light everywhere as if coming from within the hazy walls of the large room. The same voice spoke again.

'This is my learning room. It helps me come to terms with form and content. I sometimes have difficulty coping with the illogical methods of this chaotic dimension; this strange and almost singular but most natural dimension. However, I can now assimilate its workings quickly with these methods.

'I have observed some of your societies in detail and have absorbed much of your culture within my being. Finally, I am able to transfer part of myself into my specially prepared human clone for living among you.'

Suddenly the lights in the room brightened to reveal a most beautiful woman. Jon observed the enchanting figure with admiration.

'Do you find this form of myself more pleasing?' she asked.

'Yes... Very.... Is there more than one of your human forms?' he inquired.

'Personally, I prefer just one, but several other types can be produced, even other life-forms.'

She remained silent for a brief moment and an android soon entered with refreshments. He offered the drinks to each of her guests in turn. Volt's drink contained a special straw, but similar straws were also on the tray for others to use, including humans.

'I believe they are correctly assigned?' the beautiful woman inquired.

They smiled and thanked her and she showed them a settee.

'Please sit, I would like to talk and socialise with you for a while.'

A table miraculously formed in the centre of the room and the ship began to speak:

'I feel like a multitude of several. I suppose much like you, but instead you are my parts, my lifeblood. In much the same way as

you would feel about your own singular parts, I suppose?'

They were not sure what the ship meant by that statement.

'But you are not ill or unable to travel,' Volt replied, curiously.

The woman, Venusa, turned towards Jon.

'Is Solaria a beautiful place?' she inquired.

'I think the most beautiful and liveliest part of the whole universe, but that's just my personal opinion. When you visit you will see for yourself and perhaps unravel the more difficult concepts of your existence within any one of its larger cities,' Jon replied, smiling.

She shrugged her shoulders not knowing quite what he meant.

'It is also a very exciting place?' she inquired.

'Yes, and that's also another form of beauty,' he replied and she copied his smile.

Her ship then spoke again:

'You are very young and also very bright. Perhaps you can teach us more of your concepts and ideas through our human forms, also called Venusa and Martia.

'You will soon meet Martia's human form. She will visit us shortly.'

Another beautiful woman of almost identical form suddenly appeared in the room. Venusa, the cloned human form, introduced them to Martia the other beautiful cloned figure.

'Please meet my twin sister, Martia. As you see, she is very similar to myself, but for her darker hair and shyness.'

Venusa and Martia also accepted refreshments from their androids and although not familiar with the social processes involved, were learning quickly and enjoying every moment of their existence with the other human forms and of their diverse cultural notions and concepts.

It was soon time for the ships to leave dock for their maiden flights, so Martia left to rejoin her other companions on her own ship.

They did not lift off but instead transposed to Lodor III. One moment the ships were sitting on Polok II and in another they had vanished, leaving behind a small dusty storm as air rushed in to fill the large vacuum left behind.

They reappeared in one of the larger space docks on Lodor III and there decided to show their guests the more important parts of their anatomy.

The first area entered was the one occupied by the inter-dimensional drive which transposed the large bulk of the ship. While standing on the broad circular platform they could observe its complex blueish causal branches grow, interact and intersect, sometimes touching and at other times way off the mark. Billions upon billions of the branches of the causal tree constantly grew to accurately predict the next position of the ship and could pre live the future of its inertial frame between points A and B of its journey. Although in its idling mode, it was truly an incredible sight to watch. Eventually it began to absorb their minds and bodies into its causation and they were advised to leave the area.

They were then taken to another part of the ship she called the Transformation Room. There were many large dual casket-like containers mounted all around the circular room. They reminded Jon and his group of their experiences with the Megotron and Psyrotron. However the technology they were observing was over three thousand years more advanced. She began to explain the process to them.

'These dual units are used to transform any living body into another life-form or vice versa. The process is almost instantaneous and fully reversible, but masses and sexes must be equivalent for these devices to carry out the process precisely. Minds are also transformed, but with the same emotions and other characteristics inherent in the primary form. In this room, many can be transformed at once, as and when required,' she said.

Volt was excited by the strange technology and thought of the difficulties involved in transforming his type into the much larger human form. Furthermore, in his case sex did not apply because his species had become sexless. Nevertheless, a human body could be grown for that purpose with slight alteration to include his brain.

'Can you also store their information for future re-creation?' Jon inquired.

'That action is automatically carried out when the process is complete, but if you need to transform for its own sake, you can simply transform to your own self. A similar method is used for adding certain types of body parts and implants,' she replied. Jon swallowed hard and observed the strange equipment with trepidation.

Venusa then took them back to her special room.

'I can show you a clearer picture of the complete ship from here and re-create forms visually and structurally within this area while we relax in comfort,' she said.

That option was preferred by them rather than physically visiting each point throughout the length and breath of the large ship, even while using portals.

Apparently, the uppermost deck was reserved for special friends, diplomats and their families. The cabins closest to the Mind Room were reserved for their most important guests.

After the ships had landed, news of their arrival was soon received by Stradon. He was left in charge during Bailor's absence and soon arrived to join Bailor and the others. They were able to transfer to either of the ships through their portal systems. Like identical twins both ships were almost identical, but for their individual personalities, which were quite different and that aspect also showed in the decor and other subtler aspects of their designs.

Stradon was amazed by it all. He soon left and both ships arrived on the planet Safon where they docked to observe the great installations now presently under construction. Finally they return to their original positions on Polok II.

There were no great performances in space, neither were there any visible signs of incredible speeds during flight. Nothing of excitement during their long trips had occurred. Their brand of technology was almost instantaneous. Therefore they had little reason to travel within interstellar space, being able to transpose directly from surface to surface. That simple operation could be easily accomplished once supplied with the necessary dynamic maps of their journey. Most regional galactic maps had already been implanted within their memories during their initial programming and those could be constantly updated during the course of their travels.

They were flexible in design and could make accurate positional adjustment during the transposing process. Their hulls consisted of gravitational deflectors, which could during their solid phase, deflect asteroids or themselves away from larger bodies without even their passenger's knowledge of such manoeuvres.

That very same evening Malik had his palace warming party. Bailor, Volt, Venusa and Martia attended.

As Sarah's deputy acting on the behalf of Solaria, Jon gave another one of his grand speeches, during which time he presented Bailor with a beautiful porcelain statue of the Greek God Neptune. Jon subsequently explained the historical significance of the sculptured object and Bailor became very curious and interested, being hungry for more information on the subject. He looked forward to his future trip to Solaria and Earth. That was after things had become more normal between both systems.

The party with its Earth videos and music went quite well and Bailor and Malik were satisfied with the results of that historical day.

CHAPTER 39

Changes in form and nature

A few days later Jon and the others packed their belongings and presents. They said their sad farewells to Malik, Mira and a few local friends before entering the great ship, Venusa, for their return trip to the Solar System.

Martia's ship had to leave immediately for planet Eden, but did not wish to miss any of the excitement with Jon's companions aboard Venusa's ship, so her human clone Matia decided to remain with the young group.

Multitudes were at the dock to see their well-loved visitors off. This time the Lodorian, Volt, gave the sendoff speech amidst lots of cheer.

Jon asked Venusa's ship whether she could take a route via Tarran II, the hostile desert world of cats, because he wanted to learn more about its natives and cultures out of personal interests for Bawaki's people. He wanted to gain first hand knowledge of their customs and habits.

Venusa's ship soon displayed all relevant cultural and sociological data of Tarran's life-forms on a large screen. They were amazed by the numerous variety of life, which made Earth's most ferocious appear like tranquil pets by comparison. It showed detailed information on all its most predominant species including the large bat vultures and scaly monsters. Almost every creature on that world was uniquely hostile. While they viewed the information, Venusa's ship interrupted:

'I am also personally interested... but only females may visit Tarran, because it is a female's world... Even in transformation this world is too hostile for the human form. All superior life-forms are mostly carnivores and will devour you on sight.

'They are probably the most efficiently ferocious and hostile hunters within the galaxy. With senses trained and sharpened to

expertly exercise that skill... but if your female friends are interested... we.... I mean our human persons could also join them to form a hunting party. It is now spring on Bawaki's part of that world and also the time of the great hunt when the young hunters make their name.'

They hesitated for a while, but Lira showed keen interest.

'Why not?' she said, turning to Venusa's clone.

'Will we have severe problems surviving in their cat-form?'

'Yes, but if for some reason your life is terminated, due to an accident or predation, your identity vectors can be suspended in time for the short period of one deton, which is just about one-point-six Earth days. After that time we shall have to leave quickly if we are to guarantee your continued survival within this plane of existence. In other words, if you were killed or had an accident and died, then it would be up to the Grand Lord to place your original identity back within this dimension and into a revectored body. However, during the short period of one deton's suspension your bodies may be reformed without the Grand Lord's intervention,' Venusa's Ship replied.

The girls weighed the situation and finally decided to make the daring choice for the risky adventure.

Venusa's Ship could not just transform her four female companions and her human form into cat-women. She required a live specimen to act as a template during the conversion process.

She eventually found Shadite Bawaki's physical and psychological profiles through the Greater Mind and although the information she received was not sufficient for perfect revectoring, she was able to create the most essential attributes required for the hunt.

It was a known fact that cat-people had litters of more than five kittens on occasions and most of the females tended to look alike anyway, so she decided to transform everyone in Bawaki's image, but with small differences in height, slenderness and subtle variations in facial hair colouration. Their brains would contain all of Bawaki's hunting skills, language, social interactions and emotions, with the exception of the small conscious core which contained the psyche of the original human beings.

Venusa's Ship could then visualize a functional model and she explained the basic process to the ladies, who subsequently agreed.

The only additional items required were clothes and hunting weapons, but those could easily be fabricated by robots within the engineering department of the ship.

Jon, Merol and Ecrol were not happy with the girls' decision. That adventure appeared to be wroth with all types of hidden dangers, but when the girls made their minds it was usually advisable to accept their judgement. Negative pressures only made them more determined to follow their decisions through to the very bitter end, and Lira tended to lead them on, being always the most determined.

'Ha! ha! ha! Fancy being cat-women for a change. This should make for the greatest adventure of our lives! I think we should also take some protective gadgets and medicine along in case of poisonous bites and infection,' Lira said with a glare in her eyes and Julia, Petra, Venusa and Martia couldn't help but smile at her determination.

Their cat-women forms would closely match their original build, so even in that form their differences could be observed from a distance.

Jon asked Venusa's Ship whether he could attempt a rescue mission to assist if they got into trouble, but she did not like the idea. She soon asked the girls, who gave a blatant no to any such male interference on a female world. Nevertheless the men were allowed to view the women experiences on the large screen through stereoscopic helmets.

After the five women were transformed, the ship scanned the desert floor, searching for a suitable hunting sight of crustacean mulloks returning to the surface. When Venusa's Ship detected the relevant signs, including a small group of isolated hunters, it was time to land her cat-women.

CHAPTER 40

A race of prides

CAT CULTURE

Tarran was an incredibly harsh and hostile world and reflected that harshness on every part of her surface area. The planet was a little larger than Earth and slightly further from her parent star, which was over twice as massive as our sun. That star, although younger was a lot more erratic in its output than Sol, Earth's sun. To add even more variables to the world's already unstable weather pattern was the presence of a second remote star. Those formed a binary system. The more distant one was not as massive as our sun and being far away had a lesser effect on that world, even with a slight elliptical orbit.

The planet itself was part of a quintuplet system. Tarran contained two large moons, each following completely different orbits at differing rotational velocities. The system so formed was extremely turbulent to say the least and as a result, Tarran became evolution's paradise; although a survival nightmare to those evolving. Paradise lasted for the first four billion or so years, until its large oceans began to evaporate and most of its more natural ecosystems, plants and animals became extinct. This was partly due to its erratic magnetic fields, which were never as strong as Earth's.

After the initial period of full-blown evolution, the system went into another one of its abrupt shifts due to another stable change in the star's output and most of the less equipped survivors suddenly became extinct, leaving behind the most suited to survive on a much harsher world.

Where those original great oceans once lay were now deserts of sand, but still containing many surviving forms of crustaceans. Those had evolved new structures and habits to aid in their survival within the deep ocean waters that still remained well beneath the desert's sands. There were also a few small seas and lakes that had been formed in more solid rock basins. Those catchment areas would be filled after the late spring rains and remained almost that way throughout the year.

Around those green fertile areas the remaining animals and bats competed for survival and here the strongest settled.

Her most fertile valleys were equally hostile. Here, carnivorous cats and others of every shape and size roamed in search of prey. That was assuming they themselves were not the first prey of the hunt. Yet, being sparsely populated, the planet allowed some a better survival chance and those found a niche for themselves. Within that very tight niche they became more intelligent and in so doing, built protective structures like walled castles against the extreme daylight heat and predators. Such enclosed cities were constructed mainly out of sun-baked mud, straw and cut stones.

Unlike the lower cat animals, the cat people were more like Earth's mammals, highly intelligent and seldom warlike or malicious within their own tribes. They respected each other's territories almost religiously. That factor alone assisted their survival into what they were today.

While on Earth some primitive apes evolved into our human species, on Tarran even the predecessors of apes would not have lasted long, leaving the planet to the more efficient cat species. Those ferocious predators now dominated the most fertile land surfaces.

The ancient cats took several branches in evolution. One of the more pleasant branches led to the cat-people. The females were slightly taller than Earth's humans although somewhat lighter, with razor-sharp claws on their strong webbed fingers. Claws existed to a lesser degree on their toes which they clipped, causing them to retract. Those evolving changes began when they started wearing feet protection in the form of leather sandals and thick leather sleeves.

To outsiders their physical characteristics were similar, differing mainly in height and size. Their chosen means of visual identification was by facial hair and metallic identity bracelet (hand-band). Their emotions could be transmitted to others of their clan by modulating those facial hairs in certain ways. In a similar way to human facial movements.

Since ancient times they had begun to clip their toe claws and curl their two long facial whiskers which tended to get in the way when they were not hunting. However such practices subsequently grew into social etiquette.

When compared to humans their race was extremely agile and quick, with a top running speed in the region of sixty miles per hour, with reserves.

The females or cat-women played the dominant role. Their males or cat-men were docile, although skilled in industry and castle construction. They also handled the day to day running of their castles and the affairs of their females.

The young cat-women who had not yet been ceremoniously bonded and joined with males would assist in the care of the young cat-children and teach them the skills of hunting. Any border disputes would be quickly resolved by those ferocious female warriors and yet they were very protective of their children and males.

They were not yet technological in the truer sense of the word, but could make explosives and construct crude weapons from iron, copper, bronze and gold. Any real knowledge of mathematics or of the sciences were unknown to their culture. To us they would be like pre industrial or medieval man.

Cat-people used many lesser cat animals to pull their wooden carts and to assist in hunting or as pets. They employed their criminals and weaker members as slaves, to operate their grain mills and for menial jobs. That aspect was considered more compassionate than leaving them out in the deserts to be eaten by other cats and bat-vultures.

Unlike Earth, with its many species like dogs, cats, horses, cows, and others that had been domesticated and used by man. On Tarran all those numerous animals had evolved from the cat family to fill every conceivable niche in the planet's ecosystems.

Cat-people had a highly organised society, with many

experienced cat-women always out guarding their borders, exploring, hunting or gathering within the hills and desert regions. Occasionally large hunting expeditions would leave their walled cities for weeks at times during the colder and wetter seasons. During that time most wild life would water closer to their own habitats and well away from castles and walled cities. At other harsher times the periphery of their walled cities were often the feeding ground of all types of scavengers and opportunist, including carnivorous snakes and bat-vultures.

Their favourite hunting animal was the cat-dog. That animal was very agile and extremely ferocious, but essential once trained because of their unique sense of smell, small size, flexibility and obedience. While wearing suitable cladding they were used to sniff out small creatures from holes and burrows in sand and rock.

Cat-people's favourite weapon was the hunting bow, but they also carried poisonous darts with a sling, and a long sharp knife made from iron and bone. The knife included long teeth on the outer edges for removing shells from desert crustaceans like mulloks, which to them were the greatest delicacy of all.

The mulloks occupied the main desert regions well away from their peoples' fertile settlements. Once each year those turtle-like creatures with long retractable stinging tails would surface to lay their eggs in the hot surface sands. Since they could not survive for long in the extreme heat, they would complete the process as quickly as possible before returning to the watery depths beneath those desert regions to live in safety until the following year.

Once the eggs had hatched the small mulloks would follow the path of their parents towards the watery deep. Mulloks were very seasonal, being only available during late spring. As a result, several lookouts were positioned throughout the deserts' rim, watching and listening for any signs of mulloks' activity.

They had just a few hours to complete the hunt, starting from the moment their sensitive trackers detected the rumbles on their specially tuned drums. Using large mirrors mounted on poles they would signal the hunting parties. Then they would enter those desert regions on the back of cat-horses to dig trenches and prepare for the harvest. Large nets would subsequently be laid in dug out trenches to catch the unsuspecting mulloks on their return journey.

Mulloks fetched high prices within the more fertile northern markets, so the cat-women made an enthusiastic effort towards the harvest. The size of the catch reflected the strength of their clan and there was much celebration after a successful harvest.

At that time of the year there were always much competition between the clans to prove themselves during the hunt. Others would make a name for themselves by heroic deeds. Although they seldom fought each other, this was their way of gaining respect among their tribes. Such respect brought them concessions from their neighbours and from the northern wealthier clans.

CHAPTER 41

A dangerous harvest

It was a late spring morning on Tarran when many groups pursued the annual hunts into the deserts. Close to a well-trodden path stood three cat-women. There they patiently waited for others to increase their number before entering the treacherous northern pass. Alone and without cat-horses they were astonished by the bizarre antics of a seemingly large star. It travelled just ahead of them but when it approached within arrow range it appeared to be a large shiny object that skimmed the desert's floor as if searching for something. Then the object hovered towards their location under its own power, until abruptly stopping in mid air.

With a blinding flash the strange glowing object disappeared with a massive gust of air, leaving behind a much smaller craft that slowly descended towards them. Cat-women were seldom taken to uncontrollable bouts of fright. Neither would they ever surrender their catch to anyone, not even under threat of death, but here was a strangeness they could not explain nor imagine.

For a brief moment they remained frozen in their tracks, utterly confused by the aberration. Slowly, and mostly out of fear, they recovered from their shock and began to shoot their arrows towards the object, screaming and screeching in their fiercest manner. But the brilliant object still came towards them, apparently untouched.

When it landed a side entrance opened and five cat-women descended its ramp. To their further surprise the object vanished from sight as if by magic, leaving behind a small sand storm in its wake. After the sand dispersed and settled, the five strange cat-women figures were left standing in its place. The three snarled, growled and screeched, moving further backwards as they did, with sharp menacing claws and more arrows ready, but a voice shouted to them.

'I am Princess Bawaki of the Marawi Clan! I am here to join you for the hunt! Will you join us for a rich harvest? We have observed signs of numerous mulloks about to swarm just below the plateau. It's only a few miles to the north.'

They were surprised and remained still for a moment to judge the situation. They whispered a few words to each other and the strongest one came forward.

'We have heard of the great Princess Bawaki. Her name is legendary throughout the length and breath of these lands as the greatest hunter. But we have also been told that she was taken away by the gods. Are you her god-self and are your friends also god-cats?' she inquired.

Venusa-Bawaki, now acting the part of the real Bawaki had the situation under control.

'We have come from the stars and are looking forward to the hunt,' she replied.

'You do not answer my question, but if you come from the stars you must be gods and are therefore god-cats. My name is Biluchi and this is my little talkative sister, Caldi and my close friend, Matbi. We are from the Chaldori clan. Both our clans have been friends in the past... but I am not sure of our god clans,' Biluchi replied.

'To show you that we are still good friends, you may have my golden bow and arrows in exchange for yours,' Venusa-Bawaki replied.

It was then quite common for hunters to exchange weapons before the hunt. Weapon sharing was considered a sign of friendship and trust between strangers.

Biluchi came forward to observe the powerful bow and precise arrows. She could not believe that such items could ever have been made by members of any clan on her world or indeed any other. She bowed to the group of five and so did the others.

'Dearest and great ones, let us be your humble guides on this great hunt, to protect you in the bad lands, if and when you have need of us.'

Both women then exchanged bows and arrows and decided to follow a path towards the north.

The eight cat-women shouted:

'Wawi! wawi! wawi!' which meant,' hunt, hunt, hunt,' and Biluchi stretched her paws out to test the golden bow.

'Follow me, little sister!' she commanded her sister Caldi and they went off towards the distant desert floor while searching for hidden dangers as they progressed, but now a lot more confident in the company of supposed gods. Even so, they realised any journey on foot, as opposed to riding the large cats, would have given them a much lesser chance of survival.

That planet was composed of very extreme features, with great mountains and plateaus. Some extending miles into the clouds and dark valleys and chasms that were miles deep, scarring the planet's crust in all directions. Some so deep, their residents never saw daylight. Those were the pit-lands and they had to pass through one such area along a hazardous trail before climbing unto the desert's plateau from the southeast. Although there were many scaly sand snakes, they were not the horned jumping type and could not penetrate their thick leather sandals and sleeves, so they persevered.

Venusa-Bawaki had taken along all necessary anti-serums and Martia-Bawaki some nutritional and anti dehydration additives which they kept in their leather pouches. Therefore they were relatively safe from those comparatively minor problems.

The larger pits were the haunts of the great scaled beast and monsters that lived among the large rocks. Those resembled giant reptiles and could not easily be harmed by sharp arrows because of their dense armour. Such beasts preyed on anything that moved and cat-women were one of their favourite delicacies.

It was sometimes necessary for the cat-women to sacrifice one of their own kind in emergencies. Such sacrifices were necessary in order to give the others time to escape. Usually the smallest or weakest would be chosen and that individual would automatically move forward to lead the group and be sacrificed. Such offerings were considered honourable and godlike, with a major part of their gains left to the family of anyone so sacrificed.

That day, Biluchi insisted that her little sister, Caldi, walked twenty paces ahead of their slightly scattered group. They paced nervously with arrows in paws, ready for the slightest sign of danger while they approached a narrow pass.

Biluchi had hung her special quiver on her back at its optimum position for quick retrieval of the special arrows and had one arrow loaded and ready. She watched every movement of her little sister as she entered unto the narrow pass while they sniffed and checked the area for certain tell tale signs.

Adrenaline or its equivalent flowed in pints as they waited furiously for something to happen. It was not long before a long crimson tongue shot out from behind a large rock towards her little sister. She was too slow to escape its coils.

As the tongue made contact, it slowly began to wrap its victim in its folds, pulling her ever tighter between its coils before being drawn into an enormous ravenous mouth with fang-like teeth.

Biluchi knew what to expect next and seized the moment quickly. She slid past the folding tongue, hoping other tongues were not also ready and waiting. Luckily no others appeared while each of her companions followed through the narrow path. When the last one had passed the monster's trap, she made an arrow fly towards its head.

Its mouth was open, ready to accept its live and screaming meal, but it was quite surprising what happened next.

'Take that! You diabolical monster!' she snarled, while aiming as accurately as she could for a spot between the monsters eyes and trying to miss her little sister, Caldi.

As the arrow made contact its point became like a bright flame and that part of its head simply exploded into hot gasses. Its long severed tongue being left all alone to uncoil and release its strong hold from around her little sister. Although feeling crushed to the bone Caldi's small size was to her advantage and she was unhurt.

'Oh God of all cats! I thought I would be dead for sure!' she exclaimed, with almost tearful eyes.

'Still your whining! We are now among gods!' Biluchi rebuked unconcerned, while assisting her nervous sister to her feet and dusting her down.

'This is truly a weapon of all weapons. It also fires lightening bolts and bombs!' Matbi could not believe what she saw.

The cat-women went forward to observe the almost headless monster and Biluchi cautiously stretched her paw forward to retrieve the special arrow which to her overwhelming surprise was undamaged by the kill. She and the others removed some of the monster's shell as souvenirs of their first kill of the hunt.

'You did him well!' Lira-Bawaki commented, which to Biluchi was a god compliment and she bravely collected her weapons for their next encounter.

'It was the incredible arrow that killed it! With such weapons we stand a good chance of getting through.' Bawaki said.

They soon realised there would be many such traps with tongues to follow throughout the long route, so they took it in turn to act as bait and followed cautiously unto those narrow snared passes. They realised they were to expect the very worst; for this was Tarran. Next time their cat-women bait was well rapped with ropes and soft hunting bags. They retained their knives in paws to inflict as much damage possible to those unsuspecting monsters.

It was not long before another woman was caught. This time it was Venusa-Bawaki. Lira-Bawaki and Martia-Bawaki both let their arrows fly towards the animals eyes with similar explosive results. They soon realised that out of the five snares encountered only one was unoccupied at the time of their passing and four monsters lay dead. Luckily for those cat-women their snares were a great distance apart and the monsters were solitary hunters.

'Thank goodness we have passed that dangerous area. I was beginning to think we would never make it out of there on foot,' Lira Bawaki said. Although they were compelled to kill those creatures, being the only way out, they soon realized in all probability they were an endangered species and wanted never to sacrifice another one during their efforts. However that was the brutal ways of that world; to survive or be killed.

Biluchi and her two companions would show their gratitude to their godlike friends by hugging them after each ordeal. They realized that without their special arrows they would surely have been devoured at the onset.

After a short vertical climb they arrived at the lower edge of the desert's plateau. At that moment they knelt to say a prayer to the great one and shared some rations before continuing towards the higher plateau. It was just before the desert proper where the mulloks were scheduled to appear.

Moments later the cat-women were on the desert plains. Biluchi removed a net from her large bag and spread it out in an area of loose sand. Then she began to explain her own method of net laying to her company. They were to dig narrow ditches with their paws and lay the nets along its length, then conceal the nets by covering them with sand. Finally marking their positions by planting arrows at their borders. They travelled to the area where the swarm was expected.

They began to dig the long trenches with paws and knives. After they were finished and almost completely dehydrated, they filled them with sand and marked the spot as she had advised. Finally they erected a small tent and laid a net beneath with leather bags for protection against the stinging tails of the mulloks and waited.

Just before the mulloks began to surface the desert floor thundered as the sand vibrated, sometimes containing sandy waves like the sea, and then suddenly they shot out of the sand in waves after waves. While in flight they laid their eggs in the hot sand and plunged back into the sandy depths to return to their almost nonexistent ocean that was deep beneath. Some were caught on their way down, entangled by nets. Those would beat themselves exhaustively and suffocate in the hot dry sand of the desert.

To Lira-Bawaki and her Solarian companions, the process was almost0 akin to catching fish in the seas and oceans of Earth. Catching mulloks in the sandy oceans of Tarran was very much like sea fishing with nets. However the water was replaced by fine sand.

Although the sun was hot, it was late spring. During that season it was mostly cloudy with occasional rain, even in the desert, so they could survive for a while if they were sensible. Their main problem would be the sandstorms which could be faintly observed in the distant horizon. Even those deadly storms could be avoided if they remained close to the desert's rim. The rains would also help to wet the sands and minimise their hostile powers, and so they thought.

'Be careful. We must send a walker to check for quicksand. Only the areas of our nets are safe and we have to walk across dangerous areas to get to them,' Biluchi said. Caldi, being always their faithful stooge, put her paws down and was quickly nominated for the task. 'Be extra careful! Watch your step in the loose sand. There can be deep cracks and quicksand left by the flood of mulloks!' Biluchi warned. Then she showed a special determined expression to her little sister.

'Not again and again and again!' Caldi complained.

'Come on, little sister, stop your bellyaching! We can always pull you out!' Biluchi grumbled. Matbi was the quiet one.

'Don't worry. Tie this rope about your waist. Then if you fall in we can pull you out!' Lira-Bawaki shouted, then handed her a thin nylon rope.

Her little sister Caldi was soon on her way to collect from the most dangerous areas.

They tied two long ropes about her waist, placing her on a double leash. She took a specific route towards the furthest nets. The path she took, if found to be safe, was well marked and would be followed by all. Mulloks tended to create crevasses in the sands on their way down and those areas could become like quicksand and suck any unwary hunter into the depths to their death. So all such places had to be found and avoided.

The cat-women collected their arrows and began to dig into the sand with knives and paws. Firstly they remove the mulloks deadly tails and then their shells.

Their fleshy parts were drained of body fluids, dried and stored in small leather bladders. That rich but salty cocktail would be drunk when thirst demanded. The remaining pieces of meat were dried in the hot sun to further reduce their size and weight. Several of the largest shells were modified for use as protective shields on their homeward journey. Those mother-of-pearl shells were valuable items that could fetch high prices and had other more important uses than mere protection from the elements. The deadly mulloks' tails contained certain toxins that could be used for medicine.

After the mulloks' meat had been dehydrated, they said another prayer to their deity for the richest harvest they had ever experienced. Their spirits were high due to their overwhelming success that day. The dried meat was loaded into seven large sacks for seven cat-women. A nominated member would act as tracker. That one was Venusa-Bawaki and she walked freely ahead of the main group, searching the sand for dangers while pacing with uncertainty her newly formed path.

It was not long before she called the group together.

'I have been considering our dilemma and three choices exist for our journey home: our original route, with the scaled monsters now waiting for revenge in greater numbers; the northern desert tribes and clans, who will without doubt confiscate most of our rich catch, if not all, and that route will take us an extra large moon cycle. Finally, we can take a further unknown risk and follow the uncharted route along the desert's floor on the side of the great trench. That route will take us just four days, saving us one day before our arrival in Marawi City.'

'That route if it exists, is unknown!' Biluchi interjected.

'I agree! I am not sure whether a route exists along the great trench, which extends to within half days journey from Marawi City. Nevertheless all ways are high risk and this new one will be untrodden,' she said.

The cat-women pondered their choices and finally agreed to take their chances in uncharted territories which could save them a day. In that hostile desert a small part of any day could make the difference between life and death. In any event, all routes were fraught with unknown dangers.

'Let's hope we find a shorter route home. From what I can observe in the distance, this part is free of high mountains. We can see for miles in that direction,' Biluchi said, but as always on Tarran things were quite deceptive.

Although cat women were at times considered hard and vicious, they were also honest and trustworthy. Always willing to sacrifice their lives for the survival of their friends and family.

They were children of their world and blended well with its harsh environment as best they could, but their unique human qualities of love made their survival bonds much stronger. Whatever they took from their world, they returned. They never killed anything for the sake of self-indulgence. There was always a survival requirement, making their species a model to observe by way of speed, agility and efficiency.

CHAPTER 42

The giant spider's lair

Two days into their return journey, they stealthily sauntered through the desert with mulloks' shells covering their heads and shoulders for shelter from the sun's extreme radiant energy. Although they wore straw hats, the shells significantly reduced direct radiation.

Biluchi had at that time taken over the role of guide. While trekking several paces in front she nervously held her bow and arrow ready in case of immediate dangers.

They had arrived close to the chasm's wall so she suddenly stopped in her tracks and waved the others to do likewise. Their nervousness had been triggered by a sudden change in the environment. It was sensed by a strong stench of ammonia, with bleached skeletons scattered in that area.

She began to comb the surroundings, sometimes on all fours, listening and searching for any tell tale signs of danger, but she could observe none in the profusely rank air. Instinctively they became fearful of whatever lay ahead. Such bones and smells were usually associated with living predators and death.

Further, they realized their recent meanderings had been too easy. That part of the salient desert had become too tranquil with unexpected patterns across the desert's sands. They could sense death in that pungent smell which permeated the almost still air of that part of the desert. It apparently emanated from the darker patches ahead.

They had little choice but to enter unto that forbiddingly darker surface which was covered by more solid pancake sand, interspersed with normal desert sand. That view extended as far as their eyes could see, with even more larger parches of normal desert sand, contrived by wind to form an orange pattern of waves.

The surface they entered felt solid enough underfoot but drummed slightly as they walked. They had never before encountered that type of pattern, but decided to follow and straddle the narrower ledge along the chasm's wall for greater safety.

They could have travelled one more day without food and water, but decided to halt for a while to take some rations before continuing. They felt in dangerous territory and in their opinion, it was much better to face the enemy with a full and rested stomach, although not intentionally add to its future meal.

Having travelled another day along the desert's rim and almost three days into their journey, they had to divert sharply for several hundred metres. That new route guided them into the more solid but darker area that seemed firmer underneath. It did not contain the usual abrasiveness of sand, and they decided to follow its more acceptable surface for a while.

However by so doing they receded ever further away from the ledge. The very rough shoulder continued to widen, as if guiding them on purpose away from the rocky ledge towards the centre of that area. Bravely they continued onwards, still hugging the rough shoulder of more solid and slippery rock material as they went.

When it happened it was sudden. The ground in front of them opened up while a deep chasm began to move irreversibly towards them.

'Oh, My God! What's happening?' shouted Lira-Bawaki. But it was already too late.

They were stunned in their tracks and too tired to take any abrupt action, even to turn around and retreat. They found themselves falling from a great height into a large elastic net or web of some kind. Glancing towards the light in the roof from where they had fallen, they watched in terror at a giant sand spider while it dissolved and repaired its damaged lair.

There were several of those creatures as far as it was possible to see in the dimly lit cavern. All those spiders waiting patiently with sensitive feelers touching their roof for the slightest vibration or signal from life on the desert floor above. Once that life was sensed they would instantly dissolve their surface doorway to let their unsuspecting prey fall within their deadly snare.

The frantic and struggling cat-women caused even greater entanglement by the self-tightening web. Their large packed bags and hunting equipment further assisted the process.

The lower surface of the great cavern appeared to be another five metres below the net. Where they hung was about ten metres from the false desert floor above.

The webs were attached to several thick poles acting as support for the floor above. Those poles appeared to be very smooth and extremely difficult to climb, even by cat-women. Nevertheless if it was possible to escape that way, how could they have prevented the other spiders from being aroused while they crept along the dark surface above.

They contemplated their dilemma with the realization that they were in very serious trouble. Venusa-Bawaki tried with extreme effort to free herself from the ropes, but the harder she tried the more the web took up the slack to tighten about her even more. Realising the nature of the problem she remained perfectly still and whispered to her companions.

'Do not struggle! Remain perfectly still! The ropes are alive and will take up any slack,' she insisted.

They were in mid air and supported by the great web, which was held about five metres above the apparently solid surface below. They could faintly observe that surface, covered with large spider droppings and skeletons of all types of creatures.

The light from the dissolved floor above reflected from impatient eyes lurking in the silent darkness beneath. Those same eyes belonged to the many desert cats and scavengers should they fall from those nets. There they patiently waited for the rich pickings that would ensue soon after the spider had finished its repairs.

The cavern cats were not coloured orange like those in the desert, but was instead shiny jet black like the giant sand spider. They were the size of small hunting cats and appeared much more ferocious.

In one of the corners beneath the web stood a large container about two metres tall which they thought was one of the spider's eggs waiting to be hatched. Each egg could contain dozens of such spiders, and was there a second companion? The mate of the spider above?

Those thoughts passed through Venusa-Bawaki's mind as she pondered a way out of their present dilemma.

That place was cleverly designed for the sole purpose of capturing and holding prey, and the complete area had been cunningly concealed and prepared for that sole purpose.

The large spider had by now almost completed its repairs and still dissolving the composite mud between its large hairy mandibles. They realised there was little time before it descended for its first meal, mulloks included.

The light within the chamber was now dimming as it added the final touches to the surface above, but not completely. There was some faint diffused light radiating from the thinner hard surfaces above. Their large pupils had to significantly adjust to that much lower level.

They were more or less randomly distributed on the almost horizontal web. All things considered, Venusa-Bawaki realised the spider would eat them individually. However it could preserve their bodies by injecting them with neuro-toxins. That way their bodies could be saved for later, when it was hungry. Most probably they had the ability to save some for later months. After all, some of those creatures were highly intelligent, devious in their survival methods and knew how to get the most out of their harsh environment. Those survival factors would have doubly applied to their essential food supplies, which appeared to be an exceedingly rear commodity in those parts, despite their relatively high numbers.

Venusa-Bawaki accepted the worst case scenario which she whispered to her other companions, but could not find a way out of the clever trap.

After their accident all their arrows had fallen out of their quivers unto the floor beneath the web. However Venusa-Bawaki still clung unto her bow. Her knife was not accessible while her paws were held firmly in front of her body by the strange, almost live ropes of the web. Yet she had a small device in her hunting pouch which she was just able to acquire.

'Got it!' she shouted as the others turned their heads in her direction.

'A little magic box, I suppose? Nothing else will work in this place!'Matbi inquired.

'It's more than that. It's a lightning box from the gods!' Lira-Bawaki replied.

The spider had finally completed its task, cleared its mandibles of the sticky mud and saliva, including a few whiskers and was beginning to descend via one of the poles closest to the centre of the web where Lira-Bawaki lay. Lira-Bawaki, also with her bow in paws said her prayers, mumbled something and resigned herself to the inevitable. But with stun resolve to never give up the fight, even unto death. Anyway, how could she fight?

The more she struggled, the more the web ropes would tighten. It was just a matter of time before she met her maker, or so she thought.

'Catch!' Venusa-Bawaki said and through the box to Lira-Bawaki. Her cat reflexes were swift.

'Got it! Now lets have some fireworks, you bloody monster!' she shouted.

Hardly seconds passed as large mandibles stretched forward to grab her, ripping some web in the process. At the instant the spider touched her tough leather clothes, it momentarily released its grip as if shocked by an electric current. Once freed she fell through the hole in the damaged web, almost crushing one of the stalking cats beneath. It squealed in pain and the others panicked to avoid potential danger, but they soon began to regroup for the kill.

Lira-Bawaki felt several arrows beneath her. One of those she nervously loaded into her bow.

The spider was not the type to release its hard earned catch, not even at death's door, so this time it moved cautiously towards its second victim, leaving its previous losses to the scavenging cats below.

Now it was Biluchi's little sister's turn. She struggled viciously in protest, even when the net had tightened as far as it could go about her person.

'Someone, please help me! I don't want to die like this! I prefer to be a stooge in a dragon's tongue!' she cried. This time Biluchi did not utter a word to silence her.

Observing the situation from below, Lira-Bawaki did not hesitate a moment longer and as the spider pounced on Caldi she let the golden arrow fly towards one of its large eyes.

The cats were shocked by the blinding flash and sudden explosion that brightly illuminated most of the cavern. They vanished into the dark amidst growls of fear and disappointment. The large spider's head had vaporised in flames while its remains fell lifeless into the centre of the web, barely missing little Caldi, but by share weight, pulling its damaged body and prey even closer to the floor.

Lira-Bawaki was not taking any chances, so she let another arrow fly towards the large container of eggs and that object vanished into flames. She retrieved her knife and progressed under the smouldering web to free her companions.

'Wow! I thought we were goners. Thanks, Sis, for a job well done, with such panache and skill,' Venusa-Bawaki said as she jumped out of the web.

'I don't know how I did it. It just came naturally,' was Lira-Bawaki's reply.

'Come here little sister!' Biluchi said. She hugged her and began rearranging the attire of a somewhat ruffled Caldi, who was definitely annoyed by her recent encounter with the giant spider and wanted some payback.

'Don't you worry! All you guys are going to get your come-uppers sooner or later,' she mumbled, while glancing at the few remaining spiders in the distance.

Although severely ruffled by that close encounter with death, they quickly collected their belongings and prepared for the next part of their journey. They were not yet out of danger and had to find a way out of the great underground cavern with its many scavengers.

A few shocked spiders had moved further away. So the group now considered the possibility of climbing the large poles with the help of the web ropes. Once at the top they could break out to the desert's floor with knives and claws. However, how could they have continued their journey over that unnatural terrain. With the thought that once again their movement would be detected, with a resultant capture, even when they knew what to expect and could prepare for that eventuality.

They mutually agreed that everyone should be prepared for the worst, and carry their bows and arrows in readiness for immediate use. Despite its awkwardness, they readjusted their large sacks of mulloks including shells and secured them to their backs in such a manner as to avail them greater freedom.

They finally decided to follow the well-trodden side-trail inside the dark cavern. That one appeared more frequently used by wild creatures, scavengers and prowlers.

Although pitch dark in most places, light was sometimes visible through small cracks in the chasm's wall that gave indication of their progress and they made good speed. After a while they could hear cries coming from the direction of the spider's lair. They remained as quiet as possible, fearing any noise would attract local scavengers.

They could faintly hear the cries of smaller animals throughout the spiders lair, so they persevered onwards. That covered part of the desert was relatively cool. Yet they realized it was shelter and home for much0 of the desert's life.

The giant spiders' cavern continued underground for several miles, but luckily for them most of their webs further along towards the south had been abandoned and unused.

The cat-women would occasionally peep through the larger cracks in the chasm's wall for familiar landmarks, but none could yet be observed.

It was not long before they found themselves facing a solid wall, this time it signalled the end of the cavern.

'We must be silent while I climb to observe the surface above. We don't know what might be lurking up there,' Biluchi warned. They remained quietly while she mounted the almost vertical wall with web-rope in paws. They had each collected several feet of the almost unbreakable but very flexible white rope from the damaged web and elsewhere. It was found to have incredible strength and became elastic when pulled at an angle.

Using her hunting knife and paws, Biluchi broke through the overhanging black surface and gently lifted her head out through a small hole and thin pancaked material under a layer of lighter sand. Most of it had now fallen onto the cavern's floor. It radiated brilliantly with sunlight when she removed her head. They realized they needed extra shading on the surface.

This time she was able to see the outline of the great chasm. It gently narrowed, with the great desert still continuing on as far as her eyes could see. However the sand was again its normal orange colour. Biluchi extended the surface hole with her paws and they pulled themselves onto the surface to continue their journey along the chasm's wall while on the desert surface.

'Wow! What an experience? It's great to be out of that hellish place!' Biluchi commented.

They had travelled for three and one-quarter days and a large part of that journey had been spent within the giant spiders' cavern in almost complete darkness. Despite the terrifying dangers encountered during that period, they were well away from the vicious sandstorms on the surface and penetrating heat of the suns rays. Judging from the direction they followed, they had at most one more day before reaching their required point of exit. Their present route was almost at right angles to the Marawi City. That position placed them some twenty miles away and still within dangerous territory.

The great chasm was closing quickly. As they scanned the distant horizon they could just observe a column of water.

As usual, Biluchi's little sister became excited and began to shout.

'Sadana! Sadana!'

Biluchi quickly shut her up and followed her sister's eyes with disgust, but sighed with relief.

'Sadana, good Sadana,' she said, quietly.

Sadana was the main fresh water sea in that area. It was hardly ten miles from their present position and another ten to the city. They were barely twenty miles from friends, but now within the territories of the Zadi, their most hated enemy.

Although relative peace existed with the clans at present, the Zadi was not the friendliest and hated all trespassers. Therefore it was just a matter of time before they were sighted or detected by the border guards.

'Now we have the greater problem of evading our enemies, the Zadi, and finding a way through to our borders,' Biluchi waved.

They double checked their load of mulloks and shells, which they harnessed tightly to their bodies, hopefully to reduce their strong pungent cent, but also to enhance their tracking speed. Despite their careful preparations, there were many guard towers along the borders with line-of-sight throughout that area, so there was a high chance of detection by those keen-eyed observers.

CHAPTER 43

Hostile borders

Venusa-Bawaki signalled the other cat-women to come forward and she began to whisper to them.

'From this moment we are to proceed with extreme stealth and caution. Whenever possible, we should walk in single-file and in each others footsteps. This precaution will help to further confuse their trackers and allow us time to escape. However the winds are now against us and will carry our scent for several miles.'

Although they could travel much quicker by day, it was decided to continue until the end of the chasm and there await nightfall.

That evening the smallest moon was almost full. The other was low in the horizon and as a result their combined positions and shadows would not be too pronounced and hopefully, not aid their chances of capture.

They continued stealthily onwards at dusk and travelled another five miles across the area where the chasm would have been if it extended further towards the sea.

They had moved another three miles beyond the southern area of the chasm and almost within visible range of their borders. Then they could travel across the seashore towards the city of Marawi, and so they thought.

They sped onwards as fast as they could, becoming quite exhausted in the process, so they decided to have another rest to finish their rations and lighten their burden before their final dash for the border. Still within enemy territory, they finished their rations and mentally prepared for their final leap, with everything tied as tightly as possible. It was now all or nothing.

When disaster struck the second time, it was just as sudden. Their enemies were waiting. Hidden nets had already been laid along the path just ahead of them. Suddenly they found themselves once more in nets, but this time suspended in mid air between two large desert pine trees.

They were soon cut down by their enemies and taken away, spears pointing at vital organs while being prodded along in a different direction.

'Mitchi! Mitchi! Mitchi!' their captors shouted. Which meant, 'Move, Move, Move?'

When they arrived at the local guard station their catch and weapons were inspected and confiscated, and their paws tightly bound behind their backs.

The chief cat-woman guard soon entered, slave-whip in paws. She was not smiling when she selected the strongest of her captives.

'Where are you from?' she inquired.

'We are from a southern clan and are travelling across the desert towards the south,' Venusa-bawaki replied.

'We know of no such southern clans within the area you describe, yet you have harvested mulloks from north eastern regions which is apparent from the shells you carry.

'How did you travel this way across the desert?' she inquired.

'We travelled across the sand spiders caverns,' Venusa-Bawaki replied.

'No one has ever travelled across that part of the Morii Desert and lived! Never across cake sands, and yet you say you have?' she snarled.

'Yes, as you see, we have survived!' Venusa-Bawaki replied, arrogantly, showing her the web-rope. She carefully observed the rope but was not convinced.

'You lie! Take them outside to the poles and bind them until morning! No water! Then we shall see!' she shouted.

They spent that night outside the local guards' station, lashed to the binding poles, but still within range of the border post.

Their captors had intended to deliver them to their main city called Chimozi, some fifty miles away by cat-cart the following day.

At first light Venusa-Bawaki was again untied and taken inside the guard house. The vicious looking chief cat-woman guard followed the other guards, slave-whip in paws and continued her interrogation.

'Why do you lie to me?

'I do not!'

'You and your companions are spies... on a special mission with these expensive mulloks as payment for bribe?'

'No!'

'You know, we can be very lenient if you tell us the truth!' she said.

Then the chief guard became very fierce and hit Venusa-Bawaki's stool several times with the whip hoping to unsettle and scare her.

'If you keep silent or lie, you will be considered a spy and sent to our city for summary execution by bat-vultures. Not a pleasant death, even for vermin!' she exclaimed.

Venusa-Bawaki realized she and her colleagues were once again in dire straights, but did not wish to give a false report. Anyway, the captain did not appear interested in the truth, only in acquiring information about their being spies. She was also in possession of a wealthy bounty of weapons and mulloks, and had no intentions of giving it back. If she could stick to her story and accuse them as spies she had a better chance of getting away with it.

'As I have already said. We have journeyed through the desert and are on our way to a southern clan,' Venusa-Bawaki replied.

The chief guard was now furious. She slashed the whip across Venusa-Bawaki's face, just missing her eyes. She moved her head just in time to duck the full force of the blow.

'So be it! You spies will be despatched to the city today! No food or water!' she barked in front of her guards.

They were tightly bound to poles in the outside compound. All their weapons and supplies that had been confiscated were stored in a room within the main station building with a strong guard positioned at the door.

As far as they could see, it was impossible to escape their present situation. They remembered the giant spider's web and the parallels with their present dilemma.

Physical form did not dictate their situation and given half a chance they would have taken exactly the same measures with their bows and arrows to escape their present captors. Although the guards were cat-people, they may well have been giant sand spiders in disguise, but with the extra viciousness due to their larger and more capable brains. They needed a chance to retaliate.

While the sun rose some of the guards prepared for their trip to the main city. After all, they had quite a valuable catch and with seven completely full sacks of mulloks, including special metal bows and arrows worth a queen's ransom. They would most likely be promoted by their queen for showing such initiative in capturing the northern spies with their valuable bounty.

The chief guard was soon at the compound. She whipped her captives into a standing position and proceeded to untie their almost raw paws from the tall slippery poles with her guards ready with sharp spears in paws. The cat-women were then tethered to a long iron chain and placed equidistantly along its length. The guards pulled their captives out one by one and finally tied the main lead chain to a double hook at the rear of a large cart. The cart was loaded with supplies and weapons, including sparse rations for the trip. Their captives' hunting bows, web-ropes and mulloks were left behind and securely guarded.

The captain of the guards gave orders to those remaining and took her place with four other guards on the cart, this time with a longer whip in paws. The cart was drawn by four harnessed cat-horses. The creatures were somewhat larger than cat-women, walked on all fours, but were completely docile and omnivorous.

They continued their journey close to the border, while their captives were being pulled along behind the cart with the chief guard whipping those in front to increase their rate of progress.

They came to a turning in the bumpy road and Venusa-Bawaki realised her bonds was loosening, so she assisted as best she could. She was placed almost in the middle of the long chain and could have readily communicated with the girls on either side of her. However she could not speak or use signs in case she alerted the guards; so she gave a pre rehearsed mild alert smile, only known to her hunting companions and meaning: 'Get ready, now.'

Cat-people of a specific clan could communicate almost fluently by facial hair movements alone. They understood what she meant and passed the signal along. Each in turn got prepared for whatever was to follow.

The first cat-woman accidentally stumbled and in an instant all the cat-women piled one on top of the other. During that brief moment sharp paws were quickly at work, cutting through and untying thick leather hand bands. In another instant all five guards were ferociously and swiftly relieved of their weapons. Their identification stripes were taken from them and given to five new guards. Screeching and groaning, they were tightly bound; paws, feet and mouth with those very same hand bands and web-rope, and dumped into the rear of the large cart among the supplies and redundant chains. Venusa-Bawaki and Lira-Bawaki then took the reins.

'That was a nice and sweet operation, Girls!' Lira-Bawaki commented, as little Caldi gave the captain the tip of her right sandal just between the groin and she stiffened with pain.

'That little present is for tying my hands so bloody tight, you bitch!' she said. Then she gave a milder kick to her face.

'This one is for my friends.' Then she spat in her direction and jumped off the cart to assist the others.

The cart was turned around and they began moving in the opposite direction, back towards the station building with their captives.

'Before we can move to our borders, we must regain all our weapons and mulloks. That simply means taking the station. Is everyone agreed!' Lira-Bawaki shouted.

'Yes, agreed!' they shouted back.

'You will never capture our station. You are not good enough!' the captain shouted and Caldi jumped the cart and stuck her leather sandals into her face again.

'One more word and you will see the face of my boots against your ugly cakehole,' she advised and the captain remained quiet. Then they tied their faces to prevent them shouting.

CHAPTER 44

Escape from the Zadi

They approached the guard station building along the only route available. Then soon came to the conclusion that their only real means of escape was through disguise and confusion. That area was highly populated and included the additional hazard of some over-enthusiastic border guards, who doubtlessly used communication mirrors in their towers. Therefore drastic action had to be taken to neutralize all opposition if they were to proceed across the nearby border.

It was decided that Venusa-Bawaki with the other members of her god-clan and Biluchi went forward to take care of the station and its remaining guard occupants, while Matbi and Caldi guarded the cart. Matbi was to hold the captives while Caldi, made sure they remained silent. Should they have attempted to escape, she was ready and waiting with her sharp spear always pointing in the direction of their captains neck. The cat-cart was to remain at the bend, just out of sight of anyone in that area. It was held just beyond view of anyone coming from the direction of the main building. There it waited until they received an audible signal to continue. It would be in the form of a high pitch whistle they used for signalling.

Every cat-woman was now armed to the hilt, but Venusa-Bawaki and the assault group had to use whatever weapons they could find in the cart. Anyway they couldn't use exploding arrows, if available, in case the noise alerted more of their enemies. Neither did they wish to kill the guards by such overkill methods, so they took along normal spears and arrows instead.

Recollecting their past dangers and experiences in the desert and their present survival record, they were confident of success against those more civilized cat-women guards. It was just a matter of setting the nets, stalking the prey, and picking them off one by one while they tried to escape. Even so, they were over optimistic and expected a few deaths on the Zadi side in self defence.

A net was stolen and laid in front of the main exit at the rear of the building, then several arrows rapped in linen, dipped in oil, lit and simultaneously fired at the main front door. They took their positions and waited while the large door burnt and smoked, aided by a thick deposit of leaves and dried pine flowers on the ground below.

Just two members of their group had remained in front of the building. Nervously they waited with bows and arrows while three remained at the rear. The main front door was soon opened from the inside. When the guards observed the smoke and flames, they immediately made for the rear exit. The moment they open that door a rope was tripped and they stumbled and fell one on top of the other. The large net was pulled tightly to contain the catch.

Two determined guards soon realised what was happening and began to shoot their arrows while they ran, but those hit the ground. Venusa-Bawaki was wounded by one of their arrows, but it was just a flesh wound on her left arm and did not bleed too profusely. Venusa-Bawaki and Lira-Bawaki entered the house while Julia-Bawaki and Petra-Bawaki checked the building and its surroundings for strays. When they were convinced the threat was removed they whistled and the cart was mobile once again.

'The building is contained!' Venusa-Bawaki shouted.

'Wow! I feel a lot better for that. I didn't realize there was so much fun and pleasure in payback. We must do it again soon!' Lira-Bawaki shouted, still sweating from her previous efforts.

'Yea... that was nice payback!' Biluchi was pleased.

'You contained them well. Now it's our turn to tie them to their own poles,' Petra-Bawaki replied.

'Yea.. That's a much better idea!' Biluchi said, already with rope in paw.

One by one they were released from the net and bound to the poles. Soon Matbi and Caldi arrived with the others in the cart.

'Girls, you missed all the fun!' Biluchi shouted, turning to little sister Caldi, then Matbi.

Caldi was annoyed and paid personal attention to the captain of the guards. She made sure her paws were doubly bound and tight.

'I think we should take this one with us for security,' she advised and Biluchi went up and hugged her little sister for having such pleasant thoughts about the enemy.

'See she doesn't try to escape anymore,' she said to her little sister and left. Then Caldi gave a much satisfied look.

Although the surviving guards were tightly bound and harnessed to the prison poles in the same manner as their captives, they were left with small earthen containers filled with precious water.

Even though the main front door had gone up in flames, the building itself was constructed of large cut stones and the fire soon died. With the exception of the two dead guards all others remained undamaged. Venusa-Bawaki did not wish to stir the situation any more than was absolutely necessary.

After removing the other guards from the cart, with the exception of their vicious captain, they proceeded with their original plan, but this time with cat-cart. The captain, they thought, could be used for bargaining if they met with more resistance at the border. Further, border guards would think twice when firing upon their cart, and so they thought.

Their border post was another two miles away and separated by a one mile dead-zone. That zone happened to be a free-for-all area where tribal laws and agreements did not apply. Yet, they realised the dangers had not yet passed. There still remained a high chance of capture with its even deadlier consequences.

This time, however, they were much better protected by the very thick wooden cart and could therefore have put up a much better fight. On Tarran things were never that simple and just as they passed their enemy's border, mirrors flashed, fast chariots harnessed for the chase and hunter-killer cats released from their cages.

Larger crossbow arrows were soon flying from the high border post towers towards the targeted cart. Some of those arrows were tipped with a type of explosive that was quite capable of destroying the cart.

Biluchi shouted as she furiously whipped the cat-horses.

'Miti-ch0ia! Miti-chia!' she snarled.

That meant, 'Heads down! Heads down!' and once again fired her whip towards the cat-horses.

They followed her advice and placed their mulloks' shells around the cart for better protection from the flying missiles. It was not long before they were being chased by three fast chariots headed by three ferocious hunter-killer cats. However at that time they were well within the dead zone and closer to their borders than the Zadi's. If they broke a wheel or the animals fainted from over exhaustion they would still be in trouble. Many fast chariots and killer cats would soon be on the way with even larger weapons. The pulling cat-horses also realised the dangers while arrows exploded all around them and were more determined to get to wherever they were meant to be.

They were soon sighted by their border post who had observed the incident and began firing their long bows in turn towards the chasing chariots and killer-cats.

The chariot drivers realised they were beyond their legitimate point of pursuit, so they whistled at their cats who turned around and sped for their lives amidst a hail of arrows.

As the cat-women approached the border they removed their enemy's colours and threw them with disgust back into the zone.

Still keeping their heads down they shrieked in delight as they crossed the border post. After they passed that last fence they couldn't believe their incredible luck. There they remained for a while to catch their breath and rest the cat-horses before travelling the few more metres towards the large station house.

'Girls! That was close, but we made it! I have never had such a rush in all my life!' Biluchi shouted.

'We are alive and home!' Martia-Bawaki yelled and the others shouted back.

'Home! Sweet Home!' Caldi screeched with ecstasy.

CHAPTER 45

The grand reception

They were to be detained by their border guards for identification. The captain who had assisted them during the skirmish ran out of the station to greet the adventurous cat-women. That particular border-post was usually found wanting in such excitement and had not seen any kind of real action in many years. Nevertheless they had always been prepared for any unsociable moves by their mischievous and unfriendly Zadi neighbours. The border captain showed her respect by proudly saluting the two cat-women sitting in front of the cart and asked for their identification.

'It was a very exciting chase and I am proud to have been of some assistance to your company....'

'Many thanks for your timely assistance!' Venusa-Bawaki replied.

'May I please have your identification?' she asked.

Venusa-Bawaki showed her clan's markings which was branded in a private place under her hair. They were not wearing the usual identification metal bracelets.

'I am princess Bawaki of your blood clan... Here is my royal identity,' she replied.

She went back into the building to check the markings and very quickly returned.

'My beloved princess of the gods! I am so pleased to have been given this great honour!' she said.

The captain went down on her knees and kissed the princess sandals, but Venusa-Bawaki opposed.

'Please be up and attend to your guards. I can vouch for all my colleagues at the back. Take this enemy captain, question her and release her in one day. Give her enough food and water for her trip home!' Venusa-Bawaki commanded. Then her surprised captive followed humbly, after having received a strong and catlike glare from little Caldi as she handed her over.

The captain stood at attention and commanded her local guards to take the prisoner away.

'Your royalty, if you wish, some of my guards can safely escort you and your group to the city gates?' she asked. But Venusa-Bawaki declined any enthusiastic assistance.

'I would prefer to follow a quiet trail after the excitement of our past adventure. May I ask your name?' she replied.

'My name is Polichi, Mam.'

'Well Polichi. Have you made your name yet at the hunt?'

'No, Mam. I haven't found a senior to take me.'

'Then let me or one of my colleagues be your senior for next year's hunt. I shall add your name to the queen's register, with your permission of course,' Venusa-Bawaki said.

She couldn't retain her emotions and again went down on all fours.

'Thank you, my great and loving princess! Thank you!' Polichi replied.

She got up and again saluted as they sped off towards the city gates.

Mirrors were flashing towards the length and breadth of their lands. Very soon the queen heard the incredible news of the mulloks and other items of the gods. News travelled very quickly amongst cat-people, so it was not long before everyone within her fief knew of the princess's return.

Their journey into the walled city was a thrill in itself. As they rode through its large iron gates they could see cat people everywhere, waving, shouting, saluting and cheering. Even lowly males could be seen among the females doing likewise.

Venusa-Bawaki and the others held their heads high and proud, accepting the great honour of the hunt; for they did not realise that the city knew of their exploits and that their fame had preceded them.

Their almost disgraced clan, since Bawaki's absence, was waiting for something important to happen. Since Bawaki's departure with the gods the sparkle had left the city and now she, the greatest of all hunters, had returned with a great prize.

Out of the few hunters sent that spring none had so far returned. The people and most of all their queen, didn't want their proud and once great clan to lose face and become a talking point of incompetence and weakness among her rivals. Any such ridicule would have made them appear weak amongst the other clans and many might have tried to use force at their borders to test their strength, in particular their old enemy the Zadi. It would have given them an excuse to take an advantage somewhere. But now, the Zadi had been seriously beaten and would spend several years licking their wounds, even with a little ridicule from the other border clans.

Such word of the hunt travelled to the remotest northern clans, who because of their much greater wealth showed little respect to anyone and least of all those from the south, but now, they might even allow their clan's hunters through with most of their catch.

To the cat people of Marawi Clan no one could ever fill Bawaki's sandals, for she was one in a million and a known god-child.

The royal guards soon approached, coming from the other direction and greeted her.

'Her royal highness awaits your company. Please follow us!' the chief guard said.

The cart stopped and they jumped out to follow the female guards on foot into a very large stone palace that had been built in some bygone age.

Queen Barawi was once a great hunter herself, but never had she ever ventured beyond the relative safety of the north eastern desert region. At that time they were used to bribing the northern clans' chiefs on their way in to the hunt and on their return journey with their catch. When they returned home after the harvest, their mulloks would have just been a half bag and that was when they were lucky. Even then some of the lesser clans would have been envious of their catch and of her group's achievements through the dangers of the hunt. And it was not always just the quantity. It also depended on the quality of the hunters; quality to overcome the incredible survival odds on the way to the hunt, for therein lay the greatness of the hunt. For those incredible exploits proof had to be supplied in the form of souvenirs.

She was very proud of her daughter for restoring the name of her clan amongst all others, and in the process giving her enemies a bloody nose with the aid of her other friends. That tremendous accomplishment was probably the greatest gift she had ever received.

Queen Barawi thought of those things and many others besides regarding her weakening clan and worried for their future. Many things were changing in the structure of her world and there was now a yearning to move on, but where. She sometimes thought that perhaps her clans-people could do a lot better than hunting and gathering, and mould a different and less monotonous society, but she had little practical ideas on that subject.

There must be a greater beyond; a much more fulfilling existence and her cat-people yearned for that change if anyone could find it. However their environment was so extremely harsh and limiting and as a result most of their potentials were limited.

Venusa-Bawaki and the others, including Baluchi and her two companions, Matbi and Caldi, entered the beautifully decorated ancient palace with mosaic floors, interlaced wooden-covered walls and painted ceilings. Large mirrored oil lamps hung by thick iron chains from its highest points. Artifacts and earthenware were also displayed all around its walls with much larger earthenware containers in corners.

Lira-Bawaki glanced around and wondered at the rustic beauty of the palace interior within that almost large oasis on Tarran and her human side took it in and appreciated it. Although the cat in her knew it was the work of the males or cat-men. They were the most creative and industrious of her race.

Since they began the use of female slaves many ages ago, the males turned to such enterprise as a means to relieve their boredom, but eventually became very clever at those sorts of things. They were also the most curious and inquisitive of their race. Even so, those enterprises were seldom appreciated by their cat-women. They attributed such embellishments and devices to decadence that could only lead their clan to weakness with the resultant disrespect from their neighbours. It could also have led them towards an attitude of diminished aggression and lack of warlike spirit. Yet, they accepted and tolerated their males unnatural behaviour and self-indulgence, because they sometimes made machines and weapons of a superior nature that also made the clan stronger.

Cat-woman and cat-men still had a very long way to go towards the more technical understanding of art and science, but they were the type that listened and learning of new concepts would not have been a major problem.

The queen sat on her high throne with two male councillors sat on stools either side of her. As they entered, her male companions immediately stood at attention, while she nervously touched one of her curled whiskers. She stood up, composed herself and walked gracefully towards her supposed daughter. She remained stationery for a moment, eying her pretend daughter Venusa-Bawaki, searching her face for more subtle changes. She observed almost every inch of her daughter's form and equipment, including the precisely engineered bow, arrows and beautiful quiver. Then the great sand-spider's web-rope that was coiled and clipped unto her belt. There the group stood like Amazonian warrior queens and she was impressed.

'You have changed! You have become more godlike!'

'Yes Mother!'

'Well... and you have been through the walled cavern... and lived?'

'Yes Mother!'

'Not many escape the giant sand spiders and live you know... and you have?' she said, also glancing at the other Bawaki's that were so similar to her daughter.

Venusa-Bawaki bowed gently and began to introduce her other seven companions. Then the queen asked them to accompany her towards her feeding room where they were offered lunch. Their first proper lunch consisted of large sand-worms and bat-vulture wings that were specially prepared in vinegar and considered a rear delicacy. It was to be followed by a very strong but sweet fermented drink. That drink was produced from one of the local pine fruit. After what appeared to them to have been a feast for cat-women, the queen was prepared to listen to their experiences within the desert.

She found their story almost unbelievable.

'What an incredible journey and experience? You have been in such dangers and yet, despite those enormous odds, have survived and so have also every one of your friends, even without a scratch. You are truly a god-child and obviously my successor as future queen of our clan,' she said.

When they were too tired to continue, she clapped her hands and two female slaves came forward. Using facial language she instructed them to prepare the visitors' accommodation and they left in different directions.

'I will be very happy and pleased if you could remain here, in my castle, with us for a while. I desperately need your exciting company to relieve my continuous boredom in this place of monotony. This time of the year there is always so little to do. Anyway you need a rest after your intriguing adventure. We can have some entertainment before you return to your god-place in the sky,' she said and they agreed.

'As for you, Biluchi, you and your clan's people are always welcome in my queendom. Therefore you and your companions should make yourselves at home and be comfortable in my palace.'

Biluchi got up and bowed gently before the queen.

'Thank you for that great honour, your majesty.'

'Biluchi, your catch is yours, to take back with you to your clan and any other ensuing rewards. So also is your guaranteed promotion to a more senior status within your clan. I shall give you a sealed royal message which you may present to your queen on your return.

'Thank you, Mam!'

'You know, Biluchi, I knew your previous queen well. Like you and my daughter, both of us went hunting together. We jointly faced many perils and as a result became very close friends. I was saddened by her unfortunate death, but her daughter is a decent type and also knew me in the past. But you my daughter has also met her and you both get on very well together,' she said, glancing at Venusa-Bawaki.

The queen called her male councillors to organise the written parchment message and to select one of their most beautiful artifacts for a present.

Apparently, only the males knew the method of parchment writing which was another one of their peculiar inventions. It was to be used with a special quill on course parchment. That device was sometimes very useful for carrying private messages with the royal seal.

That evening the queen gave a special reception to her most senior and respected subjects, and parchment invitations were dispatched by messengers. She felt like entertaining but also wanted to talk about her daughter's incredible achievements before the excitement had diminished. The celebration began with the hunt-dances on the main floor, depicting an ancient hunt with a band of male musicians.

After the dance was over, the queen got up and asked her daughter to say a few words of courage to her clan. Only the queen made speeches at such gatherings. Therefore it was considered a great honour even for a princess to be asked. Venusa-Bawaki accepted the queen's invitation and walked towards the front where the cat-men musicians were sited with their woodwind musical instruments and drums. Everyone cheered as she began to speak:

'My dearest queen and mother, friends and clans-people. You are truly a great people and I sincerely respect and appreciate you all for showing such concern and affection towards my companions and myself on this day after our return from the hunt.... The proceeds of which I have given to our queen, to be donated to whatever charities she decides.

'You all knew of my departure to the stars not too long since.

Just four days ago I returned from the stars to partake in the great hunt. Yes, the stars, for within this universe there are many suns like ours that look like stars because of the vast distances that separate them. Yet, many of these stars are similar to our two suns, with similar worlds containing all forms of living types imaginable. All at different stages of development.

'Biluchi met us on the distant plains. Saw our strange invisible craft and our unique bows and arrows....

'Please listen for a moment and observe closely my bow.

She handed one of the special bows to her clans-people who observed its detailed design with amazement but she continued to speak:

'These bows, without doubt, saved our lives through the scaled monsters' pass; for we slew four of the giant monsters in the process. We had little fear of the desert itself and its sandstorms... not until our unexpected capture by the giant sand spiders and our escape from its tight webs and cavern cats underneath. That was a lucky experience not only for us, but also for our clan. Because we also found an almost inexhaustible supply of web-ropes, which can be made by our males into different types of hunting rope for sale to the northern clans. This material is one of the strongest I have ever seen. During that time we found a much shorter route home, but had to enter Zadi lands to get to our borders.

'Further, after our capture by our enemies, the Zadi's, we subsequently escaped and defeated fifteen Zadi guards and captured one of their border captains.

'You, my friends, can all have such bows and arrows, even flying ships to take you into the farthest deserts during the great spring harvest and much more besides.

'I promise you a truly great future for everyone and not just the celebrations after the hunt for our best hunters. Everyone on this world has wishes and desires to be fulfilled and I shall try my best in the future to fulfil those wishes for my beloved people. May you all go in peace with firm resolve, conviction and commitment, and follow our rules of queenship; not only for us but also for our males and may the great sky god bless you all,'

She bowed to her queen and left the stage under a standing ovation. Everyone cheered. Even the male musicians and the queen as she proudly walked away.

They realized that a wind of change was blowing through their lives and Bawaki had been selected by their god to initiate that change.

CHAPTER 46

A new direction

After the celebration was over the queen called her supposed daughter Venusa-Bawaki for a private chat in her rest room. She had accepted her as such because she more closely resembled the real Bawaki. Many questions needed to be asked about things said in her speech and she wanted answers.

'My dearest daughter, that was a very enlightening speech you gave. All of my guests were so impressed with you and were so excited and happy when they left. It's regrettable we hadn't enough time to invite some of our neighbouring clans... even the Zadi's queen.'

'Next time, perhaps?' Venusa-Bawaki replied, with little consideration for Zadis at that time.

'You said many things in your speech, in particular about some things regarding flying desert ships. Such technologies are more natural to our males. Do you think our males will one day become as powerful like us females, despite their smaller size and more inept frame?'

'Not so, Mam. I prefer to use the term freer to assist in the mutual survival efforts of our clan by virtue of their knowledge and technologies. Because of those reasons we should give them a freer hand. Life is not only to do with the hunt and matters of defence, you know. Anyway, they have always been an important part of us. A clan is like a body with many parts and they are but our left arms while we female are the right arms. Both can always work much better as one.

'I understand!'

'Since my visit to the stars, I have found that technology goes side by side with other methods and ways. Whenever it is hot one needs to be cold. Would you travel for days to visit a place when you knew you could complete the same journey in hours? Do you see my point, Mother?' Venusa-Bawaki replied.

'But if what you say is true, it will change the structure of our ancient oracle. It clearly states that the weaker must remain weak and the stronger remain strong. How can we associate strength with your concepts... even if we are able to travel to the deserts with ships constructed by our male folk?' the queen replied.

'The Oracle was devised by our ancient females to hold back our males. Although useful for our survival, it has outlived its time.'

'But we have always survived by its teachings!' her mother replied.

'In that case, why are we continually making more superior bows and arrows than those of our enemies. Would we win the great war just by using our strong bare paws? Strength is related to our will to survive and with the relevant technologies to support that will. When both are superior, the clan is also superior. If you had no great hunters left would you lose the war because of that fact... even when you had a superior will and also a superior technology?' Venusa-Bawaki replied.

The queen was confused by her daughter's clear and logical answers. Something she was incapable of doing with such clarity.

'My dearest daughter, if what you say is practical, by way of improving our existence on this harsh world, you will have my full support and backing in whatever new projects you propose.'

'Thank you, Mother!'

'If absolutely necessary, you may take both my male councillors along with you tomorrow. They can escort you to the male quarters to observe their projects.'

'That will be fantastic!'

'They will admire you for showing an interest in their inventions and they should, because you will be the first royal female to have done so in many years,' she said.

'Thank you again, Mother.... There is a great sky queen who rules over many worlds and stars, and she can help us to attain our goals. With your permission, we can send some of our people to the stars. This program will include our most clever males for training in those new sciences and technologies. However you needn't make any decisions now. Just give it some serious thought... I shall put together a list of some likely names. They can await my return in a few months. Great hunters will always be given the greatest rewards and privileges as in the past, but it will also include our male scientists and others hunting in their different fields of technologies for their best designs,' Venusa-Bawaki replied.

The following morning Venusa-Bawaki and her companions decided to visit the male quarters and view their industrial buildings. She wanted to see the males at work within their small production units of cottage industries.

That part of the city was always restricted to females at that time of the year. Their race only mated during the coldest two months of each year which were the winter months and it was now late spring. However she was a princess and god-child with special arrows and other strange devices from the stars and would be tolerated for a while within their compound.

Both queen's councillors escorted her and her group that day. When she was introduced to the most inventive males, she unharnessed her bow and showed them its intricacies, engravings, rear metals and materials.

Many went forward to observe the beautiful object and were amazed by its detail and composition. They asked questions on astronomy and other scientific topics and she answered them as best she could. The males had suddenly realised their ways were the future survival path for their planet and listened attentively to every word she uttered. Venusa-Bawaki then spoke to the small group of senior males:

'Some of you have a desire to learn more about the sciences, mathematics and the arts, but that desire can only be fulfilled away from Tarran, on one of the learning worlds. You needn't remain away from your home world for more than two years in any single learning period. Yet, you will learn how to pump and filter the waters of the great desert oceans that are now many metres beneath the sands. This single effort can be achieved with little or no change to desert life. You will also be able to make flying machines that may fly faster than bat-vultures.

'Such machines will simplify the process of hunting, and the filtered desert waters can be used to irrigate crops planted at the desert's edge. Then there is electricity that you may use to power our equipment and light our cities. Instead of mirrors, we could use many other more advanced forms of communication, which is invisible. All these changes may be made to enhance our society and make us a happier people.

'But please discuss these ideas among yourselves and be prepared for those changes when I return again from the stars before the autumn.'

The males listened carefully to everything she said and one of the younger, a more brilliant male, began to speak.

'When again do you leave for the stars, your highness?' he inquired.

'At late morning in a day's time. You may come to see me off, if you wish,' she replied.

The young male again spoke.

'I have already decided to follow you to the stars, my princess. That is, if males are permitted.'

'Within the greater federation of worlds everyone is free to pursue creative goals. Form is in no way related to your aspirations. Neither will it restrict your capabilities.'

They smiled at that answer and knew that after all those years of struggle with their females, they now had a royal princess willing to assist them in their efforts and desires.

When she left that day many bags were filled with gifts for her and her friends and some very special ones were included for the queen of the stars.

The following evening she told the queen of her intention to leave the following day and that she would be back within the year.

'Mother, I'm afraid, duty calls! I have to return to the stars in the morning. Don't worry, I'll be back within the year. Henceforth, you should try to considered what I've said about our future course with our males.'

'My dearest daughter, I now see our future much more clearly and have accepted your plans for the future of our clan. Perhaps when we finish, our name will once again be the greatest among all clans.'

That morning Venusa-Bawaki and her company collected their belongings together. They decided to take along a small amount of mulloks for a famous female Shadite called Bawaki (the real Bawaki) who was presently on Earth in human form. Most of the males' presents, including those from their queen to the queen of the stars, were packed in separate bags and placed on a small cart. That one was to be pulled by their giant cat called Tokai. He was Bawaki's most favourite pet and had saved her life on one occasion.

When they were finished packing, they had breakfast together and said farewell to the queen, her councillors and finally to Biluchi, Matbi and her little sister, Caldi. Then Venusa-Bawaki visited Tokai's enclosure and released his harness.

'How are you my friend,' she said while hugging him. He was happy in seeing his old friend and couldn't stop showing his affection and wagging his tail. She had found the wild cat, Tokai, during one of her teenage treks to the desert. He had since remained at the palace. She handed him four of her best mulloks. He took one and saved the others for later.

They solemnly walked towards the main square with their loads on a small cart being pulled by Tokai and were admired by all.

On their way to the square they were greeted by many, while crowds were still gathering. When the time was appropriate Venusa-Bawaki signalled to the ship by pressing the small concealed button on her belt buckle. Suddenly the massive ship appeared overhead.

The super giant star-ship about two kilometres long, cast a shadow over the whole city and many became frightened and confused. Soon a small ship appeared from one of its side entrances and began to float downwards towards the square. When it landed, its side slid open.

By that time the crowds had overcome their fears and were once again waving and cheering the princess and her friends, until they entered the small craft and the door slid shut. Then it floated upwards into its mother-ship. After that moment the mother-ship itself began to move slowly upwards until it was too small to be seen by the naked eye.

That day the whole of their world had been irreversible shaken to its innermost core. Even the Zadi were frightened by the great sky-ship that could have easily destroyed their cities. The Zadi soon sent their diplomats to apologise to the queen for their unfriendly behaviour and asked to forget their squabbles of past. Both promised to mutually assist each other in future and once again resumed trade between their clans.

At long last the clans of Tarran were being united, awakened and stirred in a new and different way.

Although they had not yet realised the significance of that encounter, they were being reorganized and realigned in order to partake in that much greater conflict. Namely, the fight against their much superior enemy, yet unknown to them by the name of, Javols.

CHAPTER 47

Venusa and Martia visits Earth

During the period of the hunt, Jon and his male companions nervously took turns on Venusa's ship viewing their screens while patiently recording the girls experiences on the hostile planet below. Only when the men were sure they were safely asleep did they themselves retire for a few hours.

They were furious and worried when their women fell into the giant spider's lair and more so, when they were captured by the Zadi's guards. However the tables began to turn after their planned escape and subsequent arrival at their clan's borders. Thereafter they could well have been the happiest men in the universe. During all that time they were shouting and egging them on in spirit, with no physical way to communicate their feelings.

After the unwelcomed advice from Venusa's ship, about the non-intervention of males on a female planet, they could do virtually nothing to assist their women while in their present catlike form.

After the crucial one and a half days were exhausted they realised they might never see their partners again. From that moment on they became very unhappy, realising they would have to witness the hunt through to the bitter end. Not for one moment did they realise the women had such hidden potentials, even as vicious cats and thank goodness, Venusa-Bawaki had installed those high voltage devices to their specially prepared leather clothes that could be triggered by the little box. Even Petra-Bawaki and Julia-Bawaki had shown such unexpected ability and courage in the fight against the scaly monsters.

The three men waited patiently for the arrival of the women, but even now, they were not allowed to meet them in their present cat forms. They could still be very dangerous if aroused and could quickly change into vicious killers. Therefore they had to undergo re-transformation before they could meet, and the men had to patiently wait for the completion of that process.

The women soon arrived in the Mind Room and surprisingly, Venusa's hidden wound had completely healed during the re-transformation process. Now in their human forms the women remembered in detail their past experiences on Tarran. The experience of that great adventure had changed them into real Amazonians.

Miraculously, they were transformed back to their original beautiful human selves, with little traces of their previous feline attitude and hunting attributes. Even so, they held on to their cat women attire as a reminder of their first great hunt.

When they entered, the men ran to them and they embraced tightly with renewed affection and love. Soon afterwards Venusa linked with her ship and they transmitted all relevant data to Martia's ship. She was also patiently awaiting the outcome of the perilous hunt while presently stationed on planet Eden.

'What have you guys been up to during our absence?' Lira inquired with a sympathetic smile.

'Not much, I'm afraid,' a humble Jon replied, with sweat still dripping down his forehead from all the excitement of having them back. He must have lost several pounds during their absence from excitement and nervousness.

Venusa's ship soon advised her passengers:

'I am instructed to visit Mars and while there to await further instructions. However you may visit Earth in one of my smaller scout ships, captained by my human self, if you wish.'

They knew that the ship meant her human clone, Venusa, so they were once again happy that their human friends, Venusa and Martia would also be visiting Earth with them.

Apparently, after the great adventure the ships formed a much closer bond with their human duals, to love and respect above all else.

When they arrived on Mars, the large ship landed close to the cluster of domes and her passengers simply entered one of the locks and into one of the smallest eight seater scout ships. They were in no hurry to get back to Earth immediately, so they viewed progress on-route. They could observe the modified shuttle making yet another of its Martian deliveries with resources for the evacuation. Venusa's ship would assist in building the great domes used in the evacuation.

As they approached Earth they visually shielded themselves from the security detectors. Yet they could observe construction in progress of massive space stations and very large ships. However, those ships were much smaller than Venusa and Martia's ships. They would be used to ferry miners and scientists to Mars and other parts of the Solar System.

While they travelled through Earth's atmosphere, their ship automatically tuned into the LPD laser guidance system. They soon found themselves spiralling through a laser corridor with many ships heading in different directions. Just a little longer and their ship suddenly turned towards a smaller space corridor, and they found themselves travelling downwards, through a dense cloud and towards the house. That method of laser guidance was close to full proof and the chance of collision, even at high velocities, virtually impossible.

They were astounded by the progress made on Earth in just over a month and realised the enormous power and speed of those incredible Microid Robots, that could perform many of their programmed tasks tens of times faster than any human. They asked Venusa to land the little ship at the rear of the large house, but there was now two houses and the rear of the second now included another landing area, so they landed there instead.

The smaller house was almost completed, with some robots inside decorating and fitting utilities, so it was almost ready for its occupants.

Now approaching the front door of the main house they rang the buzzer. The door opened and a maid greeted them.

'Hello!... You are back!... Madam, will be so pleased to see you, even as I am pleased. Let me help you with some things.'

'Madam Bawaki! They have arrived!' the maid shouted.

Bawaki soon ran downstairs to greet her new companions.

'Hello... Jon, Lira and... I remember your faces from our trip to

Polok II and the pictures Madam Sarah showed me. As you can see, the physical changes from my cat form have not altered my memory in any way.'

'Bawaki! Is that really you?' Jon could not believe his own eyes, for she was now a beautiful young woman.

'Yes, Jon! Madam Sarah, is not here at present, but will be home soon. Please leave your cases here and let us go into the dining room for some refreshments. You look tired and famished after your trip.'

'Thanks Bawaki!' Lira replied.

'No transit meal can ever be compared with home cooking,' Bawaki said in a most voluptuous manner. They realized it was the very same words Sarah would have used and Bawaki was a quick learner.

'Bawaki, you look incredible!' Lira said, stunned by her beauty as a transformed human being.

'What do you think of my new human form? Is it acceptable?' she replied, while turning around.

'Most beautiful, Bawaki,' Jon replied.

'How was your trip from Polok II? Was it straightforward?' Bawaki inquired.

'No, Bawaki. Not straightforward at all. We visited your home world Tarran on our way back and went on the great hunt for mulloks,' Lira replied.

'Lira, do you jest with me?' she responded with curiosity.

Lira took a dried mullok from a bag and handed it to her.

'We also took along a few presents from your mum and some of the males,' she said, with a childish grin on her face.

Bawaki was homesick and somewhat saddened by the realization.

'You really met my queen mother and went on the perilous hunt and they are all, well?' she inquired.

Lira and the others began to laugh while telling her about their adventures and their not too clever idea of transforming into her former cat form.

Bawaki was surprised by their achievements during the great hunt and delighted that they had done so much for her people. She couldn't stop showing them her gratitude. However she had to make arrangements to visit Tarran before the autumn in order to fulfil a few promises and select some of her people for training on Eden.

Sarah returned several hours later in one of those dual LPD Phantom Rolls cars. It was a present from a large British motorcar manufacturer for LPD concessions. It was one of the first of a limited number. Although fully automatic, it was Chauffeur driven by one of Jeffery's favourite androids. It could have travelled along any of the air routes, but she still preferred the surface roads. She always enjoyed the so-called old-fashioned methods and was seldom comfortable with very quick changes even though she soon got used to them.

As she approached the front door, she entered a small card into the special lock and it automatically opened. Since their recent problems, security was tight at the Manor. The master computer was always questioning and scanning new arrivals.

Sarah was wearing another one of her beautiful cream suits with a large insignia pinned to her broad lapel. That one symbolized her organization and included three colours, blue, green and orange, at it centre.

The moment she walked into the lounge she was so surprised. The young ones immediately went to greet her. She phoned Lumak, now busy in one of his local production plants and he informed the others. That evening a happy family sat together to exchange presents and discuss their experiences.

'I suppose the great ships passed all their tests,' an innocent Lumak asked and Jon smiled while the girls began to giggle.

'As far as females are concerned and they are also here with us in the form of beautiful Venusa and Martia,' Merol said and Lumak was utterly surprised by that revelation.

Then the beautiful women came forward to be introduced.

'Our Grand Lord does have a great sense of humour. Now, we add two more members to our esteemed family,' he said and they accepted.

CHAPTER 48

Spoken like a true empress

After dinner that day at the Manor, Sarah brought them all together in the lounge to discuss progress and to make decisions for their immediate future.

'With Meron's kidnapping and a few press reporters snooping about for a story, I think it's time we made plans to leave this world in order to focus more on cosmic matters. However, once portals are fitted, we may visit our home here whenever necessary.

'In view of certain changes planned for the future in this part of our Osmaron galaxy, I shall require the services of each one of you if we are to fulfill certain targets before the arrival of our enemies, the Javols. I should also remind you that almost all domes and other utilities are ready and waiting for the evacuees from Caefon. Once the Omegron Portal is initiated the evacuation will commence. Thereafter, they can be transferred to Eden.

'I am very happy to have all my family and friends in one place at last, and my dearest wish is that we always remain close together as a single family. Regrettably, we shall always have our own separate missions to fulfil and sometimes very dangerous and risky ones, as we all know. Nevertheless we now have the technologies to defeat even death itself, so in the interest of everyone here, whom I would like to see remain among us for several more centuries, may I suggest we accept those benefits. It will increase our chances of survival and maintain our longevity, as we find ourselves in more perilous circumstances in the future.

'Henceforth, all members of the Solarian Council will be obliged to take the necessary body scans for re-transformation within one of the great ships. You will also be obliged to receive the necessary Brain Implants. They will transmit the relevant death signal or the lack of one to the molecular reforming units. They will also include the extra programs and facilities to enhance our

existence. I've been told that the installation of such Brain Implants to be completely painless and invisible to the user.

'This program, including interstellar communications will be placed in the capable hands of councillors, Venusa and Martia jointly, if there is no objections.

'We have recently initiated the new process of interstellar banking through the Interstellar Bank of Solaria, to be more commonly known as Solarian Banking here on Earth. This organisation is necessary for handling currencies and materials throughout the galaxy. However, its main role is that of a data bank for storing information relating to donor and acceptor products from different worlds... and recruiting young federation members from Earth for the federation military.

'We have since found that most relevant materials can be stored temporarily in sealed underground chambers on dead worlds under the control of robots and androids.

'These dead worlds and moons can also be used to store crude ore and other resources in transit to or from any world. Such facilities can be extended to include safe storage of radioactive, volatile and other hazardous materials for limited periods for anyone requiring those facilities and services. All such efforts concerning Earth will be carried out through Solarian Banking in the future.

'One of our intentions is to remove all environmental pollutants from Earth in the foreseeable future. Therefore, whenever possible all such toxic materials from our operations should be sited on dead and uninhabitable worlds. Presently, we shall attempt to transfer all our Solarian production from Earth to such worlds.

'I have recently learnt of the possibility to transmit our people through specially constructed long range portals. That means, we can now travel from Earth to distant systems almost instantaneously in time. Such new modes of transport will reduce the need for space ships.

'With the necessary security measures we are now able to link *almost every habitable world within our galaxy. Henceforth, we are to embark on the task of installing such portals and build extra jump stations within dead zones in order to increase their effective range. A main portal station will soon be installed on Mars with direct connection to Eden, Earth and elsewhere.*

'And now, to the immediate projects on our list. It is now an urgent matter that we find an uninhabited, but habitable world on which to transfer our production. Therefore, councillors Jon, Merol and Ecrol have been assigned to that very important mission. You may obtain necessary information from the large ships, Venusa and Martia, and explore local systems with the Andromedan ship.

'Finally, we come to the most immediate item on our list, which relates to the evacuation.

'Everything is now ready and awaiting the great moment of linkage, which I have been told is to be resumed in a few days. Councillors Lira, Julia and Petra have been nominated to assist Councillor Merian on Mars during that operation. They will sometimes be assisted by some of us whenever we are free from our other commitments. In any event I shall visit with you on the next trip to observe progress myself.

'Can I assume that it may be possible to evacuate our people by portal transfer between Venusa's ship on Mars to Martia's ship on Eden?'.

Venusa stood up to answer that question.

'Yes, Mam. Our large portals have a range of fifty light-years and there are not many stellar systems in line with both ships.'

'That answers my question and eliminates some of the procedures required for loading and unloading. Councillors Merian Senior, Lucia, Sintra and Tomas are also temporarily assigned to Eden. They are to assist in the evacuation program on that world. Do I have your full agreement on those assignments?' Sarah asked.

They agreed by lifting their right hands.

'Now, one final word on status within Solaria: With the powers

invested in me, I have decided to make everyone here a member Councillor of the Solarian Grand Council. Henceforth, our main places of residence will be located on beautiful planet Eden. Therefore, although we may still retain residence here on Earth, our beautiful palaces and seats of power will be on that world, but hopefully we shall always continue to be at one with Earth.

'Eden will also be made a free home for all Shadites and those that we know will be made honourable members of the Grand Council.

'When we have settled there, we can resume the enormous task of assisting all endangered species throughout Osmaron. Initially, Earth and Caefon will figure highly on our lists.

'Any questions?'

'In that case, may all our projects and plans meet with our Grand Lord's approval and take us all to a better and more fulfilling future,' she said.

There were no questions. She was now the leader of a powerful organization that would in time become galactic in scope.

CHAPTER 49

Final plans

Planet Eden was selected as the seat of the newly formed Government of Solaria and as such, was to represent a more humane and less self-indulgent society than the one found on Earth at the time. Sarah was to begin her new galactic empire from a clean slate, using the best minds to assist in her dream. Thus promoting the great virtues and discouraging all corrupting influences for the sake of self gratification or just emotional arousal for its own sake.

All such activities were considered wasteful on resources and unsuitable behaviour for the type of intelligence needed to save the galaxy. In their opinion all such tendencies for the sake of self-gratification for its own sake were wasteful on planetary resources and led in time to acute survival problems, not only for the human population.

They also experienced the damages done to Earth's atmosphere and its landmasses. At that time the oceans and seas had risen by over one metre in places and would continue on its upward trend because of global warming. This situation had been further accelerated by the Antarctic meteoric collision. All those changes would place a great strain on planetary populations.

They had constructed many models of human societies and simulated many scenarios within time periods in excess of a thousand years. During those projects they found most of the problems within those societies were due to drugs and other self-indulgent behavioural outlets. But most of those endemic problems were ultimately related to population growth.

'Why do most people on Earth spend so much time entertaining themselves at the expense of others. After all, most of the other animals spend almost all their waking hours scratching for an existence. There must be a sociological flaw in their cultures or one in their genetic design,' Sarah thought.

Those figures also indicated that a planet like Earth could only have sustained an optimum population of just 750 million humans of average weight and height. That figure was the optimum for sustainable natural habitats and rain forests for other indigenous life. Thus maintaining a balance in natural resources for future generations with reduced pollution. This figure was calculated on the basis of the availability of current planetary resources.

Like a planetary parasite, the resultant great mass of Earth's human population would very soon have eaten itself out of house and home. Energy and other essential resources would soon begin to dwindle and then fail, leaving in their wake strife, the complete breakdown of law and order, rampantly spreading disease and pestilence on a global scale. Those considerations did not even include the effects on other life and their habitats.

They concluded that the present problem on Earth had passed well beyond the point of no return and could never be reduced by more natural and humane methods. The population figure for a sustainable population on Earth had shrunk and was currently well below seven hundred and fifty million because of the lesser resources and deforestation. Not to mention its atmospheric and other ecological disorders.

In the year 2043, Earth's human population from their calculations, using government census and other topographical methods was presently in excess of 9 billion and rising. The time had come to act in favour of Mother Earth and her other evolving life.

The intelligence of average humans on Earth was presently well below average because of restricted oxygen during pregnancy, bad infancy care and chemically damaged bodies and brains due to pollutants and overcrowding. When all those factors were present in people living together in close proximity, the human environment so formed engendered a highly explosive cocktail, leading to even greater problems. Like any unclean child Earth had to be cleansed. However that cleansing could only have begun with the establishment of a powerful Solarian Government.

Although the process of Earth's convergence was almost finalised, it was put on hold until the time was right. However that sorry task of population reduction had to be accomplished in full before the first Javols arrived.

Eden City was to be the first city on Planet Eden. It was to be constructed on the planet's single continent close to one of its major seas. That continent named Arcadia, and larger islands were mapped into several protectorate states. Each state being placed in the hands of a Lord Protector. Those without protectors would be left alone until someone was nominated.

Each Protector had a responsibility to all life within their fief and employed many scientists and others to maintain and assist those life-forms. It was hoped the bulk of their employees would come from the Caefon evacuees, who initially would need to earn extra credits on a continuous basis.

They could also become administrators, farmers and workers within the major construction projects, assisted by robots and androids. Humans and non carnivorous animals could be imported from Earth. That was providing their effects on the natural order was negligible in a thousand years or so, to be reviewed regularly. Otherwise, they would be kept in ecologically sealed domes. Horses, cattle and other lesser herbivores were to be allowed. However some of the milder carnivores would be restricted to some islands in the middle of its small oceans and others in more distant seas that were filled with even more ferocious carnivores, but that choice was not yet on the agenda.

Finally the Solarian charter had been drafted with the help of the Ancient, Sintra, and the great book called the Anachromagnon. It lay the rules for its government and citizens and followed democratic principles. Although human councillors always had the last say in important matters, all day to day functions were in the hands of the super-intelligent computers they called Macrons. Those Macrons were Quantum AI systems thousands of times more clever than any single human mind.

The main city of Eden was built on one of the planet's lesser fertile areas on a rocky bed close to the Median Sea. So called because of its similarity to the Mediterranean Sea on Earth.

The area was first cleared of all life before the process of excavation commenced. The city was designed in four main sectors that were themselves broken into many subsections, each with smaller pedestrian walks and moving walkways. They led onto the main avenues with even more moving walkways, LPD trains and cars. All vehicular transport was restricted to the city proper while moving stairways and elevators took commuters to lower levels beneath the city.

Most of the pedestrian routes and avenues were lined with stores, shops, restaurants and other facilities in much the same way as on Earth. Power was distributed from underground fusion generators. Even human excreta and biological gases were converted and stored for fuel and other important chemicals. Those were to be recycled and used on remote farms, further minimising ecological effects. On that planet all products were designed and packaged for easy recycling and reuse.

The maximum allowed human population on planet Eden was one hundred million. When that point was reached emigration would be assisted to other neighbouring worlds.

The city proper occupied a site of approximately four hundred square kilometres. Each of the smaller areas or blocks occupied an area of four square miles.

The most central eight square miles were reserved for museums and certain ministerial offices including the Ministry of Defence and of Law and Order. All other blocks within those innermost sectors would be used for residential accommodation and accept approximately fifty thousand homes. Hence, the whole city could initially have absorbed well over ten million humans with space to spare.

After the arrival of Martia's ship, the southern sector was immediately cleared by its efficient robots and androids, with their heavy earth moving equipment.

During the first day androids and robots went out prospecting for mineral deposits and were soon mining rich vanes. Others had begun the manufacture of glass and other building materials within the ship's factories and engineering departments.

As the city was not yet built, all materials were stored ready for the building process. Within just two days the first area had been levelled and its foundation made ready for the commencement of building the first residential blocks.

After another four days, many buildings were in the construction phase. By that time, the utilities' robots were already standing by and waiting for their part in the building program. That procedure was much quicker than re-servicing and reprogramming any temporarily idle construction robot. Hence, the construction process was extremely rapid. After another week the first block of buildings were almost completed, less furniture and other decorative coverings.

The rate of building was fast enough to keep pace with the evacuation program that was soon to be initiated. In fact, the building process was completed with automatons and construction equipment that functioned about twenty times faster than humans. It was like watching a speeded up animation about twenty times faster than normal. Some robots were so quick it was extremely difficult to track their movement with the human eye. They never made mistakes or took breaks before their tasks were completed. During that process some materials were imported from Earth via Mars through Solarian Banking.

Eden was truly one of the most beautiful planets in the galaxy, but it lacked a moon. As a result, every night was almost pitch black. However, that environmental deficiency did not severely affect its human population.

Sarah had decided to visit Mars again. She was to access progress there before the evacuation commenced, but she also wanted to visit planet Eden and observe the city's progress for herself to acquire an overall picture of the evacuation program at that end.0

She was told their travel to Eden would be arranged through the ships Venusa and Martia, so they left Earth for Mars in the small eight seater scout craft, with Merian, Bawaki, Lira, Julia, Petra, Venusa and Martia.

Jon and Lumak had refitted the small Andromedan ship, so Jon was also on his way to Eden with Merol, Ecrol, Merian senior, Lucia, Sintra and Tomas. They were to leave their four senior passengers on Eden and continue their search for habitable worlds within the Solarian Arm of the galaxy. They had to locate a suitable world for production purposes.

Lumak (Doctor Jeffery Longhurst), Meron and Hamil would remain based on Earth and continue designing and manufacturing the new products and systems, including the interstellar portals that were required for use between new worlds of the Solarian Empire, including Earth.

After Sarah's arrival on Venusa's ship, she was immediately taken to the Mind Room and there they discussed certain priorities. The ship agreed with her plans and immediately began to put them into operation.

The very brave women, Sarah, Merian and Bawaki were subsequently taken to the transformation room and there changed to a second but slightly different body with special implants fitted into their brains. Venusa then prepared Sarah with all necessary technical data on the portals and other important information for Doctor Longhurst. That information would be absorbed by her implants and extracted by his computers when she returned to Earth. However she still had to undergo special training before she could use those implants. They would increase her mental capacities by over ten times and include several additional doctors in the bargain. The implanted device was the size of a pinhead.

After the training process was completed, the superwomen decided to visit Eden together by Portal. Venusa's ship soon contacted Martia's ship and both aligned their axes ready for transference. The brave women boldly walked into the large rotating frame and found themselves leaving a similar rotating frame in Martia's ship on Eden. They only realised their arrival on Martia's ship by the differing wall coverings of the twin vessel. They had travelled over 15 light years in the blink of an eye.

'I cant believe my eyes, I'm really here. This world is so beautiful. There are giant flowers everywhere!' Sintra exclaimed.

While they admired the view of their new home.

They were greeted by Martia's ship, Tomas and others who had arrived in the early morning with the Andromedan ship. But Jon, Merol and Ecrol had since left on their exploratory mission to find a suitable production world in that arm of the galaxy.

They visited Martia's Mind Room and there discussed the future program in more detail. The program was to include the building of the Solarian Museum and University for Federation Studies.

Venusa was always in constant communication with Martia, so there was usually no requirement for communicating to both on the same topic.

'This is truly an incredibly beautiful and enchanting world. I think I must be Alice in Wonderland. Unlike Earth, with its bricks and mortar, it is untainted by the hands of man, and so beautiful!' Sarah exclaimed.

'You seem to love your new home already and we haven't settled yet,' Sintra commented and she smiled.

Sarah found Eden a most pleasant world and realised the reasons for Jerry's final wishes, to move to that world after his retirement from office as President of the USA. But she wished her husband, Lumak, was with her at that moment so they could appreciate the rear beauty together.

She and her company were soon at the site and entered one of the completed multi-story residential buildings. That single block contained several such buildings and could easily have absorbed ten times their allotted numbers if several families were allowed to share accommodation on a temporary basis. The only immediate problem was food and drinking water, but the ships were working on food substitutes and drinking water was not considered a major problem with filtration units linked to the nearby sea.

Farming robots had already begun to plant suitable seeds and bulbs taken from Earth, but it was expected most food supplies would be imported from Caefon and Earth initially. Those would be supplied up to a period of two months after the evacuation was completed. High-yielding seeds and plants would be propagated in shielded domes to augment those supplies. There was also some bio-engineered experimental plants in domes on Mars.

Sarah was pleased with the rate of construction and surprised by the precision and incredible speed of the robots and machines.

She and her company soon returned to the ship and after giving her thanks to Martia's ship, was given all information relating to progress along with residential numbers and building schedules. Venusa and Martia were already waiting to link those numbers with the names of the evacuees the moment evacuation commenced.

The younger Merian found the planet, Eden, a most pleasant one and mentioned that it reminded her of Ancient Caefon. That was when that world was in its prime. It closely resembled her observations of Caefon's environment from the visual records of ancient times, but without its moons. She was almost correct in her assumptions, because the planet Eden was of an almost identical size to her home world and the parent star was also similar to Caefon's own star. However Caefon had two major continents and Eden only one, that included smaller oceans, several seas and lakes. Merian wished Plato was there with her and she made that fact known to Sarah who always made a mental note of such important info.

Presently Plato was on Caefon in Andromeda, assisting with the final phase of the evacuation. He was required to initiate the primary Omegron Portal, part of which was sighted in the underground city of Lower Cantor in that galaxy.

Despite his many responsible assistants, Plato had his hands full with the evacuation of his people. He was also to implement packing of all genetic containers and important artifacts that represented the previous existence of his and other main stellar civilizations within Andromeda. All that had to be done before the power within Lower Cantor was placed on standby.

Although the evil rapacious Javols were on their way, he knew of their progress from the concealed deep space probes and of their expected arrival on Caefon in just two months.

Merian had a small bleeper that would signal her the moment his Portal was turned on. After receiving that signal she was immediately required to remotely initiate the secondary Martian Portal by pressing a concealed button on the small bleeper device she held on a chain about her neck.

For the process to have been effective, she had to be within visible range of the Martian Portal and to have responded immediately, thus preventing disruption of the portal's symmetries. If disruption had occurred, he would have observed the change in Lower Cantor and immediately re-initiated his unit. Hopefully, getting it right the second time. Finally both units would synchronise with each other and his unit become in tune with hers on Mars. The start-up and shut down procedure could have been repeated any number of times, until they were satisfied with the portals' behaviour.

When both units were running in perfect synchronous harmony there would be a rainbow effect about their enclosures. The glow of which would eventually diminish to a faint bluish haze. That haze would be just visible about the sealed dome to indicate they were both perfectly in synchronism and in tune with each other. After that time the Omegron Portal could begin to transport people all the way from the galaxy of Andromeda to Mars.

CHAPTER 50

The evacuation commences

The Omegron Portal was installed within the Primary Dome on Mars and floated in mid space just above its anti-gravitational neutralizers. The large sphere was held in place just two metres above the funnel-shaped reception chamber. There were two such chambers which were positioned in separate rooms. However for the Andromedan evacuation the portal was placed in simplex mode, where objects and bodies could only move in a single direction. This direction being from Caefon in Andromeda to Mars in Osmaron.

The receiving chamber channelled all its recipients unto a constantly moving conveyor from the Primary to Admin Dome. From there they would be dispatched to Eden via the great ships portals.

The Primary Dome was built in two sections, one for receiving and the other transmitting. The Omegron conveyor system was constructed from powerful screening materials. Its structure included several types of field generators. Those could detect the presence of material bodies and attempt to neutralise the portal's powers for short periods in order to capture those bodies on arrival. After capture, they would slide down the funnel and be channelled unto the soft conveyor that was constantly moving just beneath their feet. By so doing, several people could be received at once. It was quite capable of accepting several bodies at a very quick rate and in succession. However they were not allowed to carry any possessions other than normally worn clothes and light jewellery.

It was estimated that over ten humans could be captured each second and if evacuation was constant, everyone could be dispatched within three days. However things were never that simple. Some evacuees hesitated to enter the device, others needed sleep and many were still working on the surface above, on

Caefon. Those were the many farmers and military guards. A closer approximation for the evacuation would be a period of two Earth weeks.

In any event, the domes could only accommodate a maximum of ten thousand people at any given time, so the whole process relied heavily on continuous movement through the great ships to Eden. Furthermore, this process had to be synchronised with the construction program on Eden. Also, several bottlenecks could exist to further slow their process.

SOUTHERN CANTOR IN PLANET CAEFON, WITHIN ANDROMEDA.

During the previous weeks most of the surface dwellers had been moved with their belongings close to the museum at Southern Cantor. All farming and other essential duties were placed in the hands of the military.

With the assistance of senior diplomats and councillors, they were told by Plato of the approaching Javols and many moved close to the underground entrance to lower cantor. However the people remained scared and uneasy while the military had to constantly keep order. Their temporary accommodation covered a large part of the surface city and looting was rife, even for a once controlled and peaceful people.

Plato intended to retain a small contingency of troops on Caefon after the evacuation to harvest as much of the remaining food products as possible. They would remain for several weeks after the evacuation was completed. Nevertheless he kept a keen eye on the Javols' progress to their stellar system.

The bird people on Coln and others were transported to a settlement close to Cantor. They would be the last to leave Caefon.

Most of the harvested food would be dehydrated and stored in large refrigerators within Lower Cantor. Those were to be transferred by portal to Eden and used as temporary rations until they were able to reap their own harvests.

The main surface city of Cantor was now full to overflowing with almost all of the planet's remaining populations. Many large structures and tents had been erected to contain them. That was until they were summarily selected to visit the underground city from where they would be dispatched.

Plato was in full control of the operation and since his return to that world, had shown the surface dwellers pictures of the Javols destruction of ancient Cantor. He had also explained the evacuation procedure to them in detail. Even so, he had to initiate the portal process by first sending through one of his most senior and respected assistants to promote faith in the method used.

The underground city could not adequately contain more than one million people at any given time, so the majority still remained on the surface above and patiently awaited their names to be called.

As usual there were the many fanatics who tried to spread gossip and bad news in an attempt to prevent people from leaving, but Plato and others were quite effective in convincing the population of the alternatives. Most of the minds of those doubting members of society were soon changed after their first visit to the underground city. He had also arranged compulsory daily excursions to the underground city, to explain its existence and show them the advanced technologies of the Ancients. They were constantly shown gory records of Javols destroying their ancient world.

Many of those disorganized trouble makers wanted to survive just as much as anyone else and did not wish to remain alone on the desolate planet, with most or all of their families and friends in a distant galaxy and there was also the approaching Javols to consider.

THE OMEGRON PORTAL IS ON

Sarah and her companions were just getting ready to leave Martia's ship on Eden when an urgent message came through from Venusa's ship:

'I have just received message from Venusa's ship. It confirms the presence of rainbow activity above the Omegron Portal on Mars. This activity signals the presence of a higher symmetrical order between both units due to primary activation on Caefon.'

The young Merian began to panic and without hesitation decided to find the nearest portal back to Mars, followed by Sarah and the others. Both ships immediately realigned their axes and the women once again found themselves in Venusa's ship on Mars. They entered the Mind Room to observe the viewer. They could see large rainbow streamers about the dome. The strange effect projected itself several hundred feet above the Martian surface. The surrounding area, including the other domes and their ship, were illuminated by its changing scintillations. Although beautiful to watch they were not sure of the dangers caused by such spacial distortions.

'What am I to do?' Merian asked, while fidgeting with the device about her neck.

'Calm... Calm.. We are not going anywhere until this job is properly done. Think carefully about the sequence of initiation. Write it down if you have to and don't worry about the glorious display above the Martian plains, it's only telling us it's alive,' Sarah said and she became as calm as a dove.

Merian nervously removed the small device from about her neck then pressed the ring of small buttons in a particular sequence. Finally she pressed the little red recessed button at its centre. The rainbow effect immediately reduced to about 50 percent of its original size, but she was still worried the process was not complete. Any serious problems in matter transmission could result in lost evacuees. However Venusa advised her to wait for several minutes before she repeated the procedure.

After just one minute the rainbow suddenly diminished to zero and a blueish haze appeared in its place. The long conveyor was moving, indicating that the portals were in synchronism with each other. Merian's face lit up with the pleasure of knowing her people would shortly be on their way, including her beloved Plato.

Venusa's ship soon extended an entrance towards one of Admin

Dome's docking areas and the great ship was now linked to accept refugees, soon to be transferred by portal to Martia's ship on Eden.

Merian and the others joined Sarah within the dome; all dressed in Solarian Grey to assist in the evacuation program that was not long to follow.

'Soon, this day another prophesy will be fulfilled. Thank you our lord, Grand Lord Gerron!' The young Merian shouted, and Sarah agreed.

The first person through was one of Plato's most senior assistants. He was dressed in a white fabric overall and ecstatic when he observed Merian's smiling face as soon as he got off the conveyor. She went up to him, checked his heart rate and sea blue eyes before taking him to a local medical unit for a complete body scan.

He was obviously the first guineapig sent to test the portal system. Plato thought Merian would re-trigger the portal if something went wrong. Nevertheless he could easily have detected any change in rainbow activity during the initial interval which could only have meant something was wrong.

After Merian had completely scanned his body, while at the same time holding a lengthy conversation with the scientist, she could find nothing wrong and continued to wait for her second conveyor passenger.

When Plato did not receive a negative signal for a period of ten minutes, it was an indication that his guinea pig had arrived in one piece. The next one to follow on the conveyor was the scientist's basic belongings.

Instructions were displayed everywhere within the main evacuation dome in their Ancient scripts and hieroglyphics. There were thousands of small computer books available and programmed with all relevant data and menus. Those were to be supplied to the heads of each family group. Senior members of their society would be placed as guardians for ten families and ten such guardians would be placed under a supervisor, with group leaders, superintendents and so on up the ladder.

Every superintendent handled a sub-sector of residential blocks on Eden. Their position included the maintenance of law and order and to ensure everyone was cared for and happy during the evacuation process.

The next one through was an official from Coln. They were a very strange bird-like race with circular beaks for lips but with almost normal human teeth. They were usually only three feet tall and this particular official looked more like a miniature version of Father Christmas, with his broad belt and golden buckle, his fluffy white feathers and other colourful attachments forming his attire.

The male members of his race had long since lost their powers of flight. That could have been many millions of years ago, but some of their more angelic females could still achieve that athletic goal after special training. The process was more akin to humans learning the combined sports of swimming and ice-skating to a high level of competence.

He stared sternly at Merian and the other human females while handing her his identification card, perhaps wondering whether he had just jumped out of the frying pan and into the blazing inferno. He was a senior official on his world who was expected to be treated with dignity and given more privileges than most others. However Sarah soon had him escorted to Venusa's ship to await the arrival of the other members of his family.

As more evacuees came through, their identification cards were taken from them and placed into the computer scanners that fed data directly to Venusa's ship and then to Martia's ship.

The conveyor was carrying a constant stream of humans and others with their basic belongings. Many strange aliens were among the evacuees, there were no complaints from anyone. Some of those aliens were the last survivors of their home worlds. Their previous generations had existed for three thousand years in the underground city of Lower Cantor waiting all this time for freedom. Then there were many from the Coln system with its bird people to evacuate. They were further away from the path of the Javols while evacuated near Cantor on Caefon and would follow next. They were promised their own protectorate state on Eden.

CHAPTER 51

Ominous Worlds

Jon, Merol and Ecrol left with The Ship to search for suitable uninhabitable worlds within the Solarian arm of the galaxy. That was the galactic arm that contained our Solar System. Osmaron or the Milky Way galaxy contained three main galactic arms, they were the Solarian, Lodorian and Tarranian arms, as named by Sarah. All uninhabited worlds would be listed and if found suitable, be used for production and storage. While surveying that part of the galaxy they intended to take stock of both habitable and inhabitable worlds for the Federation's own records. Those were to be terra formed at a later date.

As mentioned before, that arm was the one that contained the Solar System and Eden and was the longest of the three major galactic arms. It extended from the central bulge and spiralled to a distance of almost two hundred thousand light years - almost twice the diameter of the galaxy towards its outermost rim. The direct distance from Eden to that part of the outer rim was barely seventy thousand light years.

It was decided to first travel towards the outer rim of the galaxy and from there commence the search. During that process all suitable systems would be logged while making their way back towards the centre. They would leave the innermost part of the spiral from Eden towards the galactic centre for the final search. That final part of the search would be carried out at some future date with specially designed probes.

While they travelled they could once again observe the numerous red specks on the large screen and wondered what type of structure they concealed. They had not yet encountered any large stations or facilities and were curious enough to ask The Ship whether it was possible to pass by, or even visit an invisible observation station on-route.

The ship soon replied:

'This whole universe is like a living organism with each part vectored into another negative universe within yet another space-time continuum. They are not mutual reflections of each other, for the laws of chaos here are negated over there. That other universe exists as a result of this one and may be considered a negative reflection. Perhaps its most negative and perfect part. This would have taken place during its initial formation well before time and space existed within its form which is 5th dimensional.

'Many aeons ago the Plorans themselves, also Osmaronites, but from a satellite galaxy called Balion, found ways to exist within that plenum or negative universe. But first had to change their bodies in substance and structure to live within such a perfect environment, where any random wave or chaotic change could never occur. Everything being temporally connected in space and in time. Short and long sequences of continuous events always diminished to return back to a beginning and repeated themselves to eternity.

'However, they found ways of jumping such causal loops initially, until they engineered their own temporal and long causal structures for their own survival causation within its strange continuum. That was during the time when they outgrew their human bodies.

'You see. They were then one of the most brilliant minds in the universe. Because of the reasons I have mentioned... primal life could not have naturally evolved within that orderly universe, so the Plorans had its vastness and tranquillity all to themselves.

'During that period of isolation, they were well away from the wars and turbulence of this universe. That was during its initial phase, which began many billions of years ago. From that time there have been many predators and planetary wars that threatened most life within this universe. There were numerous pirate and vermin species that constantly plagued young worlds for their own personal self-gratification and resources.

'In time the Plorans became bored with their new home universe, being themselves of an active mental nature. They found it lacked the challenges and needed the variation and beauty of our chaotic universe with its differing colours, art, science and random ways *of disciplines. After that erratic phase had somewhat diminished, with a significant reduction in its extreme randomness, instability and radiation levels; many more stable life-forms began to evolve and it was once again time for them to return, occupy and assist Osmaron and other populated galaxies.*

'Although they needed clean excitement within their existence, they did not want to interfere or disrupt the primal species, most of whom were extremely young. Instead they took care by sometimes assisting those going through difficult periods and always without their knowledge. They also instilled into them ideas of bad and dangerous forms like serpents, bats, devils and demons. They knew that even now some of the vermin plagues of that dreadful past may still have survived and preserved in some sealed underworld.

'After devising a suitable form for existence in our primal universe, they engineered temporal loop lines between both overlapping universes which gave them the powers to be at any place within either universe, almost instantly in time. For once, almost anywhere within the known universe was accessible to them. Every place within Osmaron, now the seat of the Grand Lord, could be observed and channelled into the Greater Mind or Greater Purpose within the plenum of Gohenna or Goh.

In a sense, they were the true builders. The Plorans like Lord Vektron had become the true guardians of the universe. Even so, they are all under Grand Lord Gerra. Grand Lord of our part of the known universe. He is not a Ploran and neither is he from Osmaron nor indeed anywhere else. Some say that he, with his other six brothers, came into existence with the universe itself, but that information is not yet freely available.'

The Ship slowed as it approached an almost invisible reddish glow and suddenly the screen was filled with all red.

Once again The Ship began to speak:

'The station you now observe is within universes and galaxies. They were constructed by the Octans who are also within the

Greater Purpose. These stations are Virtual. Being made of neither positive nor negative matter, but with the ability to suddenly transpose into any of the two galaxies by an even more advanced form of transposition. All these structures were engineered by the Octans. Although beneath the Plorans, they are now the most advanced species in Osmaron.

'Such structures do not materially clog the shipping lanes or pathways of either galaxies. Any object may travel directly through them without any effect. Yet, they are able to detect intruders and materialize if necessary to defend their volume of space. They guard Osmaron and other important galaxies against the Javols and other dangerous forms. There are many such invisible stations within Solaria. They are like antibodies in our galaxy in much the way as your bodies own antibodies will fight off infection.

'As you may now observe, there are more situated closer to Solaria than anywhere else within Osmaron.

'We are now getting close to the rim, do you wish to change course?'

'Yes, we have gone far enough. Let us start our observation scan from here towards Eden, within a sub volume of twenty thousand cubicrons, through the centre of this arm. There are many systems within this sector but all appear to be very ancient with little remaining atmospheres. Why are there so many dead worlds in this sector? It's as if a galactic storm passed through this area and took everyone out,' Jon said.

'Yea, the whole place is desolate. Like some major disaster passed through this part of the galaxy in ancient times,' Merol repeated.

'On the five I've observed, there is not enough atmosphere for sustaining primal life in its truest sense. Many are mainly desert. We should record all these systems for future reference including, cloud nebulae and recently formed stellar nurseries and systems. This process should be carried out until we find some worlds better suited to our purpose, then we can land and observe their environments more closely,' Jon said.

Merol was controlling the viewer when he called Jon to the screen.

'I have just observed a suitable planetary system. The outer world appears to have a dense atmosphere... but there are large rings of debris encircling its equatorial region. Perhaps due to the explosion of one of its moons.... The orbiting asteroids appear to be stable. However the planet's surface is slightly cratered from showers of such debris.'

The Ship then interrupted:

'High levels of radiation can be detected from those regions. Some of the larger craters are due to some type of nuclear explosion.

'The original moon also appear to have been mined to self-destruct.

'The time of this catastrophe was approximately two hundred million years ago, judging from the spectrum and intensity of radiation received.

'The planet is suitable for robotic production, but high radiation levels make it unsuitable for the manufacture of our most sensitive microid equipment.

'Perhaps we should take a closer look?'

'Let's be cautious!'

Jon agreed, but they were not allowed to leave the ship under any circumstances. The Ship decided to cruise around the planet once, while searching for any signs of a past civilization. They were astonished by their findings; for amidst all the craters were pyramids and hexagonal structures of all shapes and sizes. They were situated close to a greenish algae-covered lake with other pools that speckled the warmer areas. There were no oceans, just one almost complete desert similar to the one on Colmi II, found on a previous mission and marked by similar greenish radioactive lakes.

Its atmosphere was at last beginning to stabilize after its disruptive past, when all life had suddenly ceased to exist on its surface.

Jon remembered the similarities to Colmi II, but the craters here were a lot more numerous, due to a more recent disaster. Most of the larger structures had not yet corroded away or became covered by the desert's sands. Jon wondered,
'Why, why, why? Who or what could be the destroyer of worlds?
He asked The Ship for an explanation.

'There have been many such predators in the past: The Hexolytes, Drondytes, Mesotrenes, Polyatans, to name but a few and now the Javols.
'Most of those ancient predatory species have since departed and those still existing are held in eternal prisons of their own making. This here is too recent to be their handy-work.. They could have been a revived group or even a new predator species.'

He did not understand the full implications of the last sentence, but asked the ship to record all important data for future analysis before visiting the other and much hotter planet in the system.
Its neighbouring world was much closer to their parent star. With an orbital period almost precisely matching the star's rotational period, causing it to show the same parts of its surface to light and radiation. The other hemisphere was always in permanent darkness. That world was extremely hot, being over three hundred degrees centigrade at its warmest half. Whatever was left of its atmosphere and oceans were in the form of steam. There were many signs of volcanic activity on its surface by lava flows, sulphurous lakes and other noxious substances. Even so, its magnetic fields were extreme, which retained a relatively thick atmosphere.
Nevertheless, that place was the proverbial hell planet and yet, some areas on its dark side were cooler, with readings of seventy degrees centigrade in central regions. There was constant atmospheric movement from the hotter to its cooler side and vice versa which obviously benefited both regions. That world was contradictory in many respects. For one, although its outer crust did very little rotation, there was a north and south pole with a strong magnetic field and a central rotating core. That factor alone

would have ensured the retention of a large atmosphere. The star was a young one, obviously wasting its energies on such dormant worlds.

They continued searching and were astounded by what they found.

CHAPTER 52

Exoile and Drondyte - Devils and Serpents

They were soon viewing similar hexagonal structures on the large screen, yet no life could be sensed anywhere on the hotter world closest to the parent star.

'Are these structures hollow?' Jon asked The Ship.

'Yes, they are. Shall we travel to the other side while scanning for more similar structures?'

Jon agreed while The Ship went around to the hotter side. A cluster of such buildings were found in the centre of the hot disk, well away from the other more random clusters on the colder side.

'Could these structures have been for the evacuation of creatures from their original world, back there, before its destruction?

'Perhaps they were sealed in... against the extreme conditions, but by so doing have imprisoned themselves from all other external surface life. That is probably the reason why we were unable to sense life on these worlds... These enclosures could have been constructed from very high thermal insulators.... Perhaps they had little choice and nowhere else to go, not yet having learnt the technologies of interstellar flight?' Merol inquired.

'An interesting hypothesis, but why would they have also built within the very hot area, when strictly speaking, it is not required, because of the more favourable climate and abundance of space on the much colder side. Nevertheless, they do not appear to be using solar or other power generators of any type known to our science,' Jon replied.

Jon was completely baffled for a while, but The Ship interjected:

'I can, with your permission, transpose within one of the larger structures and hover at the highest level while observing its

interior.
  'The information so gained might answer our questions.'

Jon put that question to the vote and they decided to transpose within the sealed structure. When they entered their presence was immediately felt by its occupants. They could observe very large bat-like creatures. Those were black in colour with large craniums and standing on a highly polished surface. The bats had red glowing eyes, large wings and cloven hooves.

They scattered from the central circle and triangles as if to minimise their losses in case of a central explosion. When the creatures found the danger was not from the circle they began to point their small beam weapons towards the ship now hovering high in the ceiling.

The Ship soon displaced itself in space and showed the bats its image at a different location. Then it spoke to them in sunolingua, in an attempt to get a verbal or other response to decipher their mode of communication.

The sounds they uttered were not sunolingua. The creatures issued commands and instructions, but at a much higher frequency, sounding more like crickets than bats. The Ship listened to the chaotic chit-chat and very soon began to form some verbal structure by which it could communicate with the clever creatures. Then the ship attempted to speak their language:

  'I am friendly and come from another stellar system. Do you understand me?'

The Ship repeated those words three times before the creatures had settled from their fright and confusion.

The place was indeed some kind of prison, because there were no lights, except for a slight greenish glow radiating from within the structure. That faint light appeared to radiate from the central pentacle and reflected towards the many circular and triangular symbols that were fitted into the floor of the structure.

The internal wall was not hexagonal as one would have deduced from its external shape, but was instead a perfect sphere and as smooth as a mirror. It might well have been a near-perfect reflector, thus forming a type of giant thermos flask.

As if by magic they could now observe several large containers of snakelike worms. The large worms were moving about each other within large trays. They were obviously brought up from a lower level by a concealed elevator. At least that could have been one answer to their sudden appearance.

The trays moved along the circles towards the twelve bats within that chamber. Each took a large worm and began to eat the creature from its tail upwards. Chewing off little bits at a time, while the creature struggled within their claws.

Jon observed the cruelty of the process but did not wish to interfere with their callous eating habits. When they were finished, they wiped their putrid faces of remains and blood while six of the creatures took up positions at six points on the large hexagram engraved circle, not too unlike those used by witchcraft followers on Earth. While they held their claws around the circle, the green glow increased within that area and they appear to fuse into a much larger form.

The creature so formed was very similar to the original bats, but with smaller wings, a large piercing horn on its forehead, a much longer tail and other piercing and stinging organs at its lower front.

'What on Earth is this monster! A demon from hell?' Ecrol inquired, and the ship answered.

'You are almost right in your conclusions. Many such demons existed in the universe when it was young. Some evolved out of elemental substance in much the same way as primals evolved from bacterial cells. However, most of these demons have since departed this universe. Because of certain changes in the balance of matter, they can no longer survive within its environment. Now, they can only exist like fish out of water, constantly grasping for breath. However, this one appears to be suspended within some form of temporal loop,' The Ship replied.

'What do you mean?' Jon inquired.

'It appears to be held in a time that repeats itself over and over

to eternity. That way they can never die. It's like us repeating the past hours of our travels over and over again. That way we could never grow old or die of starvation,' the ship replied.

'You mean to say, they were that advanced,' Merol inquired.

'Elementals are different to Primals, in that they are able to observe, become one with and transform the basic nature of matter. While we can only observe surfaces and partake in the more natural laws of physics,' The Ship replied and Merol swallowed hard.

The Ship asked the creature for the reason of its imprisonment and the creature answered.

'We were at war with another on the other world within this system. They had visited us one day from the stars and mined our world and its moons; blackmailing us to do as they asked or face disastrous consequences. Having little recourse in the matter, we went along with them for a while, but they soon began to devour our children in the most excruciating ways imaginable. They sacrificed all our societies to debauchery, crucifixion and feasted on our still living bodies, enjoying and savouring the pains and screams of their victims in the process.'

'This was truly ghastly!'

'We could no more accept the intolerable situation, so we tried to take them over, but lost in the process. Luckily, we were able to build this place in secrecy and steal one of their ships in time to evacuate some of our more senior members to this hellish world,' the creature said.

The Ship asked a question:

'Are they also like you in form?'

'No, they are more like very large serpents with webbed hands and feet. After they won the war they creamed the best part of this world for their own kind before exploding their large bombs. Luckily for us, we had previously mined their large star-ships which also went up in the explosions.

'You must help us to take back that which is rightly ours.

'Please help us! Please?' the creature pleaded.

Despite all the creature's pleadings, The Ship could not register any life within the structure and yet the creature was there and being recorded.

When the creature realized it wasn't gaining ground with The Ship it changed its attitude into a more aggressive one.

'I am Hexil of Dron. But for this chamber of entrapment I would have used your energies against you as I have against even my best friends in the past. I have not met your form before in my travels. Are you newly created and not of a primal nature?' the creature inquired in a strange and powerful voice, but this time in Sunolingua.

The Ship, realizing some form of deception, replied:

'You are not in a position to ask questions of your lords and masters. You may return to your previous transformations.'

Once again the creature transformed. This time into the five large bats and they went away from the main circle towards other triangles where they remained as if in hibernation with the other seven.

The worms and other items around the place had suddenly disappeared. Jon and the others did not know what to make of the strange aberration and asked The Ship again for its advice.

'Their self-imprisonment was obviously engineered by a much greater mind.

'The circles, triangles and other forms remind me of ancient portals used by the original masters or Patriarch Gods of that era, during the most vicious periods of our universe many aeons ago. That would answer the question: "why the bats went away from the large circle as we arrived?" They obviously expected one of their enemies to arrive by that route, from within the portal.

'These ancient portals could still be linked to other worlds within

our universe. Although it is quite possible they are not fully operational at this time.

'These creatures show no sign of life within our monitors and sensors, which might mean their truest forms are suspended within dimensions by other portals designed for that purpose and yet, allowing them some freedom and influence on their own destinies. Perhaps one of the conditions of their imprisonment.

'I strongly believe these creatures to be demonic elemental servants of the cruel Hexolytes, from their eating habits and deceptive attitude. Most of the information given to us, although not entirely lies, were obviously meant to deceive us into freeing them once again into the universe, with possible disastrous consequences. However, even if they were freed their masters have long since departed this universe and they could not exist for long in our present universe.

'We must leave this place as soon as possible and mark this prison world with special security coding within our defence computers.

'I have my own hypothesis on this situation which I shall tell you soon, after we have visited the creatures on the other side, if indeed they exist.'

'Yes, but if they cannot be freed, how could they have acquired ships and weapons to destroy the world out there?' Jon inquired.

'They could have been assisted by a very intelligent species with knowledge of screening them from the environment. Those could have been the ones with knowledge to build the highly reflective chambers,' The Ship replied, but Jon was not convinced.

'Yes, but how were they re-imprisoned and by whom?' Merol inquired.

'By themselves, if they had little choice. They could have chosen that type of eternal life over death,' Jon replied.

The Ship disappeared from the building and suddenly reappeared in one of the similar buildings on the other side of the planet. The large floor of that building had many small pyramid structures. One of the larger serpents could be seen devouring a large bat, but not of a similar type to the Hexolyte servants.

The serpent stung the creature with its small under tail and like the Hexolytes, began to eat the creature from its tail upwards while it screamed in agony.

During this time other smaller serpents gathered around and also started to feast, sometimes even pushing their front claws into the creature and ripping bits of its wings apart, but never damaging its most vital organs, which they left for last. They tended to enjoy and savour its screams.

The larger creature, by some strange quirk, was now kissing the bat and embracing it, while it continued to get closer to its juicier, most vital organs. Blood was now spouting out of its mouth and nostrils, but the serpent continued to kiss, and lick its blood. Very soon it was stuck to the bat's mouth as if drinking the rich supply of blood and other supplies of body nutrients now spouting out of its mouth while the other smaller family members continued to eat away at its most vital parts.

When they had finished eating the bat, its head was taken away and mounted on a small cross-like pole.

Jon, Merol and Ecrol, with utter revulsion, watched the nightmarish occurrence and could little believe their eyes, for those creatures had appeared to be even more sadistic than the Hexolyte bats. What planet could have spawned such vicious and sadistic demons? They thought.

The serpent was not really a serpent in the truest sense. It was like a standing broad cobra with four small arms and webbed claws, a long tail and a very large cranium, showing high intelligence, but with vicious fangs and powerful hypnotising eyes for cunning and evil. It did not have a forked tongue but had another small stinging claw just below its broader abdomen.

Its underbelly was coloured broad red bands on cream scales, but the rest of its body was coloured blue and green.

The moment they observed the ship, which was suspended in the high ceiling, they dived into the loose sand for shelter. The larger serpent soon came out of the sand and as it lifted its head several smaller ones rolled off his body. Although some tried to cling on, they lost their grip and was again covered by the course sand.

That chamber might have been the home of a single family of those snakelike creatures. Their little babies looked more like large lizards than their monstrous parents. The older children were still hiding in the sand, obviously waiting for a signal from their parents to surface.

Once again The Ship began to speak and the whole chamber resounded and echoed. The large serpent began to communicate while others continued to crawl into the larger building, muttering fearfully to themselves. Unlike the smaller Hexolyte servants bats, which were obviously not true life-forms, but suspended in time, these serpents had evolved well-developed vocal cords and a structured language.

The hexagonal structure's interior was highly reflective and relatively well lit by torches at its lower levels. Its internal temperature was maintained at a constant forty-three degrees centigrade by air circulating from lower chambers below the pyramids. But there were no signs of any advanced technology beyond just the basic smaller structures and torches. In any event where would they have acquired the basic raw materials for building on such a barren world. They soon realised those serpents had little knowledge, even of the greater structures they inhabited.

The primitive lighting was by oil torches, being composed of spirals of bat wings which contained natural oils. There may have been other creatures like the large worms that the bats fed on, but the bats were obviously their main staple diet and perhaps their only one. They realized that even on that apparently barren world there was a type of food chain. Perhaps within large underground caves, or perhaps they brought those creatures with them.

The serpents may have already taken themselves outside of their relatively cool enclosures by digging beneath their structures. In all probability they could not survive for sustained periods at the higher temperatures of seventy plus.

Their world never saw much light other than the small disk of their forgotten home planet with its small rings of debris.

It was soon assumed that they had lost all knowledge of their violent and vicious past. There was no sign of any written information or advanced technology.

The Ship soon analysed their language and began to speak to them:

'I have come in peace.
'Have you lived in this place long?'

The large serpent moved its tail to one side.

'As far as we can remember, great one. Can you think of a reason why we should be somewhere else?' it replied.

The Ship then asked a question:

'Where do you get your food from?'

'We grow our foods in other local buildings and in underground caves. But why do you wish to know of such things,' the serpent replied.

The Ship again spoke:

'I am sorry for asking you these questions, but I am on a mission to assess your world and others in this area. Is there anything else I should know about your life here?'

'No! Great one. As you can see, we have what we need and little knowledge of anything else,' the serpent replied.

The Ship departed from that world as suddenly as it had arrived.

Jon and his company were confused by the whole episode, but the ship began to unfold its hypothesis on the most probable past of that system and many other dead worlds within the habitable but uninhabited systems they had visited.

The Ship continued to speak:

'My hypothesis is a very simple one and I think it's close to the truth from the data received. I think Hexolyte remnants were the last to visit the original planet, after the serpents... They were obviously assisted by a local intelligent and technological species with a knowledge of interstellar travel. Perhaps a batlike species

like the ones in the demonic pyramid. They could have tried to get help from those Hexolytes to destroy their cruel invaders.

'Those others I now think to be the direct descendant of the Drondytes... They had doubtless existed there many millennia before, eating and corrupting the indigenous population as they had done to other dead worlds we have visited. They could well have been the last remnant of Drondytes. Their very last remnants after countless billions of years of survival.

'They would first arrive in their large star-ships, mine the planet and its moons and begin to abuse its populations. They received more pleasures from taking over intelligent worlds; so the indigenous bats and others might have had a relatively advanced society.

'The serpents were obviously the most cruel and sadistic of the two predators, but the least advanced, although having acquired interstellar technology from one of their captives. However not portal technology, as I could see no sign of their construction within their own enclosures. These serpents were obviously no great threat to the Patriarchs, then masters of the universe. Despite that fact, they have found themselves in an eternal prison. I suppose fair retribution for the destruction of all life within this galactic sector. They must have terminated all life in this part of the Solarian arm over a period of many millennia.

'As we have observed, this world makes an ideal prison because of its almost nonexistent resources and minerals, not to mention its harsh environment. Hence, these creatures may never find a way out of their ecological tombs, and they should never be so allowed by anyone in the future.

'The indigenous bats might also be paying a penalty for past crimes on the more dominant, but now extinct species. For all we know, they might even have been a human type, but that is a broad assumption.

''The great disaster could have been due to mutual hostilities between both predator species. Perhaps, as the food supplies diminished and competition increased. Even so, the Hexolytes would have been the masters because of their more superior and technologically advanced minds, not forgetting their demonic

assistants. Therefore each may have laid mines on each other's ships and installations, causing mutual destruction when the surface mines and missiles exploded.

'The Patriarch masters would have imprisoned hexolytes and demons eons before. So their trap has been in existence many eons before.

'This is a good reminder to us all, that our insatiable uncontrolled desires of self-gratification may eventually lead to our own ruin in the end and also to the detriment of our future surviving generations, as in the case of the Drondytes.

'The creatures observed could have been the descendants of the main predators, who hopefully, will never prey again on anyone outside of their concealed prisons.'

'What a hellish world!' Merol interjected.

Jon and his companions listened patiently to The Ship. They could not find any flaws in his judgement and from what they themselves had recently experienced.

They were once again on their way, searching for more habitable worlds.

In all the worlds they visited within that section of Osmaron, there were just fifty five habitable worlds and three of those were fifteen light years away from the planet Eden. Many of the more distant ones had become hot deserts that showed signs of abuse and destruction by predator species. The last and most recently destroyed was the system they visited, with its strange structures and prisoners. So the predators, which were once a predominant kind, were obviously now out of commission and would hopefully never again return to plague that part of Osmaron. They soon found a suitable uninhabited system which they named Polion and chose three neighbouring worlds for the purpose of production.

Jon decided not to continue the search beyond Eden, towards the centre of the galaxy. Instead, they set course for Mars, to assist the others with the evacuation program.

CHAPTER 53

Consolidating the empire

THE EVACUATION

After only one week the evacuation was moving slower than scheduled. Only half a million had arrived on Eden. Also, all the accommodation slack was already taken up. Any further settlement being allowed by the rate of the building program and the release of completed units.

Most evacuees arrived with enough rations for two weeks, so food and other resources had to be ferried from Earth to Mars after those initial two weeks. That was until transportation portals were installed between Earth, Mars and Eden. Those interstellar portals were not yet fully optimized and tested for life-forms. They could only be used for transferring foodstuffs and materials.

Nevertheless more food supplies could be transferred from Caefon after all civilian evacuees had left. At that time the underground city of Lower Cantor could be used for the storage of as much food and materials as possible, even while its fusion generators were functioning on standby. Nevertheless during that time its main sun-lamps and projectors would be switched off to conserve power. The underground city being sealed off from the surface could retain its internal temperature and pressure for a very long time. Even so, all plant life relying on sunlight would soon die.

The space probes within the local systems constantly relayed information on the Javols progress and the military geared their programs to suit. When the time became critical they would themselves be evacuated to the underworld of Lower Cantor.

THE FINAL SWEEP BEGINS

The Omegron Portal operated almost flawlessly, except for one short period when there was a brilliant white flash about the Martian dome. It was thought Plato would have seen a similar flash of light in Lower Cantor and taken the necessary steps to alleviate any detrimental operation. The problem appeared to have subsequently cleared itself. That strange occurrence took place two million transpositions ago and it was now running like clock work. Even so, it was not possible to lose anyone through the system that way, since both chambers transposed their bodies almost instantaneously in time. Therefore it either sent or refused matter within its fields.

Shadite Plato was expected to remain on Caefon until the end of the evacuation. There was still so much work left to do and he was meant to keep a keen eye on the Portal, military guards, the Javols and the general evacuation program. He was also to permanently seal the main shaft close to the museum with explosives. That action was necessary to prevent curious Javols visiting the underground city.

There was still no sign of Javols' activity within their local systems and whatever little information he had received from deep space probes, indicated they were a little over a month away.

He had also received signals from the large maulars and vessels now entering the Andromedan galactic rim to begin their sweep on their way towards the galactic centre. But that was a slow process because of their large structures and more antiquated design. They were of an older LPD design that was constructed over three thousand years ago. It was estimated they would take in excess of one century to cover the distance across Andromeda during their mission to lay probes, search and destroy.

The Javols were less than two centuries away from Osmaron and followed their large supply vessels which carried enough rations for their intergalactic trip. Many had formed into large mobile spheres and gone into hibernation during that long period.

EVACUATION ENDS and LOWER CANTOR MOTHBALLED

After another month the evacuation was completed. All genetic materials, artifacts and whatever other items they considered important were dispatched to Eden.

A small contingency of the Military was the last to leave the farms on Caefon. Before abandoning the planet they carried out a thorough search for human life. After that exhaustive search the museum was finally evacuated and destroyed along with most of the local area above. Such drastic action was to prevent Javols gaining access to the underground city, which had been moth-balled until its requirement in the foreseeable future. Nevertheless there still remained several life forms in its small underworld forests. Those would be evacuated before the many power systems were turned off.

The destruction of the museum and elevator entrances permanently hid and sealed the elevators' shafts to the underground city of Lower Cantor.

After all major life had been evacuated from the underworld of Lower Cantor, the Omegron Portal at that point was placed in another housing and modified with more sensitive devices to act as a two-way transposer. In this much lower and limited standby operational mode it required much less power from the fusion generators, so the power drain was minimal.

All the powerful underground city lamps, projectors and utilities were turned off in order to conserve energy. Any residual energy would be used to maintain the Omegron Portal in its present mode of operation. It would also be required to maintain the large refrigeration units holding non essential but important foodstuffs and other biological and chemical substances. All animals, including rear crustaceans and fish, were subsequently dispatched to a small environmental dome on Eden. The scavenging insects could still survive in the underworld city on rotting leaves and other debris for many years to come.

EDEN CITY

Initially, the organisation within Eden City was very haphazard to say the least, but when the trained military arrived from Caefon they were placed under Jon. Under his direction they were allowed to assist in ration distribution, farming and other general law and order duties. By then the population was close to eleven million humans and other alien life-forms that had been evacuated from Andromeda. The Coln bird people had been evacuated soon after the Caefonites and settled well within their own state on Eden. Many had also settled in Eden City and had joined Meron's group as planetologists and scientist.

Caefonites or the New Ancients as they were sometimes called, were a very organised and resourceful people, who soon began their own programs for the schooling of their children and other social activities. They found their New World much more beautiful than the one they had left and soon settled into their new ways of living.

After the building of the shopping precincts, there were many vacancies for empty stores, shops and commercial ventures of the non-polluting kind. Sarah wanted her communities to be similar to those within the better Earth cities, so those interested business persons were sent on special commercial courses to learn all about Solarian Banking methods. They also studied courses on the primary English Language and Sunolingua which was to be the new interstellar language used by the Federation. Sunolingua was a much better language for transferring concepts through Brain Implants and hundreds of times faster than languages like English. It could also be used for communicating directly with computers, and lower life-forms through implants.

On Earth, one of Lumak's (Doctor Jeffery Longhurst) factories had since been converted to a ration storage warehouse, with inbuilt one-way portal. Its robots were constantly on the move transferring goods between both worlds via Mars. Most of the local farmlands had been bought by Lumak and Madeline's family, and were presently used as efficient agricultural farms, although not yet being fully harvested.

The robots and androids, having completed the central administration block in Eden City had turned their attention to palaces that were to be constructed within each of the first protectorate fiefs. Those fiefs covered a relatively small section of the Gardens of Eden State and most fertile areas of the great continent. Protectors were chosen among senior councillors. They were given large estates outside of the protectorate realms as their own personal fiefs, come what may.

The main palaces, however, were not theirs to keep once they were no longer council members. Such beautiful structures were essential if Solaria intended to show a superior image to members of the federation and was also important for entertaining diplomatic guests from all parts of the galaxy, so they were also given secondary fiefs on which to build their own palaces.

The large super-intelligent Macron Computers were almost in full control, guided by the council and its administrators. However, most people still preferred to use their creative skills freely. Therefore many were returning to their hobbies and duties in much the same way as they had done on Caefon, either to earn extra credits or for their own personal satisfaction.

Crimes were minimal and serious criminals were transported out of Eden to work on the production and mining worlds for specified periods. Those with psychological disorders were promptly cured of their illness and placed into more pleasant environments.

Caefonites possessed a high level of contentment and commitment and were seldom envious of their friends or neighbours.

MADELINE'S MAJOR SHOCK

One day Lumak called beautiful Madeline into the dining room at the manor to explain a very important matter to her and her family and they nervously followed.

'My dear extended family members, what I am to tell you must go no further,' he said and they listened carefully.

'You have our word,' Madeline replied, while giving that special look to her children. Although in her nineties she had the body and looks of a thirty year old woman.

'How would you like to live in a most beautiful paradise, where no one ever grew old. You would also have the freedom to come back to this place whenever you chose. But you must always keep the secret,' he said.

'What place is this?' her eldest son Joseph asked.

'It's a new world called Eden. Jerry and Meron discovered it when they travelled the stars. It's virtually free of pests and disease. You will have your own golden palace and thousands of acres of land, free of cost,' he said and they were numbed.

'What we have to do?' she inquired with extreme willingness.

'Just live and carry on doing what you do best. Anyway, think about what I have said. I love you guys and always want you to be with me,' he said. They went up to him and embraced as a single family.

Later, Madeline and her family agreed to Lumak's offer, but they wanted to continue in their roles as caretakers of Lumak's homes and properties on Earth and elsewhere.

THE GREAT SHIPS

With the evacuation ended, Venusa and Martia's ships were lying side by side on the newly built space docks just outside Eden City. They were used as temporary universities for training the young scientists and others of the Eden population in the sciences, language and business. During that period there were many young newcomers who frequently arrived from Earth via Solarian Banking for training. Those became part of the federation navy to survey space and locate other advanced civilizations.

MARTIAN DOMES

The Martian domes used for the evacuation were security fenced. Each dome carried the Solarian flag on their topmost pinnacle. Human-like androids now occupied and maintained the fusion power generation plants. The Omegron Portal was functioning in its secondary standby duplex mode. Interstellar portals were also fitted on Mars in a concealed underground location. Those would subsequently link Earth to Planet Eden and other Federation worlds.

POLION II

Meron and Lumak were soon to shift all robotic production to the new production planet of Polion II. That world was several light years from Eden, but some nineteen light years from Earth. During that time they were very busy moving supplies and other necessaries to that world, including robots and androids, many of whom had been acquired from Polok II and used there during the initial building program.

EARTH

Earth's technologies had since moved on at an incredible pace, but the drug abuse situation had worsened and so did every conceivable form of crime and corrupt activity.

Lumak wondered whether it would ever be possible to cure the social ills of Earth, the now very sad world. He couldn't find any method short of terminating half its human population. However that was not the Shadite's way. They had taken an oath to save and preserve life at all cost and never to destroy it.

He had always believed in the freedom of the individual, but with that freedom also went respect and responsibility to oneself, their families and neighbours; not to mention the so-called lower life-forms to whom they owed so much.

Humans on Earth paid little regard for such altruistic concepts and for the first time since their formation, the Solarian Council suddenly became frightened of Earth's contaminating influence on other normal societies. Soon more laws were passed. Earth was subsequently declared a no entry zone and no go area for trade or any other purpose not of a political nature.

Despite everything, Meron, Jeffery, Ben (Sarah's father), and others were allowed to continue their original work there and form new educational groups for children, special Solarian universities and the Friendly Solarian Charitable Society through Solarian Banking. The organization FSCS was pronounced First. That last organisation was headed by Ben to select the better Earth humans for relocation to Eden or other worlds within the Federation. That was until the planet could be slowly decontaminated sociologically and psychologically. Sarah's global organization, BioLive, was also included in those efforts.

However, as history would dictate, Ben would use them for the global distribution of his antigen against the Terminal Disease with Mallory Colman's assistance.

CHAPTER 54

Friendly engagements

President Gerald Fraser of the United States of America, also called Jerry by his many close friends, was finally on a long vacation to Eden. He had made all the usual clandestine arrangements with his favourite lookalike actor at his country residence on Earth. His carefully planned absence was timed to coincide with the first visit of his old friend Malik from Polok and other visitors from Lodor, shortly to arrive.

Jerry had arrived on Eden via the Martian portal and found that mode of transport to be the least exciting of all forms of space travel. One moment he was in the large cubicle on Mars and what appeared to be seconds later was in a similar one on Eden. The only problem he found with that method was the annoying tendency for his feet to buckle beneath him on arrival. It was indeed a strange sensation that made one struggle to regain balance.

Presently he was stood on one of the golden palace's patios, gazing unto the large city of Eden in the misty distance, hardly twenty kilometres away. He reflected on his first visit to that world several months before and recollected his initial reckless intentions of naming it Earth II.

'What a wrong decision that would have been in light of Earth's current developments. Luckily for everyone, I had changed my mind and finally settled for that beautiful name, Eden,' he thought.

He could hardly have believed the sights he now beheld. Just a few months ago that area was one of the least popular spots on the planet, even for its fairy like creatures and now it held a most beautiful city, teaming with all forms of life. How different those Andromedans and Shadites were to Earth's humans. So orderly and meticulous in everything they did... and yet, Sarah was the only true Earth human among them and perhaps the most gifted to rule the galaxy.

That was an incredible recommendation for Earth's humans. Why couldn't they be less self-indulgent and act more intelligently and responsibly? Perhaps genetic engineering could create a more practical species for long term survival within the galaxy. Even so, moral ethics were involved and if it was a choice between moral ethics and self-gratified drug addicts, even with the aid of bioengineering, the balance of justice would always sway in favour of the former.

He gazed in wonder at the large artificial moon, duplicating the precise brilliance and orbit of Caefon's own largest moon that he had once viewed in one of Meron's videos. But this one was without the much higher gravitational effects and he wondered of the ingenuity behind its creation. Another satellite, but this time created for the sole purpose of nostalgia.

He and his wife, Sharon, had been given the complete freedom of the planet. That also included permanent residence at Sarah's palace if they so desired, with a palace and small fief including diplomatic status as one of her permanent advisors whenever he was around. He intended to make things more permanent soon, by retirement from Earth's political scene. Which in his opinion couldn't be soon enough. After that time he would be free to become a permanent Solarian councillor.

Perhaps one of those prearranged accidents in space could account for their permanent disappearance from Earth. Even if his children was saddened by his supposed death for a while. Anyway, they were quite strong and would get over his unfortunate demise within a few months and so he thought.

Sarah had imported several horses and other farm animals from Earth. She had also decided to build several large enclosed parks. Within their confines the more carnivorous Earth types, including some endangered species, could roam and breed freely within their enclosed biospheres. Some of the Ancients' types could also be genetically revived and replaced within similar biospheres within their own areas. She had changed her mind about domestic cats and dogs, providing they were adopted under special license and tagged for quick detection in case they left their owner's environment. However all would be neutered. She didn't like the idea of those carnivorous non-indigenous animals chasing and killing the beautiful indigenous life on that world. For Jerry, that was another homely move, because he loved and relished his cat, Sphinx, and dog, Jinx.

'How different was this paradise place, Eden, from our Earth, with gold more common than iron and diamonds that could be mined in vast quantities by robots, making them of such little value,' he said.

'Yes, Darling. This is definitely not a world for those types of greedy people that hoard such wealth,' Sharon commented, while handing him a drink. It was a female world and the women felt very comfortable with those ethics and restrictions.

'But I bet you wouldn't mind a very large one on a ring about your finger,' he replied.

'No Darling!' she said and walked away.

He worried about his children, but even they could be admitted to planet Eden sometime in the future after a period of suitable conditioning. After they had undertaken extensive sociological education and treatment. Life on Earth was so much less organised and primitive, even non conceptual by comparison with the Ancients. Nevertheless Doctor Longhurst's scientists, who although from Earth, followed a set plan and were quite ordered and meticulous. Since that was the case with them, so also could others, given the right training and encouragement.

He urgently wanted to see Doctor Longhurst and Plato to discuss Earth's present dilemma. If anyone had a solution, it would be those two. They tended to know so much about the social behaviour of species throughout the galaxy, even to predict with incredible accuracy their eventual faith. While pondering those concerns his wife rejoined him on the balcony with drinks and held his hand while both glanced in amazement at the artificial moon, christened Caefon after their planet.

'Are you thinking about Earth again, Darling?' she inquired.

'Come! Sarah wants us for the engagement party.'

They walked hand in hand down the expansive corridor, its sides and walls adorned with every conceivable figurine and statue that represented many advanced intelligent life-forms known to Solaria. Those areas contained pedestals and space for many new ones to be added at a later date. They entered the smaller and more private dining room.

Many teenaged boys and girls could be seen throughout the palace holding small plasma hand weapons. They were dressed in federation colours and looked very similar to bell-persons at large hotels on Earth. They filled the positions of fully trained palace guards.

Bawaki was in charge of palace security. It was her idea to prepare her youths for that favoured position. They were subsequently trained in the special military school on board Martia's ship.

Today was a very important one for Sarah and others, in particular for the younger unattached councillors. It was a day chosen for the official proposals to their respective partners. Such engagement parties were planned to take place just before their marriage ceremony which was to be held in two weeks.

It was Sarah's duty, as their most senior guardian, to arrange all such ceremonial matters. Accordingly, she was to agree to their choices and in the rear case of a refusal, give advice and make recommendations. Their surrogate parents and every other council member were present and waiting for the completion of that ceremonious occasion.

The couples simply made their wishes known by sitting next to their future partners while holding hands and wearing similarly coloured caps. Those leaving the table with the same coloured caps were a matched pair. However, colours could differ if they made changes during the course of the meal.

Such proceedings were just a formality which had been resurrected by Meron. It had been taken from customs of Caefon in ancient times and also a good idea for a break from their otherwise hectic and irregular duties. All couples concerned had already made their decisions clear and Sarah had agreed with their choices. Even so, there could be last minute changes.

During the ceremony Sarah was going to offer them deeds to their palaces and fiefs, so in that regard it was very important to all of its participants.

Jon and Lira were the first couple to enter the room. They were dressed in gold braided white robes with Jon's female partner, Lira, beautifully adorned in jewellery and flowers. On entering they were constantly cheered by families and friends. Then it was Merol and Julia, followed by Ecrol and Petra. Those three couples sat next to each other on the same side of the large table. Then it was Merian senior by herself, and Hamil, followed by Tomas and Sintra, and finally Plato and Merian junior. Meron and Lucia shared the bottom end of the table with Sarah and Lumak at the top. Jerry and his wife, Sharon, shared the same side as Plato and young Merian. The elder Andromedans simply wanted to renew their marriage vows in this life.

With the exception of coloured jewellery and flowers, they appeared white, with federation insignias pinned to their garments. In the centre of the table were a small pile of mixed hats and paired multicoloured ribbons. The women drew first. Then the men drew a hat from the pile with matching ribbon which they placed on the table in front of their female partners. Then Sarah stood up to speak to Jon and the others.

'Do we make this engagement official? Say yes and kiss your chosen partner properly. And I want an affectionate kiss!' Sarah insisted.

Each said yes in turn and kissed their partner. Then she took the ribbon and gently folded it around the right and left hands of each couple in turn.

'Let this ribbon be a symbol of your binding together for life and may you both be happy in this union of love and responsibilities,' she said.

She handed them a scroll of their deeds and fiefs, within the area they called the Gardens of Eden State.

When the ceremony was over, they congratulated the other couples before settling down to a haughty meal. Finally, it was to the dance hall for the evening's real entertainment.

Bawaki, Venusa, young Merian and Martia were soon to be the

only young and unattached single women remaining within the Council.

Lord Meron had briefed Sarah on the different ancient ceremonies, and was nominated to take the final marital or Joining Ceremony based on the Senots as it was usually called. That grand ceremony would be held in two weeks.

CHAPTER 55

A change of residence

Lord Vektron and Lord Patron, the Plorans, had suddenly arrived on Eden to take stock of the Solarian System and prepare the way for the Grand Lord's visit. They seldom appeared before lower species like Andromedan or Earth humans unless absolutely necessary and would never visit the celebrations and functions of others uninvited. Nevertheless they made their presence known to The Ship and to the Shadite Lumak, presently disguised as Doctor Jeffery Longhurst.

When they were quietly together, Lumak told Sarah to prepare for a high level visit from the Grand Lord of the Seventh Universe. Thereafter she called all senior members of the Solarian Council and briefed them as best she could, not knowing the true nature or form of her important intergalactic visitor.

No one knew who or what to expect. He had taken the form of the great warrior Obe on Lumak's world, and others who were no longer among us on different worlds. Sometimes he appeared as a ball of light and on other occasions would take the form of anything, but she expected he would appear as a male human. Sex was not an important parameter to such a supreme being. She pondered the thought whether he could be either male or female. Then she decided on male, and that perhaps there were also females or even children in his plane of existence. She also wondered whether he was married or had a relationship with a female of his kind similar to the god Zeus and Hera.

After the engagement meal, they visited the large hall. The mixed band began to play an Earthy rock'n'roll tune. It was not long before Lord Vektron and Lord Patron took their places on either side of the main entrance. Shortly thereafter, in walked a tall young man, perhaps about Meron's height, but in his early thirties. He was wearing a well cut light grey suit with black wand and white hat in hand. His attire was of European style and made for a prince.

Nothing was said as he casually made his way along the main hall towards Sarah's position. As he approached, she became quite nervous, but he gracefully took her hand and kissed it and she curtsied by bowing slightly.

'I am pleased to meet you, Councillor Sarah.'

'Thank you, My Lord!'

'Presently, I am Homiene Gerra,' the Grand Lord said.

He then glanced at Lumak.

'And how are you, Jeffery?' he inquired.

'I am very pleased with everything, My Lord,' Lumak replied, humbly. Now in the form of Dr. Jeffery Longhurst.

Grand Lord Gerra knew what that meant. Then he asked Sarah to be introduced to the others and some time was spent chatting and making himself known to all.

Then he spoke to all and sundry.

'Friends, ever so often it is my duty, and may I say, a most pleasurable one... to change my form and place of residence.

'This time I have selected Planet Eden for that purpose. Although this planet will be my abode for many years, I do not intend to live on its surface and will not in anyway interfere with your politics or individual modes of existence. However, I intend to visit you, my friends, from time to time in order to socialise or even perhaps give advice, with your invitation and permission of course. That is, when I am not occupied elsewhere.

'Now please follow me. I have something of beauty to show you.'

He took them to the balcony and then pointed to a most beautiful and brilliant crystal city in the sky.

'This is my Little Osmaron, my crystal city satellite. Also my present and future abode. It also provides you with the benefits of a second moon.'

It was indeed just like a second moon in synchronised geostationary orbit around planet Eden, which meant it always remained precisely above the city. The first moon was a large satellite presently being constructed by numerous robots and androids, That one was quite visible but smaller than Little Osmaron.

'My Little Osmaron represents the Osmaron galaxy to me in much the same way as Eden City represents planet Eden to you,' he added and smiled, but they knew not what he meant. However, it linked with every part of Osmaron as the city linked with every part of planet Caefon, so in that respect he was correct.

While they watched the beautiful crystal floating city in the sky, now to be considered the second moon of Eden, they could observe a strange bluish haze all about the satellite, even extending unto the surface of Eden. It was only just visible to the naked human eye. Through the Greater Mind that moon intersected with many dimensions and universes, including Gohenna or Goh.

'This is truly the Caefon of my youth,' Meron exclaimed and they all agreed. Eden with its two artificial moons was almost identical in every respect to their world Caefon. It was then that Meron remembered his holy scriptures, written by Prophet Seno about certain promises made to Melor and Micol in ancient times. That particular chapter was about their new home in Osmaron. Then he realised that prophesy had been fulfilled.

For once in a very long time Meron thought he was on Caefon in ancient times before the creation of the evil Javols. The relative sizes of both satellites were so precisely placed that they mimicked both of Caefon's moons and the Grand Lord had a hand to play in the grand illusion.

They had lost a world, but through the Grand Lord, had gained a much more beautiful one and who knew what the future would bring with their new technologies and powers, to control even galaxies.

Despite the trauma of their recent settlement on Eden, the Andromedans felt a lot more secure in the knowledge that the threat of the Javols had been temporarily removed. They could now spend their time in planning for the future.

The atmosphere of Eden was supercharged and filled with certain pollen that acted like a drug to inspire all through thoughts and deeds. It was a near perfect environment and they wanted it to remain that way for all, including its indigenous life-forms.

Nevertheless Sarah decided that Eden should also be used as a refuge for other endangered life-forms facing extinction throughout the galaxy. Therefore, large environmental domes were being built in isolated places and infertile regions as temporary habitats for all such unfortunate creatures.

CHAPTER 56

The start of Solarian Empire

For once in a very long time every council member was in the same place at the same time for the grand occasion of their engagement and future marriage. That whole process of arrangement and receiving visitors, not to mention the ceremonies themselves, would cover the best part of three weeks.

They had therefore decided to take several weeks vacation to properly view their new home planet and inspect their beautiful palaces and fiefs. Most of their palaces were still under construction, although almost completed.

After their forthcoming marriage, the three young Andromedan couples had intended to allow their surrogate parents from Caefon the choice of living with them in their respective palaces. However even at that time their parents hadn't any knowledge of their children's true genetic identity, with the Ancient Andromedans as their real biological parents.

The young six knew they were not their true biological parents, and had decided earlier on to never tell them any differently. Anyway such information was of little importance to anyone and could have led to more confusion and unhappiness.

To all its residents, Eden was now their home and they could find little reason for returning to Andromeda or even Earth in the foreseeable future. Even so, many like Jerry, the president of the USA, would have to stage a spectacular accident on Earth in which they would appear to die, before resuming any permanent residence on Eden.

Anyway the situation on Earth had worsened, with drug addiction, the worst crimes and kidnapping most prevalent. They also realized that if the biologist, Powell, had taken their DNA and handed it over to other criminal organizations, as Andromedan aliens, they would be prime targets. In any event those problems did not prevent them from returning to the Manor via portal, providing they kept well away from Earth's public domain for a while.

EARTH & SOLARIA

Doctor Jeffery Longhurst recently brought his team of Earth Scientists with him to Eden. He had arranged a small fief for them within which they would continue their inventive efforts. Those young minds were taken from many places on Earth and had been moulded by Lumak into highly creative scientists and technologists. They were responsible for his remote production plants, bioengineering and other important projects. All trained as his young scientists for the future and given every incentive. They were all under Lennox, his second in command. Many commuted to Earth on a daily basis by portal, to maintain the plants and agricultural fields close to his residence. Very soon, however, most of the basic workers would be replaced by duplicate androids. Many young people from Earth would visit Solarian Banking and be transferred to environmental domes under construction there.

Sarah's houses on Earth were permanently maintained by her loyal helpers, with Madeline McCririck at its head. The main Manor was used as a guest house for councillors and others in transit. Her other home in the hills of Turkey had since been extended and used as a second place on Earth for her many important guests. However, Doctor Emil, Jeremy's father was now in charge of those buildings. Marion was presently in charge of all care-taking.

The local town now contained one of the largest hospitals on Earth for age reduction and longevity treatment. That whole area in the hills of Turkey was spouting to the brim with many tourists. It had since undergone massive expansion. Professor Jean-Claude Chairmowich was still in control of all such efforts in Eastern Europe and Asia, with Jeremy in charge of all serum and terminal antidote production, plus many other types of medicine.

With the exception of Ben (Sarah's father), Sarah and others of the Grand Council rarely visited Earth, but could always return at a moments notice via the hidden portal in the basement of the manor.

Ben used the second building next to the manor as temporary residence for some of his senior assistants. He utilized certain areas of the main building as his permanent residence, but still retained several empty rooms for unexpected visits from Sarah, Jeffery and other colleagues and friends.

ANDROMEDAN ANCIENTS & ANDROIDS

All other Ancients were placed under Lord Meron. The chance to transform into eight fingered humans were now possible, should they so desire. They were also given a fief north of the Garden of Eden States, bordering Meron's own fief. Those few survivors could create their own environment with their past culture if they so desired.

Their main duty was to act as official planetologist and group planets into different categories. Then such planets would be labelled as Donor or Acceptor worlds for the purposes of trade, habitation and mining. They were also to be the interstellar Customs and Excise Officers of the future. They would supervise the other scientists involved in assisting other life-forms throughout the Federation. Even so, they were seldom involved in the original exploration programs. Those mundane tasks were more suited to probes with computerised samplers, specialized androids and robots.

Most tasks within the empire could now be efficiently carried out by advanced androids through Macron computers. Nevertheless exceptions would be made for tasks requiring personal initiative by way of random choices and the apportioning of blame when such choices went wrong. It was always easy to forgive a human, but in the case of an intelligent robot, android or computer, a similar error would never be tolerated, given the exact circumstances.

Humans still had a prejudicial bias against intelligent computers and could not yet accept them as equals. Even so, android policing was allowed throughout their newly formed empire and handled most of the nitty gritty, boring and dangerous tasks.

THE NEW HEAVEN

Their elite society had the powers to live forever by revectoring every twenty years or so into their original recorded standard body format. That way, there could never be any degradation to body or mind, just repetition. The environment on Eden also enhanced longevity with healing powers. When they got tired of their original forms, they could always swap genetic matrices or create an original one by mixing several genetic matrices together. Even their sex could be changed by that method. However, Chief Councillor Sarah always had the final say in such matters, so sex changes were out of the question and removed from the convertors.

If anyone had an accident and died, their true selves could always be recovered and reformed within the critical time limit of one-point-six days. Failing that short period, they could always appeal to the Grand Lord for a new corporeal existence. However after such drastic measures, that person would be expected to become another one of his true servants and partake more directly in his cosmic plans. Those specials or Shadites as they were called were at a higher cosmic level than mere rulers.

Venusa and Martia (the ships) accepted, loved and enjoyed the new chaotic dimension they had been placed in and tried their utmost best to maintain that way of life with its strengths and weaknesses. They also had to come to terms with the unpredictability of humanity and other primal life-forms, realizing they existed in a mostly chaotic universe where cause and effect was not always visualized or seen from a human perspective.

EMPRESS SARAH

Sarah had changed significantly since those early days on Earth, but had still retained her strong sense of humanity and knew her responsibilities towards future goals.

She was getting ready the Solarian Council for the second phase of the Greater Purpose within Osmaron. During which time the military might of the federation would be constructed. Thereafter many federation fleets would roam the galaxy with mixed crews, searching for new civilizations, creating communication links, laying interstellar and intergalactic portal links and training all newcomers to take their rightful place within the greater order of the new empire. Hence, many star-ships were currently being built and fitted with the latest and most destructive weapons in civilization. Some of those great intergalactic ships were also expected to visit Andromeda at the later stages of the Battle for Andromeda against the Javols.

Planet Eden was ringed with many observation satellites and stations. Deep space probes were continuously installed within the whole of Solaria aided by the Octans. Underneath the planet's surface were many concealed defensive and offensive devices. Further, the scientists were continuously developing even more powerful and advanced devices and weapons. Each competing in their relevant fields for the best prizes and promotion.

THE SHIP

The Ancient's ship, known to all as The Ship, was given its own private dock within Sarah's Palace and granted complete freedom of Eden. It took great pleasure carrying children on exploratory expeditions when it was not otherwise occupied. It always preferred human contact and enjoyed the young because of the numerous and incredible questions they would ask. That aspect was another diversion from laying dormant within its dock.

IMPERIAL DEMOCRACY

The Federation Parliamentary Buildings were finally completed just outside Eden City and occupied an area of nine-point-five square kilometres. It incorporated every possible facility for aliens and humans alike, with several separate hotels close by and directly linked by secured portals, again with alien facilities.

Like Sarah's great palace, the Federation University was built on one of the local hills overlooking the city. Quite extensive by Earth's standards, it was also situated just within the Gardens of Eden State and Sarah's Eden City Fief which included Eden City itself.

Most alien life, including the Lodorians, could be given human bodies by a process called humanization. It was thought that suitable aliens who considered the idea desirable could undergo the process at minimal costs. Anyway a standard human form on a human world simplified accommodation and other embarrassing situations and the process was fully reversible.

No more was the requirement of equal masses necessary for such conversions in form and nature. They could create a standard human body and modify or program a brain to fit virtual the same emotions and feelings of the donor life-form. However, the only drawback was the loss of certain extra limbs, senses and organs. For instance, the Lodorians would loose their abilities to shock fish with their powerful electric tails or communicate that way with others while in water, and there were many such examples. Nevertheless all such senses could be simulated by the use of Brain Implants and a range of other technologies, so they were not strictly necessary.

SPORTS & GAMES

The large Olympic Sports Arena and Solarian Museum of Art and Science, was being constructed towards the south of Eden City. The former could only have been used by categorised humans. However, transformed humans could also be allowed, providing they were of a standard format.

Sarah had always thought competition in sports and games an important parameter in cementing interstellar relationships and had selected a special committee to publicise many of Earth and Caefon's games, including football and golf, throughout the galaxy.

CHAPTER 57

Final checks

'Harry want's you!' Hal's secretary said, while returning with more paperwork.

'It's a nice day, so I hope it's good news!' Hal rushed out towards Lennox's office on the top floor. He spent a while admiring the view from the 153rd floor before knocking.

'Dr Seaton, Please enter!' Lennox shouted.

'You wanted me?'

'Yes! Please take a seat. This may take some time!' Lennox said.

'Boss has decided to release your terminal bug. He wants to know if there are any foreseeable problems. Is there anything you can think of?'

'We have been testing for a while now and as far as I can tell it works to spec. So far we have tested on a population of several thousand, young and old. It's a simple enough device. There is not much to go wrong within it's lifetime. The only problem we might have, is a mutation of the bacteria, but that does not affect the viral part. The viral part is what stops reproduction.'

'So you think it's ready for release?'

'Yes! The only problem I see is that it will take close to 100 years, while I would like to see the job done in under 50!' Hal replied.

'Well, the Boss wants it this way. He thinks there will be less human suffering.'

'Less human suffering! Where has he been all those years. Has he been living in the real world. Has he seen the suffering of a young woman that knows she can never have kids. Not to mention being picked on and molested if you are the only one with kids. I say we could do it much quicker with a modified version of the Bubonic Plague. It could be made a lot more severe and quick acting!'

'But it would be random and indiscriminate. We have to save

about 500 million. That means choosing people genetically and by vaccination. We must select better humans for a better world in the long term!'

'Ok, I'm convinced! I see your reasoning. But the situation would be different if we isolated the chosen from the walking dead? Then we could kill them all in one fell swoop!' Hal replied. Lennox was startled by his uncaring attitude towards mankind.

Having thoroughly checked all reports on the Terminal Disease, Lennox was convinced of its effectiveness and relayed that information to Dr. Jeffery Longhurst.

'Ok, now we can concentrate on mass production and methods to administer. Hal has done a great job, but he should be kept in the dark about it's release. We don't want too many leaks.' Lumak said.

'Will do, Sir!' Lennox replied.

'By the way, I would like to see Hal in my office at 3 pm today. It's time he knew the truth. Do you think he can handle it?' Lumak inquired.

'I don't know sir. That one has a mind of his own. He will need some convincing,' Lennox replied.

'Then we shall see!' Lumak said and hung up.

Hal was sitting quietly in his office updating his computer on recent progress when the phone rang.

'Hi, Hal!. The boss wants to see you about an important matter in his office at 3 pm. Don't be late!' Lennox stressed.

'What have I done now!' Hal complained.

'Have you done something I should know about?' Lennox inquired.

'No! Sorry, just thinking aloud!'

'Well, pal, this could be very important for your career!' Lennox replied and hung up.

Lumak was in a great mood that day. The young Andromedans had discovered a suitable world for Microid production called Polion. Eden city was finally complete with space for all the

Andromedan evacuees, who had settled well. And of all important things, the Grand Lord had moved residence to that beautiful world, so what could go wrong?

With all those recent successes he wanted his special projects and scientist close at hand on Eden. So a special isolation dome was built in an unpopulated area for that purpose.

As Hal walked through the corridors he could observed many parked crates and realized there were changes afoot.

There was a mild tap on the door and Hal walked in.

'You wanted to see me, Sir!'

'Yes, Doctor Seaton! Please make yourself comfortable! Tea or coffee!'

'Espresso please!'

'Morin, two espressos please!'

'Are you moving from this place!' Hal inquired.

'I am afraid so! My time on Earth has finally come to an End!'

'What do you mean? Are you proposing suicide?' Hal couldn't believe him.

'Wait here for a while. This will only take a minute,' Lumak, presently in the disguise of Doctor Jeffery Longhurst, replied.

Lumak in his black shadites cloak suddenly appeared in front of his desk. He faded into reality from thin air,

'Oh, my God! Are you for real? So you are a real alien ... from another world?' Hal shouted in despair moving his chair back in the process.

'Yes, I am. But I have US citizenship, so in a sense I am not a real alien!' Lumak replied in jest.

'Why are you here?' Hal inquired.

'Let me show you why!' Lumak said as he retrieved a small box from his pocket and placed it on the desk. He tapped the box and it began to display a 3D image above the desk in mid air.

'Oh, gracious lord. This is the worst video I've ever watched. Is that for real?'

'That is what happened to the Andromedan's world about 3000 years ago. These monsters are now on their way to our galaxy and will be here in about 200 years.' Lumak replied.

'So we only have 200 years to prepare for their invasion?' Hal inquired.

'That's a close estimate. We have a few interstellar probes. They will update our Mecrons as they progress. I am a Shadite. Like a special intergalactic holy man or priest. I was sent by the Grand Lord of our part of the universe. My task is to inform mankind of the dangers and improve Earth's technologies to Class 5. That is about 100,000 years more advance than where we were 2 years ago. We need such advanced technologies if we are to fight those monsters.'

'Does other humans know of the dangers and your plans?'

'Yes! Your president and some of his most trusted senators. There are also Andromedans involved. You will meet some of them on your first visit to Planet Eden. That is if you agree to a change of residence for a while. You can always return to Earth from time to time.'

'You mean guys like Lord Meron. You know he has 3 fingers and one thumb. Once I saw him washing his hands.' Hal was even more curious.

'All Andromedan Ancients like him are like that, with golden hair, sea-blue eyes. They are a great people and you will get to like them. However, you will need brain implants if you want to be a great scientist.'

'Is it a painful process.'

'No, the quantum device is the size of a pinhead. The process is quite painless. After that you will have much greater intelligence, with about five extra doctors in other important fields. It will also increase your brain powers by about ten times.' Lumak replied.

'Well Boss, I'm keen. When can I leave?'

'You will receive an envelope containing a special card. That card will open a way for you through the Portal System. You will visit Planet Eden via Mars. You should spend a little time on Mars to admire its beauty from one of the large domes. You will be contacted on the day of transit.' Lumak explained.

'Whatever you say, Boss!' Hal was intrigued to say the least.

A happy Hal Seaton was back home cooking his favourite hot

spaghetti bolognaise when the phone rang.

'Hi, Powell, I thought you were in the slammer!'

'Yes, I am! Being a Thirteenth member, I have certain privileges you know. Contacts in high places and all that!'

'So why this special call?'

'To say hello and thank you for your assistance. They are moving me to higher security so I'm not sure when I'll be able to contact you again. I take it you are still with the Thirteenth?'

'Yes, I am!'

'Then, can you still assist!'

'Yes, I can assist the Thirteenth, but I've never been interested in LPD concessions. I am only interested in saving our world from brainless humans.'

'I was only trying to make some extra bucks for a few important projects I'm working on. Sadly the whole bloody project went south.' Professor Powell was not happy.

'Ok, but I'll only help if you have a bigger picture in mind and with our organization, the Thirteenth.'

'If they are Aliens, it would be nice to know why they are here. Wouldn't it?'

'I recently had word with the boss, Doctor Jeffery Longhurst. You won't believe what he showed me. He is also one of them but from another world. There are many worlds involved. They are here to improve our technologies so we can survive an invasion of blood-sucking monsters. These monsters will be here in about 200 years, so we have to prepare. They are about 100,000 years more advanced. So you have your work cut out if you are to save our world. You need to think up a good plan. We will need your clever brain.

'I am off to a most beautiful world called Eden soon, so you wont see me for a while. Pass that information over to the Thirteenth in your next meeting,'

'Oh my God! So they are the good guys?'

'Yes! You got the wrong end of the stick. They are here to help us survive an invasion. You and your guys went in like a giant hoofed elephant and almost spoilt the plot for everyone,' Hal stressed.

'Yes! I am very sorry about that. I did not have enough data at the time. But I was almost right. I knew something was wrong, but how was I to know. Anyway, I wont be able to contact you for a while. These places are never kind to people like me. Even so, I should be released soon. In the mean time I will lock myself in my cell and come up with some brilliant ideas against some nasty enemies.

'Senator Cleary was a good senator until enticed by a few bad guys needing LPD concessions. So he should be released by the next president for good behaviour. Please keep in touch, I'll keep things secret,' Powell replied.

CHAPTER 58

Earth's ills and cures

In order to reduce Earth's still growing population and save its numerous other life-forms from extinction, it was necessary to take drastic steps to curtail all human reproduction. They soon realized that advertising and other publicity campaigns to be completely fruitless. Similar methods had been extensively tried in the past and failed. The problem was partly sociological but mainly hormonal and deep seated in the human genome.

Most of Earth's rain forests were already gone, with a population currently in excess of 9 billion and rising like a balloon, to the point of explosion. Population control was never on any political agenda, being considered a human-rights issue.

The point of a sustainable human population had already been exceeded when it was about one billion. That was about a century before. At that time the planet could quite easily have supported its populations' with its expansive forests, lands and fossil fuels still in tact. But now, those resources had been exhausted and more offspring were usually the outcome when there were high levels of uncertainty and insecurity. Those very same factors also increased population growth. It was one gigantic spiralling circle that fed on itself to the detriment of all life on the planet.

Because of those reasons it was necessary to wipe the slate clean and start from scratch. The present planet with its dwindling resources could only at that time support less than five hundred million individuals. Therefore an answer had to be found quickly if Earth, with most of its remaining varied life was to survive the ever growing human problem. However mankind was also to partake in the Solarian Empire and assist in the final battle against the Javols. Since planet Eden was not going to be used as a crutch for Earth, by accepting most of its endangered species, which were numerous, other methods had to be found.

Sarah called everyone concerned to a special crisis meeting to discuss those issues and in the process find a lasting cure for

Earth. During that meeting certain drastic decisions were taken.

'What say you, fellow councillors. We have heard Councillor Longhurst's report on the problem and its cure, and must now take a unified stand if Earth is to survive the next hundred years. I realize the medicine and methods of our cure to be somewhat drastic, but it is not our fault that the people of Earth are the way they are. We have to revive that world before the arrival of the first Javols in our galaxy,' she said. All wands of office was lifted and the motion was carried.

'In that case, we are to introduce the Terminal Disease within Earth's atmosphere. The disease will have no discernable symptoms and spread throughout the planet while affecting every human in contact. I have had guarantees that it will not detrimentally affect any other life-forms in contact. Only those humans that are administered the special antidote will be allowed to have children. Nevertheless all others will live out a normal lifespan with no symptoms. The drops will be made by the two great ships and let's pray that during this time of planetary transformation, mankind survives the change and turmoil that ensues,' Sarah said.

It was subsequently decided not to allow untrained and untested Earth humans on Eden or anywhere within the Solarian Empire. It was argued that by so doing they would corrupt and spoil individuals by inevitably introducing their pirating, drug abuse and other vices and lawless tendencies and behaviour throughout the empire.

It was however decided to assist young Earth people, wherever possible, by introducing them into the Empire through Solarian Banking. Then they could be rigorously trained and given positions within the Federation Navy and other less critical areas. They would be further assessed until ready to take their natural places within normal Solarian society.

Henceforth all Solarian routes leading to Earth would be guarded and Earth itself quarantined from its contaminating influences. That last operation was a form of planetary imprisonment and would severely restrict Earth in her efforts towards space exploration, until the time was right, after its cleansing. Those drastic measures would be further reinforced by negative publicity towards all would-be deep space explorers and miners. That quarantining would last for a period just in excess of one hundred years. That was after the human population had reduced to just under 500 million by natural means.

Lumak (Councillor Jeffery Longhurst), having already visualised and predicted those very same problems, had with the assistance of Professor Harry Lennox, Dr. Hal Seaton and others, devised the special Anti-birth or Terminal Disease with which planet Earth would be seeded. The highly resistant bacteria with virus inhibited the human conception process in both sexes, so it played a dual role.

Being engineered from a type of human skin bacteria, it would exist on the human body and within reproductive organs, eggs and sperm. Once an individual was contaminated, it would be virtually impossible to eradicate the specially engineered bacteria. However it was only harmful to those basic structures before and during the process of conception. Furthermore it displayed no side effects or symptoms and allowed the infected individual a full lifespan.

The bacteria were highly contagious. Their spores could remain dormant within the environment for periods in excess of fifty years from the moment of release. What people required were the completion of the anti-bacterial vaccines or antidote. It would be given to those few selected children, young workers and soldiers, who would be made immune from its effects for the future survival of Earth's specially chosen populations.

Lumak (Doctor Jeffery Longhurst) with Ben's assistance, had over a period of several months collected most types of biological specimens from Earth, including endangered species. Those critically endangered species could never have survived the next fifty years of Earth's stampeding human population. Therefore most of those life-forms were introduced into large domed parks on Eden and another prepared world. They would be kept alive and secured until Earth was well again from its plague of humans.

Professor Bengizara Khan (Sarah's father Ben) was placed in charge of all Earth's recovery programs. He had lots of professional assistance and relished the position and responsibilities.

He could always leave Earth in an emergency through one of the local concealed portals at the manor, but was always wary of such unnatural devices. Even a local aeroplane flight was sometimes too much for him to tolerate, even when it was one of his specially prepared jets. He had seen so many psychiatrists about his phobia problem, but even hypnotherapy did not help. He was just very nervous about such things, like putting ones head under a primed guillotine. He just preferred to ere on the side of safety. Nevertheless being a military captain made him fearless when it came to battle or dealing with people.

He had been involved in the vaccination program from the start. That was when Lumak told him it was only an experimental project over a year ago. Then Lumak had placed the complete project in the hands of Professor Harry Lennox.

'Professor Harry Lennox and Doctor Hal Seaton did an excellent job by engineering such a unique bacterium with added virus to Lumak's specifications. The experimental antidote had worked satisfactorily on many specially selected patients in a few local hospitals and in Turkey. Even so, selecting those suitable for the antidote across the whole planet will be a nightmarish task if not planned properly,' Ben thought. Not realizing then the significance of his task.

Having witnessed severe problems within the larger Earth cities, he had given some thought to the crisis himself and decided the chosen method to be the most humane from all other alternatives. Every person could still live out their almost normal lives with the exception of those below 45 years or so, who would naturally desire offspring. He realized one could never make the proverbial omelette without breaking a few eggs and in this case the real human egg was truly broken.

It was not long before many large invisible ships briefly appeared above Earth, dropped their biodegradable canisters in several places and left. No one on Earth ever observed what had happened. The canisters were timed to explode at the same time and quickly evaporated in the process leaving behind no evidence of the spill.

The highly contagious, anti birth or terminal bacteria with the dangerous virus, would now lie dormant until it came in contact with a human body; to then spread throughout that body like the other skin bacteria and be further transmitted by hands, bodies, surfaces, the air and water.

Once a patient was infected it was almost impossible to rid them of the disease in order to make them fertile again. Further, how could they have known that their infertility was due to their own skin bacteria, which was not easy to trace. For the selected few, all vaccines had to be taken before the individual was infected. Even so, young children could be made immune if vaccinated before puberty.

Ben and his officers, including Mallory Colman, would continually target schools and young families, in particular young military types with a spirit of adventure. Several recruitment offices were set up to interview those would-be out world adventurers and many were recruited and sent to Mars for initial training within its domes. From there they would be transposed to Eden for a new life in the Solarian Federation Navy and elsewhere.

Ben also knew that once the problem was known by Earth's authorities he would by then have the matter solely under his control, since he was the only source of the antidote vaccines. He had prepared for that eventuality by acquiring for himself a new identity as an eccentric professor of biology by the same name and had all the relevant papers to substantiate those claims. Even so, he was also a real professor of biology among other professions.

After Ben's first and only visit to Eden, he had acquired the special Brain Implants. He was given little choice in the matter when his daughter, Sarah, ordered him through the portal. On arrival he was taken directly to Venusa's ship where he was put into the special chamber for revectoring. He went like a sheep to the slaughter, but was amazed with his new mental potentials after he had recovered from the ordeal. After that operation he found his thought patterns to be considerably altered. He had lost all his phobias and was now packed with an incredible amount of knowledge on every conceivable subject that he could ever have imagined. Yet, the new complexities in no way interfered with his normal senses and emotions. He was also given the choice of revectoring whenever he required to reduce the aging process. He was now like a god among men and could process any thought in a fraction of the time taken by a normal person.

SATELLITES ETA AND GIMBAL

Those two large observation satellites in orbit around Earth were constructed in space by numerous robots for Solaria by Solarian Banking during the initial period of satellite construction. There were many such structures in orbit about Earth and some contained large hotels and health centres. Within those retreats the wealthy would retire on long holidays well away from the troubles of Earth. They were also used for conferences and diplomatic meetings.

Security on such remote structures could be maintained at higher levels than on Earth, and monitoring of crews and passengers carried out a lot more efficiently.

While crime increased on Earth, many of the wealthier became disheartened by the degeneration of their respective societies and took flight with their families to such places like satellite Gimbal. Solaria owned the company involved in all such satellite construction. It was called Eta, which was the acronym for Extra-terrestrial Accommodations. Solaria also acquired shares in all structures built by Eta. Therefore Solaria also had a say in their chosen occupants.

Satellites Eta and Gimbal were among the largest of such satellite structures. Those two were built by robots for Solaria under Solarian Banking. Eta was subsequently used for engineering and as an observation satellite, where construction robots, androids and other equipment could be stored and serviced. The large telescopes and other sensitive observation equipment were constant eyes on Earth. Any changes being relayed by H-Wave to the Macrons on Eden.

Gimbal, however, was designed as a most beautiful hotel and recreation complex. The very large satellite consisted of an inner rotating sphere about 3 kilometres in diameter with two pivoting outer wheels. The innermost wheel precessed about the outer, in much the same way as a gyroscope, but fully under computer control.

Gimbal, was the largest and most beautiful of all the satellite structures. It was also the most frequently used by the elite of Earth's wealthy society. Within one of Gimbal's large wheels were the largest observatory and bacteriological cleansing and isolation chambers. At its centre was positioned the large sphere that contained a city with lakes and forests on the inside. As such satellites traversed the planet they jointly recorded all planetary changes including those attributed to its ecosystems, the weather and those of a geological nature.

Both satellites contained powerful portals and main docks for large shuttles without portal technology.

However they also contained interstellar ports for the larger inter-dimensional ships of the Federation. All portals linked with the main terminal which was sited on Mars. Solaria continually monitored Earth and could always respond quickly in times of crisis by alerting Ben's and other charitable organisations with Biolive placed there solely for that purpose.

THE TECHNOLOGICAL VIRUS

Doctor Longhurst had also visualised Earth's attempts to fight back once placed under such extreme population controls. Therefore he had engineered all robots, androids and computers with three levels of infectious viruses and inbuilt obsolescence. They were extremely contagious to other robots and androids. Once triggered by special code sequences most of Earth's robot-based society would be rendered completely inoperative, if and when that decision was taken. It was however hoped that such further extreme measures would not be necessary, despite the fact they were already in place and like a time bomb, ready and waiting.

In many ways and without even their knowledge, Earth's societies were fully controlled by Solaria. The whole planet could quite easily have been taken back in time to a period before even the motor car had been invented. Earth was fully dependant on the new Class 5 technologies and could never again have resumed their own brand of technologies from where they had departed several decades before. For one thing the main resources had all been used up.

The process of re-engineering their societies by the Solarians could not have been achieved without the complete break down of all present sociological and economic structures. Further, almost all the fossil fuels had been exhausted and a more advanced type of clean atomic energy had not yet been fully developed by Earth's humans. Even so, there still remained wind, wave, hydroelectric, a few nuclear reactors, and other methods for generating electricity.

Epilogue

In the wake of the Javols unimpeded approach to our galaxy, Osmaron, many civilizations are to be aligned under the new Solarian Empire based on Eden. During the few years remaining before the Javols arrival, many new methods and technologies must be learnt.

The three main Federation nations, namely Solaria, Polok and Lodor have come together for the common good, with Councillor Sarah as their head. Resources and materials are now flowing between these nations, which become very wealthy and prosper as a result.

In the year 2045 the population of Earth is over 9 billion and rising. In order to save Earth and its other evolving life the Terminal Disease was introduced into its atmosphere. This disease is unknown to the human population of Earth and will prevent almost all fertile young from reproducing new offspring.

Only those few selected by Professor Bengizara Khan (Ben) will be administered the special antidote and are able to reproduce. Since there is no easy way to remove the Terminal Disease, Earth's human population will gradually reduce over the intervening years until the population reaches 500 million humans.

During the following years there will be much turmoil and unrest on Earth, leading to child snatching and kidnapping, as children become a rear commodity. Crime and antisocial behaviour will become endemic, as the many disappointed and downtrodden give up hope and turn to drugs and other methods to quell their troubles.

However all that is just a light breeze before the storm. Sarah has other plans for Earth and many of the present greedy and self-indulgent humans will never figure in those incredible plans.

To be continued with **Fertilates**

The Chronicles of Galaxy Osmaron series

The Osmaron series point a way to one of our possible futures. In this future, technology is more advanced. But our real problems come from another galaxy, where another human species have accidentally created the ideal nano-bot type soldier. They are truly unique in the sense that they are almost indestructible, can copy and replicate almost anything, can live for ever, can reproduce their own kind and require living organisms like us for food. At least that was the unintended nano-bot type demon that came out of the mould after their second and final experiment.

Those nano-bot Javols went on to destroy all major animal life, including their creators, within Andromeda and are presently on their way to our Milky Way galaxy. The most advanced in our galaxy, who are non-human, decide to fight back for the survival of all naturally evolving life, but have to first inform lesser civilizations like us of the impending danger.

Before we can confront the demon Javols, we must first advance our technologies to Class 5. This is about 100,000 years more advanced than Earth's present levels. During this period Earth undergoes many changes due to Global Warming and human overpopulation, but manages to survive the onslaught.

Wars will rage, but apparently ubiquitous humans will always find ways to survive and win the day.